Love's Labour's Won

The Secret Life of William Shakespeare

William Gray

Orlando, Florida

Publisher's Cataloging-In-Publication Data
(Prepared by The Donohue Group, Inc.)

Names: Gray, William, 1959- author.
Title: Love's labour's won : the secret life of William Shakespeare / William Gray.
Description: First edition. | Orlando, Florida : William Gray, [2020] | Includes bibliographical references.
Identifiers: ISBN 9781734189001 (trade paperback) | ISBN 9781734189018 (ePub) | ISBN 9781734189025 (mobi)
Subjects: LCSH: Shakespeare, William, 1564-1616--Fiction. | Dramatists—England—History—16th century—Fiction. | Dramatists—England—History—17th century—Fiction. | LCGFT: Biographical fiction.
Classification: LCC PS3607.R3969 L68 2020 (print) | LCC PS3607.R3969 (ebook) | DDC 813/.6—dc23

Library of Congress Control Number: 2019918020

ISBN: 978-1-7341890-0-1 (trade paperback)
ISBN: 978-1-7341890-1-8 ebook (epub)
ISBN: 978-1-7341890-2-5 ebook (mobi)

Front and back and cover design by: word-2-kindle.com.

The William Shakespeare poetry and play excerpts in this book are from *Shakespeare's Works. Dramatic and Poetic.* R. Worthington, New York, 1881. The other historic poetry, song lyrics, inscriptions, and play excerpts of Shakespeare's contemporaries are from public domain sources.

The front cover image is of Stratford's Guild of the Holy Cross Almshouses, which are near the site of New Place, the large home Shakespeare brought for his family in 1597. The back cover image is a portrait of Shakespeare. The title page illustration is of the Shakespeare childhood family home on Henley Street.

First Edition

Published by: William Gray, Orlando, Florida, billpgray@outlook.com.

DEDICATION

For Elsie: All my love, now and forever.

I don't have much to offer
Except this silver pen.
From this amber sundown
One doesn't come back again.

I've seen the blazing sunrise
And welcomed in the dawn.
I know that Heaven smiled
On the morning you were born.

You are a ray of sunshine
That brightens up my life.
I love to see you laughing
In the pale moonlight.

Your voice is like an Angel's,
So clear and pure and true.
It reveals all the beauty
That is inside of you.

The gates of Heaven opened
To bring your soul to life;
And I am blessed to know you
In this earthly life.

The Globe Theater

TABLE OF CONTENTS

Love's Labour's Won

Anne Hathaway's Cottage

CHAPTER I
RETURNING HOME

A large black coach slowly rolled its way along the rutted tree-lined road in the English Midlands in June of 1662. It was pulled by a team of four sleek and powerful horses with jet black coats of hair that shimmered as they were struck by rays of sunlight streaking through the canopy above. Tom skillfully used the reins to manage his team. His friend Jack rode shotgun. They were bringing Lady Elizabeth Barnard back to Stratford-upon-Avon to visit the remaining members of her family and pay her respects at the grave of her recently deceased Aunt Judith. Sir John Barnard, Lady Elizabeth's second husband, was occupied with urgent parliamentary business preventing him from making this journey.

Sir John entrusted Tom and Jack with the care and protection of his esteemed wife. Wrapped in a tarpaulin, among numerous pieces of luggage secured to the roof, was an elegant hardwood chair. The chair back contained separate engravings of a shield, and a falcon holding an upright spear. They comprised portions of the hard-won coat of arms of Lady Elizabeth's grandfather, Stratford poet and playwright, William Shakespeare.

A generation ago, Shakespeare's fame was far greater than it was now. He and his fellow playwrights Christopher Marlowe, Ben Johnson, Francis Beaumont, and John Fletcher were the leading cultural lights of their age. For theater was by far the most popular form of public entertainment during the reigns of Queen Elizabeth and King James.

Among his contemporaries, Shakespeare's fame was greatly enhanced by his astonishing versatility. He was a fine actor and poet, as well as a great playwright. As Ben Johnson said, Shakespeare was "not of an age, but for all time!"

The cultural light created by Shakespeare and his colleagues could not last forever. Storm clouds of immense proportions merged, creating one of the worst tempests experienced by any nation. With the increasing dominance of the black garbed and narrowminded Puritans in English society and politics, the theaters, which the Puritans called hotbeds of sin, were closed in September 1642. They remained shuttered through the bloody and protracted period of the Civil War and the dictatorial regime of the self-styled Lord Protector, Oliver Cromwell.

The atrocities of the war years and the Cromwell regime were too numerous to catalog. The most earth shattering was the execution of King Charles I. Such atrocities prove the truth of the adage that mankind's capacity for brutality is limitless.

Although much of William Shakespeare's work was a plea against the violence and destruction which would be brought upon the realm if Civil War occurred, given the silence forced upon the theaters and the playwrights making their living in them, his mere words, printed on aging pages, were powerless to stop the scourge of war from riding forth.

After twenty years of chaos and repression, the people and their ruling elite grew weary of the bloodshed of war and joyless oppression. Following Cromwell's death in 1658, they invited the exiled son of the executed King back to assume the throne.

With the return of King Charles II in 1660, a new day arrived for the nation. Since John's and Elizabeth's families had been strong supporters of Charles I, John became a member of Parliament and obtained the title of baronet. Given this good fortune, Elizabeth and John moved from Stratford and took up residence in John's family seat, an elegant manor house in Abington, thirty-five miles east of Stratford.

If this were not enough to give Elizabeth cause for thanksgiving, shortly after assuming the throne, Charles II, a man who thoroughly enjoyed good living and entertainment of all types and fashion, reopened the theaters. The nobility, gentry, and commoners once again enjoyed the plays of William Shakespeare and his contemporaries. If not yet in the ascendant position they once occupied, William Shakespeare's name and reputation were on the rise. At least that was the opinion of the elegantly dressed and coiffured Elizabeth as she sat silently in the coach watching the mossy tree trunks stream by.

Despite the causes for celebration, Elizabeth's heart was tinged with wistful sadness, a longing for the people and places making up the daily fabric of her life in days gone by. Like most of us, Elizabeth viewed her days of yore through rose-colored glasses — filtering out the difficult and unsavory portions of her early life — while preserving what was good and worthy in the treasure chamber of her mind. The wooden box resting on the cushion beside her contained keys which would open a way back to those precious memories.

Lifting the hinged top, the first item she saw was a fashionable pair of kid gloves, a gift from her grandfather to her grandmother, Anne Hathaway, during their Stratford courtship in 1582. The exquisitely stitched gloves had cuffs fringed with delicate lace. Just before her death, her grandmother told Elizabeth they were made by her grandfather in the family glove shop on Henley Street. Placing one of the gloves on her left hand, Elizabeth marveled at its suppleness.

Elizabeth next retrieved a finely made bugle-beaded purse. Her grandmother told Elizabeth her grandfather brought it for her from his brother Gilbert, who once made his living as a peddler. Great Uncle Gil was a kind and funny man who loved to play harmless pranks upon family members and friends. He knew skillful card tricks. And he once discovered a penny behind Elizabeth's ear, giving it to her as a birthday present.

Elizabeth smiled as she opened the purse, revealing an exquisitely engraved silver gilt locket. It contained a beautiful miniature portrait of her grandfather by society artist Nicholas Hilliard. The portrait was set in the locket and given to Elizabeth's grandmother as an anniversary present during her grandfather's first taste of fame in the early 1590s.

In Mr. Hilliard's painting, Elizabeth's grandfather sports the reddish, curly-brown hair, neatly trimmed beard, and mustache he wore in his twenties and early thirties. He is stylishly dressed in a beautifully textured and rounded grey hat with an ostrich feather cockade and felt brim. He wears an elegant dark doublet jacket with a white collar and cuffs of knotted lace. His bright eyes have a look of steady intensity.

Gazing upon the portrait, Elizabeth remembered her grandfather's friendly manner, twinkling eyes, and joyful laugh. In his later years, he loved to tell jokes. Like his brother Gil, he enjoyed playing little pranks upon everyone in the family, especially her grandmother. She would scowl playfully, calling out: "Will Shakespeare, stop pulling my leg!" Her grandfather would saunter over and give her grandmother a hug saying: "Don't take it seriously. Just a jest!" Pretending to fuss a bit, her grandmother would relent, joining in the laughter.

How fast the years flew by. The eternal clock keeps ticking no matter how much one wishes to slow it down. And here Elizabeth was now, in this coach, with the trees passing by and sunlight splashing in the coachman's eyes. Sadly, there was no way to return home again. She was the sole survivor of her immediate family. She would not live forever. While still here, she must do her best to finish the remaining duties owed to those who raised her and preserve her family's hard-won reputation.

With joyful anticipation, Elizabeth turned her attention to the remaining item in the box. It was a dog-eared manuscript in old fashioned secretary hand. This simple sheaf of aging papers contained the most important legacy her grandfather left Elizabeth and the other members of his family — the true and secret history of his remarkable life. The stories it contained were a precious lifeline to the ones she loved best on this earth. Unfortunately, the manuscript also created great risks for Elizabeth and her husband.

For there were facts, beliefs and opinions expressed within those pages that could damage John's career and their family's hard-won social status. Now that Elizabeth and John were finally able to bask in the rays of success, something must be done to extinguish the risk posed by the contents of this memoir.

In years past, Elizabeth, her parents and other members of the family would sit around the parlor fire in New Place, their spacious home in Stratford, reading portions of this precious manuscript. They were the stories she and the others in her family circle knew by heart. Elizabeth's grandfather wrote it during the last three months of his terminal illness. He left it to them as a parting gift — a little piece of his heart and soul containing the essence of his wit and wisdom.

As Elizabeth picked up the first page and began reading, a secret door opened to reveal the brilliant vistas of the past. It was one she walked through enthusiastically as she began a final journey into the true map of her family's heart.

Chapter II
All the World's a Stage

I once wrote a play called *As You Like It* which spoke of the joys of true love and a simple pastoral life. In that play, a character called Jaques, whose view of life somewhat mirrors my own, spoke the following lines:

"All the world's a stage, And all the men and women merely players: They have their exits, and their entrances; And one man in his time plays many parts."

Like each of us in this world, I have been called to play many parts in the drama that was my life. Whether that drama was a comedy, a tragedy, or a tragi-comedy, I leave to you, the heirs and readers of this manuscript, to judge. That it was also a history filled with adventure, love, sadness, and some success, is not to be doubted.

I begin the story of my life at its beginning, on a cold April St. George's Day in 1564. The year of my birth was unforgiving for the twelve hundred or so souls dwelling in our town of Stratford. The plague took the lives of over ten percent of Stratford's citizens. My mother, Mary Arden Shakespeare, and my father, John Shakespeare, who already lost my two older sisters, Margaret and Joan, to the Black Death within a year or so of their births, were fearful they would lose yet a third child to the virulent disease that has taken the lives of countless millions.

Consulting with other family members, my parents decided it was best for my mother and my wet nurse, Margery, to temporarily take me to my mother's family home in Wilmcote, a few miles outside Stratford. My father remained in town to oversee his glove-making business. As a rising member of the Town Council, it would have damaged his public image and political future if he ran out at the first sign of the pestilence.

It might seem old-fashioned to those of us survivors living in the present age, but personal courage mattered a great deal in those times. As my parents taught by example, when a crisis occurs, one owes it to one's family to bear it as best one can and carry on with the business of living.

My father did what came naturally to those like him; he showed courage and fortitude during the plague year, continuing to operate his business while fulfilling his civic duties, and trusting in God to protect and preserve us. Fortunately, his and my mother's prayers were answered. The plague eventually drifted off into the mists and miasmas from whence it came.

Once the threat of plague subsided, my mother and I returned to Stratford and resumed residing with my father in the fine home they owned on Henley Street. A marvelous house it was, with parlor, kitchen, dining area, a large workshop located on the ground floor, several bedrooms on the second story, and a spacious loft on the third. There were numerous windows at front and back. I recall spending many a contented hour as a child in my "box seat" before a large front bay window that looked out upon busy Henley Street — watching the world go by.

Go by it did, in what seemed to be a never-ending cavalcade of people, animals, costumes and faces. There was an old man named Adam, who strolled by the house every day playing his flute, his equally aged but energetic mutt, Crab, barking and dancing beside him. There were sunburnt farmers leading work horses pulling produce-filled carts to market, straw-hatted shepherds and cattle drovers driving flocks and herds down the street, and stylish gentry riding sleek coursers.

Young, attractively dressed saleswomen came sashaying by selling flowers, cherries, apples and pears. "Sweet pears!" And the occasional jingle chiming peddler singing out, leading his gelded pack horse carrying leather clad trunks filled with needles, pins, ribbons, bows, caps, bonnets, fringes of lawn and lace, and sundry other items gathered from far and wide. The sales pitch of a peddler named Jimmy, who I saw hawking his wares on numerous occasions, went like this:

> Lawn, as white as driven snow;
> Cyprus, black as e'er was crow;
> Gloves, as sweet as damask roses;
> Masks for faces, and for noses;
> Bugle bracelet, necklace-amber,
> Perfume for a lady's chamber:
> Golden quoifs, and stomachers,
> For my lads to give their dears;
> Pins and poking-sticks of steel,
> What maids lack from head to heel:
> Come, buy of me, come; come buy, come buy,
> Buy, lads, or else your lasses cry;
> Come, buy, come buy!

On occasion, one of these peddlers would stop at our door. If my mother thought she could get away with it, she would listen to the latest gossip gathered by the peddler on his travels down the highways and byways. Perhaps she would purchase a little trifle or bauble before my father would discover there was another of those "ragged solicitors" trying to take advantage of "your mother's exceedingly kind heart."

Shooing the peddler out of the house, my father would say: "Mary! How many times do I have to tell you not to give these vermin the time of day? They part foolhardy housewives from their purses. Despite the drabble and babble, they're silver-tongued thieves!"

"John! You're exaggerating. They're fun to talk to. Gentlemen like that are the only source of news we have around here about what goes on in the outside world. The trifles I buy brighten up the day. They don't cost much in the grand scheme of things," my mother would say, arching her eyebrows, and giving an "if looks could kill" stare.

"Gentlemen! News! You call the trashy rumors those arrant knaves pass on news! They're better at lying than Satan himself!" my father would continue his peddler bashing, before turning his attention to the "poor quality" of whatever it was my mother obtained from the peddler.

Because everything my parents did and said was laid upon a firm foundation of love and respect, the squabbles they occasionally had over such things as soliciting peddlers never worried me much. Given the creative language employed in their verbal duels of wits, it was often quite entertaining.

Most often, my silent sympathies were with my mother in these domestic squabbles. For some of the purchases she made, including colorful marbles, a spinning top, and a small set of carved wooden chessmen, were for my benefit.

Despite my father's outward protests of "You're spoiling the boy!" I sensed he inwardly approved of those purchases, although the position he took on peddlers and such "riff-raff" prevented him from publicly saying so.

CHAPTER III
SISTERS AND BROTHERS

Looking back upon those days four decades ago, there was never a dull moment. My brothers and sisters came into the world like clockwork; Gilbert in 1566, Joan in 1569, Anne in 1571, Richard in 1574, and Edmund, nicknamed "Babe," in 1580.

As the first child to survive infancy, I occupied a special place in my parents' hearts. But, as all oldest children know, there was a heavier burden of parental expectations placed upon my shoulders. The oldest is expected to be the trailblazer. The one the younger children are supposed to emulate. The example setter. The name bearer. The carrier of Great Expectations.

Whether those expectations are fulfilled, or founder upon the inevitable rocks and shoals of life, is completely out of one's hands. As the Good Book says, the rain falls upon the just and the unjust. The obverse is also true. The sun shines upon the deserving and undeserving.

Each of my brothers and sisters were special and unique people in their own rights. Like lilies of the field, no two of us are exactly alike. It takes all kinds to make the world a place of wonder. But, due to our nearness in age, the sibling closest to me during my youth was my brother Gilbert. With only two years between us, Gil and I shared the same circle of friends and we struggled through school together.

I was the better student. Gil was more athletic. For years we were inseparable: sleeping in the same bedroom, taught in the same schoolroom, memorizing and reciting Latin ten hours a day, six days a week, learning our father's trade as a glover, hunting, hawking, fishing, practicing archery, playing at chess, bowls and football with our schoolmates, and at childhood games like leap frog, hoop rolling, spinning tops, marbles, and hide and seek, with our younger siblings.

Despite limited time for play, Gil and I formed a circle of friends called the Henley Street Gang. It included a baker's son, Hamnet Sadler, and Robin Wright, a butcher's son a year older than I. Though my closest friend is Hamnet, Robin was the most intelligent and clever. Our verbal sparring matches were essential to honing my own wit.

Robin and I challenged each other in contests to determine who could tell the better jokes, jingles and stories. Gil, Hamnet and some of our other schoolmates acted as judge and jury. Robin had an edge in jokes and jingles. I often won when it came to storytelling. Forty years later, I can still recall Robin's jingles. I can hear him singing as he skipped along a leaf strewn road in an outfit that made him look like a pied-piper.

Where's your silly nightcap?
Put it on your head.
Tuck yourself right in,
When you go to bed!

First you slurp your porridge,
Then you crunch your greens.
The sound I hate the most,
Is when you eat your beans!

Whistles made of tin.
Patches sewn with thread.
Better watch your step,
That's what Mother said!

I often wonder where Robin's talents would have taken him if he lived to adulthood. Sadly, that was not to be. Robin died of the flu when only ten years old. When I heard the news, I cried myself to sleep.

It seems the Grim Reaper is never far from our doors. Our family is not immune from his terrible visitations. When I was fifteen, his scythe took the life of my sister, Anne. Anne was the gentlest soul in our family. She loved every person and everything she encountered. They say St. Francis spoke to the animals. At times, it seemed Anne had a similar gift. Our cats, dogs and horses showed her more affection than they did the rest of our family combined.

Anne's mind was a fine one in other respects. I was teaching her to read and she was making good progress. She was a talented artist. As young as she was, Anne already drew a fine line. The drawings she made of our cats, Sheba and Calico, and our dogs, Gabriel and Troubadour, still hang in my study. Fortunately, it will not be long before I have the pleasure of seeing Anne's smiling face again.

Chapter IV
The Old Religion

As well as being astute businesspeople, my parents were devout Roman Catholics. In the times in which we live, this is not only inconvenient, it's illegal. Fortunately, in the early part of her reign, Queen Elizabeth's government practiced a less coercive policy of enforced religious belief and repression of "recusants" who refused to attend government mandated services than they did later on.

Even in those early years, my parents took precautions. They hired servants and apprentices from Roman Catholic families. The few items associated with Catholic worship we owned, such as my mother's crucifix, rosary beads, and the small statuette of the Blessed Virgin Mary, were hidden and kept under lock and key.

The early instruction in the faith we children received came from our parents. They limited the daily prayer we said out loud as a family to the Lord's Prayer because it was said by Protestants and Catholics alike.

Once or twice a year, when we conspired to get the servants and the apprentices out of the house, my mother would remove her crucifix, rosary beads and painted statuette of the Virgin from their hiding place. We would say the five decades of the Rosary, including the Apostles' Creed, the Our Father, and the ten Hail Marys per decade. We children cherished these moments of special family unity.

I thank God we grew up in a town as tolerant of differing religious views as Stratford was in the days of my youth. Over half the town's population was Roman Catholic or Catholic leaning. If we lived in a less accepting part of the country, I am sure our lives would have been much bleaker.

Because my parents were both good and decent people, none of our neighbors ever informed upon us to the authorities. Live and let live was the order of the day for most people in Stratford.

And live we did, through many revolutions of the ever-changing seasons. As a boy, my favorite time of year was early summer. The leaves were green and bright rays of sunlight sparkled off the ripples in the current of the steadily flowing Avon. On rare days when I had time to myself, I would run down to the banks of the river, lie under the shade of one of the nearby trees, and bask in the warm weather. As I did so, I daydreamed of the future, singing little songs to myself. One of my own compositions I later used as a song in a play went like this:

Under the greenwood tree,
Who loves to lie with me,
And turn his merry note
Unto the sweet bird's throat,
Come hither, come hither, come hither;
Here shall he see
No enemy,
But winter and rough weather.

Another song I sang was one I learned from a wizened, cross-eyed shepherd we nicknamed Tom O'Bedlam because he looked and acted a bit zany.

When daffodils begin to peer, —
With, heigh! the doxy over the dale, —
Why, then comes in the sweet o' the
year;

For the red blood reigns in the winter's
pale.
The white sheet bleaching on the hedge,—
With, heigh! the sweet birds, O, how
they sing!—
Doth set my pugging tooth on edge;
For a quart of ale is a dish for a king.
The lark, that tirra-lirra chants,—
With, hey! with, hey! the thrush and the
jay:—
Are summer-songs for me and my aunts,
While we lie tumbling in the hay.

My youth was lived in a joyful age of song!

Chapter V
The Farming Life

Since my mother and father were children of farming families, it was only natural I was exposed to a life of tilling, sowing, reaping and threshing from an early age. My father's family farmed in Snitterfield. My mother's in Wilmcote.

My father's brother, Henry, had a beautiful baritone voice. Uncle Henry entertained those of us working beside him with a variety of old folk songs, as well as some of his own invention.

Sitting here in my book lined study, with the mid-afternoon sunlight streaming through the expensive swirled glass window, I can picture Uncle Henry singing away, looking like a sun burnished sailor on the deck of a rolling ship far from home.

Crack your cheeks!
Four winds blow!
Through the icy
Sleet and snow!

Cast your rake!
Tend your hoe!
With the scythe
We cut and mow!

Yoke the Ox!
Plow the field!
Comes the rain,
Our yield is sealed.

Sow the corn!
Scare the crow!
Watch the seedlings
Grow and grow!

Thresh the Wheat!
Sort the chaff!
With our merry
Wives we laugh!

Ground the flour!
Knead the dough!
Through the mill
Our grain does flow.

Dance a jig!
Roast a pig!
Cause the Harvest
Is so big!

Pluck the strings!
Play the harp!
Feel the music
In your heart!

Like most who make their living on the land, my Uncle Henry was a simple man. He led an uncomplicated, honest and God-fearing life. What you saw is what you got. There is much that is virtuous in the rural way of living.

My father left the farm at an early age. But he married a farmer's daughter. Both my parents passed on to us children the straightforward, hard-working traits that are part and parcel of country life.

My father's deep-seated knowledge of the way the country mind worked was invaluable in what was by far the most lucrative part of his business. Although he began life in Stratford as an apprentice to a glover, and he achieved financial independence by being admitted to the Glover's Guild and opening his own glove and leather goods business, once my father achieved sufficient capital, he dealt in wool.

Though my father did not have a license to do so, during the early days of my childhood, there were great fortunes to be made in the wool brokering business. It was worth risking fines and imprisonment to those desiring to get ahead, and get ahead fast!

Given my parents' country roots, they had an extensive network of kith and kin in the Warwickshire countryside. Just as we closet Roman Catholics stuck together, so did those in the black-market wool trade. Shepherds could obtain a higher price for their wool by dealing with black-market "broggers" such as my father than they could selling to licensed wool dealers.

As my father traveled a good deal in his wool-brokering business, when I was old enough to do so, I had the privilege of accompanying him on occasion. I enjoyed these trips because they gave me a rare opportunity to see and experience the surrounding villages, towns and countryside. On several of these journeys, my father and I attended the colorful festivals associated with shearing the sheep that produced the precious bales of wool purchased by my father and his fellow broggers.

To a boy like myself, these festivals were marvelous. There was a cornucopia of entertainment, singing, dancing, drinking, and eating to one's heart's content. Jugglers, clowns, wrestlers, puppeteers, blind harpers, bonfires, and fabulous storytellers enlightened the evening with their performances, ballads and rhymes. After filling my belly with pork, poultry, and cider, I would go to sleep dreaming of knights, jousts, and fair maidens with ribbons in their flowing hair, longing to be rescued by sweet and charming princes!

CHAPTER VI
THE MYSTERY PLAYS

One of the memorable journeys I took with my father was to see the renowned Mystery Plays staged every Christmas season in the town of Coventry. These plays retold the story of the Savior's Life and Passion. They had been put on by the Coventry guildsmen for hundreds of years. Members of the various guilds played the Biblical saints and sinners, and acted them to the hilt, with all the bombast and braggadocio one expects from butchers, bakers and candlestick makers on a brief holiday from their day jobs!

The most visually impressive mystery play I attended was one portraying the Passion and Crucifixion of Our Lord. Seeing Christ scourged, crowned with thorns, and crucified between the two thieves, while one mocks him, and the other asks for his blessing, brought the Gospel Message home to my young mind with an impact mere words on a page could not achieve.

I will never forget seeing the carpenter on the cross, straining against the weight of his body, saying the most sublime words ever uttered to mankind, "Father, forgive them, for they know not what they do." Words as relevant today as they were when Our Savior said them over 1500 years ago!

Although the most visually inspiring scene was the Crucifixion, the most fascinating play I saw was the one depicting the journey of the Wise Men and the massacre of the innocents by King Herod. The most memorable performance in that play was given by the rotund baker portraying the King. I can still see him strutting his huge carcass across the stage, roaring at the top of his lungs: "Kill the innocents! Kill the babies! Put them to the sword! Let the curse of their blood be upon my hoary head!"

This performance was so bad, it was good. Ever afterwards, when I felt an actor in one of my plays was performing in an absurdly exaggerated manner, I would call out: "You sound like you're trying to upstage Herod!"

Because we arrived in Coventry the day before the plays began, my father and I had the good fortune of seeing the rough and tumble rehearsals of several productions. Watching these amateurs work as hard as they did in their eagerness to put on the best show their abilities would allow, is something I drew upon years later when I wrote the rehearsal scene of the honest tradesmen preparing to put on the "Pyramis and Thisbe" interlude in *A Midsummer Night's Dream*. Bottom the Weaver and his rustic cohorts owe a deep debt of gratitude to their fellow tradesmen in the Coventry Mystery Plays of 1578.

I was fortunate to have made the journey with my father to see the Mystery Plays that year. The following year they were suppressed, cruelly shut down by government authorities as another instance of "Popish Knavery."

Accompanying my father on these business trips made me feel important. It also brought us closer together. I was proud of my father and everything he did in his business and public life. What a public life he had! Within a few years of my birth, he became the town bailiff, the highest and most powerful civic official in Stratford. When his term as bailiff concluded, he remained an alderman on the Town Council throughout my childhood.

Having held such high office, my father was entitled to be called "Mister Shakespeare." He was presented with a large agate stone ring that, when I was still small enough to do so, he occasionally allowed me to play with while I sat on his lap.

The perks and benefits of my father's success were many. They included a free seat at the command performances of the plays and entertainments that came through town. Before the troupes of entertainers could give a play for the paying public, they were required to perform for the bailiff and the councilmen of the Stratford Corporation.

As my father enjoyed plays and entertainments, he often allowed me to tag along. What shows they were: Biblical stories brought to life, historical figures from the nation's past, reliving their famous and glorious battles and victories, and pleasant pastoral comedies, concluding in joyous weddings.

My father and I were not the only ones enchanted by these performances. My mother, Gil, and my sister Joan loved them too.Our family was creative and artistic by nature. In fact, several times a year we would entertain each other in family talent contests with small prizes going to the winner.

Chapter VII
A Talent Contest

Another cherished memory of my early life is the family talent contest held in connection with the celebration of my tenth birthday. After my father completed his work in the glove shop, and Gil and I returned home from school in the company of my closest friend, Hamnet Sadler, our entire family enjoyed a feast of roast lamb, chicken soup, good-quality ale and cider, and candied pastries baked in the brick ovens of the bakery owned by Hamnet's family.

While we all sat around the fire roasting crab apples, sharing the gossip and news of the day, my father cleared his throat and said: "Hamnet, we're honored to have you join us this evening. The gift of friendship you and Will share is among the greatest one can give another. In honor of Will's birthday, we invite you and the other children here to enjoy a Shakespeare family tradition — a talent show! Since it's his birthday, Will has the honor of being the first to take our hearth stage."

Looking around sheepishly, I took my position in front of the fire. Summoning up my courage, I began reciting a ballad I had written the day before in honor of my little dog Troubadour.

> Troubadour and I went walking down the street.
> One had paws, the other had feet.
> Suddenly he started barking at some sheep,
> Waking a lazy shepherd from his drowsy sleep.
> He chased us for a while with his crooked staff,
> Before we shook his tail with yelping and a laugh.

We weaved our way through town,
And stopped at Clopton Bridge,
To watch some working men,
Who were digging in a ditch.

In the world of dogs,
Sir Troubadour is best.
He flushes out the fowls
And ferrets out their nests.

I love to throw him bones
And watch him run and fetch;
But now we'll go on home
And get ourselves some rest!

Finishing my performance, I was relieved to see everyone laughing. Troubadour, who was now in Hamnet's lap, barked his enthusiastic approval.

My father said, "Mary you've got quite a task to try and better Will's performance."

"I do," my mother answered as she moved over to the center of the room while my father provided a stool for her to sit upon. He handed her the small embellished Irish harp she would often play in the evenings when we sang songs and told tall tales.

My mother was a slender woman, with a pearl-like smile, violet eyes, high cheek bones, and shimmering dark hair. She had a clear sounding voice which perfectly complemented the rich tones of the harp strings.

As she took her seat, giving me a wink and a nod, I sensed we were in for something special. She began:

"Will, I'm going to sing a song for you this evening I learned from your grandmother. I heard her sing this often when I was your age. It's called 'The Lover's Lament.'"

Her fingers began to slowly pluck the taut harp strings, creating a haunting melody. After a beautiful prelude, she began singing:

A beauty born and bred,
Among the memories of the dead,
Turned her head once and said,
A strange vision haunts my bed,
And keeps this lonesome head,
From the bliss of eternal sleep.

It was long, long ago,
When the sea did swill and swell,
By the endless wishing well,
Underneath a sad willow,
Where our love did slowly grow,
That a promise he did keep.

He was pure, lean and tall,
And my name he would call,
Among the great and the small,
In the hills and mansion halls,
In the sunshine and the squalls,
While the Evil One did creep.

A jealous envy led,
To the garden of our bed;

He raised his serpent head,
And very slyly said:
"Your lover is quite dead,
Drowned in the ocean deep."

My heart it was torn,
By the love that was shorn,
From the life that was born;
And I bled from the thorns,
On the path that was worn,
Down to a castle keep.

Now I sit all alone,
As silent as the stones,
While the wind wails and moans;
And I have no hearth or home,
While my spirit longs to roam,
To my love in eternal sleep.

My mother put a great deal of feeling into the lyrics. I could imagine her as the lady depicted in the song, lamenting her long-lost love. After accepting our little audience's appreciation, she said:

"All right, John. Now that you've heard our performances, it's time for the man of the house to step up to the plate."

Taking his turn in our "bull baiting ring," my father said: "I will entertain you tonight with a tale of the warrior days of old, when the redhaired demons called Norsemen wreaked havoc throughout this land of Angles, Saxons, Jutes and Celts. And every merchant cleric and yeoman trembled in their beds!"

With that, he picked up an ancient hunting horn that he kept on the fireplace mantle. Puffing his cheeks, my father gave it a powerful blast that resonated throughout the room, bringing Troubadour instantly to life. As Troubadour danced around my father's legs, yelping his approval, my father began chanting his ballad in a bellowing voice.

In the old Norse Viking time,
When mermaids sang upon the Rhine,
Ships went gliding through the mists,
With Dragon faces, and lines so crisp.

Bows first rise, and then they dip,
As curses fly from sailors' lips.
On this weird and fateful trip,
Leagues fly by, clip by clip.

Loki the Jester, Thorgard the Lame,
Sit at the foot of the Hammer of Flame,
Scourges of West, eaters of fame,
Gods of raiders who kill and maim.

From fjords of Norway, to coast of Spain,
Them with swords and axes came,
Splitters of oaks, berserkers insane,
Slavers of peoples, binding in chains.

Stoners of hearts, makers of blame,
Slashers of hope, bashers of brains,

Drowners of youths, hewers of shame,
Demons stoking Hell's red flames!

Erik the Red, Hrogar the Dread,
Always to lead, never been led,
Tearing the virgins off the bed,
Knocking the merchant over the head.

Sanguine fountains, colored in red,
Nightmare's children, bearing the dead;
Rounding the cape, scaling the tower,
Counting the griefs, hour by hour.

Craving the gold, stealing the dower,
Brazing the blood, feeling the power,
Kindle the fear, hide in the bower,
Casting the tears onto the flower.

Kneel at the Cross, pray for the lost,
Summon the souls, sum all the cost,
Bring up the Knights, mounted on horse,
Cut down the heathen, far off the course.

Slaughter the swine, give them the dowse,
Roust all the ghosts out of the house,
Frozen in time, blood-colored wine,
Split all the skulls authoring crime.

In the Old Norse Viking Time,
When mermaids sang upon the Rhine,
Ships lay sunken in the mists,
With Dragon faces, and lines so crisp!

Finishing the last line of his mesmerizing chant, my father gladly accepted our enthusiastic applause and cheers with a deep bow. When he rose back up, he said: "Ladies and Gentlemen, I'm glad you enjoyed my performance."

Walking across the room, opening the lid of a casket that sat on a side table, he continued, "In this little treasure chest, we have a special present for the birthday boy." As he spoke, he lifted a rectangular wrapped package tied together with string out of the casket. Walking across the room, he handed the package to me, giving me an affectionate pat on my shoulder.

I realized, from the shape, weight and method of wrapping, it was likely an expensive book. Filled with eager anticipation of further armchair adventures, I undid the string, quickly removing the packaging. Much to my amazement, there in my hands was, to my way of thinking, the book of all books of fantastical creations, Ovid's *Metamorphoses*. Until this point in time, I had only been able to whet my appetite for Ovid's tales of magical transformations through brief borrowings of the copy of the book owned by my schoolmaster, Simon Hunt. Now, I would be able to delve into this treasure trove of myths and stories to my heart's content.

Filled with excitement, I embraced my father and my mother, thanking them for this generous gift. My father responded with a characteristic flourish:

"We wisheth well the well-wishing adventurer, as he sets forth upon his travels to the world of creative glory and endless story!"

Just as I imagined, the magic carpet of *The Metamorphoses* transported me to other places and times, entertaining me with legends of Greek and Roman mythology for countless hours during the remainder of my youth. The book and its tall tales became a touchstone for my imagination, a source of seemingly endless inspiration for my own plays and poems.

CHAPTER VIII
SCHOOL DAYS

Another critical factor in my development as a writer and creative artist was the positive influence of Catholic schoolmaster, Simon Hunt, my instructor at Stratford's King Edward VI's grammar school from 1572 to 1577. Even though it is a standard practice, I never saw Master Hunt beat any of his students. He relied upon positive motivation. The enthusiasm and passion he brought to his lessons made them enjoyable.

Following the educational tenants of Richard Mulcaster of the highly respected London Merchant Taylors School, Master Hunt incorporated role-playing and play reading into his lessons. This gave me a dramatic foundation I used throughout my career as an actor and playwright.

Simon Hunt believed I had great academic potential. And he took his Roman Catholic faith seriously. As a result, he was an occasional guest in our home for supper.

Unfortunately, nothing good lasts forever. It was with great sadness I learned Simon was leaving his post as Stratford schoolmaster. Although he could not announce it publicly at the time, Simon left his teaching position to pursue a higher calling. He traveled to the Continent to enter seminary, beginning the process of becoming a Jesuit priest.

I greatly admired Simon Hunt's intelligence, kindness, and courage. Because he was a one-of-a-kind person, it was impossible for our next schoolmaster, Thomas Jenkins, to fill Master Hunt's shoes. Master Jenkins was a decent person, but I was by this time an advanced student, while Master Jenkins was a young, inexperienced teacher.

Making matters worse, he was a Welshman, and he spoke with an accent we Warwickshire lads found amusing. The fact

Jenkins was a proud man, who, like the pompous and conceited steward Malvolio in my play *Twelfth Night*, had an exaggerated opinion of himself, while Hunt was modest and humble, letting his intelligence and talent speak for themselves, confirmed my initial opinion of Jenkins's aptitude and abilities.

Years later, when writing *The Merry Wives of Windsor* in response to Queen Elizabeth's command I show the comic knight Falstaff in love, I parodied Jenkins's personality and manner of speaking in a scene where the Welsh parson and teacher of the local grammar school, Hugh Evans, foolishly tries to demonstrate the effectiveness of his Latin teaching skills to the mother of young student, William Page.

Though I did not admire Master Jenkins, I had enough common sense not to be openly antagonistic towards him. Instead, I focused my efforts upon assisting my brother Gil and some of the younger students in the class to make the most out of a less than optimal educational opportunity.

Fortunately, for those of us who were not great fans of Master Jenkins's educational skills, his reign as the lord of our grammar school was short. He left Stratford after less than two years and was replaced by John Cottam, a man much more to my liking. Master Cottam was cut from the same cloth as Simon Hunt. He was intelligent and good-natured. He was also a devout Catholic.

Master Cottam's family were such firm Catholics that his brother became a priest. Master Cottam came from Lancashire, one of the remaining bastions of the Old Catholic Religion. The connections John's family had to the Lancashire aristocracy and gentry were to prove instrumental in my education and development.

Although I enjoyed having John as a teacher, and he and I quickly developed a great rapport and respect for each other, I was soon at the end of my studies at the Stratford Grammar School. I completed all classes and obtained the highest form.

The problem is I was like a wannabe dandy who purchases a new doublet and pair of silken hose, but has no place to show them off.

This unfortunate situation was partly a result of my father's slow decline in fortune and status, but mostly a consequence of our Roman Catholic faith. For, as the Queen's reign progressed, the repression of Catholics and other religious recusants by the government grew in vigor and intensity, until it reached even small towns, affecting lives as distant and remote as mine in Stratford.

Chapter IX
The Death of Katherine Hamlet

The death of Katherine Hamlet is a strange and haunting incident from my late childhood. Her body was found floating in the reeds beside a shallow bank of the Avon. Although the coroner's inquest concluded she drowned accidentally, falling into the river while attempting to fill a pail with water, there is a bias in favor of finding such suspicious deaths "accidental."

Suicide is considered a mortal sin by the English and Roman Catholic churches. Many consider the tragic loss of faith and hope inherent in a suicide the sin against the Holy Spirit Jesus warned against. The bodies of those who take their lives are not permitted to be buried within churchyard grounds.

This was all a great deal for a young impressionable mind to digest. Especially when I heard rumors the verdict rendered by the coroner's jury whitewashed the true story. If the rumor mill was correct, Katherine was involved in an affair. Jimmy Rogers was the son of a vinter known to liberally partake of his own merchandise. The son inherited the father's penchant for vice. When nature took its course, Katherine became pregnant. Jimmy refused to marry.

Driven mad by rejection, and the shame she would bring upon herself and her family for giving birth out of wedlock, Katherine drank a large quantity of aqua-vitae stolen from her father's strong box. Drunk and despondent, she plunged into the Avon in the dress she planned to wear on her wedding day, a wreath of flowers wrapped in her hair. That's what the fireside gossip said.

Wherever the truth lies, Katherine's premature death left a lasting impression upon me. I spoke with Kat on several occasions. She was outgoing and had a friendly smile and sparkle in her eyes. It was shocking such a beautiful person in the prime of life should end it in such a manner.

I have reflected upon the circumstances of Katherine Hamlet's death quite a few times over the years. One of my earliest poems, "A Lover's Complaint," is about the feelings of a woman jilted by a deceptive lover. She conveys her story to an old sage who encounters her on the banks of a river. The poem is an imaginary telling of a tale like the one Katherine might have told had she been able.

Although "A Lover's Complaint" is a long poem I revised several times before publishing it with my sonnets in 1609, the following stanzas convey its essence.

Well could he ride, and often men would say,
"*That horse his mettle from his rider takes:*
Proud of subjection, noble by the sway,
What rounds, what bounds, what course, what stop he makes!"
And controversy hence a question takes,
Whether the horse by him became his deed,
Or he his manage by the well-doing steed?

So on the tip of his subduing tongue
All kind of arguments and question deep,
All replication prompt, and reason strong,
For his advantage still did wake and sleep:
To make the weeper laugh, the laugher weep,
He had the dialect and different skill,
Catching all passions in his craft of will;

So many have, that never touch'd his hand,
Sweetly suppos'd them mistress of his heart.
My woeful self, that did in freedom stand,
And was my own fee-simple, (not in part,)
What with his art in youth, and youth in art,
Threw my affections in his charmed power,
Reserv'd the stalk, and gave him all my flower.

For lo! his passion, but an art of craft,
Even there resolv'd my reason into tears:
There my white stole of chastity I daff'd,
Shook off my sober guards and civil fears;
Appear to him, as he to me appears,
All melting; though our drops this difference bore
His poison'd me, and mine did him restore.

O, father, what a hell of witchcraft lies
In the small orb of one particular tear!
But with the inundation of the eyes
What rocky heart to water will not wear?
What breast so cold that is not warmed here?
O, cleft effect? cold modesty, hot wrath,
Both fire from hence and chill extincture hath!

Thus merely with the garment of a Grace
The naked and concealed fiend he cover'd,
That the unexperienc'd gave the tempter place,
Which, like a cherubim, above them hover'd.

Who, young and simple, would not be so lover'd?
Ay me! I fell; and yet do question make
What should I do again for such a sake.

The melancholy madness and manner of death allegedly chosen by Katherine is mirrored in the conduct of Ophelia in my *Tragedy of Hamlet*. Perhaps a fitting epilogue to Katherine's story is the ancient song Ophelia sings in the depth of her grief at Hamlet's cruel rejection and his murder of her father.

Good morrow, 'tis Saint Valentine's day,
All in the morning betime,
And I a maid at your window,
To be your Valentine:

Then up he rose, and don'd his clothes,
And dupp'd the chamber door;
Let in the maid, that out a maid
Never departed more.

By Gis, and by Saint Charity,
Alack, and fie for shame!
Young men will do't, if they come to't;
By cock, they are to blame.

Quoth she, Before you tumbled me,
You promis'd me to wed:
[He Answers.]
So would I ha' done, by yonder sun,
An thou hadst not come to my bed.

CHAPTER X
REFORMATION DESOLATION

Certain things move one in this life. Events and people crystallize in the fiery forge of memory, converting a black lump of coal into a glistening diamond. For me, the Mass said by the Jesuit priest, Edmund Campion, one evening during his mission to England in the spring of 1581, was one of those precious moments.

The Reverend Campion was a brilliant Oxford intellect given the further gift of a unique charism by our Lord and Savior. Through a combination of grace and mercy, he was able to cross the English Channel in June 1580, landing at Dover. Although initially detained for questioning, he managed to outwit his would-be captors, convincing them he was merely a country gentleman who had been traveling on the continent for business purposes.

Upon his release, along with other Catholic priests, Campion quickly made his way inland from Dover, weaving through the web of spies and mercenary priest hunters lying in wait to detect, capture, and turn them over to the Regime's torturers. As is true in all times and places, there were many willing to betray a "friend" with a kiss to have an opportunity to collect thirty pieces of silver. Bloodhounds sniffing and yelping in search of blood money!

Some say Edmund Campion was a traitor, seeking to overthrow the Queen. That is a lie. Campion's heart and soul were pure. His mission was simple: to bring a beleaguered Roman Catholic flock the sacraments they were dying of thirst to receive. Freedom to practice our religion in peace was denied.

Our altars were desecrated, rood crosses torn down, stained-glass windows broken and dismantled, murals and frescoes whitewashed, statues hacked into pieces, relics destroyed, chalices and plate auctioned off to the highest bidder, rosary beads forbidden, priests and nuns made into outlaws, our glorious monasteries and convents confiscated and laid waste — turned into bare ruined choirs where late the sweet birds sang!

It was artistic and cultural assassination, a repudiation of all that came before. Our ancestors are surely rolling over in their graves. Some might call the times we live in the birth of a new age, a new way of looking at the world. But, to me, we threw the baby out with the bathwater. Everything is inverted. Fair is foul; foul is fair; and the cry of the Banshee shrieks through the air!

The course of events leading to the crossing of my life path with that of Edmund Campion was a fateful one. The year 1580 was significant for my family. Through our connection with John Cottam, I was able to secure employment as the tutor of the children of the Hoghton family in Lancashire.

Earlier in Elizabeth's reign, the Catholics in the North revolted against the Queen and her government. This Northern Rebellion occurred in 1569, when I was five years old. I still remember my father and mother anxiously praying for a successful conclusion. One allowing them freedom to practice their religion in peace. Unfortunately, the rebellion was brutally put down and over five hundred rebels were executed.

Despite their defeat, the government had neither the troops nor the power to completely suppress the Northern Catholics. These families had held their seats of power for many generations. Among them, the Hoghtons were significant. The place where their current patriarch, Alexander Hoghton, lived, was a fortified residence called Hoghton Tower. I would journey there to assume my position as the children's tutor.

John Cottam's recommendation helped me secure the position. He knew my ambition to attend Oxford was thwarted by a combination of factors, including my father's business difficulties and the statute enacted to prevent Catholic families from sending their sons to university.

As my father explained on numerous occasions, the economic system was rigged to keep Catholic families impoverished. The prohibition against Catholics attending university made it impossible for ambitious young Catholic men like myself to gain entrance into the professions of lawyer or doctor. We could not become clergyman of the state enforced religion. We could not obtain positions in government.

Making matters worse, Catholic tradesmen were prevented from bettering the lives of their families. Since the regime was Protestant, doing all it could to remain in power, the odds of a Catholic obtaining a wool dealing license were about as likely as a snowstorm in June. Given the stacked deck against Catholic merchants like my father, what was a man to do? The answer for many was to live beyond the pale, dealing on the black market. But if one got caught, it could be financial ruin for you and a stroke of good fortune for the government informer who turned you in.

Pick up any rock in the garden. You never know what you will find. Deal enough hands at cards, you're bound to lose. During the 1570s, my father's number came up several times. Betrayed by informers, he paid severe fines for dealing in wool and lending money at interest.

These business setbacks pale in comparison to the fines and restrictions imposed upon my father due to his refusal to conform to the state religion. He had to cease attending Town Council meetings because he would not take the Oath of Supremacy requiring civic officials to acknowledge the Queen as the supreme authority of "God's Church on Earth."

Though my father did not lose his head for failing to take the Oath, he suffered economic slow death by degrees. As the government continued to raise the fines for recusancy, it caused my parents to sell the parcel of land my mother inherited from her father. The worst of those fines came in June 1580, but I am now getting ahead of my story.

CHAPTER XI
JOURNEY TO LANCASHIRE

The best thing that happened to our family in 1580 was the birth of my brother Edmund. Edmund was my parents' last child. My mother's pregnancy at such an advanced age was a surprise. We all prayed for the health of Mother and the baby. Edmund's March delivery was a cause for celebration.

Now that there was another family mouth to feed, I felt it was imperative I find a way to support myself. So, after Edmund's baptism, I set out with John Cottam to assume my position as tutor of the Hoghton children. My father was able to purchase a small pony named Nutmeg to carry me on the journey. John rode a fine black stallion named Mercury. Although we slowed them down, John and Mercury enjoyed the company.

Given the threat of vagrants, John carried a rapier and dagger. I carried a bow and set of arrows made by our local fletcher. Though we were not professional soldiers, John was a good swordsman. I had won several local prizes for archery. Any vagabonds we met along the way were going to get more than they bargained for.

Highwaymen were a different matter. They carried pistols and muskets. Given their firepower and experience, they would have the upper hand. We would give those brigands what they wanted.

To decrease the probability of being waylaid, John and I resolved we would stop traveling several hours before sundown each day. John was going north to spend some time with his family. They lived only a few miles from Hoghton Tower. He had come this way on his journey to Stratford to accept the teaching position at King Edward's School, so he knew of several inns along the way with decent food and stables for boarding our horses.

The journey to Hoghton Tower was the longest I had undertaken without the protective presence of my father. Traveling at a reasonable pace of twenty-five miles a day, it would take at least four days to get there.

Roads throughout the realm are unpaved and poorly maintained. Many sections turn into impassable quagmires on a rainy day. Given the length, comfort, and, even the success or failure of our journey, depended upon the weather, John and I began and ended each day with a prayer for blue skies. My parents provided me with the generous sum of one pound to finance my journey north. Each day of rain delay would eat into more of this precious allowance.

Thankfully, the weather remained unusually dry and warm, allowing us to make good progress. At the end of our first day, we arrived at the Red Fox inn and tavern.

The Red Fox's proprietors were Joseph, a middle-aged man, and Agnes, his young, freckle-faced wife. Agnes had a winning smile, red hair, green eyes, and a small straight nose. She wore a dress showing three quarters of her ample breasts. For Joseph, his wife's style of dress was good business. Having an attractive young wife was not just an asset to a tavern owner, it was an asset to anyone in a trade catering to male customers.

Many a goldsmith, haberdasher, bookseller, and cobbler owe much of their success to the youthful beauty of their wives. On a sunny day, you will find these women sitting in front of their husbands' shop windows. It's a step above the advertising going on in doorways and windows of stews, but it operates upon the same age-old principle.

Not only was Agnes an alluring beauty, so was the bar maid working the tavern room with her. Although Sylvia was not as buxom or sharp featured, she was more attractive to me. While Agnes had a mature woman's figure, Sylvia was lithe. Her blonde hair shimmered in the candlelight.

Fortunately, Sylvia served us. When we finished our meal, I paid the bill, giving her a sizable tip. While the crowd thinned out, I chatted with her — making an instant connection. I discovered her father was a joiner who died several years ago. Sylvia and her mother now lived in a cottage nearby. As I suspected, she had not yet turned seventeen.

As young as I was, my heart went out to Sylvia. Without a dowry and a father to protect her, she was vulnerable to being taken advantage of by men. Though she was very beautiful, I sensed it was a fragile beauty. One which could easily be destroyed.

On a sudden impulse, I asked Sylvia to meet me outside the tavern for a few minutes when she was allowed a break. Much to my surprise, she accepted.

A quarter hour later, I was standing in a brisk wind, shivering on the outside, simmering on the inside with a strange brew of emotions, leaving me tongue-tied when my own version of a youthful Venus emerged from the front doorway of a slightly run-down Warwickshire Tavern. Breaking through the invisible current of emotion leaving me speechless, I suddenly grabbed Sylvia by the shoulders. Looking directly into those beautiful blue eyes, I blurted out:

"Has anybody ever told you you're beautiful?"

"A few," she answered. "Not for the right reasons."

"Trust me," I replied. "I'm not trying to deceive you."

Sylvia giggled. Placing a hand over my mouth, she said:

"Don't be silly. We've only just met. I like you so far. You're witty and handsome, in a certain sort of way. But I've heard you talking with your friend about going to Lancashire. I may never see you again!"

"You will!" I protested. "I'm not going there forever. I'll be back in a year or so. You're only a day's journey from Stratford. I pray you'll give me the opportunity to woo you properly!"

"Your intentions may be sincere," said Sylvia. "But promises, promises, promises are what we young women hear from young men like yourself — and you're younger than most!"

"Don't feel that way!"

"You must come from a respectable family. I'm sure they'd feel I was unsuitable."

"Don't say such things," I implored.

"What's your father's name? How does he make his living?"

"John Shakespeare. Owns a glove shop in Stratford."

"Will you be a glover too?"

"Doubt it," I responded. "I don't know what I'll eventually do. I'm on my way to tutor children up north."

"Ah! You read and write. If you're to become a teacher, you know Latin as well?" Sylvia asked.

"I studied Latin at the King's School in Stratford."

"As I thought," she said with an air of resignation. "You're above my station — there's no future for us."

Though what she said was logical, I desperately wanted to throw caution to the wind.

"I don't believe that. Love can overcome all obstacles. We can remake the world instead of allowing it to shape us."

"Oh, Will. I wish that was true. You're a prince at heart. I'll not soon forget you."

"I can't forget you!" I said. "Listen to your heart. Love will prevail!"

At this, Sylvia again put a hand over my lips, whispering, "Hush."

She threw her arms around my neck and gave me a quick kiss. Just as abruptly, she gave me a playful wink, and sprinted back into the tavern, leaving me with a taste of ambrosia — wanting more!

We humans are strange that way. Most often, it's the illogical rather than the logical that adds spice and flavor to our lives. It's the happenstance meeting on a street in London, the Stratford horse fair, or at a tavern on the road to Lancashire, which touches off sparks kindling flames of passion that make life worth living.

Journeying through time, I have found there are many degrees of that exquisite gift from our Creator called "Love." And, there is a rare version of that precious commodity called "Love at First Sight." I first experienced it with Sylvia on that cold April night.

CHAPTER XII
A TASTE OF AMBROSIA

After my beautiful encounter with Sylvia, I made sure Nutmeg and Mercury were being well cared for in the stables and headed back to the tavern to retire for the evening. When I entered the great room, with its roaring fire, I was surprised to find John had not turned-in for the night. He was standing before the crackling flames, color in his cheeks, a gleam in his eyes. I had seen him look like that before, so I knew something was up.

John was much admired in Stratford for his singing voice. I sometimes encountered him serenading himself on one of his habitual walks in the countryside. John's intellect was flexible and ingenious. He could begin with the opening line of a well-known song and go on to create one equally as good as the original. As I came into his line of sight, he smiled and began singing in his unique, raspy voice:

I spied a fair young bonnie lass,
Traipsing out upon the grass,
With her eyes she made a pass,
But I knew the flame could never last.

Cause when we hear the trumpet blast,
And the noisy cymbals clash,
We know we've gone and run too fast,
And he's that's first must come in last.

When a sailor climbs upon the mast,
And tries to use his looking glass,

To divine the future from the past,
All his hopes they wind up dashed

Upon the rocks that ring the seas,
That crash against them ceaselessly,
While lonely mermaids pine and sing,
Of treasures that drowned sailors bring.

When masts and spars are cracked and
split,
Our trusty ship is so unfit.
Like stallions chomping at the bits,
We charge too fast and lose our wit.

Well, send me hope from far above,
And, like two lovesick turtle doves,
We'll hop and laugh, and dance and sing,
And bathe in Bath's eternal spring,

Whose waters are so warm and soft,
They wash the dirt and grime right off.
They slake your thirst, and heal your sores,
And leave you off at my front door!

During John's performance, Sylvia paused from her work cleaning tables to stand beside me. I was not sure whether she picked up on the "look before you leap" message John was sending.

I vehemently disagreed with his analysis and the cynical worldview it implied. Like many other young adults, I believed he underestimated the intelligence and understanding of those of my generation. I wanted to prove John wrong. There was more to life than the accumulation of wealth.

Gathering up my courage, I took to the floor to try my own hand at improvisation. I was shooting for something to demonstrate what occurred between Sylvia and me this evening was pure and life-changing.

With a heady mixture of thoughts and emotions, I gave Sylvia a friendly nod, and began.

Thank you for the kiss,
That serves as a bridge,
Between what is ours,
And between what is His.

Thank you for the kiss,
That floats in the mist,
And hovers over me,
Like halos angels see.

Thank you for the kiss,
Which fell from your lips,
Like music from the stars,
Or magic candy bars.

Thank you for the kiss,
From a sweet princess,
It tasted of true love,
And knowing innocence.

Thank you for the kiss,
That shattered all the bricks,
And brought down the walls,
That locked me in so long.

Thank you for the kiss,
It brought me such bliss,
And opened-up the door,
For me to love you more!

As I finished singing, I saw Sylvia brush back a tear and begin clapping enthusiastically. When our eyes met, her face lit up. John was gently shaking his head back and forth with a wry smile.

While I made a little bow, Sylvia stepped forward. Taking my right hand in both of hers, she gave it a gentle kiss.

"That's your reward for standing up for me. You're a sweet angel!" she said in a trembling voice.

I felt like a god newly ascended to Mount Olympus! I respectfully draw the curtain on a magical evening. Ah! The joy there is in being young, when the world is still one's oyster!

CHAPTER XIII
HOGHTON TOWER

The next morning John and I awoke before dawn, enjoyed a hearty breakfast of cheese, milk and bread, and went to the stables to saddle up the horses, preparing for departure at sunrise. To my surprise, Sylvia was waiting for us with a wineskin, a small round of cheese, and a slab of wrapped bacon to place in our satchels.

"Are you sure you want to do this?" I asked her earnestly. "I don't want you and your mother going without for our sakes."

"Don't think that way. If we couldn't afford to give it, I wouldn't have brought it here."

"Then I accept. But I insist I pay you for it," I said, extracting three silver pennies from my purse, placing them in her hand. As I did, I said: "What you have given me from your heart is beyond recompense."

Accepting the pennies, Sylvia kissed me on the cheek.

"A third kiss!" I laughed. "I've died and gone to heaven!"

"Let me bring you down to earth," interjected John. "Although I hate breaking this up, it's time we moved on. We've a long way to go. We can't afford to lose any daylight."

"Will you send word back to me? Let me know how you're doing and when you'll return?" Sylvia requested.

"Of course! I'll send you word as fast as I can." Leaning close to her, I whispered: "I want you to be part of my life. Forever."

"I want you to be part of mine too," she answered, adding, "I'll wait for you."

After we shared a long embrace, Sylvia left the stable yard to return home.

While John and I walked our horses to the outskirts of town, I could not help feeling partings like this were such sweet sorrows. It was touching to know Sylvia loved me as she did. I had never had a woman outside my family care for me like this before. It gave me a feeling of great elation. At the same time, the thought of having to leave her was gut-wrenching. But I had no choice. I could not yet support myself, let alone a wife.

My education left myself and my family feeling I was too good for an apprenticeship. I was not eligible to enter a profession. I was a fish out of water.

So, I reluctantly continued the journey to Lancashire with John. Our horses trudged on monotonously. The next few days seemed like they would never end. But, as we approached our destination, our spirits began to rise. One day, off in the distance, we watched the high ramparts of the entrance gate to Hoghton Tower come into view.

As John explained during our journey, Hoghton Tower was originally built in 1109 by one of William the Conqueror's comrades, Count Harvey de Walter. The current owner counted Lady Godiva of Coventry, as well as Count de Walter, among his ancestors.

For defensive purposes, the tower was built atop a hill from which there was a panoramic view of the surrounding countryside. The present large manor house, and surrounding stone buildings, were built in 1565. They gave a traveler like me the impression the owners of this fortress-like manor possessed immense power and wealth.

Fortunately, John Cottam was a frequent visitor to the manor. After we dismounted from our horses, he was able to gain admittance from the gate keeper in short order. Before entering the main house, we walked Mercury and Nutmeg around to the spacious stables. The head groom assured us they would be well cared for.

I confess I felt a bit uneasy as I walked with John from the stables to the back entrance of the main house, a meager satchel and bedroll in hand. Other than the riding boots I wore for the journey, I only had one pair of semi-respectable shoes with me. My mother had packed a nightshirt, three shirts, two pairs of breeches, some stockings, a clean jerkin jacket, and several pairs of matching hose. But, other than the clothes I was wearing on my back, these would be all I had to get started in my new teaching life.

Once we had an opportunity to clean up, the Hoghtons' butler escorted us through a long hallway to meet with the master of the house, Sir Alexander Hoghton. Although he was never officially knighted by the Protestant Queen, John said everyone in the household called him "Sir" out of the deep respect they had for this prince of a man.

We found Sir Alexander working in a large room that served as his library and study. To a lover of books like myself, the room was spectacular. It was lined with several built-in bookcases, chock-full of leather-bound volumes. Within those bindings were the thoughts, hopes, and dreams of the best of our human race. I was fortunate to live in a time where a common person like myself could have access to books such as this and even own some himself!

Movable type made this immense transmission of knowledge possible. This type of printing had only been conceived of for a little over a century — a drop in the bucket of the human chronicle. Our culture owes a great debt of gratitude to the goldsmith, Johann Guttenberg of Maines, who perfected the concept of movable type printing in the 1440s and 1450s.

Sometime later, William Caxton brought this technology to England. He established the first English printing press in Westminster in 1476. Caxton published numerous English masterpieces, including Chaucer's *The Canterbury Tales*, and Sir Thomas Mallory's *Le Morte d' Arthur*. One hundred years later, one of the heirs of this printing ingenuity was Alexander Hoghton's impressive library of beautifully bound classics.

My thoughts were soon interrupted by our greeting from the master of the house.

"John! Good to see you."

"You too, Sir Alexander."

"Life in Stratford agreeing with you?"

"Certainly."

"Beautiful town. Pretty good angling. Been there once or twice. Had good luck with flies made of sleeve silk. Casting for trout in the shadow of the picturesque church. What's its name?"

"Holy Trinity!" I blurted out without thinking.

Before either of them could speak, I began apologizing "Sorry sir, for interrupting your and Mr. Cottam's conversation."

Acknowledging my apology with a nod of his head, Sir Alexander asked: "Who do we have here?"

John said: "Master William Shakespeare. Son of the former Bailiff of Stratford, John Shakespeare."

"I met your father back in the day. Good Catholic."

"Yes sir," I replied. "In fact, my father is intending to make the pilgrimage to St. Winifred's Well this year. He's going to give thanks for the protection of my mother during her pregnancy and the successful birth of my brother last month."

"St. Winifred's a fine Saint to have as one's patron. I've made the pilgrimage to Holywell several times. From what John's written, your mother's a member of the Arden family."

"True," I said enthusiastically. It felt so good to be in a place where I could acknowledge my Catholic lineage with pride.

"You're from good stock. John said you were his top student."

"Yes sir," I answered. "My family and I are grateful to you for giving me this opportunity. I'll do my very best to teach the children. I'll not let you down."

While making this pledge, I looked Sir Alexander directly in the eyes.

"That's good enough for me. I cannot ask more. You'll meet the children and give them their first lesson tomorrow morning. I've asked John to draw up a curriculum of study.

After we review it this afternoon, John will deliver it to you. In working out your lessons, you'll have free access to the books in this library.

"I expect you to give the children four hour-long lessons a day — two in the morning, and two in the afternoon. The lessons are to occur six days a week. Sundays you'll attend Mass with us in the morning. And have the afternoon free. Understand?"

"Yes Sir," I smiled.

Compared to the schedule of the Stratford Grammar School, Sir Alexander's was a version of heaven on earth. Only four hours of instruction a day, access to a priceless collection of books, and Sunday afternoons free to do as I wanted! All this, and Mass on Sundays too! But how?

Summoning up my courage, I asked: "Sir, you mentioned Mass on Sundays?"

"You must wonder how we manage that. A gardener named Gerard works here on the property. He's a Catholic priest, ordained during the reign of Queen Mary, the good ruler who blessedly, but briefly, returned England to the Catholic Church. Father Gerard remains an ordained priest in the eyes of Rome. He says Mass for us Sunday mornings. I must have your solemn vow you'll never reveal the true identity of Father Gerard, or that Masses are said here, to anyone outside this house."

"As God is my witness, I'll not reveal the secrets of this household," I swore.

"I appreciate your sincerity and good faith. I know you've had a long journey. I'll let you get some food and rest. Please follow our butler to the kitchen. Let our head cook, Geoffrey, know I'd like him to prepare an early meal for you."

"Thank you, Sir," I replied. As I met the butler, I glanced back towards the library and saw John Cottam writing notes while Sir Alexander dictated instructions to him.

CHAPTER XIV
SETTLING-IN

Upon my arrival in the huge kitchen, with its numerous brick bread ovens, roaring fireplaces, simmering kettles, and freshly slaughtered pig roasting upon a spit, the large, cherubim-faced, white-aproned cook, Geoffrey, prepared me a generous meal of freshly baked bread, milk, cheese, salted beef, and a large tankard of small ale.

Placing the pewter plate containing the food on the table, Geoffrey patted me on the back, saying: "Welcome aboard, Me Laddie! I hear you'll be learning the children. You're lucky. They're a sprightly, happy band. No need for rod or switch, my man. They respond best to a gentle hand!"

"Thank you for this excellent meal," I responded, gratified by the warmth of the greeting. "And for your sage advice regarding the children. I'll keep it in mind."

The cook's round face broke into a wide, toothy grin.

"By our Lady, I believe John Cottam's found a good one! I can tell you one thing about the Hoghtons. If you do right by them, they do right by you. They're one of the few remaining families of the Old Guard. Loyal and true as the day's long. I've been with Sir Alexander over twenty years. Been with him through thick and thin. By the Grace of God, we're still here to tell the tales!"

Between mouthfuls of hearty brown bread, and soft, creamy cheese, I rejoined: "By the look and sound of it, I'm sure you have interesting tales to tell."

"Certainly do, me Laddie. Stop by some evening after day is done. We'll sit by a country fire, roast some crab apples and drink honeyed mead like warriors of old. I'll regale you with stories of Sir Alexander and I that will make your hairs stand on end!"

"I'll take you up on that offer," I called out, as I watched the cook go about his business.

While he basted the succulent pig, Geoffrey glanced at me with a knowing grin. He began singing a ballad, entertaining the kitchen maids and helpers:

> There was a fair, young bonny maiden,
> Who found herself in my safe-haven,
> She was a dove, and I a raven,
> But, by God, I loved that fair young maiden.
>
> We danced and pranced the night away,
> Like young colt and mare at play,
> And, like two kids on the first of May,
> We jumbled and tumbled in the hay!
>
> Hey nonny no! Hey nonny neigh!
> Watch what we do, and watch what we say,
> The sun may set, the ship sail away,
> But no one can change what we shared that day.
>
> So God bless you, and God bless me,
> And let us both be fancy free,
> I'll sing for you; you sing for me,
> With hearts that beat most lovingly.
>
> Hey nonny no! Hey nonny neigh!
> Whatever the gossips and old men say,

Leaves will rustle, boughs will sway,
And boys and girls in love will play!

As Geoffrey finished this shimmering song, chock full of the *joy de vivre* which poured out of every pore of his bear-like body, we all broke out laughing.

By the time I made it back to the room I was sharing with John Cottam, I was ready to hit the sack and get some shut-eye. Thanks to the Hoghtons' generosity, the room was fitted with a sizable bed with a pull-out truckle bed underneath.

Getting into the surprisingly comfortable truckle bed, I said a prayer of thanksgiving to the Lord, asking Him to protect Sylvia and my family. Then I pulled the thick woolen blanket over my head and slept like a baby.

CHAPTER XV
CULINARY REVELS

I awoke the next morning to find a shapely, flaxen-haired chambermaid using an ember to light the kindling in the small fireplace. As I lay under the blanket, silently watching this morning angel going about her business, I smiled, relishing the moment.

Although her back was towards me, using a mysterious sixth sense, she somehow became aware I was observing her. Women are wise that way. From an early age, they learn we men initially prefer visual form to substance. Like master musicians playing finely tuned instruments, they intuitively know how to do the things necessary to pluck at the heart strings of a man's psyche, leaving him desiring more.

This thin and agile chambermaid, poised on the brink of full womanhood, instinctively knew how to play the age-old game of courtship. Once she successfully kindled a growing fire in both the fireplace and my mind, she turned and flashed me a coquettish smile worthy of the finest courtesan in a lusty bachelor king's court.

Had my heart not already been filled with the white-hot flames, dreams and visions of a supremely powerful love goddess named Sylvia, I might have, like a ravenous trout in a mountain stream, avidly taken the bait. But, instead of allowing her to set the hook, and beginning a conversation with this bewitching rival goddess, I nodded, rolled over, and pulled the blanket back over my head, hoping to blot out the image of her large green eyes, coral lips, and winning smile that had already imprinted itself into my imagination.

As I lay under the blanket thinking, I resolved to return to Sylvia unscathed. Like everything worth having in life, truth and beauty require sacrifice. Love and life are a series of choices. For better or worse, I made my first love choice that morning.

By the time I roused myself out of bed a quarter hour later, the Circe-like chambermaid had vanished. But the crackling fire she set made the room significantly warmer. After using the chamber pot to relieve myself, I poured some fresh water from the ewer into the pewter basin and washed my hands. As I was drying them, John Cottam rolled over, stretched his arms out wide, and called out: "Good morning!"

"Sir John!" I returned in jest. "I trust you slept well. Sounded like you did!" I said, referring to John's habitual snoring.

"Slept like a newborn in swaddling. You?"

"I was so tired I believe I would have slept soundly if the bed and pillow were stone. As they were soft and clean, there was no need to test that theory," I replied, continuing the friendly banter that characterized our conversations during the long journey from Stratford to Hoghton Tower.

"Will, I envy you. This is a special opportunity you have here," John said, getting out of bed and beginning his morning toilette.

"Sir Alexander and I worked yesterday to develop a curriculum for the students. In addition to Latin and Greek, it includes Geography, English History, and the History and Literature of the Roman Empire."

"Sounds great," I replied.

"It will allow you the opportunity to utilize the resources of the Hoghtons' excellent library to develop your lesson plans. Although you're not able to attend Oxford this year, having access to the Hoghtons' library, and the time to study the books within it, will be almost as good. Yours will be a university of the mind!"

"Hopeful." I replied.

"There's more," said John. "I explained my practice of having students act in plays to Sir Alexander. Sir Alexander's given his blessing. I know how much you enjoyed being part of the school productions in Stratford. You'll now have the opportunity to put on some of your own plays with the children here at Hoghton Tower. Even better, when I discussed your love of playacting with Sir Alexander, he offered to introduce you to the lead actor in a local group of Catholic players that often perform here. If things work out, you might have an opportunity to act and teach."

"Fantastic! I can't thank you enough," I told John.

"You're heartily welcome. In times like these, we Catholics must support each other. Your father's been of great help to me. He's a special person."

"He is," I agreed.

"Let's finish getting dressed and see what Geoffrey and his motley crew are fixing for breakfast," said John.

"Sounds like a plan. Geoffrey's one-of-a-kind."

"I think he's as interesting as any character that ever graced the stage. He's the salt of the earth, and the spice that gives life to the soup in the kettle. He puts meat on the bones, and strengthens the mettle!"

"Well said," I responded. "Now let's get down to the kitchen, and fill our gullets with bread, eggs and chicken, that leaves our fingers fit for licking, our bellies fit for hitching, our legs fit for kicking, and our candles fit for wicking!"

"By fair young maidens that work in yonder kitchen!" said John, completing the sentence with a bawdy flourish, demonstrating, in the kingdom of wits, he was still the sorcerer, and I the mere apprentice.

Arriving in the kitchen, we found Geoffrey immersed in his role as a master magician, casting spells and whipping up culinary dishes that would make even the laziest child wake-up, take notice, and jump into his britches. Ever the entertainer, when Geoffrey saw us, he smiled, and broke into a sea chanty he learned from an old sailor.

I was knocking on my noggin,
Whistling up the wind,
Dreaming of my paradise,
While living here in sin.

The mermaids on the rocks,
Throw back their golden locks,
And watch the drunken sailors,
Careening on the docks!

So keep your bearings up,
Though your flag be struck,
And drink yourself some wine,
From your favorite stein!

The King lives in his castle,
The deaf they lead the blind,
Through the lanes and alleys,
Till the end of time!

And if you cut and run,
You're going to have some fun.
But when you need an anchor,
Then your days are done!

So, when it's touch and go,
Just move on with the flow.
And when the wind runs out,
Then tack yourself about!

And if you cannot fathom,
The curse of Eve and Adam,
Find yourself a maid,
And turn her into Madam!

So when you're high and dry,
Don't go out and cry,
The tide will wipe the tears,
From your salty eyes!

And when you fight your battle,
And you take the prize,
You'll find the hidden treasure,
Concealed by all the lies!

I was knocking on my noggin,
Whistling up the wind,
Dreaming of my paradise,
While living here in sin.

As Geoffrey finished this sea chantey, I applauded. John whistled his approval. As the noise died down, I called out: "Well done, my man! Sung as only a true sailor can!"

Geoffrey replied: "If you enjoyed that one, here's a bawdy little ditty I learned years ago while on a cruise with an Old Salt from the Isle of Man.

The master, the swabber, the boatswain, and I,
The gunner, and his mate,

Lov'd Mall, Meg, and Marion, and Margery,
But none of us car'd for Kate:
For she had a tongue with a tang,
Would cry to a sailor, Go, hang:
She lov'd not the savour of tar nor of pitch,
Yet a tailor might scratch her where'er she did
itch.
Then to sea, boys, and let her go hang.

When Geoffrey finished, John and I rose out of our seats, clamoring for more. Bowing, Geoffrey said: "No more encores for now, my friends. You'll have to come back for a second helping. I've got some savory dishes to prepare. A man's mind's no good without food in his belly!"

For some reason, Geoffrey's last little ditty remained "knocking on my noggin" for years on end. I finally exorcised it by using it as a drunken sailor's song in *The Tempest*.

CHAPTER XVI
FATHER TOM AND LITTLE MARY

After our rollicking breakfast, John escorted me to the schoolroom in the second story of Hoghton Tower. To my pleasant surprise, I was to have a comfortable chair, an oak table, and a portable desk box.

The room also contained several long benches where the students would sit. The lighting was provided by two windows covered with expensive panes of glass capable of being swung in on their hinges. Most wonderful of all was an ornately carved wooden chest containing hornbooks, Latin grammars, comedies by Platus, tragedies by Seneca, wax tablets, styluses, paper, inkhorns, and quill pens.

If this were not enough, in the center of the table was an exquisite, imported globe, which could be spun on its axis to illustrate the geography lessons I would give the children. As I traced my right index finger across the equator, I marveled at the knowledge of the world we had obtained since Vasco de Gama rounded the continent of Africa, and Christopher Columbus discovered the New World less than a century ago.

For a country boy like myself, to have such a rare object as a globe to let my imagination run wild upon was nothing short of a miracle. The hours I spent studying it led to my lifelong fascination with the voyages of discovery that opened-up countless new horizons to those willing to take the risks. As Miranda says in *The Tempest*: "Oh! wonder! How many goodly creatures are there here! How beauteous mankind is! O brave new world that has such people in't!"

Finally, along a side wall, there was a beautifully painted virginal and instrument stands housing a lute and finely crafted viola. Although I did not yet play an instrument, I hoped to learn to do so.

Not long after I inventoried these educational treasures, the five Hoghton children arrived. I still remember their names: Christopher, James, Abigail, Anne, and "Little Mary." The fact the Hoghtons insisted their girls should be as well educated as the boys was an admirable family trait. One I did my best to later emulate with my own daughters, Susanna and Judith.

Proving God does not discriminate between the sexes, my best student turned out to be Abigail, the oldest girl in the class. Abigail was tall, fair skinned, with raven dark hair and light blue eyes that sparkled with intensity and love for learning. Though she was my favorite, like all conscientious teachers, I tried not to show it.

At that point in my life, I was still more boy than man. But I took my teaching responsibilities most seriously. I knew the good names of my father and my mentor, John Cottam, depended upon my holding up my end of the "bargain."

One day, when we finished our morning lesson, Abigail and her younger sister Mary, accompanied me to the stables to visit Nutmeg. Like many little girls and boys, Mary loved animals, particularly horses. With her mother's and father's authorization, and the assistance of the Hoghton's groom, a burly, baldheaded Scandinavian name Oswald, today would be a special day for six-year-old Mary. She was to enjoy a ride on her favorite steed, the magnificent Nutmeg!

In anticipation of this marvelous event, Little Mary donned the princess dress the Hoghtons' French seamstress, Madame Françoise, painstakingly stitched. Being the "baby" of the family, Mary received special treatment all around. The dress was a case in point. It consisted of a blue satin skirt, off-white ivory colored sleeves, and was ringed with a snowflake lace collar. To top it all off, Mary wore a faux tiara, made by the village silversmith, using colored glass in place of diamonds, emeralds, and rubies.

Ever the watchful older sister, Abigail held Mary by the hand while Oswald led the gentle Nutmeg out of his stall. I assisted

Oswald with securing a child's version of a woman's saddle upon Nutmeg's back. The saddle was marvelously tooled, made of the finest grades of leather. It was designed to allow Mary to securely ride Nutmeg sidesaddle. Once we had the saddle, bit, and bridle fastened in place, it was time to place the Little Princess upon her charge.

While I held the reins, gently patting Nutmeg on the side of his head, Oswald carefully lifted Mary and placed her in the saddle. Then, with Oswald and Abigail on either side, and I leading Nutmeg by the reins, we took Mary for a leisurely tour of the grounds. As we did so, Mary called out to all who could hear: "Look at me. I ride horse!" The joy she took in something so simple was beautiful to behold.

One afternoon, not long after Mary's first ride on Nutmeg, and John Cottam's departure for Stratford with a letter I asked him to read to Silvia, I heard an intriguing tune being played upon the schoolroom virginal. Curious, I left my room and strolled down the hallway. The door was half open. Abigail and Mary were standing beside a seated, well-dressed young man. He had his back to me while his fingers danced upon the jacks of the instrument keyboard.

When he finished playing, Abigail and Mary clapped enthusiastically. Abigail shouted, "Fulk, play us another tune!"

"I will if you can convince Father Tom to sing the song he wrote not long ago," Fulk answered.

At this, Fulk faced the schoolmaster's table, where a man with a strong resemblance to John Cottam sat, arms folded across his chest, an enigmatic smile on his lips.

"Oh, Father Tom! Would you sing for us?" Abby pleaded.

"Yes! Please!" Mary joined in.

Standing up, Father Tom said, "Fulk! You know I can't refuse these two!"

Crossing the room to take his place before the virginal, Father Tom caught sight of me.

"Who could that young man in the doorway be? Master William Shakespeare?"

"At your service," I answered. "I've heard much about you."

"Good?" asked Father Tom.

"Surely. Your brother holds you in the highest regard."

"As he does you," Father Tom Cottam answered.

"How about that song?" Abigail insisted.

"Okay!" Father Tom reassured.

Addressing Fulk, he said: "I assume you were referring to 'The Kingdom.' Ready?"

Fulk began playing a slow, rhythmic melody. At the appropriate point, Father Tom began:

I do not know the time;
I do not know the place;
But I know You'll call me
To Your endless Grace.

The myths of time and distance,
Keep us all apart;
But Your Spirit moves me,
To open-up my heart,

To feel the love and mercy,
You spread upon this earth,
To bring us all a Springtime,
Of new hope and rebirth.

The Golden Age is coming
When You will arrive,
To free us from our bondage,
And let our spirits rise,

To join You in the Heaven,
That comes down from Above,
And revel in Your Kingdom
Of Faith, Hope, and Love!

Father Tom sang his song in a graceful, conversational baritone.

When he finished, he said his goodbyes to the girls, and excused himself. With the center of attention gone, the girls soon went their own way. I found myself alone with Fulk Gyllome.

"You're a master on the virginal. Do you play the lute too?" I asked, pointing at the beautifully crafted instrument resting on the stand beside the virginal.

"The lute's my favorite. You can't take a virginal on the road."

"Do you spend much time traveling?" I asked.

"Quite a bit," said Fulk. "I journey from manor to manor giving music lessons, as well as playing in the Hoghton's troupe of actors. We put on a number of religious based plays every year. Music's always part of the entertainment."

"Sounds exciting," I said.

"Life on the road is not what you imagine," said Fulk. "I looked forward to it when I was young. Now that I've added a few years, the bloom is off the rose. But I've been able to put food on my plate and clothes on my back. Compared to dangers faced by priests such as Tom, my problems are insignificant."

"Is Father Tom in danger here?" I asked.

"He's always in danger," Fulk answered. "Government spies and informers are everywhere. Even in Catholic households. You sleep with one eye open.

"Fortunately, Sir Alexander's created an excellent priest hole; a safe space where Tom and other priests can rest, sleep, and enjoy some decent food. They're all brave men. They occasionally travel with us, posing as players. Being Catholics ourselves, we feel it's our duty to offer them what protection we can."

"It's courageous of you," I remarked. "You wouldn't, by any chance, have room for another player?"

"It's not out of the question. But you would need Sir Alexander's permission. It's my understanding you have great responsibilities here. At your age, you don't have any experience as a player, right?"

"Other than acting in plays at Stratford's King Edward's School, under the tutelage of John Cottam and earlier schoolmasters, I have no experience."

"Don't worry. All's not lost," said Fulk. "My suggestion is to make the best of your present situation. You can start learning to play an instrument, a valuable skill for any player. Perhaps you can assist us with some playwriting responsibilities. A little editing would be helpful. Most plays we perform have been written hurriedly by priests like Tom. Given the constant turmoil in their lives, it's catch as catch can."

"Anything is fine with me. And I'd love to learn how to play an instrument. Perhaps the lute. Like you said, a lute can travel with a performer."

"It's a deal. I look forward to working with you."

Bargain concluded, Fulk went on: "No time like the present to begin." He picked up the lute and began showing me how to tune it.

As the days of Father Tom's visit went by, an air of anticipation grew within the Hoghton family. As our friendship deepened,

Fulk shared a great secret. Edmund Campion would soon pay a clandestine visit to Hoghton Tower. While Father Tom was visiting us, Father Campion had been staying at the home of Alexander's brother Thomas.

Finally, the great day arrived. There was much hustle and bustle. Geoffrey and his mighty crew were busy cooking, baking, and brewing, fixing a feast fit for a king!

CHAPTER XVII
THE SERMON

As Edmund Campion stepped up to the makeshift pulpit to begin his homily, I could feel my heart palpitating. He was a lean figure in the prime of life. And the eyes set within the features of his finely chiseled face sparkled with the perfect mixture of faith and courage.

Father Campion was more than a simple soldier in the spiritual warfare occurring around us. He was a general, about to give the final speech to his outnumbered troops before leading them into a monumental battle.

One could read about mythical heroes until the wick in the candle expired, but standing before me, clad in the vestments which were his armor, was a real hero, a flesh and blood leader, able to look the Queen and her government in the eyes, facing the imminent threat of death without flinching.

In the history of Christianity there have been many great preachers of the Word. St. Peter, inspired by the Holy Ghost, spoke brilliantly at the first Pentecost. St. Paul's preaching led to the formation of many of the early churches. St. Stephen's preaching of the Word led to his martyrdom. St. Ambrose's led to the conversion of many, including St. Augustine. St. Augustine's sermons were legendary. Of course, the greatest sermon of all was Christ's own Sermon on the Mount, in which he gave us The Beatitudes. The way those disciples in the crowd on that mountain must have felt when Jesus spoke to them, is the way I felt now as Edmund Campion began to speak to us.

"I wish to begin my sermon today with a note of gratitude."

Extending his left arm in a welcoming gesture to the crowd, he continued:

"First, I thank everyone in the Hoghton family for hosting us and making our visit here today, and this Mass, possible. I appreciate the great risk to treasure, life and limb they willingly take upon themselves for the greater glory of God and his Church here on earth!

"Second, I want to thank each one of you who have had the faith and courage to attend this service. Like the early Christians of Apostolic Times, you know what it is like to be considered outlaws on account of your faith. I know many of you have suffered greatly for it. I want to assure you, God is all seeing and all knowing. The slings and arrows of misfortune you suffer here in His name are storing up many treasures for you in Heaven. God the Father's mansion has many rooms, and the rooms reserved for those who remain faithful through times of persecution are among the most sumptuous in the City of Gold that will someday be our eternal home!"

After pausing for effect, Father Campion went on:

"Regarding the claims of allegiance other so-called churches try to enforce upon you, remember it is Peter God entrusted with care of his flock! Despite what any king, queen, or government may say, the Pope is the only legitimate successor to St. Peter. The Pope holds the Keys to the Kingdom Not of This Earth. Kingdoms and empires made and ruled by men and women will rise and fall in the ever-shifting sands of time. But the Kingdom of our Lord and Savior Jesus Christ is for all time. It shall never pass away!

Although it was not customary for a Catholic congregation to do so, many began clapping and shouting, "Praise the Lord!" "Thank you, Jesus!" and other devout exclamations. Allowing the congregation to quiet down, Father Campion resumed:

"I liken the times we are living in to the period the Israelites spent in the Babylonian captivity, praying for deliverance and return to the land of milk and honey promised by God the Father.

"God loves us. He knows how many hairs we have on our heads. If he grieves to see a sparrow fall, imagine how much more he grieves when he sees one of us fall!

"Just as God was never deaf to the prayers and lamentations of the Israelites, answering their prayers, and allowing them to return to Jerusalem, God is listening to our prayers and lamentations. He will free us from our own captivity, and lead us to the New Jerusalem!"

Father Campion stopped for a moment to allow a young mother in the congregation to sooth her crying baby, before continuing:

"Like the Pharisees and the Sadducees, the greatest enemies of the True Faith come from those who profess to follow it but change or pervert it for their own self interests. The Evil One takes immense pleasure in seeing God's True Church fractured and divided.

"Lest we fall into the same snare which has enmeshed those who persecute us, we must not strike back in anger. Revenge is mine saith the Lord! It is not our role to play God. Only God can judge the living and the dead!

"Instead, our role as Christians is to love one another with the same depth and intensity we love ourselves. To do unto others as we would have done unto ourselves. We must love and pray for our enemies and turn the other cheek when struck by them!

"This command is the most difficult Our Lord gave us. If we fail to honor it, the consequences will be dire. As the Lord said: 'for all that take the sword shall perish with the sword.'"

Adjusting the tone and delivery of his message to that of an admired professor addressing a group of his favorite students, Father Campion went on:

"In reflecting upon the parables and sayings of our Lord Jesus, it is apparent he is not just a man. A mere man could not and would not promulgate a way of life and thinking that contradicts the natural instincts of mankind to pursue wealth, power, pride, and glory in all its forms. A mere man would never tell us to love our enemies and turn the other cheek — even as they laugh at and spit upon us, even as they torture us. And, yes, even as they execute us!

"Only God could devise a system of conduct that rises so far above man's selfish and bestial inclinations it raises us to the status of His true sons and daughters."

Father Campion caught his breath, gathering his thoughts, before beginning the final portion of his sermon.

"For, through the thunder and rain, the panoply of war and persecution, the wheat mixed in with the chaff, the green grass and flowers choked by the rank weeds, the cankers devouring the petals and the bulbs, vice eating virtue out of house and home, there is a Guiding Light, a North Star, which allows us intrepid Christian sailors to find our way home, a Compass to guide us through the tempests and vicissitudes of the raging seas. A Certainty which drives out the uncertainty of the rolling dice. Guideposts which lead us through the marshes and the bogs, away from the lethal mists and miasmas that hover over the quicksand of unbelief. That Star, that Compass, those Guideposts, and that Certainty, is found in the Word and teachings of the Living God, as given to us by our Lord and Savior, Jesus Christ!

"In conclusion, I ask that you all pray for me, as I do and will continue to pray for you. And that each of us may have the faith, courage and strength to pick up our crosses to follow our Savior, wherever he leads us, to the ends of the earth, and to the end of time!

"May the grace, protection, love, and blessing of our Lord and Savior be upon you now and forever!"

When Edmund Campion finished his sermon, I wanted to burst out cheering. His content and delivery were like nothing I had heard before. Here was an incomparably intelligent man of courage and faith! The words he spoke, and the message they contained, penetrated to the inner core of my being. In many ways, I felt transfigured. The sermon that day changed my life.

As could be expected, I was not the only person affected. When the Mass concluded, Father Campion was mobbed by those wishing to speak with him. Given my position as a servant in the Hoghton household, I stood in the back of the group.

One of the men traveling with Father Campion was handing out small pamphlets which turned out to be printed copies of a Catholic Spiritual Will and Testament. When I finally had a chance to ask Edmund Campion for a blessing, which he happily gave, there were no spiritual testaments left for distribution. I asked Reverend Campion about the pamphlets. He informed me they received them from Bishop Charles Borromeo when they stayed with him in Milan during their journey to England.

The testaments were prepared to allow English Catholics, who had infrequent access to priests, The Eucharist, and the other Sacraments, to declare their allegiance to the Church and its teachings. Edmund Campion had the original document translated from Latin into English and printed for distribution to the English Catholics he met during his mission.

Given my interest in obtaining a copy of the Spiritual Testament, Father Campion told me he would speak with Alexander Hoghton, and ask him to allow me to make a handwritten copy. Sir Alexander permitted me to do so. I spent a good portion of that evening copying the inspiring words.

Given what my father sacrificed to remain loyal to his faith, I knew this would be a gift dear to his heart.

I was not the only person writing by candlelight. When I met with the Hoghton children the next morning for their daily

Latin lesson, the oldest boy, Christopher, informed me he had spent the evening composing a poem based upon the portion of Edmund Campion's sermon concerning the Israelites and their Babylonian captivity.

I was so impressed with his effort, I made a copy for myself. The words of Christopher's poem follow:

The slaves in Babylon lay
By their huts in the month of May.

They turned their heads West,
Uttering sighs of loneliness.

The tears from their eyes fell,
Like drops in a wishing well.

Like tigers which are caged,
They remembered freer days,

When David played his harp,
Under Jerusalem's stars;

And Solomon's wisdom ensured
Their Kingdom would endure.

Then their Rabbi sang a song,
In a tenor voice so strong,

The blood in their veins was drawn,
While their heart strings were torn.

And the babes in their mothers' wombs,
Cried out as from their tombs.

The cries of His children were heard,
By the Nameless One of the Word,

Whose hand wrote upon the wall,
In the artful Heavenly scrawl;

And He caused the King to say,
"The Jews can go on their way;"

And they thank Him till this day,
In the songs they sing and pray!

CHAPTER XVIII
LOVE AND LOSS

Many people say the most important lessons they learned in life were taught by the school of hard knocks. Although I wish it were otherwise, that saying applies as much to me as it does to anyone. Just as the sparkling sun of my youth reached its zenith early in 1580, I watched it steadily descend into a dark nadir over the next eighteen months.

With a deep sense of piety and gratitude, my father joined other pilgrims on the roads and paths leading to Saint Winifred's shrine in the spring of 1580. He hoped to bring back a precious vial of healing waters from the famous holy well that sprang up at the site where the martyred virgin had given up her life at the hands of a rejected suitor. My parents believed those healing waters would help protect my infant brother from the numerous maladies that threatened his life.

This was not the first time my father travelled to Holywell. His initial pilgrimage occurred shortly after my birth. He and my mother had lost my two older sisters to the plague. They vowed to do everything in their power to prevent losing another child. When I survived infancy, it was only natural to seek similar divine aid for each of their subsequent children.

As Queen Elizabeth's reign wore on, the risks of making pilgrimages increased. But my father persevered. He said he would "not put the life of his child in jeopardy just to satisfy the whim of an earthly queen." So, he left Stratford on a fine early June morning, carrying his walking staff, wearing his floppy, wide-brimmed pilgrim's hat, and sporting his cockle-shelled necklace.

Shortly after arriving at the shrine, he and a large crowd of fellow pilgrims were surrounded by a force of pike and sword-wielding militia. The pilgrims were herded into a nearby church and interrogated. Those suspected of being priests were kept for further questioning and imprisonment. Those like my father, who were mere lay persons, had their names and addresses taken down and were released on bond. They were summoned to report to the Queen's Bench in London on a certain day later in June.

The forfeiture penalties for not reporting as ordered were extremely severe. In my father's case, he faced a fine of twenty pounds for not appearing. Additionally, he was forced to stand surety for an additional twenty pounds for another pilgrim, John Audley, a Nottingham hat-maker.

On the other hand, the consequences of appearing before the court as ordered were life threatening. The likely result would be imprisonment or worse. Given the horrible conditions in the London prisons, we might not see my father again.

My father chose not to appear, as did Mr. Audley, resulting in a total fine of forty pounds. We faced the difficult task of liquidating many of our family's hard-earned assets at fire sale prices to pay the immense fine and avoid a prison sentence that could be my father's death knell.

Not long after this horrible news reached me, the Hoghton household went into a state of apprehension and mourning. Shortly after Easter 1581, Edmund Campion was arrested by the authorities while staying at another Catholic safe house. News of his arrest, and the torture likely to be inflicted upon him, sent a chill up and down the spines of the entire household. Despite Campion's obvious strength and courage, few could avoid being broken by the regime's sadistic torturers. After the torture would come the show trial, and the gruesome execution of this great and holy man.

We all knew when Father Campion was broken, he would probably provide his torturers with information that would lead to a governmental raid upon Hoghton Tower. In preparation, the priest who worked as a gardener was relocated to another

Catholic safe house in Rufford. Geoffrey hid many of the family's Catholic religious objects in a place they could never be found.

Just when it seemed things could not get any worse, at the beginning of August 1581, Sir Alexander was stricken with a terrible case of gout. It worsened in pain and intensity as the days wore on. Despite the entire household's prayers, it became apparent Sir Alexander might not survive this latest illness. Sir Alexander's long-time friend and lawyer was summoned to Hoghton Tower. They began drawing up his will.

Like the great man he was, Sir Alexander not only provided for his immediate family, he also remembered even relatively insignificant servants like myself and Fulk Gyllome. He requested his brother Thomas take us in if he was able. If not, he asked his friends, the Catholic Hesketh family in Rufford, to do so. He also left Fulk and myself a gift of our instruments, including the finely made lute I was learning to play.

Sadly, shortly after completing his will, Sir Alexander passed on into what I hope is a much better Kingdom. His funeral was a magisterial event. At the head of the procession, his groom, Oswald, led Sir Alexander's riderless white war horse, Galahad, followed by a sleek team of jet-black coursers pulling a heavy cart with Sir Alexander's black draped coffin resting upon the cart bed. Beside the cart marched Geoffrey, dressed in a black wool jacket and kilt, playing a series of mournful dirges on the bagpipes.

Behind the cart walked Sir Alexander's veiled widow, children, and grandchildren. They were followed by a mass of local gentry who came to pay their respects to this giant of a local hero. Bringing up the rear of the procession were the family servants including myself and Fulk.

Marching beside Fulk, I prayed for the soul of Sir Alexander and those who had to soldier on without Sir Alexander's benevolence, love and guidance. Ahead of me, I saw Abigail comforting Little Mary. Despite her big sister's best efforts, she was crying profusely. I was sad for them, and sad my own small part in their lives was ending in such a tragic manner.

When the solemn, black-clad service was over, we made our way back to the great house where a veritable feast of food and refreshments awaited. For once, Geoffrey was able to partake of the food and drink rather than having to serve everyone else before he could enjoy the meal he had prepared.

As the crowd began to disperse, Geoffrey and I found ourselves alone beside a table arrayed with sweetmeats and conserves. I proposed a toast: "To Sir Alexander Hoghton, a man greater than ourselves."

Finishing his tankard, and filling himself another, Geoffrey gave his own toast honoring Sir Alexander: "To a great friend, and true Christian warrior!"

After finishing my own tankard, I asked Geoffrey, "Now that the great man's gone, will you be staying on with the family?"

"For a short period of time. Just long enough to make sure the new head cook is competent to carry on. When I'm satisfied, I'll be moving on.

"Why? Everyone here loves you so!"

"It's the perfect time for leaving. It's always better to go out in a blaze of glory while one is still on top of one's craft."

"Do you have enough set aside to take care of yourself and your wife?" I asked tactfully.

"Don't worry about us Laddie. Sir Alex purchased a fine cottage for me and mine years ago. He gave me a purse full of gold crowns I've socked away for such a rainy day. The clock of my life now stands at ten minutes before midnight. It'll not be long before I'm babbling about green fields, and resting in King Arthur's bosom, along with mighty Sir Alex.

"Yes sir, I suspect St. Peter's ears will turn red before Sir Alex and I finish telling the tales of our lives — the dances we've danced, the adventures we had, the things we've done and said. But, then again, maybe St. Peter will laugh so hard, he'll have to work just to keep his britches on! I hope I get to heaven before Old Scratch knows I'm gone. May Saint George slay the dragons that seek to do you harm, may your barns always be full, your hens lay golden eggs, and may your feet always be warm! Farewell, me Laddie! God Bless you and all that's yours!"

After saying my goodbye to Geoffrey, and my tearful, gut wrenching farewells to the children, it was time for Fulk and I to hit the road for Rufford, where we would join the Hesketh family's acting troupe. The journey was a long one, and we would make it on foot. Although I still technically owned Nutmeg, I could not break Little Mary's heart by separating them. I tempered the sadness we all felt by gifting Nutmeg to her. The tears of joy the news brought to Little Mary's eyes made what was unacceptable, bearable.

By the time we arrived at the impressive Hesketh Hall, we were completely exhausted. The saving graces were: we were both healthy young men; we were lucky enough to be travelling during September; and the weather was almost perfect — pleasantly brisk in the mornings and evenings, sunny and warm in the afternoons.

Strolling through the countryside carrying our instruments on our backs, we admired the colors of early Autumn. The leaves were a beautiful melody of greens, golds, yellows, reds and browns. It was harvest time, and there was plenty of bread, beer, ale and cider available at reasonable prices.

When we arrived in Rufford, we went directly to Hesketh Hall and met our new master, Sir Thomas Hesketh, a polished and urbane man. He welcomed us with generosity, providing us with a warm, dry room with its own fireplace.

The acting troupe we joined was top-notch. It contained several members I would cross paths with later in life. Despite the hopeful beginning, my time in Rufford turned out to be exceedingly short, a mere matter of months. The tightening noose of the government crackdown on Northern Catholic families soon found its way into Rufford. One day, not long after our arrival, the house was raided by a group of government troops. The urbane and generous Thomas Hesketh was thrown into prison for harboring "Popish Traitors."

For the second time in less than a year I became a physical and spiritual refugee, a fugitive from what passed for "Justice" in an age of intolerance.

This time around, the only refuge I could find was to return to Stratford. I had saved some of the wages I had been paid by the Hoghtons and Hesketh. Given the setback my father suffered due to being arrested and prosecuted for making his pilgrimage to the shrine of Holywell, I knew what I had saved would be put to good use back home.

After sharing a fond farewell with my dear friend Fulk, I began the journey back to Stratford. Much to my amazement, Fulk had managed to procure a pistol which he lent to me to provide some "extra protection" on my long journey. Where he obtained it, I'll never know. I suspect it was part of a cache of arms hidden by the Hesketh for such a day as they were now experiencing.

Walking along the half-frozen road out of Rufford, I could not help but dwell on the irony of my position. It seemed, like tens of thousands of other suffering souls, I was just another powerless creature trapped in the endless game of cat and mouse played by the Regime. The persecution my family suffered led to my travel to Lancashire. Now, the persecution of my employers necessitated my return journey. It seemed, wherever a Catholic went, the path was strewn with mousetraps. We were blind mice, tracked down by an ogre's queenly wife, with her murderous carving knife!

Somehow, I'd have to find a way to keep the dogs of war at bay and survive to see the dawning of a new day. For I was still in the welcome spring of youth, and there was a magnetic light named Sylvia shining on my horizon — leading me on to love and glory. Or so I hoped.

Happily, I had received a letter from Sylvia while at Hoghton Tower. It was transcribed by John Cottam when he stopped at Sylvia's village during his return journey to Stratford.

In that letter, Sylvia assured me her heart remained true. She would wait for my return, however long that might take. She still worked at the Red Fox, and she was continuing to support and care for her widowed mother. She prayed for my health and well-being, and she hoped I was getting along well with my employer and students.

John Cottam carried that letter home to Stratford.He sent it north a few months later with a post courier carrying business correspondence to Alexander Hoghton.

I cherished it, carrying it in a pouch I wore close to my breast. As my path took me ever closer to Sylvia's village, my heart beat faster in anticipation of seeing her angelic face. I had preserved my shimmering vision of Sylvia for the many months I was away. It grew more beautiful each passing day.

When I finally arrived at Sylvia's village, I made a beeline for the Red Fox. Joseph was pouring drinks while Agnes ferried tankards of ale to a group of boisterous customers.

Noticing me, Joseph's face took on a look of serious concern. Ignoring it, I said: "Good to see you. Sylvia working tonight?"

"I'm afraid not," Joseph answered in a tone best described as tinged with sadness.

Agnes arrived to pick up the remaining tankards. With a frown, she asked, "Have you told him?"

"No," Joseph murmured, lowering his eyes.

"Someone has to do it," Agnes said in a manner sending a

jolt of fear through my body. Looking into my eyes, she said, "Sylvia's no longer with us. She passed away a fortnight ago."

In shock and disbelief, I found myself asking, "How?"

"A sudden fever. Took her fast. She was working when it came on," said Agnes.

"One minute she's fine, serving guests. The next, she feels faint. Had to rest on that bench over there," Joseph added.

"When we realized it was more than momentary, we helped her best we could. Gave her a cup of ale. Helped her up to a bed in one of our upstairs rooms," Agnes said.

"We hoped she'd be able to sleep it off," said Joseph.

"Checked on her a few hours later. She wasn't any better. In fact, she was worse. We sent a message to her mother," said Agnes.

"With the help of our customers, we carried the poor girl down the stairs and out the tavern. Placed her in our cart. Drove her to her mother's cottage, a couple streets over," Joseph explained.

"Never saw her again. Late next day we heard she was gone. We took up a collection from our patrons to pay for the burial," said Agnes.

"I feel so sad for that poor girl's mother. Lord knows how she's going to survive without Sylvia's income," Joseph remarked.

"Where did they bury her?" I asked, feeling sick to my stomach.

"A short distance inside the churchyard gate at old St. Sebastian's. I'll have someone show you if you'd like," Agnes offered.

"I'd appreciate it," I said, beginning to feel numb.

A few agonizing hours later, I found myself approaching the gate to the churchyard of St. Sebastian's chapel. I had just finished paying my respects to Sylvia's grieving mother, giving her some of the money I had saved to help get her through the remainder of the winter.

Walking through the gateway, I spied a grave with newly turned earth in the front row to my left. From the description I had been given, this was Sylvia's resting place. There was no headstone. I would see to that before I left town. Sylvia was someone who deserved to be remembered. It was the least I could do.

Standing beside the grave, in the spiritual Hades of my own turmoil, I murmured the Lord's Prayer and the Hail Mary. I asked the Lord to hold Sylvia in his arms and keep her close in the same way I would have done had she remained here with me. I prayed from the depths of my soul she was now safely in Heaven. Holding hat in hand, I burst out sobbing. I felt the terrible sword of anguish pierce my heart, leaving a wound that would never completely heal.

When I was finally able to tear myself away from the grave, I went to see the parson. I left the aged man with enough funds to obtain a gravestone. Then I reluctantly set off on my return trip to Stratford.

Upon my arrival, my parents, brothers and sister greeted me with jubilation. It was a happiness I could not share.

I fell into deep depression, remaining in bed for days on end, until my father finally rousted me out, mandating I work with him in the shop. I found myself slaving away, laboring night and day, trying to grind myself out of my seemingly endless grief.

One evening, long after everyone else had turned in for the night, I found myself in the parlor reading my copy of Ovid when my thoughts again returned to Sylvia. With tears in my eyes, I retrieved pen and paper and began writing in remembrance of my first love.

When life was young and shining
And love was still brand new,

The world was such a playground,
Filled with games and clues.

Within the age of lightning,
You lit my heart anew;
And I was never lonely
With the thought of you.

The seashells by the ocean
Are white and brown in hue;
I hear their echoes calling
In siren songs so blue.

You are the fairest Angel
Who ever rose and flew;
The gates of Heaven opened
To one so brave and true.

So, as the sea rolls over,
As oceans often do,
I search the face of mystery
For a sign from you.

Chapter XIX
Anne Hathaway

Now we journey through the mystic rites of marriage, misunderstood and most disparaged. Bouncing through the rolling carriage, making love, not doing damage. Knitting up the bonds of peace, ensuring life's eternal lease. Beyond description and common speech: breathless, deathless, and sometimes reckless!

Cupid's arrows fly through the air, pierce our hearts, and make the pair. Petals of roses strew the ground, and pave a path of great renown. Flames of passion fill the night, and crackle in the morning light. Vows and banns create the strength, that gives the fruitful marriage length!

So it was, a number of months after my return to Stratford in early 1582, while I was still in mourning over Sylvia's untimely death, Providence mysteriously intervened, and sowed the seeds of circumstance which led to my marriage with Anne Hathaway.

Although Anne was eight years older, our parents had known each other for many years. I often saw her when she came to Stratford on market days. Anne was a comely girl who had grown into a handsome woman. She attracted her fair share of admirers.

The fact Anne lived outside of town, had the reputation of holding herself aloof, and would only have a modest dowry, resulted in her remaining single until now. Because of our age difference, I never dreamed we would one day marry. But many things that seem improbable occur in this world.

One unusually warm spring morning, while I was tending the shop window at the house in Henley Street, Anne came calling to buy a new purse. As she stood at the counter, examining the wares we had to offer, we engaged in pleasant conversation.

"I'm glad to see you're back in town, Will Shakespeare," Anne said, lifting her slate gray eyes off the purses to meet mine. "How did you enjoy your time in Lancashire?"

"Very well," I answered in a superficial manner.

"I heard you were teaching children up North," Anne said, as she returned the purse she had been examining, and pointed to another hanging from the rack at the top of the shop window.

Handing her the other, I replied, "I had bright students. Free time to pursue my own interests. I even learned to play a few tunes on the lute."

"That's wonderful. I love music, and dancing too," said Anne, flashing a smile. "I hope I'll be lucky enough to hear you play a song very soon," she said, as she looked inside the purse. Closing it, she asked, "How much?"

"Three pence," I replied matter-of-factly.

"That's higher than I expected," Anne answered. Biting her lip, she said: "I'll make a deal with you. If you'll play a song for me on your lute, I'll pay you the three pence you're seeking. What do you say?" she asked, extracting three silver pennies from her worn purse.

"My sweet lady, you've made me an offer I can't refuse! When would you like this performance?"

"There's no time like the present. As the blacksmiths say, strike while the iron is hot!"

I laughed spontaneously. "Okay, we've got to make our hay while the sun's still shining."

"Here today, gone tomorrow, said Anne."

"If we don't act now, there will only be sorrow," I added, completing the thought with a saying that brought a knowing laugh from Anne.

Then she said, "I like your attitude."

"I like yours too. If you go over to the front door, I'll let you in. My lute is in the parlor."

While Anne began walking along the long front of our home towards the parlor door, I could not help but admire her trim figure. There was something about the way she moved, spoke, and carried herself that stroked a resonant chord in me.

After admiring this angelic creature for a few seconds, I went to the back door of the shop, and asked my brother, Richard, working near the leather treatment pit, to take my position at the counter for a couple of minutes. Then I rushed back through the shop and entered the main house where I found my mother preparing the noonday meal with our kitchen maid. As I came into the kitchen, my mother interrupted her work, looking at me inquisitively.

"Nothing to worry about," I reassured. "Just a customer I need to see to complete a sale. I'm meeting her in the parlor. Richard's covering the counter."

Satisfied, my mother resumed her work. As I proceeded through the parlor and approached the front door, I could hear Anne's knock. I quickly opened it. Seeing her standing there on the threshold, in her pretty dress, white cap and shawl, made me unexpectedly nervous.

Ushering Anne into the parlor containing our best chairs and the best bed in the house, I frantically reviewed the songs Geoffrey taught me. They were all unsuited to the occasion. After what seemed an eternity, I settled on a simple song the great soul, Edmund Campion, composed for the Hoghton children during his brief stay at Hoghton Tower.

As Anne settled comfortably into the rocking chair my mother often used while singing lullabies to Edmund, I picked up my lute, and started fine-tuning it, while I improvised an introduction I hoped was entertaining.

"Dear Anne, I 'm just a novice. A pure amateur. But, I really want to make this sale. So, I'm going to do my best to give you your money's worth. I'll try to earn my pay so you'll come back someday! I 'm going to sing you a song I learned from a great and holy man. I used to sing it to my students, and it pleased them well. I hope it will please you too. With that minor ado, I'll now play for you!"

I began playing the song's simple melody as carefully as possible, trying not to miss a note. When I reached the proper point, I began to sing the lyrics in an earnest falsetto:

When you're happy, smile;
Also when you're sad;
Wake-up every morning;
Give us all a laugh.

Look upon the earth;
Gaze upon the sea;
See the Highest Love
That lives in you and me.

We're on a great adventure;
We're reaching for the sky.
You've learned your ABC's,
And earned your cherry pie.

Always live for truth,
And never tell a lie.
You know that there's a King
Enthroned up on high.

He'll love you till the end;
His Love it never dies.

He loves you like a child,
With a Father's pride.

So, when you're happy, smile;
Also when you're sad;
Wake-up in the morning;
And give us all a laugh!

During the rendition of this song, I had my head bent down, intently focusing on the correct placement of my fingers on the strings. As a result, I had not been able to observe its effect upon Anne.

Finishing the song with a brief strumming flourish, I was finally able to look up. When I did, I was delighted to see a light in Anne's face which was not present before.

"Will, that was exquisite. The melody and words go so well together. Your singing voice was perfect for the sentiments of the song."

"I'm glad you enjoyed it. A performer always appreciates his audience. I assume I've passed muster and earned my three pence, and you are now the proud owner of a purse made by the most reputable firm of John Shakespeare & Sons."

"John Shakespeare & Sons indeed!" My mother's voice resounded. Turning towards it, I saw her standing at the entrance way to the parlor with what I knew was a feigned scowl on her lips and her hands on her hips.

"Ask your brother to cover for a few minutes, did you! Just so you could serenade Miss Anne Hathaway. I see what you're up to."

"Aw Mother! Stop pulling my leg," I said, feeling a faint blush coloring my cheeks. "It's not what you think. Anne's buying one of our purses.

"Hearing I learned to play the lute, she asked me to perform a quick song. That's all!"

"I see. Well Anne, how are things going on the farm?"

"Very well, Mrs. Shakespeare. We're getting ready to sow the corn," Anne replied with a broad smile.

"I remember that well," my mother said. "You know I was once a farm girl too! Before I moved into town to start my life with John."

"I've heard that. A great life it has been from everything I've heard," said Anne.

"You mustn't believe all that you hear," replied my mother. "Like everyone's lives, ours have had their ups and downs. I guess there's been more good than bad."

"One thing I can say," said Anne. "To have a son as handsome and talented as Will is a blessing!"

At this comment from Anne, the blush in my cheeks went from carnation pink to rose red. If this gabbling gossip continued, soon this blushing violet would be good as dead. The invisible communications going on between my mother and Anne as the banter progressed was proving to me once again that true power in this world rests in the shapely hands of women. They were the omniscient authors, directing the puppet play. They were the Amazon huntresses, circling the cornered prey. They were the fabulous fencers, proud to shout "touché!" While I was a prisoner of desire, roasting in love's fires!

Chapter XX
Betrothal

Anne Hathaway and I were soon an item of discussion by the local town gossips. My mother was one of the more secure links in the information chain that wound its way from house to house, and street to street, ensuring nothing Anne and I did was private for long.

As our romance blossomed, I came to believe Anne was a person I wanted in my life for the long-term. She understood my ambition to use my education and learning to make my way in the world. She also knew I was not cut out to be a tradesman like my father, or a farmer, like her father. Like myself, Anne wanted children. And, since Anne was twenty-six, we could not wait long.

Although Anne and her family were ostensibly Protestant conformists, their allegiance to the New Faith was lukewarm. So, the closet Catholicism my family and I professed was not a significant barrier.

Since Anne's father died a short time before my return to Stratford, the person I would technically have to obtain permission from to marry Anne was her brother, Bartholomew. Bart inherited the bulk of his father's estate. But Anne was left a small portion for her dowry. Given my father's history of having been a former bailiff of Stratford, and a still serving member of the Town Council, it was unlikely Bart would object.

During our courtship, I made several visits to the Hathaway home in nearby Shottery. I drank copious amounts of ale, played primero with Bart, chess with Anne, who was very good at it, and roasted crab apples in the parlor fire.

The Hathaway cottage was a fitting abode for a family that made their living from the land — which is the way most people in this world make their living. After over twenty years living in the city, I have come to appreciate the simple virtues of farming life. The plow and the furrow do not fuel one's vanity.

Wherever the many twists, turns and vicissitudes of life took me, I was fortunate both my heart and my soul were firmly rooted and anchored in my hometown of Stratford and the surrounding Warwickshire countryside. Anne was a pure country girl at heart. She was never a fan of the dubious attractions of the big city where one's every waking moment seems subject to the tyranny of time and the winds of fashion.

Like many others of our time, neither Anne nor I believed a formal church wedding was needed to consummate our marriage in the eyes of God. If we committed ourselves to each other, we each had a high enough level of trust to know it was true and unwavering.

It is with these thoughts in mind, one Sunday, in a meadow on a meandering bend in the Avon River, I asked Anne to be my partner and my truest friend for life. When I popped the question, I did so with some trepidation. Although I knew Anne was attracted to me, I also knew her acceptance of my offer would inevitably result in unpleasant gossip:

"There goes the lass that robbed the cradle," and such sayings. Darts thrown to the heart. Jealousy and envy are as old as the hills,

To express my feelings for Anne in the most elegant way possible, I spent several weeks working on a special poem to accompany my marriage proposal. As an 18-year-old, whose father had lost much of his wealth and power due to adherence to the Old Faith, I knew I did not have much to offer in the way of worldly goods.

At twenty-six, with a recently deceased father, and a brother who inherited the bulk of her father's estate, Anne would not be bringing a fortune to the marriage either. What we lacked in riches, we would have to make up for with passion, enthusiasm, and faith in each other.

So, when the time was right, and there was a break in the witty small talk we had been engaging in until that point, I said, "Anne, there's something important I want to say to you."

Anne focused her eyes upon mine in a way that let me know her woman's intuition had tipped her off to my intentions. She simply asked, "What do you wish to say?"

"I'm not the best at speaking off-the-cuff. I thought it better to express my feelings in verse," I said, pulling a thin sheet of folded paper out of a pocket of my jerkin jacket. Looking into Anne's eyes, I began:

> Shall I compare thee to a summer's day?
> Thou art more lovely and more temperate:
> Rough winds do shake the darling buds of May,
> And summer's lease hath all too short a date:
> Sometime too hot the eye of heaven shines,
> And often is his gold complexion dimm'd;
> And every fair from fair some times declines,
> By chance, or nature's changing course, untrimm'd;
> But thy eternal summer shall not fade,
> Nor lose possession of that fair thou owest;
> Nor shall death brag thou wander'st in his shade,
> When in eternal lines to time thou growest;
> So long as men can breathe, or eyes can see,
> So long lives this, and this gives life to thee.

When I finished reciting the final line, Anne exclaimed, "That's beautiful! I can't believe you wrote it for me!"

"I'm glad you like it!" I said, feeling relieved. Reaching into my pocket again, I removed a simple gold ring which had our initials "W" and "A" inscribed on either side of an engraved heart. As the yellow band of gold gleamed in the sunlight, I knelt on one knee, and said in the most confident voice I could muster, "Anne, will you marry me?"

"Yes! Yes! Three times yes!" Anne said, throwing her arms around my neck and giving me a passionate and enthusiastic kiss. The joy and excitement she brought to that moment is something which touched my heart forever. If Cupid's love shafts had not pierced my breast already, the little love god's hot arrows of desire now found their mark, branding me forever as one of his most ardent disciples!

Chapter XXI
Wedding Bells

As the betrothal poem I wrote conveys, summer is the true season of love. The long, languid, light and heat filled days allow young couples to spend more time together out of doors. The countryside is lush, green, and teeming with life. The birds serenade their mates, while the bees jauntily hop from flower to flower, and, through alchemical magic, produce the sweetness of honey in the hive.

It was on such a summer afternoon, under the shade of an ancient oak, next to a little gurgling brook, on the fringe of a flowering meadow, not far from Anne's home village of Shottery, that Anne and I physically and spiritually consummated our union of bodies and souls.

Within the meadow, beside the brook, immersed in the perfumed sent of flowers, and our mutual passion for each other, I began to understand the eternal truth of the words of God the Father in the Book of Genesis: "It is not good for man to be alone." And, as Eve was made from Adam's rib, Adam called her "bone of my bone and flesh of my flesh." For, as the Good Book says: "Wherefore, a man leave father and mother, and shall cleave to his wife: and they shall be two in one flesh."

In the aftermath of our lovemaking, while we lay beside each other, enjoying the sense of peace and contentment which is part of God's gift to humanity, Anne began humming to herself. Looking at me with an air of playful mischief, she began softly singing the words of a country song I had not heard before.

> A lad and his lass were playing in the grass.
> They tumbled in the hay, in joyful, merry May.
> La La, La La, Leigh Leigh!

They fed on love, in bright and sunny days.
Their hearts intertwined, like fruit on a vine.
Seigh seigh, Heigh heigh, Seigh Seigh!

Soon there came a son, filling life with fun.
He keeps his father busy, his mother on the run!
Teigh dum, Teigh dum, Teigh deigh!

He's playing on his flute, he's beating on his drum.
They pray for relief and hope that Kingdom comes.
Hurray, Hurray — Hurray!

As Anne finished, I laughed, and said playfully, "Good song! Are you trying to foretell the future?"

"Perhaps, Will Shakespeare, perhaps. None of us know such things with certainty. But we all have hopes and dreams!"

Within a few months of our conversation, it became evident Anne's hopes and dreams of becoming a mother would be fulfilled. Of course, when it became apparent Anne was pregnant, the pressure for us to make good on our pledge to each other, and get married in a church wedding, grew, especially on Anne's side of the family.

Although my mother supported my match with Anne from the beginning, it took some time to win my father over to the idea. His primary objection was I was too young to take on the responsibility inherent in being a husband and father. He also pointed out I had yet to establish myself in a career, and I had neither the income nor financial assets to support a family.

My father wanted our engagement to be a long and well thought out endeavor. But, reckless or not, Anne and I felt otherwise. I had always been one of those children who wanted to grow up fast and enjoy all the perceived pleasures the adult world has to offer.

Of course, the greatest forbidden fruit in the pantheon of adult pleasures is the joyous wonder which occurs between a man and a woman. Once Anne and I tasted the joys of our passion for each other, there was no way to turn the clock back.

The fact a woman as beautiful and intelligent as Anne cared enough to commit to marrying and starting a family with me, was something of which I was rightfully proud. I did not know what future God might have in store for us, but I felt, one way or another, the Lord would guide our footsteps along the straight path that leads through the narrow gate.

Despite my best arguments, I could not win my father over to my way of thinking until he was faced with the inevitable. Once he resigned himself that, like it or not, if he did not sanction the wedding, his first grandchild would be born out of wedlock in the eyes of the law and the church, he caved in, and got involved with the planning for the great occasion. He even made arrangements to have an addition built on the home on Henley Street to provide an abode for Anne, myself, and his first grandchild.

While we were waiting for construction to be completed, we would reside with Anne's brother, Bart, in the Hathaway family home in Shottery.

As Anne's pregnancy was starting to show, and marriages were not permitted during the season of Advent, our wedding arrangements had to be made quickly. Because there was not enough time for the banns to be read in church on three consecutive Sundays before the wedding occurred, a bond would need to be posted to cover the costs and damages which could be suffered by the church and any injured parties if the marriage turned out to be unlawful.

The bond the church required to be posted was so enormous it was beyond my father's means. However, two of Anne's father's friends, who owned substantial farms in the neighborhood, were kind enough to act as bond sureties. They had known Anne since her childhood, and they also knew my father. I'm sure the fact I was only eighteen made their decision easier. There are not many eighteen-year-old bigamists!

Regarding the ceremony itself, my parents wanted us married by one of the few remaining priests in our area ordained during the reign of Elizabeth's half-sister, the Roman Catholic Queen Mary. The closest, was the aged John Frith, vicar of the nearby church at Temple Grafton. Our family knew Father Frith well. We had journeyed to Temple Grafton to attend many a Mass said by him over the years.

In addition to being a good vicar, Father Frith was well known throughout the local community as a person with a special gift for healing injured hawks. In fact, when I was thirteen, Father Frith was kind enough to sell my father a hawk my father gifted to me. In those days, there was nothing that gave me more joy than returning from a successful hunt with game that could be dressed, cleaned, and prepared for the family table.

So, it was fitting Father Frith married us. By adhering to my father's and mother's choice of a priest to perform the ceremony, Anne pleased them greatly.

The church at Temple Grafton was austere but elegant. Father Frith did a fine job of making the ceremony meaningful and memorable. When it concluded, both our families and friends went to the Hathaway home for the traditional wedding feast. At the celebration, our guests enjoyed main courses of venison, coney rabbit, and stuffed goose, as well as cider, ale, and Canary wine.

When the feast concluded, Anne and I retired to the bedroom Anne's family specially prepared for our use. Its main feature was a large four poster "tester" bed, with a unique and beautifully carved headboard that had originally belonged to Anne's father and mother. The most remarkable feature of the headboard were three mysterious figures, standing with their arms folded across their breasts. Anne's brother had graciously given her this family heirloom as a wedding gift to grace our new home. It later went from our home in Henley Street to our present home, New Place. It not only is our marital bed, but it's the bed in which Anne gave birth to each of our three children.

Given the state of Anne's pregnancy, our church wedding night was nothing like the day we first pledged our troth to each other. But, like all rites of passage, it was something which occurred once in one's life. I wanted to make it as special as I could.

As I got undressed and prepared to jump between the sheets, I asked Anne, "Did you enjoy the day?"

Removing her dress, she replied, "Yes. It was nice. Everyone was gracious and happy!"

"On their best behavior. No drunkenness, or arguments!"

"That's a blessing!" Anne said, as she finished undressing, lifted the sheet, and slid her soft body into the bed beside me.

Leaning over and giving her a kiss, I said, "I have a special present for you, Mrs. Shakespeare!"

"I wonder what it can be?" Anne said, smiling mischievously.

"I don't mean *that*!" I said with a chuckle. I've composed a poem for you in honor of our wedding."

"I must warn you, flattery will get you nowhere!" Anne said.

"Okay, Madame. I see my audience is wise to the ways of this world."

"Maybe so," said Anne. "But this audience is one which will always be excited and happy to listen to anything you've written."

"I hope that's the case," I answered. "Here it goes."

> Those lips that Love's own hand did make,
> Breath'd forth the sound that said, *I hate,*

To me that languish'd for her sake:
But when she saw my woeful state,
Straight in her heart did mercy come,
Chiding that tongue, that ever sweet
Was us'd in giving gentle doom;
And taught it thus a-new to greet:
I hate she altered with an end
That follow'd it as gentle day
Doth follow night, who, like a fiend
From heaven to hell is flown away.
I hate from hate away she threw,
And sav'd my life, saying — *not you.*

Before I could say anything further, Anne said, "As much as you believe I saved your life, I believe you saved mine!"

We embraced, intertwining our hearts as only true lovers do.

Chapter XXII
Bundle of Joy

The first year of our married life was hectic and eventful, filled with the highest of highs and lowest of lows. Before the chilling frost settled on the pumpkin, the bloom was on the rose.

First the petals, then the thorns. We had a blessed winter and spring. By the end of February, the renovations to the family home in Henley Street were complete. A now very pregnant Anne and I were able to move from Shottery to Stratford — just in time for the arrival of the newest member of the Shakespeare family.

Anne's first pregnancy was surprisingly smooth and uneventful. Blessed with a positive spirit and outlook upon life, Anne managed to bear the aches, pains and discomforts of her pregnancy while maintaining her good-natured sense of humor.

Still largely in the blissful ignorance of youth, I enjoyed playing the part of proud expectant father. The thought of the new life miraculously forming within Anne's womb filled me with a profound sense of awe and thanksgiving for the gifts of our Creator. If anything can bring a man closer to God, it is the birth of a child. Becoming a father was the most significant event in my life. It was an important part of the plan God had for me, and it is the best method we humans have to pass the torch of the divine flame to the next generation. There are few joys greater than seeing a reflection of our own good attributes and qualities in our children.

Our time on this earth is short. The time we have to procreate is even shorter. Reminders of our mortality are everywhere. It is part of our obligation to get on with the creative process.

My feelings on this issue are so strong that, some years after I became a father, I decided to accept a commission to write a series of sonnets directed to a young bachelor reluctant to marry. His mother, a great patron of the arts, paid me a generous sum to try and convert her handsome son to my way of thinking on the duties and the benefits of procreation. One of the best of those sonnets went as follows:

> When forty winters shall besiege thy brow,
> And dig deep trenches in thy beauty's field,
> Thy youth's proud livery, so gaz'd on now,
> Will be a tatter'd weed of small worth held:
> Then being ask'd where all thy beauty lies,
> Where all the treasure of thy lusty days:
> To say, within thine own deep-sunken eyes,
> Were an all-eating shame, and thriftless praise.
> How much more praise deserv'd thy beauty's use,
> If thou could'st answer — This fair child of mine
> Shall sum my count, and make my old excuse —
> Proving his beauty by succession thine.
> This were to be new-made when thou art old,
> And see thy blood warm when thou feel'st it cold.

I am pleased to say the object of my entreaties eventually succumbed to the angel of his better nature. He threw off the fancy-free lust of bachelorhood, and put on the mild and pleasing yoke of fatherhood.

Perhaps I digress too much. If so, I beg your indulgence. It is one of the little pleasures of the retired playwright to so digress, while my beautiful mistress, Fortune, finishes weaving my silver thread.

Returning to the events of 1583, fickle April came and went, giving way to the darling buds of May. In imitation of the new life emerging around us, the time arrived for Anne to give birth to our first child. A beautiful day it was, sunny, clear and warm, with a gentle breeze blowing from the west.

I was working with my father, repairing the wheel of the cart we used to transport our product to market, when my sister Joan came running out the door of the cottage-like extension where Anne and I lived. Her face was flushed with excitement as she shouted: "Anne's gone into labor!"

Wiping the sweat from his brow, my father said, "Lord protect her and the baby!" Turning to me, he said, "Son, go to your wife."

While I ran towards the house with a mixture of joy and apprehension, I heard my father say, "Joan, fetch the midwife. Be quick about it!"

By the time I reached the open doorway, my mother and her kitchen maid were assisting Anne up the stairs to the bedroom.

I shouted Anne's name and asked if there was anything I could do to assist.

Reaching the top of the stairs, my mother glanced back saying, "We could use a pot of small ale and some clean cloths. Once we get Anne settled in, you can come by for a visit."

Happy to have something to do, I quickly exited our little home and fulfilled my mother's requests. When I returned, Joan arrived with Liza Richards, the middle-aged midwife who assisted at the birth of Edmund three years ago.

Seeing the items in my hands, Mrs. Richards instructed, "Joan, take the ale and those cloths. Today you'll learn a great deal about what it means to be a woman."

As I handed the ale pot and cloths to Joan, Mrs. Richards said, "Don't worry. I've helped over a hundred babies enter this world. This one will be no different!"

Despite these reassuring words, I knew giving birth involved a considerable amount of risk for Anne and the baby. Within the last year, several Stratford women and their infants died in childbirth. With these thoughts swirling through my head, I said: "God bless you, Mrs. Richards. Please take good care of my wife."

"I will, my boy," she reassured, as she and Joan went upstairs to join Anne and my mother for the "great event."

While they labored courageously above, I paced back and forth along the paved stone floor of the small parlor. I quickly made the sign of the cross and recited numerous Hail Marys memorializing the words of the Angel Gabriel's annunciation to the Blessed Virgin. With its focus on the Savior's incarnation in St. Mary's womb, it seemed most appropriate for this occasion.

A short while later, my prayers were interrupted when Joan, standing at the top of the stairs, called out: "You can come up here if you want."

"If I want!" I echoed, bounding up the stairs two at a time. Inside the room, Anne lay in bed wearing only her night shift. Tracks of drying tears streamed down her cheeks.

Concerned, I tried to reassure her, "Don't worry. It'll be over soon."

"Easy for you to say!" she replied with the trace of a smile.

Fortunately, my words proved prophetic. Within several hours of my visit, I heard the slap and cry signaling the birth of the newest member of our family.

But, of course, today was merely the crossing of an important threshold. Our child had been developing inside Anne's womb for many months. I remember the excitement I felt when Anne told me she suddenly felt the child quicken. And how, lying in bed beside Anne that evening, I had placed my ear upon Anne's stomach, hearing and feeling the child move inside her. Very few things in life can equal the joy I felt that moment.

As I once again bounded up the stairs towards the landing and closed door, which opened to reveal the freckle-faced smile of my sister Joan, I said a heartfelt prayer of thanksgiving to our

Lord and Creator.

Entering the room, I saw the midwife hastily draping a comforter over Anne's exhausted body. On the far side of the bed, my mother stood holding the newest member of our family, crying, and gently wrapped in a blanket. My mother said, "You're the father of a healthy little girl."

All I could say was, "Thank God! Can I hold her for a moment?"

My mother answered, "Her mother hasn't even had that opportunity."

"It's fine," said Anne. "Let her meet her father." As Anne smiled, and my mother handed the baby to me, the baby stopped crying."

"Welcome to the world, Susanna Shakespeare!" I said, using the name of the great Biblical heroine Anne and I selected in the event our first child was a girl.

When the baby responded with a tender little cry, my mother quipped, "Daddy's girl, isn't she?"

"You've got that right," Anne said.

I laughed at the gentle ribbing I was receiving, enjoying the precious never-to-be-repeated moment with my firstborn.

Just as quickly as the sun had peeked its precious face through the clouds, a little squall arrived. Susanna began sobbing gently.

"She's calling for her mother now," I said, as I walked over to the head of the bed, handing our bundle of joy into my wife's waiting arms. As Anne cradled Susanna, I kissed Anne on the forehead. So the curtain descends upon that ancient spring afternoon — one which will always mean a great deal to me.

CHAPTER XXIII
THE SOMERVILLE PLOT

Like the slow-moving waters of the Avon, the late spring and summer of 1583 meandered on as future became present and present became past.

When Anne recovered from the birth of Susanna, we occasionally had a few hours to ourselves. We would wander along the banks of the river, stopping to enjoy a picnic lunch we packed in a wicker basket. I can still picture Anne sitting on the river bank in her slightly faded dress, undoing her white linen cap, allowing the tresses of her long dark hair to flow freely over her shoulders and shimmer in the bright sunlight. Those were our salad days!

Unfortunately, nothing lasts forever, including peaceful late spring and summer afternoons. Not long after the harvest, the weather of our lives began to change, and darkness began to descend upon our family.

One of the things my mother was proudest of was her membership in the Arden family. The Ardens were old time Catholic gentry of the highest order. They could trace their lineage to before the arrival of William the Conqueror. Back when there was a forest in the vicinity of Stratford, it had been called the Forest of Arden. The current Arden pater familias was Edward Arden. He lived with his wife, Mary, and their secret Catholic chaplain, at a mansion called Park Hall. Although I never visited Park Hall, my mother had. She loved to regale us children with stories of the Arden's glittering wealth and history.

Of course, the Protestant government hated Catholic gentry like the Ardens. It sought any opportunity it could to destroy them. I saw the vicious nature of such persecutions during my time in Lancashire. Now, the iron fist of the Queen's gauntlet struck much closer to home.

John Somerville of Edstone had the good fortune to marry Edward Arden's daughter. When he saw how the government's taxation and fines were eroding the Arden family fortune, it began to drive him crazy with hatred of the regime and Queen Elizabeth.

I met John Somerville when he ventured into Stratford to purchase a pair of gloves. He dressed the part of a provincial dandy. Local gossip held he was a hothead. But no one ever thought he was off his rocker until he embarked upon his suicide mission to take justice into his own hands by killing the Queen!

On October 25, 1583, an insanely angry John Somerville began his one-man mission to "cut the head off the snake" squeezing the life out of the English Catholic community. Like the crazy man he was, he let every person he met along the way know exactly what his intentions were.

Inevitably, one of the ears John Somerville poured his venom into summoned the authorities and Somerville was soon in custody. When they determined Somerville's relation to the Arden family, the wheels of the persecution gristmill were set in motion.

In short order, Park Hall was raided. Edward Arden, his wife Mary, his daughter, and eventually their priest, Father John Hall, were arrested and transported to London where Edward Arden and Father Hall were subjected to the rack. After a brief trial of Somerville, Edward Arden, his wife, and Father Hall, Somerville and Edward Arden were sentenced to be hung, drawn and quartered. On the evening before their scheduled executions, John Somerville cheated the executioner of his fee by hanging himself, although there were rumors he was murdered.

On December 20th, just five days before Christmas, Edward Arden was hung, cut down alive, castrated, disemboweled, and had his heart cut out. His head was cut off and placed on a pole atop London Bridge.

One of the investigators, charged by the crown with ferreting out Somerville "plotters," was our local Protestant gentryman, Sir Thomas Lucy. Under Lucy's direction, his gang of hired thugs and priest hunters began raiding the homes of anyone even remotely connected with the family of Edward Arden. The houses of many of those we knew were the subject of these unwarranted searches and seizures.

Unfortunately, the aura of suspicion and fear resulting from these investigations changed our lives significantly. To avoid being sucked into the ever-widening whirlpool of destruction, we hid our Catholic devotional aids including my mother's rosary, the statuette of the Virgin, and the Spiritual Will and Testament of my father I copied while working in the Hoghton household.

One morning, my father removed the Spiritual Will from its strong box and handed it to me. With the aid of a lantern, I went into the attic and wedged it between the roof rafters and tiles. Sadly, I did such a thorough job, we were never able to retrieve it. My father assured me that was all right. The protection of the family was paramount.

In the late afternoon of a cold day in the last week of November, there was a series of sharp, incessant knocks at our front door. I was sitting across the dining room table from my mother, finishing a late afternoon snack of peeled apples and cold milk. Hearing a second set of even louder knocks following quickly on the heels of the first, my mother said, "Will, get your father!"

As I left the dining room, I could see my mother approach the front door. When she asked, "Who is it?" I heard a muffled reply: "Open up, in the name of Her Majesty!"

I ran down the hallway until I reached the door to the workshop. Seeing my father working on a soft kid glove destined to grace the hand of a gentleman, I shouted:

"The law's at the door!"

Placing the glove and sowing needle on the table, my father whispered, "God protect us!" as he rushed by me.

By the time he arrived in the parlor, my mother had opened the front door. Several armed men entered the house with their hands on the hilts of their swords. Seeing them, my father blurted out: "What's the meaning of this?"

A third man stepped into the entranceway announcing, "You, John Shakespeare, are a well-known recusant. Your wife is an Arden — a nest of vipers if there ever was one!"

The man speaking these words was dressed impeccably in a black and silver threaded doublet. He had a closely cropped beard and mustache. As he looked me over with the hard and unforgiving stare of a wolf, I recognized the infamous scourge of the Catholic community, Sir Thomas Lucy!

When my father saw his accuser, he hesitated before asking, "By whose authority are you here?"

"Her Highness the Queen," Lucy curtly responded. "I've been charged with ferreting out those involved with the Popish Somerville Plot. As I'm sure you're aware, John Somerville and his father-in-law, Edward Arden, are in custody. They will soon stand trial for undertaking the assassination of our blessed Queen. Soon their heads will be impaled on pikes atop London Bridge. As will the heads of anyone else in league with them!"

"I assure you sir," my father answered, "there are no traitors here. We're loyal subjects!"

"We'll see about that. You've failed to pay anything to support the militia established to put down a potential Catholic uprising. You were fined an additional forty pounds in connection with the unlawful pilgrimage to Holywell. Your history of knavery is well-documented. May God have mercy on you if we find Popish relics or other evidence of your participation in this plot against the Queen!"

Once Lucy finished, my father said in a steady, grave voice: "You'll find no such evidence in this house. My wife Mary is only a distant relation of Edward Arden. We're not part of any plot."

"Let's test the truth of that statement," Lucy said. Addressing the men who entered the house with him, he ordered: "Search this place from top to bottom. Bring anything suspicious to me for examination."

Spying the locked chest holding my father's business papers and our few precious valuables, Lucy said, "Unlock it. Bring the contents to your dining room table for me to review."

My father reluctantly unlocked the chest. He and I carried the books, papers, and the purse full of gold and silver coins that comprised my parents' life savings, over to the dining room table where Lucy sat looking like the "master" of the house.

As we approached, Lucy said, "Let me see that purse." Taking it in his hands, he poured the assorted gold and silver coins it contained out upon the tabletop. "You have quite a nice collection of crowns here. Looks like you still have some of your ill-gotten gains from wool brogging and money lending. You shouldn't mind paying your dues for the maintenance of the militia here and now!"

Lucy quickly placed five of the gold coins in a pocket of his black doublet.

"Sir!" my father protested. "What you've taken far exceeds any amount I might have been legally assessed."

"I just charged a little interest. Like you've done to victims before! Who's a Papist going to complain to anyway? You'll be lucky to come out of this alive!" Lucy said with a smirk.

I saw my father's face turn beet red. I knew he wanted to strike the foul interloper sitting at the table. I also knew his concern for the rest of our family would prevent him from doing so.

I wished I could strike out at Sir Thomas Lucy too. But I also needed to bide my time. For I now had a wife and child to protect. However, I would not soon forget the insults and indignities Lucy was heaping upon us.

To make a painful memory short, neither Lucy nor his lackeys were able to find any Popish relics, books or pamphlets in our home.

CHAPTER XXIV
LOWSIE LUCY

The government crackdown on Catholics resulting from the "Somerville Plot" lasted throughout the winter and well into the spring of 1584. Notwithstanding the efforts of Thomas Lucy and his paid informants, very few practicing Catholics were found. Most of the people of Stratford were sympathetic towards the Old Religion.

Despite the persecution surrounding us, we pressed on with the business of life. In the aftermath of the Lucy raid, we continued running the glove shop. But sales were not what they once were. Over the course of the next year, it became clear the shop was not generating enough income to support us all.

Given our narrowing circumstances, my father, Gil, and I took to hunting. We had an eagle-eyed hawk, and a pair of hunting hounds Gil and I trained. They performed well during our forays into the countryside around Stratford.

My mother and Anne were excellent cooks. They made use of every part of the hares, squirrels, and fowls we brought down. On a couple of occasions, we were even able to bring home larger game, including small deer and a wild boar. Unfortunately, due to centuries of clearing, farming and enclosing land, the game around Stratford was not nearly as abundant as it had once been.

Although six months had passed since the invasion of our home by Sir Thomas Lucy, we had not forgotten the disdainful way he treated us. Being young and impetuous, I determined Lucy's treatment of our family, and his outright theft of our money, should not go unpunished.

Sadly, I had neither the social standing, training, nor equipment to challenge Lucy to a duel. Had I done so, he would have had me run through or shot dead like a mad dog.

There was one gift I possessed which could be used to exact revenge upon this monster of a man. My dexterity with words. My family and schoolmates had, on occasion, felt the barbs of my acerbic wit. One who possesses such a gift must be judicious in its use, for the tongue and pen inflict wounds as grievous as those of the dagger and the sword.

So, when little Susanna had been put to bed, and Anne was catching up on some much-needed sleep, I stole away and fashioned a revenge ballad by candlelight. Though not a magnificent achievement in the art of posey, I believed it would serve its purpose, hurling a dart of sarcasm into the greedy heart of Sir Thomas Lucy!

The next night, long after midnight and well before the dawning light, I stole away from my wife's side again. Donning a hooded jacket and dark set of breeches, I ventured out into the deserted streets of Stratford. Careful to avoid being noticed, I attached the "Curious Ballad of Thomas Lucy" to the doors of all the taverns in town.

While gliding home, I whispered the ballad to myself with inner satisfaction.

> A parliamente member, a justice of peace,
> At home a poor scare-crowe, at London an asse;
> If lowsie is Lucy, as some volke miscalle it,
> Then Lucy is lowsie whatever befall it:
> He thinks himself greate,
> Yet an asse in his state
> We allowe by his ears but with asses to mate.
> If Lucy is lowsie, as some volk miscalle it,
> Sing lowsie Lucy, whatever befall it.

After planting these "seedlings," I waited a month or so to let the roots begin to grow. Then I sowed another batch. When I subsequently traveled to neighboring villages in the following weeks and months, I would leave a copy or two in a place they were sure to be found. As the seeds grew sprouts, the ballad found its audience and took on a life of its own.

Thomas Lucy had only himself to blame. He was the type of man everyone loves to hate.

Gradually, summer turned to fall. Our family received some needed good news when Anne announced she was pregnant. While Anne's pregnancy with Susanna had gone smoothly, this was the exact opposite. Anne suffered through several months of intense morning sickness. She was confined to bed for days at a time. After the fourth month, her symptoms subsided, and our life together returned to normal — or at least semi-normal. For we both sensed there was something very unusual going on

One night, Anne felt some movement within her rapidly expanding belly. She gently placed my hand on her stomach. I felt what seemed like two kicks, followed by a series of further kicks on the other side.

Lifting my head, I said in a whisper low enough not to wake Susanna, "Have you noticed this before?"

"Several times when you were out working," Anne whispered.

"Twins?" I excitedly asked.

Anne giggled. "I think so. I can't imagine what the delivery is going to be like."

"Don't worry," I reassured. A million women have safely delivered twins. With God's help, you'll do so too."

After praying together, we returned to the land of Nod.

CHAPTER XXV
TARLETON'S JESTS

The most entertaining jig I've seen is the one the great comedian, Dick Tarlton, performed on the improvised stage of the Stratford Guildhall shortly after Anne gave birth to our twins, Hamnet and Judith.

At that time, I was still assisting my father in the glove shop. Everyone knew my pulse quickened on the rare occasions a troupe of players arrived in town. There was nothing like a play to take one out of the claustrophobic experience of small-town life.

For me, seeing a professionally produced play was an opportunity to experience a taste of the action, excitement, and sophistication flourishing in the ever-expanding City of London. It seems those born and raised in the country dream of making it in the city, while those born and raised in the city long for the imaginary simplicity of country life.

Being a typical country lad, I arrived early at the Guildhall, gladly handing over my hard-earned pennies for a premium seat just behind the Bailiff and Aldermen. From the news circulating in Stratford's taverns, the play to be performed this afternoon was about an old king named Lear, who gives away his kingdom to two ungrateful daughters, and the price he pays for doing so. Although the story was interesting, most of my excitement arose from the opportunity to see Richard Tarlton.

Dick Tarlton was one of the most famous persons in the realm. Some of his popularity stemmed from the fact he looked different. His large, bulging eyes, perfectly round face, block-like head, and wide, flat nose, gave the audience the impression he was always a bit out of kilter. His baritone voice and wacky persona animated the crowd.

Like most comics, Dick was not leading man material. But he had an irresistible magnetism. He could draw a roar from an audience by popping his head out between the curtains and making a series of funny faces just before the show began.

True to form, Dick did not disappoint. Before the show started, Dick jutted his head out from behind the curtains, drawing roars of laughter as he contorted his lips, nose, eyes and ears in a carefully choreographed display of anger, laughter, fear, astonishment, frustration, and love-sickness. Concluding this little performance, he gave us his legendary tilted head wink, raised eyebrow, and gap-toothed smile, before tucking his head back out of sight.

How unlikely was his rags to riches story. Several years ago, he was a mere tavern keeper who enjoyed entertaining his patrons with spirited duels of wit. Over time, he became so good at delivering hard-hitting one-liners more people began showing up in his tavern to hear the repartee rather than to drink the middling ale.

Given that the newly built Theater and Green Curtain were always looking for new ways to put fannies in the seats, it was only a matter of time before Dick was performing a version of his stand-up comedy on London's stages.

Although he played clowns and wise fools, Dick's greatest strength was improvisational comedy. When he improvised dialog, he always drew laughs. The sheer power of Dick's charisma and wit could overshadow the other actors' efforts and change the entire meaning of a scene in a way not intended by the playwright.

At the age of twenty, these were not my concerns. I was just there to enjoy seeing a master craftsman perform his work. And what a magnificent job he did. His role in the play was that of the wise fool who reminds Leir who the real fool is. Several of Tarlton's quips remain with me until today.

The world is topsy-turvy,
Like rabies and like scurvy.
But when you lose your mind,
Your Father's love is blind!

As well as,

The brightest, sweetest fruit,
Conceals a rotten rind.
And even those who kiss,
Can sometimes be unkind!

And,

The Kingdom's at your feet,
In your salad time,
But, when you step on down,
You're kicked in the behind!

These rhymes brought much laughter while reinforcing the play's central theme. When it was finished, we all clapped enthusiastically, while awaiting the most anticipated part of the two-hour entertainment.

Suddenly, from behind the curtain, Dick Tarlton emerged in a brown monk's robe, dancing a Morris Dance of his own invention, while playing a pipe he held between his lips, and drumming away on the small tabor drum strapped to his waist.

Concluding his dance, Dick welcomed the applause of the audience, launching into a stand-up routine filled with many of his best-known jokes.

Next, Dick was joined by a boy actor, dressed as a well-endowed young maiden, with a bump around her midsection that made her look like she was very pregnant. As she pranced between Dick and the audience, flitting and fluttering her eyes, Dick, holding an open hand beside his pursed lips as if he was sharing a gossip's secret, whispered in a studied manner allowing his voice to be heard throughout the room:

"It's hard to look real svelte when you're wearing a chastity belt!"

His one-liner left us rolling in the aisles. While the laughter subsided, Dick and the girly boy began a courtship dance, with high-stepping, hands on the hips, and exaggeratedly happy faces, reminding us of the antics of intoxicated couples at country weddings.

When Dick and the boy finished dancing, they faced us holding hands. Dick let loose another well-known quip: "A little titillation is sure to grow the nation. It gives bread its butter and sizzles up the bacon!"

Removing the tabor from his waist, Dick exchanged it for a lute. As he began gently plucking the strings, Dick said, "I guess you good people of Stratford are wondering why I'm wearing this outlawed monk's habit while performing in this beautiful hall.

"There's a simple and, I hope, satisfying explanation. For this song I am about to sing concerns the life of a wandering monk like Robin Hood's Friar Tuck. He's not just any monk. Like many who roamed the land in the days before Good King Henry, he doesn't take his vows seriously. His name is Gyrovagi, and here's his song."

He began to chant in a lilting voice, with a faux Welsh accent that tickled our English funny bones.

Love's Labour's Won

I was born in Wales,
Son of a merchant burgess,
And journeyed to Shrewsbury,
To don the brown robe of Francis.

We traveled to Canterbury,
To bow before relics,
And returned to The Boar,
To kiss lilac scented harlots.

I've been successful on the lecture circuit,
Winning women converts from the virtuous.
At sunrise, commons till the Lord's fields,
At noon-tide, they fall to their knees.

A threatened charge of witchcraft
Quakes the legs of a peasant,
Stuffs my purse with shillings,
And fills my moaning belly with pheasant.

Yes, I've trampled Louie's Realm
On a pilgrimage to Rome,
And drank red wine from an urn
While heretics burned.

Oh, my life has been a magnific feast,
Of tender fowls and roasted beef,
But now, I'll make my peace.
Brother! Please! Call a Priest!

When he finished, Dick was joined on stage by the other actors in The Queen's Men. As they bowed, we gave them a standing ovation. After the applause and cheers died down, Dick led us all in a prayer for the health and well-being of the Queen.

Chapter XXVI
Contest of Wits

As the prayer concluded, the crowd began dispersing. Approaching Dick, I introduced myself, offering to pay for dinner and drinks if he would discuss what it was like to be an actor in the City of London. To my surprise, he agreed. Dick said he was staying the night at Burbage's Tavern, a few blocks from our home on Henley Street.

An hour later, I found myself sitting across a table from the great comedian.

"What would you like to drink?" I asked, in a voice carrying over the tavern's background chatter.

"Sack my boy! Sweet Spanish wine. Sad Sack! Happy Sack! Hot Sack! Dry Sack! High Sack! Hack and Sack! That's my drink of choice!" he answered, before asking: "Have you visited Spain?" He went on before I could answer, "I've heard they have some fine-looking women there. Fiery and hot. With the flames they engender, they send even drunken sailors on a bender!"

"I wouldn't know about that. I've never had the opportunity to travel outside England, Mr. Tarlton," I said, motioning to the bar maid, raising two fingers, and calling out: "Sack!"

"Mr. Tarlton my foot! Call me Dick. Everyone who loves me does. As to traveling outside of England, it's not all it's cracked up to be. There's plenty of fun to be found right here. There are beautiful women by the score in London town. That's where you want to be. Right?"

"I think so," I answered, as the bar maid brought us our cups of sack and we began drinking.

Finishing my first draught, I continued, "But the primary reason I would like to go to London is not for wine, women and song. It's to learn the trade of being a player."

"I have to tell you, young man, there are quite a few ambitious lads like yourself that flock to the city with similar dreams but end up crashing into the many rocks and shoals awaiting the greenhorns in our business. I don't want to discourage you, but most who set out on the primrose path you're considering come home with their tails between their legs. What gives you the idea you can make a go of it? Have you acting experience?" Dick asked, with a skeptical expression.

"I'm not a complete novice," I explained. "Not long ago, I returned to Stratford after serving as the tutor of children of a wealthy family in Lancashire. While there, I performed in the Manor's troupe of actors."

"Ho! You're a Popish Catholic!" said Dick with a look which made me queasy.

"Not really," I said, telling a white lie.

"I don't care if you are one!" said Dick, causing me to breathe a sigh of relief.

"A lot of our best players are Catholics. To be worth his salt, a man, even a young man like yourself, has got to have some vices. All of us players have something to hide. Most of us found ourselves on the wrong side of the law one time or another. The trick's not to get caught! My own theory is the more you have to conceal from the world, the better player you'll turn out to be. Living life as an outlaw, hiding in plain sight, is the best training you could ever have to act on stage. I call it The School of Night."

"That's unique," I said.

"You've had a little acting experience. That's a start. Any other talents?"

"I play the lute."

"Music livens up a performance. Can you sing?"

"Reasonably well," I answered. "Many people here in town believe I'm a talented writer of jests and poetry."

"I'm always looking for good material to work into my jigs. Let's put your wit to the test." he said. "I'll clink cups with you, and give you a taste of my wit. Then give me a taste of yours. Okay?"

"Sounds good," I said.

Dick and I clinked cups. Licking his lips, he exclaimed:

"Sack! The elixir! The ambrosia! The spice of life! The rival to the happiness in bed with one's wife! The burier of axes! The maker of hatreds and stripes! The peacemaker, marriage breaker, and undertaker! All rolled-up in one! And so, I make my jest, in this time of fun!" Dick said, joy in his eyes.

"I see you like your work," I smiled.

"I certainly do. Now, it's your turn! Let's see the quality of your wit."

I lifted my own cup, clinked it with his, and began a short improvisational sketch. I hoped like hell Dick Tarlton would find it amusing. As I spoke, I employed a slight Germanic accent, adding some extra "sauce" to the dish.

"The old man and the maiden sailed to their safe haven. First, they hid in Hamburg, then they hid in Leiden. On the ship they traveled with buxom bills of lading, with buttons, beads and baubles, exchanged in their fair trading. The master and the maven tricked the fair young maiden. And the old man's face was craven, while golden horns were graven. So I tell my tale, a whopper of a whale, that glides on through the seas, and leaves its hearers pleased!"

As I finished speaking, I looked at Dick Tarlton with breathless anticipation. He placed an index finger and thumb on the point of his chin, tilted his head to one side, and gave the impression of a man deep in thought. Then he burst out laughing, saying, "Not bad for a novice. It shows promise. It has the flavor of Chaucer's 'Miller's Tale.' And it's light enough to be acceptable to burghers out here in the hinterland."

Catching his breath, he continued, "It never ceases to amaze me. The jewels one sometimes finds in small towns. I'll tell you what. If you really want to come to London, I'll put in a good word for you with the right people."

His words filled my heart with joy. "Thank you!" I exclaimed.

"Don't think too much of me," Dick said. "There's something I wish in return."

"Anything you desire?" I replied.

"That you serve as one of my jig writers. I have several young men with fine wits like yours. They provide me with jests, ballads, humorous poems and skits, to supplement the ones I write myself. For each one I accept, I'll pay you a penny."

"That's generous," I said.

"Further, if and when you decide to come to London, I'll introduce you to its greatest theater owner and impresario, a person who could be of great assistance if you decide to pursue a career as a player."

"Who's that?" I asked.

"James Burbage," he said with a smile. "A cousin of the Burbages who run this tavern! He owns the Theater in Shoreditch, just north of the City. If Burbage takes a liking to you, you could go places. Now, to strike fast our bargain, let's drink to our mutual success, and then write down your little story of the old man and the maiden. I'll work it into my act in Warwick tomorrow afternoon!"

Walking home that evening, inebriated but happy, I could not help wondering how I would explain all this to Anne and my parents. I felt I was being drawn to London by an irresistible force. It was where I believed my destiny awaited. Come hell or high water, I would have to find a way to get there!

CHAPTER XXVII
CAT O'NINE TAILS

Being a typical country squire, Thomas Lucy enjoyed hunting and hawking with a passion. He jealously defended his property from poaching by the "riff-raff" local townsmen. To prosecute such "worthless vagabonds," he employed several wardens to protect the game on his property.

Lucy's grand, recently built home, a sprawling brick mansion called Charlecote, was located beside the banks of the Avon about three miles from Stratford. In addition to this huge mansion, Lucy owned many of the remaining tracts of forest land around Stratford. Although he had not yet stocked and fenced a deer park, he kept a rabbit warren, and many of the remaining deer in the area naturally gravitated to Lucy's forested land. There they could find the shelter, food and water necessary to survive. In addition to being a natural haven for the remaining deer in the area, Lucy's tracts of land were a natural habitat for wild hares, foxes, squirrels, and pheasants.

Lucy's wardens were brutal men without land of their own. They drank heavily and had nasty reputations for gambling, brawling and bullying. That's the way he liked them. Lucy bragged his men had "cracked more heads" than he could count.

To further discourage poaching, Lucy armed his men well. They each were issued muskets and wheellock pistols from Lucy's private collection. And they carried rapiers, clubs, and daggers, as well as birches and whips, to administer country justice to transgressors. Although Lucy, who had recently been selected for a second term as one of Warwickshire's two MPs, might not technically have the legal authority to whip a poacher found on his land, outside the Stratford town limits, Sir Thomas Lucy was the law.

Brutal as it was, it was sometimes better to be beaten or whipped, than to be formally prosecuted under the harsh laws of the Crown. Or so young men like myself, my brother Gil, and our friend, Hamnet Sadler, thought on a cool October day in 1585, seven months after the birth of my twins, Hamnet and Judith.

The three of us met up at our home in Henley Street at the crack of dawn. Hamnet brought several loaves of bread he had baked in one of his family's numerous bread ovens the day before. After consuming fresh milk, curds, and whey, and placing the loaves of bread, and some generous hunks of hard cheese in a satchel, we slung the straps of our wineskins over our shoulders, along with quivers of arrows made by the local fletcher, and picked up our trusty bows.

We headed out the back door, and gathered the hawk, two horses, and our hounds, Brace and Hold-Fast. As Hamnet's horse had recently come up lame, he was riding with Gil. I was riding alone with our hooded hawk on my forearm. We were prepared for whatever game we found. In such times of scarcity, that was the only way we had a chance of success. But, despite our best efforts to flush out game all morning, we came up empty-handed.

Frustrated, we took a lunch break in the shade of a broadleaved tree by the banks of the river. As we ate our bread and cheese, washing it down with swigs of wine, we lamented our bad luck.

I must confess, I was the one who first broached the idea of making a foray into the forest land owned by Thomas Lucy. Of course, the idea of our taking something belonging to Lucy was attractive to me, as an additional piece of the revenge I had begun to take by writing and publicizing the by now infamous "anonymous" ballad.

Gil, who shared my hatred of Lucy, was all for the idea of spending the afternoon hunting on our persecutor's land. This would not be the only time we had done so. On previous forays we had successfully taken hares, pheasants, and even a good-sized buck, without encountering Lucy's wardens.

Although Hamnet had no love for Sir Thomas Lucy, he sounded a note of caution. In his opinion, the benefit of returning home with a few meals for our families was not worth the risk of being caught by Lucy's henchmen. Despite Hamnet's reservations, in this case my bad angel fired my good angel out. I was hell-bent on filling my stomach at Lucy's expense.

So, after finishing our rustic meal, Hamnet went his way, while Gil and I went ours. Hamnet gracefully agreed to walk the three miles to Stratford. We promised to bring his gear back to town. This would allow him to travel quickly. Hamnet and I had traversed similar distances in less than an hour on many occasions.

While Gil and I watched Hamnet fade out of sight on the worn path back to Stratford, we loosed the hounds and resumed the hunt. After proceeding a mile, and verifying Lucy's mercenaries were nowhere to be seen, we crossed onto Lucy's land. Our luck immediately began to change. We soon bagged several hares and our hawk brought down a plump pheasant.

Not wanting to press our luck, Gil and I had just decided to call it a day when the otherwise peaceful afternoon was shattered by the sharp report of a discharging pistol. Turning towards the gunshot, I saw two horsemen rapidly galloping our way. I instinctively shouted to Gil: "Get outta here! Head to Stratford. I'll lead them astray!"

"I'm not leaving you!" Gil shouted back.

"Don't be stupid!" I yelled, steering my nervous horse towards Gil's,drawing my sword, and striking his horse's hindquarters.

The high-spirited temperament of the horse Gil was riding did its job. Despite my brother's best efforts, the horse galloped off towards Stratford, Gil holding on for dear life. Our barking hounds followed, chasing after them. Had the situation not been desperate, it would have been hilarious.

Quickly removing its hood, I released the hawk, hoping I could later retrieve it. With a last glance at our pursuers, now within a hundred yards of my position, I spurred my horse to action, heading away from Stratford. I prayed our enemies would take the bait and follow me into the brush where I could shake them. Leading my horse off the trail gave me the best chance of escape. None of our horses were bred for racing. The one I was riding had seen better days.

After galloping a few hundred yards down the trail, I sharply pulled on the reins, spurring my reluctant steed through the brush. Undeterred, my pursuers followed. One right, one left.

As the distance they were trailing me closed to twenty yards, they began shouting: "Stop now! Yield! You cur!"

I did not have the opportunity to respond. Frantically turning to see how much ground they had gained, I was struck squarely in the upper chest by the branch of a tree my horse passed under. The sudden blow threw me from my saddle. I was knocked unconscious when my head impacted the leafy ground below.

I was fortunate to have landed where I did. A fall like that could easily have broken my neck, and the fragile thread of my earthly existence would have parted.

How long I remained unconscious, I do not know. It must have been several hours. When I came to my senses, I found myself tied face-first to a post outside the stables of Sir Thomas Lucy's imposing red brick mansion. The occasion of my regaining consciousness was a drenching with a cold bucket of water. As I came to, I felt intense pain in my right ankle. I did not know if it was broken or just a severe sprain. A cold chill coursed through my entire body. I soon realized I was stripped down to my waist.

Snorting and shaking the water out of my hair, I heard a gruff voice behind me say: "Well gentlemen, what type of rat do we have here?"

"A drowned one," said another deep voice, punctuating the sentence with a gleeful laugh.

A third chimed in saying, "Like all rats, this one's a thief! And a Papist to boot!"

"A thief, and a Papist too!" Said the gruff voice I now realized belonged to the master of the house.

As this dawned upon me, I heard footsteps approaching. A moment later a hand grabbed the wet hair at the back of my head and yanked it around until I came face-to-face with Sir Thomas Lucy. Lucy's grey eyes looked at me intently. With a cold sneer oozing hatred and contempt, he said: "Well, young Master Shakespeare! We meet again. I've heard it said, in addition to being a poacher, you fancy yourself a balladeer!"

Hearing the word "balladeer" sent a chill down my spine. I knew there was going to be hell to pay.

"You know what balladeers need to do to survive in this world?" Lucy asked with a malevolent glare.

I did not give him the pleasure of an answer.

"They need to learn new songs to sing. I'm going to help by teaching you one. Do you want to know its name?" Not bothering to wait for an answer, he continued, "It's called the song of the cat. They say cats have nine lives. This one has nine tails, and nine claws," he said, thrusting his instrument of torture, a nine stranded whip known as a Cat O' Nine Tails, in my face. As he did so, he snarled: "You better hope you have nine lives to live, because I'm going to take eight of them!"

With that sadistic flourish, Thomas Lucy stepped back away from me with an eerie laugh. A few moments later, I heard the swish of the strands of the whip speeding through the air, followed by the beelike stings of the small knots tied into each strand of the cat cutting into my skin.

Again and again, Lucy drew back the cat, unleashing its nine vicious claws upon my raw and bleeding back. Despite my best efforts at suppressing a scream, by the tenth strike I could no longer avoid crying out.

Pausing, Lucy said, "That's better! Now you're starting to cry like the whimpering weasel you are. You Catholics are all the same. Even your so-called martyr, Campion, gave up his friends to avoid a little pain. You spent some time employed by the Hoghtons and the Heskeths. Didn't you? I can see you're cut from the same cloth. Let this be a lesson. Amend your ways, or you'll end up butchered on the scaffold, flesh food for carrion, just like Campion's!"

Finishing this speech, Lucy continued whipping me for what seemed like an eternity. In between blows, I could feel rivulets of blood streaming down my back. After twenty more strikes, everything went black.

Late that night, I was returned to our home in Henley Street by a Stratford carter who happened to be making a delivery at Charlcote that afternoon. My father and Gil carried my limp body to the bedroom in the addition to the house my father had built for Anne and me.

My mother and Anne spent the better part of the next week doing their best to tend to my dangerous wounds and nurse me back to health. Despite their efforts, I have never been quite the same. I permanently lost some range of motion in my right ankle joint, and I carry the unsightly scars on my back until this day.

CHAPTER XXVIII
TURNING POINT

After the severe whipping I received at the hands of Thomas Lucy, it became more apparent than ever, for the sake of my and my family's well-being, I needed to get out of Stratford. But such a move was not an easy thing to manage.

Of course, I did have the open invitation of Dick Tarlton. I had been supplying Dick with a steady stream of jokes and a few short comic skits. But the remuneration I received from these efforts was not enough to provide for myself in London, let alone enough to support my wife and three children back in Stratford.

Fortunately, Lucy's persecution of my family resulted in a wave of sympathy among a sizable number of the people of Stratford. But, in the immediate aftermath of my incident with Lucy, there were few willing to be seen entering our home for fear of being reported to the authorities. However, after a month passed without further episode, some began to feel more comfortable interacting with us.

One evening, when I had recovered sufficiently to resume most of my daily activities, my father invited me to join him for a couple of drinks at Burbage's Tavern. By the time we arrived, it was a half hour before closing late on a Tuesday afternoon. The place was nearly empty. We had just received two mugs of ale from the bar maid, when the owner, William Burbage, came over holding a cup of ale. He took a seat beside me, across the table from my father.

"Hello Will! Thanks for joining us," said my father.

"Glad to, John," replied William Burbage. Looking my way, he said, "I hope you're ready for an adventure?"

"Adventure?" I asked quizzically.

"I see you haven't told him about the arrangement?" said Mr. Burbage looking at my father, a big grin lighting up his face.

"I decided to keep it a surprise," replied my father.

"What mischief have you two been up to?" I asked.

"Nothing to worry about, son. I think it's going to make you very happy," my father reassured. "Because Mr. Burbage has done us such a gracious favor, he should have the honor of telling you about it."

With that, Mr. Burbage simply said: "Your father shared your desire to work in London some time ago. When I heard about your recent misfortune with Lucy, I took the liberty of sharing your story with my London cousin. Do you know who James Burbage is?" asked Mr. Burbage.

"I do!" I answered, a wave of excitement building inside me. "He runs the famous Theater. Dick Tarlton's told me about it. It has room for several thousand people!" As I spoke, a smile spread across my father's face.

"Dick Tarlton's part of the story. He put in a good word for you with James. Said you have an excellent wit. Show great promise," said Mr. Burbage.

"Tarleton's a special man!" I said.

"There aren't many young lads your age who can earn a recommendation from Dick. He's the true English King of Comedy. Everyone else pales by comparison. Here's the upshot of it all," said Mr. Burbage. "My cousin James has agreed to employ you. Just as importantly, He'll let you reside in his home as a member of his household while you learn the trade."

"I can't believe my good fortune! Thank you for all you've done. I'll never forget it."

"Neither shall I," said my father.

"Although I appreciate your thanks, there's no need. I know you and your family would do the same for any of us if we were in similar circumstances," said Will Burbage.

Looking back upon that evening three decades later, it was a turning point in my life and the life of my family.

CHAPTER XXIX
SETTING-OUT

On the way home, my father surprised me. He told me my mother and Anne knew about and fully supported the plan. They concluded my best hope for a safe and decent future was to get out of Stratford and Warwickshire. And the only real place a young man like myself could find employment outside of Warwickshire was in London, which had fifteen times the population of the nation's second largest city, Norwich.

The fact my father, mother and Anne pooled their resources to come up with enough to send me to London with sufficient funds to pay for my first three months room and board caused my heart to soar!

When I returned home, I sought out Anne and my mother, thanking them profusely. Only a fortnight later, after a farewell dinner presided over by my father, a heartfelt send off by the entire family, and a hug and kiss from Anne, I set out for London on a rented horse in the company of the Stratford-to-London courier and family friend, William Greenaway.

The time-honored route Mr. Greenaway took to London included an overnight in Oxford. Although the trip so far had been uneventful, it seemed the greater the distance from Stratford, the less exuberance I felt. It was the beginning of my realization this was just the start of a long haul. Not weeks, but months, perhaps years, of spending large stretches of time separated from those I loved.

I already missed the hugs and kisses of the children, their sweet smiling faces, and the whispered pillow talk I shared with Anne before we nodded off to sleep. Feeling her warm body beside mine, and the steady rhythm of her heartbeat. Enjoying the wit and banter I shared with my father and brothers as we worked together. Savoring a bowl of my mother's hot pea soup on a stormy day. Yes, at the very beginning of this new phase of my life, I was already experiencing my first bout of homesickness!

In the middle of a spell of insomnia brought on by that homesickness, I found myself taking up pen and paper in the small room at the inn where William Greenaway and I were staying. I wrote the following poem which I gave to Mr. Greenaway to convey to Anne upon his return to Stratford.

Weary with toil, I haste me to my bed,
The dear repose for limbs with travel tired;
But then begins a journey in my head,
To work my mind, when body's work's expired:
For then my thoughts (from far where I abide)
Intend a zealous pilgrimage to thee,
And keep my drooping eye-lids open wide,
Looking on darkness which the blind do see;
Save that my soul's imaginary sight
Presents thy shadow to my sightless view,
Which, like a jewel hung in ghastly night,
Makes black night beauteous, and her old face new.
Lo thus by day my limbs, by night my mind,
For thee, and for myself no quiet find.

It was the beginning of a correspondence between Anne, myself, and the other members of our family which would span a quarter century.

After completing this poem, I was finally able to get some sleep. Surprisingly, I woke the next morning feeling far more refreshed than I ought to have felt under the circumstances.

For resilience, and a seemingly boundless fountain of energy, are two of the supreme gifts of youth. The others being optimism, and a sense of innocence which goes along with it.

Oh, how many visions of our youth turn out to have been mirages? And how fortunate we are we did not know then what we know now.

CHAPTER XXX
THE BURBAGES

So, with the welcoming world arrayed before us, we completed our trip to London. After dropping off the horses at the stable of the Bell Inn, we proceeded through the streets of the city to the neighborhood of Shoreditch, where the Theater and the Green Curtain were located, and where many of those in the theater industry, including James Burbage and Dick Tarlton, lived and worked. Mr. Greenaway knew the way to James Burbage's spacious three-story home on Holywell Street.He sometimes carried letters and messages from the Burbages in Stratford to their illustrious relatives in London.

Travelling through the streets, lugging the small chest containing the bare-bones belongings I brought from Stratford, I was overwhelmed by the hustle, bustle and sea of humanity surrounding us. The constant clatter and rumble of horses, carts, and coaches, along with the cries and jingles of salesmen and saleswomen selling their wares, hawking, bargaining, chattering, and haggling, created a cacophony which required a period of adjustment before the ears of a country boy like myself grew accustomed to the clamor and din of this giant beast of a city.

As we approached the three-story, half-timbered home of James Burbage and his family, my heart beat faster. Much depended on our first meeting.

Fortunately, I did not have to wait long. Mr. Greenaway's knock at the door was quickly answered by a bearded, thick-bodied, middle-aged man of average stature, who turned out to be the master of the house.

"Hello friend," said James Burbage.

"Good day, James. I trust you're well," Mr. Greenaway responded.

"Still alive by the grace of God!" said Mr. Burbage, with a hearty bellow. With a glimmer of mischief in his eyes, he continued, "What baggage have you brought from Stratford this time?"

With a half-toothless grin, Mr. Greenaway announced, "A fugitive from Mighty Lord Lucy."

"Hah! A fugitive from Loosey Goosey! Trying to stay one step ahead of the law, are you?" Mr. Burbage asked, relieving the growing tension in my breast with a wink.

Carefully laying the chest I carried on the hardwood floor, I replied, "Maybe so, maybe no."

"Well, young Mr. Maybe! I don't give a hoot in hell who or what you're running from. What I want to know is what you can do for me?"

Thinking on my feet, I answered, "just about anything. I can cook, clean, write, tend to your horses, hawks and hounds..."

"Hawks and hounds!" Does it look like I have those here in the city? A real greenhorn, aren't you? And a jack of all trades to boot!"

"Yes sir!" I answered. "I'm at your beck and call."

"Well Mr. Maybe, *maybe* we can find something you can do to earn your keep. Do you know what I do for a living?" James Burbage asked, with a skeptical air.

"You run a theater business," I answered hopefully.

"Ever seen a theater?" he asked.

"No sir."

"Then come with me tomorrow for a grand tour of one. Afterwards, we'll find some things to keep you busy. Now let's get you fed and assign you a place to sleep," Mr. Burbage said, placing a hand beside his mouth, and calling out in the voice of an actor accustomed to projecting over great distances:

"Richard! Get a move on! I need you down here. Pronto!"

What seemed like an equally powerful voice reverberated from above, "Hold your horses, Father! I'll be down in a minute."

"The sooner, the better," Mr. Burbage answered. Turning to William Greenaway, who was observing the proceedings with an air of amusement, he said: "I've been so occupied getting to know young Mr. Maybe..."

"Shakespeare," I interjected, drawing a stern look from Mr. Burbage, causing me to regret making the interruption.

"The young Mr. Shakespeare," Mr. Burbage corrected before continuing, "that I haven't had a chance to catch up with you and hear the latest from Stratford."

While Mr. Burbage spoke with Mr. Greenaway, a handsome, impeccably dressed young man of less than average stature came down the stairwell located on the right side of the room.

Seeing him, Mr. Burbage interrupted his conversation with Mr. Greenaway. "Dick, this young man from Stratford is here to work with us. Take him back to the kitchen, and have Rebecca fix him something to eat. Then get him a bed back in the servants' quarters."

"Aye, aye Father," said the young man with a mock salute and a touch of sarcasm. With a gesture of his hand, he beckoned me to follow.

While Mr. Burbage continued his conversation with Mr. Greenaway, I picked up my small chest and went with Dick Burbage to the kitchen at the back of the house. When we arrived there, Dick introduced me to their stout, strong-armed cook. She served me a generous helping of mutton stew, a half loaf of rye bread, and a tankard of small ale. Richard sat down opposite me at the kitchen table with his own tankard.

As we ate and drank, we introduced ourselves. Much to my heart's content, we got along famously. Like his father had done, Dick was working his way up the corporate ladder in the hope that, in the not-too-distant future, he would earn the right to be the company's leading man.

When Dick spoke about the roles he already played, and those he aspired to, his energy and enthusiasm were contagious.

I felt this person pouring his heart out to me was someone very special. He seemed to have the aura and demeanor of what the old wives of the villages would call an "Old Soul." God further gifted him with good looks, and a beautiful baritone voice.

What he lacked in height, Dick more than made up for in humor and a genial nature. It is said first impressions are most important, and the first impression Dick made upon me was that of a fiery comet, streaking across a dark night sky. I felt he was destined for greatness.

Although the judgments of one's youth are often inaccurate and prone to excess, in this case, my first opinion of Dick was straight and true. The acquaintance we began that day blossomed into the most artistically creative and productive friendship of my life. One that made the future financial well-being of my family possible.

When I finished lunch, Dick escorted me to the quarters I would end-up occupying for the next five years. It consisted of a small room, barely wide enough to contain the cot-like bed running along the far wall. Although the mattress was stuffed with straw, it was snug. And there was enough space at the foot of the bed for my small chest of belongings.

After making sure I was settled-in, Dick said his temporary adieu. Once he left, I unpacked my personal belongings, placing some of them, including my precious books, pen, paper, and inkhorn, on the shelves above the bed. Then I lay down and took a nap to recover from the fatigue brought on by several days of rough road travel. I awoke in time to enjoy supper in the kitchen with the servants. I later found time to dash off a letter to Anne before retiring for the evening.

CHAPTER XXXI
THE THEATER

The next morning I felt refreshed. After a hearty breakfast of toast and scrambled eggs, I accompanied James Burbage, Dick, and James's eldest son, Cuthbert, on the walk to the Theater through the fields of Shoreditch. Even from a distance, the Theater was most impressive. It was a huge octagonal building, three stories high, topped by a thatched roof and small wooden tower and flagpole. Cuthbert explained the flagpole was used to fly the different colored flags signaling comedy or tragedy.

As we approached, I saw a long row of stables. Cuthbert said these were built to accommodate the nobles and well-off gentry who rode their horses to performances. When I asked why the Theater was located so far from the city center, he explained, due to the influence of Puritanical sects with members at all levels of our society, as well as a fear of the effect of large gatherings like those which occurred when several thousand people attended a performance of a play, the city fathers banned the construction of playhouses within city limits. When Cuthbert's father built the Theater back in 1576, he had to construct it out here beyond the city's jurisdiction.

Not far from the Theater was a building of similar construction. Cuthbert explained it was the rival theater called the Curtain. When the Theater succeeded, it was inevitable another venue would be built to offer the public a choice of entertainment.

"Are the performances always in the afternoon?" I asked.

"Yes. We need the light. And the statutory curfew requires everyone to be back within city limits by sundown," Cuthbert responded.

Stepping through the large double doors at the entrance to the Theater, I was awestruck. Before my eyes was a huge stage six feet above ground, supported by four pillars and covered by a large canopy. The stage, the pillars, and the canopy looked like a giant tester bed. The columns gave the appearance of marble, although I subsequently discovered they were masterfully painted columns of wood.

Behind one side of the stage was a large shed-like structure Cuthbert identified as the tiring house. There the players put on makeup and changed into costume before and during each performance. As I turned to obtain a panoramic view of the interior of this huge building, I saw stairways leading up to three tiers of galleries spaced at intervals along the side walls. While I admired the craftsmanship of the carpentry and the efficiency of the design, Dick and Cuthbert explained the structure of the seating pricing.

"It costs the groundlings, on the entrance level where we are now, a penny to see a performance. Those on the second level pay two pence. Those on the upper level three," said Cuthbert.

"For the young dandies looking to display their fine taste in fashion, there are a limited number of seats allowed to be placed on stage for the substantial price of six pence," Dick added.

Above the stage canopy, against the far wall, was a long, covered gallery. Cuthbert explained it housed the players who entertained the audience with music before and during performances. They also provided the music for the comedic jig closing every performance.

Once my awe over the enormity and uniqueness of this specially constructed structure subsided, Dick joined his father and the group of actors already on stage preparing for a rehearsal of this afternoon's performance of a play about the life of Henry V.

When I asked Cuthbert if his father still took on roles, he laughed.

"Not often. He used to be one of the best players in the land. But years of living on the road in a traveling troupe took its toll. And the pressing concerns of running this enterprise don't leave much time for anything else. Rarely, he plays an old king or jester."

"Is that why he's there today?" I asked.

"No. He's directing," Cuthbert answered. "My father's teaching them how to charm an audience."

While Cuthbert spoke, I watched James Burbage take a rapier out of the hand of one of the young actors. Moving to center stage, he gave a tour de force tutorial on the thrusts, slashes, and stances necessary for convincing swordplay.

"There's more to performing those moves correctly than meets the eye," Cuthbert commented. "Dick has been studying with a fencing master for six months. He's still nowhere close to my father's proficiency."

When James Burbage finished his demonstration, Cuthbert led me up a stairwell and down the gallery to a room at the end of a hallway. Inside were shelves full of bound hand-written scripts and a large collection of small blue ceramic jars with coin slots in their fat, little bodies. There also were numerous large wicker baskets filled with broken jars and blue ceramic shards.

Noticing my quizzical expression, Cuthbert explained, "We call those jars 'boxes.' This room is called the box office. Patrons place their coins in the slots of the boxes as they enter. Once the play begins, the gatherers bring the jars to the office. My father and I break them and count the coins. The jars keep the coins from being filched by the gatherers, and the numerous cutpurses and pickpockets lurking in the audience."

Listening to Cuthbert, I couldn't help wondering whether there was a more economically efficient way to provide the security they sought without having to destroy scores of these blue ceramic jars at every performance. But I was here to learn. I did not want to bite the hand feeding me by questioning a tried-and-true method.

Pointing to the row of leather-bound books stacked on the top shelf of the far wall, Cuthbert explained, "those contain a record of receipts for every performance here since the Theater opened in 1576, as well as all financial transactions associated with the business, including purchases of costumes and props. You may be surprised to learn we pay more for the costumes than we do for the scripts."

"I never would've guessed," I said.

"The velvets, silks, satins and lace royalty and members of the aristocracy wear cost a pretty penny," said Cuthbert. "Cheap imitations stick out like sore thumbs, breaking the spell of suspended disbelief our plays depend upon. Although our players are commoners, it's vital for them to authentically look the part of the members of society they're playing. Since women's' roles in our plays are acted by boys, we purchase both men's and women's clothing. Keeping up with the endless whims of male and female high fashion is financially burdensome. From a practical standpoint, it's nearly impossible. We do the best we can. But it's a constant battle," Cuthbert said, catching his breath.

"After the immense cost of the costumes comes the expense of the props. In addition to the bows, arrows, halberds, rapiers, daggers, old-fashioned broad swords, suits of armor, crowns, scepters, tankards, pots, cups, and chalices, we have purchased several bronze cannons we can fire off during battle scenes and ceremonial occasions!"

"Wow!" I exclaimed, imagining the thrill that must run through an audience hearing the booms of cannon reverberate throughout the circular echo chamber of the Theater as tongues of fire emerged from the bronze barrels during a performance.

"It's about as good as it can be. We spare no expense giving our audiences an experience they will not forget," said Cuthbert proudly. "It doesn't just include the show. We provide food and drink for our patrons, including beer, ale, hard cider, oysters, walnuts, tasty apple pippins, and even clay pipes and tobacco — all at reasonable prices! For those well-off enough to ride horses to the show, we have stables, with water, hay, and grooming for their steeds. Like many of us before you, that's where my father has decided you'll start."

"As a groom?" I asked, crestfallen.

Seeing my disappointment, Cuthbert said, "Yes, but don't look sad. You'll have plenty of opportunities to prove yourself and move up in our organization. If you want to be in the acting business, especially working with our family, you've got to start out on the ground floor.

"Once you prove yourself with the care of our most important patrons' horses, you'll move on to work as a gatherer, and seller of food and drink. If you prove to be trustworthy, and reasonably free of vice, you'll progress to supporting the actors, taking care of the costumes and props. Eventually, you'll move up to preparing the prompt books, the rolls containing the actors' lines, and giving the actors their cues. Finally, assuming you stick it out, and we believe you've got what it takes to be successful on the stage, we'll give you some minor roles to cut your teeth upon."

"If I prove myself worthy, how long will it be before I can begin training as an actor?" I asked.

"For a person of average talent and ability, I would say two years. If you devote all your efforts to the work at hand, it could be shorter," Cuthbert responded. Then he added, "There's a way I believe you can make it very short indeed."

"How?"

"You've been providing Dick Tarlton with material for his jokes?"

"He pays handsomely for ones he accepts."

"We always need good jokes. Humorous sketches too. Some old manuscripts sitting on the shelves over there aren't long enough for two hours entertainment. So, we work on finding ways to lengthen the shows. On the front end, the back, or both.

"On the front end we have something called an induction. It's a ten minute sketch that gets the audience in the right mood for the major work which follows. Light humor works best. If popular, it can be reused to introduce a variety of plays.

"When the play concludes, we serve the audience a light chaser called the jig. It can take two forms. For plays on serious subjects, it's an elaborate and formal dance in which the characters in the preceding play take the stage again and symbolically reenact the performance.

"The most moving I've seen occurred about a year ago, at the end of a play dramatizing the love triangle between King Arthur, Queen Guinevere, and Sir Lancelot. Seeing the story in dance brought the audience to a high pitch of emotion. There wasn't a dry eye in the house."

"Sounds impressive."

Cuthbert continued, "the second and more common form of the jig is a comedic sketch. It's sometimes combined with a slapstick folk dance. For these, we need scripts and well-written jokes. Working with Tarlton has given you a good writing foundation. It could enable you to quickly establish value with my father. If he likes your inductions and jigs, he may engage you to revise and expand the scores of old plays which are company property."

"I can't thank you enough for explaining all this to me," I said with an air of gratitude. "I feel there's a future here. I'll work as hard as I can to justify the investment your family is making in me."

"I'll convey what you've said to my father. I know he'll be glad to hear it," said Cuthbert. "Now it's time for you to head on over to the stables and begin your apprenticeship. Our head groomsman is expecting you."

So ended my first glimpse of the inner workings of the business which would become both my livelihood and my passion for the remainder of my working life.

CHAPTER XXXII
A PROMISING INDUCTION

After the inspiration of that first day with the Burbage family, the next year went by with the speed of a relentless tempest. The more intensely I threw my body and soul into my work, the more I felt God had gifted me with the grace of finding my true calling in life.

As Cuthbert explained, during the first year I was in their service, the Burbages made sure I had the opportunity to perform all the tasks necessary to the successful operation of the Theater, short of performing with the actors on stage. Although I took satisfaction in ascending each of the necessary rungs on the ladder of theatrical success, the top rung remained elusively out of reach. But this is how it was meant to be. A pearl of great price is worth the labor needed to obtain it.

One benefit I received from that gradual ascent is the opportunity to see a huge number of plays. From this experience, I learned the type of writing and acting which works well with an audience.

I also had the opportunity to study many of the leading writers and actors of the age. Among the writers I came to admire were the members of a loose social circle known as the University Wits. These included Robert Greene, George Peele, Thomas Nashe and the charismatic, boyish-looking playwright, Christopher Marlowe.

Despite my admiration, I knew the chances of my being accepted within their circle was remote. I lacked the prerequisite of a university degree.

The actors I came to admire most during this period included the well-established Ned Alleyn, my incipient friend, Dick Burbage, a young comedic actor named Will Kemp, and my great mentor, Dick Tarlton. But I knew I had neither the exceptional good looks, charisma, and stentorian voice necessary to be a leading man like Ned Allen or Dick Burbage, nor the gift of Average Joe looks, and comedic timing and delivery, possessed by Dick Tarlton, and his protégé, Will Kemp.

One night, when success and security in this challenging business seemed most out of reach, and my effective banishment from those I loved in Stratford was weighing heavily upon my mind, I tried to purge myself of such pessimistic thoughts, penning the following lines to Anne:

> When in disgrace with fortune and men's eyes,
> I all alone beweep my outcast state,
> And trouble deaf heaven with my bootless cries,
> And look upon myself, and curse my fate,
> Wishing me like to one more rich in hope,
> Featur'd like him, like him with friends possess'd,
> Desiring this man's art, and that man's scope,
> With what I most enjoy contented least;
> Yet in these thoughts myself almost despising,
> Haply I think on thee, — and then my state
> (Like to the lark at break of day arising
> From sullen earth) sings hymns at heaven's gate;
> For thy sweet love remember'd, such wealth brings,
> That then I scorn to change my state with kings.

Fortunately, such dark thoughts were more the exception than the rule. For, along with the occasional blue days, there was also sunshine and excitement. Speaking of the sparkling sun, there was none whose illuminating rays shone more brightly on his fellow man than the scintillating Dick Tarlton!

Since arriving in London, I had kept up my correspondence with Dick, supplying jokes and jests, while also working on a myriad of tasks for the Burbages, including occasionally trying my hand at writing inductions and jigs.

Although my first few efforts in these genres had not tickled the fancies of the ever-fickle crowds that frequented the Theater, my third attempt at writing an induction scene struck a chord in many. I cannot explain why this work succeeded while previous efforts did not. All I can say is, after a quarter century in show business, it is impossible to predict what will become a hit with any certainty. To attempt to package a formula for success is to play Don Quixote among the windmills.

Be that as it may, it was one of the greatest honors of my life when I saw my friend and mentor, Dick Tarlton, act the leading role in the third induction scene I had written. For lack of a better title, I call it "The Drunken Dream of Christopher Sly."

Dick read the script shortly after I wrote it. In the presence of myself and James Burbage, he said, "The soused tinker has comic potential if played right!"

"You're the man for the part," I said with the enthusiasm of a young writer.

"Playing drunkards is my specialty.I kept an alehouse myself before I got into this business. Being a tapster gives a man the opportunity to get to know all types. The high, the low, the rich, the poor, good, bad and everything between!" Dick said, with a great bellow of a laugh.

True to his word, when Dick played the role of Christopher Sly several nights later, it was a performance for the ages!

Much to my surprise, Dick was joined on stage by James Burbage. Mr. Burbage was making one of his rare appearances, acting the role of the Lord who, arriving at the inn after a long day hunting with hawks and hounds, finds the tinker, Christopher Sly, passed out near the doorway. Seeing an opportunity for some amusement, the Lord decides to play a practical joke, removing the tinker to the Lord's own home, dressing him in fine garments, and putting him in a luxurious featherbed. When the Tinker awakes, he is treated as the master of the house arising from a long bout of moonstruck madness.

Christopher Sly is waited upon hand and foot by the Lord's own servants, who assure him his belief he is a tinker is merely a figment of his imagination. The Lord has one of his servant boys dress-up as the comely woman of the house. After his initial bewilderment, Christopher Sly looks forward to the enjoyment of connubial bliss. A sentiment not shared by the servant boy playing his wife.

Fortunately for "her," the other servants convince Sly that too early enjoyment of wedded bliss could throw him back into his recent madness. Instead, they offer him an entertainment by some traveling players. He gladly accepts. So, the playlet within a play begins.

Although, for everyone in the audience except me, the main attraction and purpose of being in the Theater was the Robert Green pastoral comedy which followed my interlude, Dick Tarlton, James Burbage, and the other actors that performed my work made this evening one of the highlights of my life. To top it off, after the play concluded, Dick asked me to join him, his wife, and James Burbage for dinner at his nearby home.

Chapter XXXIII
Dick and Em

After James Burbage finished accounting for the proceeds of the performance that evening, we took the short walk to Dick Tarlton's house. Upon arrival, Dick and his live-in lover, Emma Ball, welcomed us into the elegant dining room of their mini-mansion.

Despite the somewhat gentrified surroundings, to say Dick was a person who never let fame and fortune go to his head was an understatement. It was evident from the fact the person he chose as his partner was a former "working girl." True to form, Em's personality was, like Dick's, larger than life. I had seen her on numerous occasions attending performances at the Theater. Although she had retired from the world's oldest profession when she moved in to keep house with Dick, she still carried herself with the confidence and in-your-face swagger that made her a Shoreditch legend.

Although many of a more puritanical streak than myself believed the union between Dick and Em was one fashioned in Hell, I believed it was made in Heaven. Em was the perfect mate for Dick. She was clever and tough enough to give him as good as she got.

Once, when Em was in the audience while Dick performed a lackluster jig, and I was dispensing tobacco to some well-heeled patrons, I heard her shout at the top of her lungs:

> Tarleton's a clown,
> That Joker's not wild;
> The sauce that he's selling
> Is not spicy, It's mild!

Much to my surprise, upon hearing this brassy jeer, Dick turned his head toward Em, smiled his characteristic gap-toothed smile, and gave her a one-eyed wink, before wheeling around on his ox-like legs, dropping his trousers, and showing her the moon, bringing the house down with cheers and tumultuous applause. Whether or not this was a pre-planned set piece or spontaneous, it had the effect of turning an otherwise lackluster performance into a memorable one in the twinkling of an eye.

Besides having witnessed this incident, I heard many apocryphal stories about Em that were in circulation in the demimonde. One of those legendary stories had to do with the humorous advertising "slogans" Em would shout before, during, and after theatrical performances in the heyday of her working life. Among her many alleged slogans were the following:

Some like to cry,
Some like to pout,
But I'll put a smile,
Right on your snout!

Pass me the plaster,
Hand me the grout,
I'll fix what ails you,
Inside and out!

Come with a grimace,
Leave with a smile,
You'll lie in a hearse
After a while!

And the most sassy of all:

Whether you're better,
Whether you're worse,
Hand me the money,
Or I'll cut your purse!

When I first heard these sayings, I had serious doubts about their authenticity. After hearing Em's outburst in the Theater, I'm more of a believer. Sometimes truth is stranger than fiction!

Fortunately, everyone at the dinner table was in high spirits. The box office take was better than average. It had been a good week. I'd been around long enough to know James Burbage's moods fluctuated with the ups and downs of attendance at the Theater.

Dick Tarlton was one of those fortunate people who are always in high spirits. He perpetually saw the glass as half-full. More often than not, things worked out the way he wanted. Em was as positive and as brilliant a raconteur as he. For them, the sun was always rising, and birds were on the wing!

The conversation that evening was engaging and entertaining. James and Dick regaled Emma and me with tales of their early years in the theater business, when both were members of the same troupe of actors, crisscrossing the country in search of patronage, their next meal, and roofs over their heads. Playing in inns, taverns, town halls, mansions, country fairs. Anywhere that they could find an audience. Unlike many of their contemporaries, they were lucky enough to come through those days in one piece. They were now enjoying what was, for actors, a relatively comfortable old age.

Towards the end of the evening, the conversation turned to the short piece I wrote for the induction scene these two veterans graced with their talents earlier that evening. Much to my gratification, James, Dick and Em, who had attended to see Dick's performance before heading home to oversee the preparation of the roast duck dinner we just enjoyed, all praised the sketch. James suggested I should think about trying my hand at writing a full-length play. He also told me he was going to cut back on my other job responsibilities to allow me enough time to doctor older play scripts owned by the company.

As James Burbage spoke, Dick Tarlton nodded his approval. At the end of the conversation, Dick raised the goblet of sack he was drinking and toasted me: "To my young friend, Will Shakespeare. May Lady Luck be your mistress, and may you achieve all your desires!"

None of us knew that would be the last time I would have dinner with Dick Tarlton. For the good luck that graced him all the days of his life finally came to an end. Within three months of that marvelous evening, my dear friend lay in his grave, another victim of the scourge of the Black Death!

CHAPTER XXXIV
THE SPANISH ARMADA

Sometimes, in the depths of my imagination, I can hear the chop, chop, chopping of the wood. I can see the thousands of whetted axe blades slicing into the meaty hearts of the trees. And watch them teeter and fall, crashing to the ground, while the lumberjacks scamper away from the falling timber.

Before the Spanish can cross the channel to invade this sceptered isle, a veritable army of trees must be felled to build the necessary Armada of ships and troop transports. The Iberian shipyards, rope and sail makers' shops, cannon foundries, gunsmiths, and bullet makers, are working day and night.

For even an army proposing to do God's work, must still be provisioned and outfitted in the way all armies are. And there is much profit to be made. The clash, which must inevitably come, has been building to its crescendo since before the day I was born. And now, in the summer of 1588, the cauldron has boiled over into a witches' brew.

The impetus for the invasion has come from the beheading of Mary Queen of Scots. Whether Mary posed a significant threat to Elizabeth's rule, or she was a victim of Protestant paranoia, is hotly debated on the streets and in the homes of Londoners.

The government has supported the Protestant armies opposing the Spanish forces in the Netherlands for many years. The Spanish want to put an end to it now. Elizabeth's execution of Mary, a divinely anointed Roman Catholic monarch, allows Philip II to obtain the Pope's blessing for his mission to overthrow the Protestant "Usurper" who sits on the English throne. The Pope has promised Philip he will contribute two million ducats to the Spanish war chest if the Duke of Parma's forces ever reach the shores of England.

The Spanish plan is simple in concept, but requires close coordination and luck to be successful. The Spanish fleet will travel from Southwest Spain to the English Channel to provide support and protection for 30,000 battle-hardened soldiers from the Duke of Parma's army. They will cross the channel on vulnerable barges. On board the hodgepodge of ships comprising the Armada are an additional 20,000 Spanish troops.

Given the lack of preparedness of our government's own army, it is likely the sheer number of Spanish forces will overwhelm the smaller and ill-equipped English army if they can successfully cross the channel. But crossing the channel with a force that large is easier said than done. Especially when one is opposed by the very capable English fleet commanded by Lord Howard, John Hawkins, and Francis Drake. We English have almost as many ships to bring to the fray as the Spanish. And, what our ships lack in size, we make up for in maneuverability and firepower.

While the storm clouds are coalescing, I am going about my business, keeping my nose to the grindstone, working for the Burbages. Like most Londoners, the Burbages hate the Spanish, and pray for the success of our English fleet. They fear a Spanish victory will result in closure of the Theater — their lifeblood. The government is using the Theater in its propaganda efforts. It has even hung a Catholic priest, who was, according to the Government's Proclamation, a Spanish spy, within the precincts of the Theater itself.

As a Roman Catholic, I am disgusted by this cruelty — and realize the executed priest was just a pawn in the larger chess game being played by the competing powers that be. He is one of many thousands on all sides of the conflict who become victims in this battle of titans.

But, if I want to keep my own neck from being stretched, it is essential to keep such thoughts locked within my head. The air around us is so thick with tension you can cut it with a knife. For a fortnight or so, everyone is on edge as the Armada makes its way up the southern coastline and over to Calais, harried by the swiftly moving and better armed English fleet.

The Spanish make it to Calais pretty much intact. But the Duke of Parma's forces are not ready to launch their troop barges. While the Spanish fleet is stuck waiting at anchor, the English launch a line of eight explosive laden fire ships into the anchored Spanish fleet. Although the fire ships are lost, and sink no Spanish galleons, they bring about much chaos. Many panicking Spanish captains cut their anchor chains. The next day, the English fleet engages the somewhat disorganized Spanish fleet at Gravelines, sinks one of the Spanish ships, and causes damage to others.

Now that there is no chance of a successful rendezvous with Parma's forces, the Spanish fleet sails north. They eventually round the northern coast of Scotland and return to Spain by sailing along the west coast of Ireland. They are without adequate provisions, charts, or the primary anchors cut loose to avoid the fire ships. Running into a series of storms, many of the remaining Spanish ships are wrecked upon the coasts of Scotland and Ireland.

The English provincial government in Ireland pursues the shipwrecked Spanish sailors with a vengeance, placing a price on their heads and executing all those who cannot afford to pay a ransom for their freedom. Many Spanish sailors, on ships which do not wreck on the Scottish or Irish coasts, die of starvation or disease.

Unfortunately, our own English sailors do not fare much better. Because of contaminated provisions, disease runs rampant. Thousands of English seamen die earning the "Great Victory." Adding insult to injury, the crown never fully pays the sailors for the work they performed saving the nation from the calamity of Spanish rule.

Much of what I have written about this attempted Spanish invasion is done with the benefit of the knowledge I have been able to obtain over the many years since these events occurred. It is the product of numerous conversations I have had with participants and sympathizers of both sides of a conflict which did not end in 1588, but went on for another 16 years with numerous "victories" and "defeats" for both sides.

Of course, my feelings about the engagements of 1588 are different today from the way I felt then. At the age of twenty-four, I was more idealistic and less jaded than now. I was then fervently devoted to the faith of my father and mother. I still felt deeply hurt by the persecution my family and I had suffered at the hands of the Queen's enforcer, Thomas Lucy.

But, despite my adherence to the Roman Catholic faith, I also had a deep devotion to this land and people. I am English by birth, and English at core. Although I wanted the freedom to practice my religion without interference or persecution, I did not want to submit to foreign rule to achieve it. I hoped, as I did for many years afterward, for a uniquely English "solution" to the "Catholic Problem." The fact such a peaceful solution was not achieved is one of the great disappointments of my life.

Back then, I was rather relieved when news the Armada had been defeated reached London. Although I could not bring myself to join in the jubilant and intoxicating celebrations of many of those who surrounded me, I was happy the Theater would not be closed, and my job with the Burbages was secure.

CHAPTER XXXV
CHRISTOPHER MARLOWE

It was not long after the Burbages allowed me to try my hand at writing plays I got a once-in-a-lifetime opportunity to collaborate with the most popular and controversial playwright of our time — Christopher Marlowe. When God made Kit Marlowe, he broke the mold. There was no one like Kit who came before, and it is doubtful anyone like him will come again.

Like myself, Kit was an out-of-towner. But, while I came from the rather obscure Warwick town of Stratford, Kit came from one of the most important towns in all England, Canterbury, with its beautiful Cathedral, and the history that went along with it. Canterbury was the scene of Archbishop Thomas Becket's murder by members of Henry II's court. And, over two centuries after the death of St. Thomas, the Old Master of us writers, Sir Geoffrey Chaucer, wrote his unforgettable tales about a group of diverse pilgrims journeying from Southwark's Tabard Ale House to Canterbury to visit the shrine of St. Thomas. In doing so, Chaucer created the greatest work of poetic beauty in our language, painting a magnificent portrait in words of a venerable and Catholic English society that now is just a faded memory, receding into the smoky twilight of the past.

For the shrine of St. Thomas Beckett was mercilessly desecrated, and the pilgrimage to Canterbury cruelly abolished, during the early throes of the English Reformation. Despite the destruction of the shrine, Canterbury Cathedral was still the seat of the highest prelate in the new English Church established by Henry VIII — the Archbishop of Canterbury.

In this ancient, historically important city, Kit Marlowe was born in February 1564. Kit's cobbler father was, like mine, a common tradesman. Kit's parents wanted a better, more refined life for their son. So, off to Canterbury's King's School Kit went, for six days a week of repetitious learning and memorization of Latin.

Like myself, Kit showed great promise. Kit was fortunate enough to be awarded a scholarship to attend Corpus Christi College at Cambridge University. From Canterbury, Kit journeyed to Cambridge—a young Adonis if ever there was one!

Although he may not have distinguished himself academically, Kit made a splash socially. Handsome in a gamine sort of way, Kit was naturally endowed with a scintillating, acerbic wit. This made many of Kit's fellow students want to be around him just to hear the next quip he would utter. His exotic allure was enhanced for some by the rumor he was bisexual, with a marked preference for boys rather than girls.

In addition to his social charisma, Kit Marlowe was one of the greatest writers of our age, and one of the greatest of any age. His poetry was well-known and circulated in manuscript privately among his friends and admirers. He was also famous, or infamous, depending upon the social circle one traveled in, for translating Ovid's sexually explicit "*Amores*" from Latin into English.

And this was just for starters. For, along with the scintillating brilliance, there was a dark side to Kit Marlowe. It was rumored, between receiving his Bachelor of Arts degree in 1584, and his Master of Arts in 1587, Kit helped make ends meet by engaging in anti-Catholic espionage activities in England and the Netherlands for Elizabeth I's treacherous but grimly effective spymaster, Sir Francis Walsingham.

Like a giant octopus in search of its prey, the tentacles of Walsingham's network of spies and informers operated relentlessly to ferret out and destroy any persons and activities that might threaten the stranglehold the Protestant aristocracy had upon the wealth and power of the English nation.

If his cloak and dagger espionage activities were not enough to give one pause, Kit was also a person who had a hair-trigger temper. He was quick to give and take offense. And the consequences of Kit's anger could be deadly.

In late September of 1589, Kit was involved in a fight in which an innkeeper's son was stabbed to death on the street in Shoreditch where both the Theater and the Curtain were located, and many of us actors lived.

Kit, and a man named Thomas Bradley, got involved in a violent sword fight. Kit's friend, the poet Thomas Watson, attempted to intervene to separate the combatants. Giving proof to the adage "no good deed goes unpunished," Bradley turned his anger upon Watson, and beat him severely. Having temporarily taken Watson out of commission, Bradley turned his anger back upon Kit. Regaining his senses, Watson rejoined the fray, and obtaining the advantage on Bradley, ran his rapier deep into Bradley's chest. Bradley died. Kit and Watson ended up in Newgate prison until things could be sorted out.

I later used the facts of this three-way combat as the basis of the fight scene involving Mercutio, Tybalt, and Romeo in my play *Romeo and Juliet*. The character Mercutio in that drama shares much in common with the attitude, demeanor, and worldview of Kit Marlowe.

Unfortunately, the brawl in Shoreditch was not the only violent fight Kit was involved in over the years. A number of others spilled over into the courts. Fortunately, they did not result in the death of a participant.

The tainted aura surrounding Kit's hair-trigger temper and reputed spy activities added to his notoriety and helped him become a dark star in London society. Rumor held Kit's spying had proved so valuable to the Queen and her Privy Council, they had written to the powers to be at Cambridge to ensure Kit's work for the Crown would not detrimentally affect Kit's ability to obtain his master's degree.

Upon receiving that degree, Kit put his tremendous intellect to work, writing astounding plays which changed the world of the English theater. Kit's first blockbuster was a play called *Tamburlaine*. It was a fictional retelling of the tall tale of the Central Asian conqueror, Timur. The play is complex and plot driven. And it is written in glorious unrhymed blank verse, which, at that time, was cutting edge.

The mighty lines of its protagonist, Tamburlaine, were blasted across the stage of the Rose theater by the greatest actor of the age, Ned Alleyn. Seeing Ned strut across the stage, arm upraised towards the heavens, uttering Kit's immortal lines was mesmerizing. Tamburlaine was so successful, the owner of the Rose, Philip Henslowe, asked Kit to write a sequel. That was just as successful, giving birth to several of the most famous lines ever uttered by an actor. As Tamburlaine's chariot is pulled by a "team" of his captive kings, I can hear Ned Alleyn's whip cracking across their bleeding backs, as he calls out:

"Holla, ye pamper'd jades of Asia!
What, can ye draw but twenty miles a-day?"

Kit followed up the success of *Tamburlaine* and its sequel with a series of additional blank verse plays, including, the *Jew of Malta*, the *Massacre at Paris*, *Edward II*, and, last, but not least, what I consider his greatest masterpiece, *Dr. Faustus*.

The mind-blowing power of *Dr. Faustus* is best conveyed by a story I heard from the lips of Ned Alleyn himself, while we were both at the wedding feast of an actor friend. While giving a performance of the last act in the town of Dulwich, the act in which the Devil's part of the bargain with Faustus being complete, demons materialize to carry off the soul of Dr. Faustus to Hell, Ned, and many of the other actors in his company, saw a Witches' Sabbath of leering demons appear on the stage among them! If the play had not been concluding, they would have had to close the curtain and shut it down.

After pulling themselves together, Ned and the other players concluded the demons were made to appear as a warning to them to repent and ask forgiveness for the many sins they had committed in the theatrical life. As part of the penance he assigned to himself, Ned set out to found a college in Dulwich, and endow it for posterity. Apparently, his sacrifice proved acceptable. When the company resumed their performances of *Dr. Faustus*, the demons were gone.

As for the author of the play, like many of us, Kit fell upon hard times when the theaters closed due to the terrible outbreak of the plague in 1592. Strangely enough, we both tried to generate income by writing long poems for publication and patronage. In the time-honored tradition of artists and writers trying to put food on their table and roofs over their heads, both of us wrote on the subject of erotic love, using classical settings and characters. While I was writing my poem about the unrequited love Venus had for Adonis, Kit was writing his on the love of Hero and Leander.

CHAPTER XXXVI
TITUS ANDRONICUS

It was during this time of plague that Christopher Marlowe and I worked on writing a play together. Being the more successful and experienced writer, Kit took the lead in developing the plot.

I remember the day we first met to begin work as if it were yesterday. Kit sent word he would meet me at a favorite pub of his in Shoreditch called the Burning Candle. As I walked from my lodgings to the pub, I thought how appropriate its name was. For, if there ever was a person who burned the candle at both ends, it was Kit Marlowe.

By the time I arrived with wax tablets and stylus in hand, Kit was already seated in a booth enjoying a pot of ale. An open, dog-eared book lay flat on the table before him.

Seeing me approach, he looked up, saying, "Hello Will!"

"Great to see you. Hope life's treating you well," I answered, sitting down on the other side of the table.

"Treating me well? I don't know about that. I'm alive and kicking. But who knows for how long?"

"What do you mean?" I asked.

"I assume you've heard Tom Kyd has got himself arrested. He's in a jam with the authorities over that ballad found on the door of the Dutch Church threatening violence against foreign refugees."

"I've heard the rumors. It's hard to believe the author of as successful a play as *The Spanish Tragedy* would stoop so low as to be involved with rabble rousing of that nature."

"Don't believe every rumor you hear," said Kit looking at me intensely. "I want you to know, I had nothing to do with that doggerel poem, or anything else Kyd may be involved in. I've got enough of my own problems without taking on his. He's got plenty!"

"If you're not involved, it should blow over soon," I remarked. "You've been in many tough spots before. You've always come out unscathed."

"True. But this has a different feel. When a man as spineless as Kyd is backed into a corner, there's nothing he might not say to avoid torture or the noose."

"Is it that bad?"

"Could be!" said Kit, with an uncharacteristic frown. "The ass that wrote that libelous poem signed it Tamburlaine! The danger's enough to make a man want to find his faith in God again. But I'm too far gone!"

"Now you're exaggerating. I'm sure there's light at the end of the tunnel."

"I hope so. Except you don't know the half of it. There are things I can't share."

Seeing the open book and wanting to change the subject, I asked, "What have you been reading?"

"Something fueling my ideas for the new work we'll be collaborating upon," Kit said. "It's Ovid's tale of Philomena. Are you familiar with it?"

"Yes. I love Ovid. I call his *Metamorphoses* my magic book!" I said, relieved the conversation was now focusing upon the scriptwriting we would be doing together. "Let's see if I remember the story correctly. Philomena's a royal princess brutally taken advantage of by her lustful brother-in-law. He assaults and rapes her while taking her to visit her sister."

"Right," said Kit. "To try to prevent her from telling her story, her brother-in-law cuts out Philomena's tongue. But she still finds a way to convey what happened to her sister using her hands," said Kit.

"Then the two sisters take revenge upon the perpetrator by killing his son, and feeding his son's remains to him. When the rapist seeks revenge upon the sisters, they escape his murderous wrath by transforming into birds."

"You remember your Ovid well," said Kit.

"I ought to. Ovid was my salvation. An escape mechanism. An oasis of imagination, saving me from the monotonous drudgery of endless school days!"

"I second that," Kit said. "I was birched on a number of occasions for reading Ovid on the sly during my lessons. I ended up with some patches on my britches and caught hell from my mother for it," Kit said, breaking into a captivating smile energizing his features.

"You know what The Good Book says," I retorted.

"'Spare the rod and spoil the child.' In theory, there may be some truth in that saying. But, I think it does more harm than good."

"You may be right," I answered. "Returning to the story of Philomena, what in that bizarre little story is spurring your imagination?"

"I've been trying to figure out how to turn the public's seemingly insatiable appetite for shocking horror stories to our advantage. Sex violence, blood and gore never fail to sell well among certain segments of the population. If we throw in the fig leaves of classic references and allusions, it gives an excuse for the highfalutin among us to go slumming with the groundlings. You with me?" Kit asked, raising his eyebrows.

"I'm following your line of thought," I assured.

"What have our stages' two biggest hits been these last few years?"

"*The Spanish Tragedy*, and *Tamburlaine*," I answered.

"A revenge play and a classical blood spectacle. What if we combined the two? What will result? You know the answer, don't you?" Kit questioned, rapidly answering the question himself: "An addictive mixture of sex, murder, maiming, blood, and gore, the likes of which has never been seen before!"

"Sounds like a recipe for box office gold," I said.

"I can hear the coins jangling in those little blue ceramic money banks. It's enough to bring tears to a miser's cheeks!" Kit said, working himself up to a fever pitch.

Sensing he was coming to the heart of the matter, I picked up my tablet and stylus as Kit began.

"Now, to lay out the essence of the plot. The setting is ancient Rome. The protagonists, an aging Roman general named Titus Andronicus, and his mortal enemy, Tamora, Queen of the Goths. Titus returns to Rome in triumph, having won a stunning victory. Despite the victory, Titus has lost his eldest son in battle. The Goths' Queen and her three sons are his captives.

"Titus plans to bury his son in the family tomb. But, according to Roman custom, to properly honor his son and the gods, Titus must offer a human sacrifice. To fulfill his duties to his son and the gods, Titus selects Tamora's eldest son as the sacrificial lamb. Tamora begs for her son's life. But her desperate pleas fall upon deaf ears. Titus kills Tamora's son.

"The Emperor suddenly dies. The people want to make Titus Emperor by acclaim. Titus refuses to usurp the throne. Instead, he foolishly urges the people and nobles to make the Emperor's cruel and degenerate eldest son king. In a show of insincere gratitude, the conniving new Emperor offers to marry Titus's daughter, Lavinia, as a check on Titus's power. Lavinia will not play her part in this political game because she's in love with the Emperor's younger brother, Bassinius.

"Lavinia elopes with Bassinius. Titus is angry. The Emperor is distrustful of Titus. In a shocking twist, the Emperor marries Tamora. This turns Titus 's world of custom, honor, and duty, upside down."

Kit paused for a few seconds to catch his breath, while I continued scribbling away, changing tablets as I tried to catch up.

As I did so, Kit asked, "What do you think so far?"

"Wonderful!" I replied. "It gives people what they want! Sex! Action! Violence! More sex! More action! More violence! You're outdoing yourself this time!"

"Glad you like it, my friend," Kit said. He continued speaking so fast I had trouble documenting the ideas that seemed to sprout from his head.

In no time at all, Kit finished laying down the remainder of the surrealistic plot, describing how Tamora and her two remaining sons kill Bassinius. To silence Lavinia, Tamora's sons rape and mutilate Lavinia — cutting out her tongue and cutting off her hands. Then they proceed to frame two of Titus's remaining sons for the murder of Bassinius.

Tamora's illicit lover and partner in crime, Aaron the Moor, murders two of Titus's remaining sons. He sends their severed heads to Titus, after first fraudulently inducing the deceived Titus to sever one of his own hands in exchange for the lives of his sons.

Meanwhile, using a stick to write their names in the sand, Lavinia reveals the identity of her rapists and mutilators. Titus takes his revenge by killing Tamara's two sons, grinding their bones into meal, and feeding them to Tamora in a pie.

In the final plot twists, Titus kills Tamora. To free her from her pain and misery, he also kills the maimed Lavinia. The Emperor kills Titus. The Emperor is killed by Titus's remaining son, Lucius, who plans to execute Aaron, after promising to protect the illegitimate infant son of Aaron and Tamora.

As I finished the plot notes, I burst out laughing. Kit smiled. He said matter-of-factly:

"So I see I have brought you some joy in this life. I guess there are worse things I might have done!"

When I stopped laughing, I said, "The thought of it strangely does make me happy. The plot's crazy. Crazy good! It's so over the top, it's farce! A black comedy that drives a stake through the heart of convention. Kit, you're like a fox that has found its way into the henhouse. It's ingenious!

"Well, well, well," said Kit. "Who knew you were a man capable of appreciating *Titus Andronicus* in the manner you have? Now I know why our play-writing comrade, poor Thomas Greene, described you as having a 'Tygres hart wrapt in a players hyde' before keeling over after gorging himself on pickled herrings and Rhenish wine. Behind your meekness and good manners lives a ravenous wolf, ready to pounce upon its prey. Lying in wait to trap the coney rabbit and roast it on a spit! Who would've thought it?"

"There are more sides to me than you'll ever know," I replied, good-naturedly, before taking up the creative challenge in Kit's words, waxing poetic myself.

"The plot you've laid out is a glistening diamond, with many sparkling facets to admire. But, it's not the type of maudlin fare to which country bumpkins aspire. It's got enough sex, revenge and hate to set the world on fire, and all the blood, guts, and gore that sanguine hearts require. It has murders and crimes to pale the face, and draw the lines between love and hate. It's certainly not to Puritan tastes, but there's plenty to savor on that plate."

"A speech worthy of one of the Nine Worthies. It makes the hairs on my head stand on end, go kinky and go curly. Like the boy actor on the stage whose voice must turn girly!" Said Kit.

I burst out laughing, and then said: "'Touché! Touché! I concede the field to the one more worthy!'"

"As you should, my young friend."

"Young indeed!" I replied. "You're barely two months older."

"Perhaps," said Kit. "But much more water has flowed under the spans of this bridge."

"True. But my wherry is ready to shoot the rapids running under those arches," I said.

"You must be careful it doesn't run aground." said Kit. "Enough of this idle nonsense for now! Let's divvy up the writing assignments and meet here again in two weeks to measure our progress."

With that, we went about our business. I bid Kit adieu and headed home to my lodgings where I began enthusiastically working upon this fantastic project of Kit's imagination.

Chapter XXXVII
An Unexpected Visit

The days and hours of the next week flew by like quicksilver. I wrote day and night — doing my best to bring the characters that were the creatures of Kit's imagination to life. Only stopping when necessary to refuel my body and sleep. Burning through numerous candles, squinting to eke out the words in the flickering light. As often happens with me, some of the characters seemed to take on a life of their own.

In this case, the most enigmatic character, and the one to whom I gave the most thought, was Aaron the Moor. The Moors were the ultimate outsiders in our society, separated from the majority, by culture, race, and religion. And, although the story line called for him to be an unrelenting monster, I found I could not help but imbue him with a trace of compassion for another human being, his illegitimate son by Tamora. He barters with Titus's son, trading the confession of his crimes for his son's life.

Despite the hard work, I was looking forward to my next meeting with Kit, to compare notes and see what progress he had made. After our first meeting, I heard Kit had returned to the mansion of his patron, Thomas Walsingham.

One morning near the end of May, there was an unexpected knock on the door of my room at the Green Dragon Inn, where I had been lodging for a few months after moving out of the Burbages' home. After rolling over in bed, yawning, and calling out, "Hold on! I'll be there in a minute," I quickly rolled back the grey woolen blanket, strolled across the room, and opened the door, bleary-eyed. Standing in the doorway, dressed in a brass-buttoned blue and white cut-sleeved doublet that had seen better days, was Kit Marlowe.

From the way Kit brushed me aside, he was in a hurry. As he crossed the room and took a seat behind my writing desk, which had many of the draft manuscript pages for "Titus Andronicus" laying upon it, I noticed he carried a satchel under his right arm.

As he silently eyed me, I said, "What brings you back to London so fast? I thought you would be at Walsingham's another week?"

"I was brought here under arrest."

"Why?" I asked incredulously.

"It's a mess.I'm a mouse scrambling beneath elephants."

"Who are the elephants? What do they want with you?"

"Essex, the Cecils, Raleigh. You name it, they're involved," he said.

"That's a short list of aristocratic movers and shakers. I thought Raleigh was your friend."

"He is. That's the problem," said Kit. "He's out-of-favor, banished from the court because of his secret marriage to lady-in-waiting, Elizabeth Throckmorton. He's not able to help!"

"I'm so sorry," I said.

"It's Raleigh they really want. I'm just a pawn," Kit blurted, banging his fist on my writing table. "That sorry bastard, Kyd. He put the finger on me in Bridewell prison to cover his own butt. I'm innocent! I'd like to whip him like the beadles whip the whores! Tie him to the back of a cart. Go at him to my heart's content!"

"What are you accused of?" I asked. The fact the Cecils and Essex were the most powerful forces in the land did not bode well.

"They're alleging I'm a goddamn atheist!" said Kit, a pair of tears beginning to stream down his cheeks. "They've twisted all the facts. They say I read a manifesto to Raleigh, converting him to my supposed godless philosophy. It's a bunch of bull shit!" Kit lapsed into profanity as people do when they are angry, scared out of their wits, or both. "I may have an inquisitive mind, but I'm no atheist. I didn't convert Raleigh to anything, let alone atheism!" Kit said with a tone of finality.

"Let's hope the truth wins out. What's the current status of the case?" I asked.

"I'm out on bail. But required to check in with Privy Council officials daily. I expect the trial will occur next week. Looks like the deck is stacked against me. If my answers don't satisfy, the consequences could be deadly."

"You've done some secret work for the Cecils before. Will they protect you?"

"Maybe," Kit said. "But the trumped-up counterfeiting charges brought against me while I was spying for the government in the Netherlands last year may have cut into any goodwill I have left with them. I believe the only reason I'm not already in Bridewell is because of the Cecils. But I don't know how badly they want Raleigh's head on a pike. There's no honor among politicians!"

"True," I said. They see how the breeze blows , seizing any opportunity to fill their sails. And salt their tails."

"I've got to find a way to thread the needle. There's a good chance, whatever happens, I'll be out of commission for a while. So, I want to leave what I've written on *Titus Andronicus* with you. If I can't finish it, at least I'll have the satisfaction of knowing my work didn't go in vain. We might not see eye to eye on some things, Will, but I respect your work."

"Coming as it does from you, Kit, that's a high compliment. I consider you our greatest playwright. Don't despair. It's darkest just before the dawn."

"Perhaps you're right," said Kit. "A ray of light may be shining through the clouds. An acquaintance named Ingram Frizer has invited me to have dinner with him and representatives of Lords Essex and Cecil tomorrow. Frizer wants to broker a deal concerning my testimony before the Privy Council."

"Sounds hopeful," I said in the most positive manner I could muster.

"Wish me luck," Kit said, removing a sheaf of manuscript pages from his satchel, and placing them on the table.

"I do. I have a feeling it will turn out fine. We'll soon be working together again," I said, as Kit stood up and began walking towards the door.

As we shook hands, he said, "I hope you're right, Will Shakespeare. I hope to God you're right. If this doesn't work-out, a plague upon both Essex's and Cecil's houses!"

Those were the last words I heard Kit Marlowe utter on this earth.

Chapter XXXVIII
Murder, Mayhem & Marlowe

The next I heard of Kit he had been killed in a knife fight by the person who invited him to the fateful "feast" at Eleanor Bull's boarding house in Deptford. The news was sadly conveyed to me by Dick Burbage. Together with Dick, I journeyed down river to Deptford to attend the hastily arranged funeral and burial of Kit in the churchyard of St. Nicholas.

The funeral was held immediately after the conclusion of the coroner's inquest. After hearing the testimony of those involved, the members of the jury concluded Kit's killer acted in self-defense. Given my final conversation with Kit, I knew that verdict was suspect.

By the time Dick and I arrived in town, Kit's death was the only thing anyone was talking about. Given its seamy, sordid circumstances, wild rumors abounded.

But our first priority was to get to the church and participate in the prayers for the repose of Kit's soul. Kit's family in Canterbury was too far away to travel to Deptford in time to attend the service. I was glad Dick, myself, and other members of our theatrical profession, including Ned Alleyn, were able to do so. Given the attacks made upon Kit's religious beliefs, I was relieved to see the authorities and the rector of the church allowed him to be buried in the consecrated ground of the churchyard.

Pursuant to custom, Kit's body was transported to the funeral service in a painted black coffin placed on a horse-drawn cart. When it arrived at the churchyard gate, the rector asked for volunteers to act as pallbearers. Dick, myself, and four other actors from the company of Lord Strange's Men carried the coffin through the churchyard to the newly dug grave.

After the prayers for the dead contained in the Book of Common Prayer were read, the hinged cover of the coffin was opened, revealing Kit's body wrapped in its white winding sheet and shroud. Using the ropes already tied around the rigid body, we were able to lift Kit's corpse out of the coffin. As gently as possible, we lowered it into the new grave. As we did so, the bell in the church tower tolled its mournful knell for a talented artist tragically deprived of the opportunity to reach even greater heights of brilliance.

When the funeral concluded, Dick and I went to a nearby tavern for food and drink before beginning our journey back to London. While we were there quenching our thirsts with a potent brew called Left Leg, we ran across several locals who served as members on the coroner's jury at the inquest earlier that day.

At our request, one of the jurors, a tinker by trade, began to share some of the testimony presented to them.

"The first man to testify was Nicholas Skeres, a servant of Lord Essex. He said he and another witness, Robert Poley, were invited to the feast at the widow Eleanor Bull's house by Ingram Frizer. Frizer is a servant of Christopher Marlowe's patron, Sir Thomas Walsingham, and a relation of the deceased spymaster, Sir Francis Walsingham. Skeres testified all four present at the feast, Marlowe, Poley, Skeres, and Frizer, had a merry time playing primera and backgammon, conversing on subjects of common interest and court gossip.

"Then they all sat down and enjoyed a hearty dinner of roast turkey and fixings prepared by Mrs. Bull and her kitchen maids. Since her husband's death a few years ago, Mrs. Bull has made ends meet by renting out a room and providing food and drink for parties and feasts, such as the one organized by Mr. Frizer.

"When they finished the meal, they took some air in the garden and smoked several pipes of tobacco. Skeres further testified they went back to the room and enjoyed pints of ale and cups of wine. Christopher Marlowe lay down on the bed in the room, while Skeres, Poley and Frizer played backgammon. A little while later, the conversation turned to how Mrs. Bull's bill for the room, food, and drink, was to be divvied up.

"Christopher Marlowe and Ingram Frizer got into a heated argument. When it escalated into personal insults of the worst sort, Marlowe leapt off the bed. Coming up behind Frizer, Marlowe grabbed Frizer's knife from the sheath on his hip. Using the pommel, Marlowe struck Frizer on the top of the head several times, causing several cuts to Frizer's scalp.

"Frizer, a stocky powerful man, rose up out of his seat and began fighting with the lanky Marlowe. After a few moments, Frizer wrested control of the knife. With a quick thrust into Marlowe's face, Frizer stabbed Marlowe in the upper portion of his left eye. The blade of the knife penetrated Marlowe's brain, killing him instantly."

"Terrible!" said Dick Burbage. "To think such a valuable life was lost over a petty argument about a bill for food and drink!"

It's a pity," I remarked, before asking the talkative juror, "What did Frizer say?"

"He backed up Skeres's story to the hilt. He said Marlowe started the fight and continued cursing Frizer out in the most abusive way right up until the end."

"How about the other person in the room?" I asked.

"Poley didn't add anything new," The juror replied. "He made it a point to say he was not involved in the argument or the fight. He was certain Frizer acted in self-defense. In Poley's opinion, it was kill or be killed."

"Were there any other eyewitnesses?" I asked.

"None," the juror answered.

"The Widow Bull testified she delivered the invoice into the hands of Frizer about a half hour before the fight began. She overheard screaming voices, banging and knocking. She rushed up the stairs shouting, 'is everything all right?'

"By the time Robert Poley opened the door, Christopher Marlowe was already lying on the floor, stone dead. A stream of blood flowed down the side of Marlowe's face from his pierced eye. Nicholas Skeres stood over the body, shouting, 'You stupid bastard! Look what you've done!'

"Ingram Frizer sat on the bench, head in hands, moaning. Realizing a murder occurred in her home, the widow Bull sent her servant boy running to the authorities."

"Was there any other testimony?" I asked.

The juror took a long draught from the tankard of ale we paid for before answering, "Just an investigator from the coroner's office. His testimony was routine. He said he found Frizer's knife lying beside the body. The blade was covered with blood. He also gave us the dimensions of both Marlowe's and Frizer's wounds. Marlowe's wound was two inches deep, and Frizer's wounds from the pommel of the dagger were two inches long, and a quarter inch deep."

Some years later, reflecting upon the death of Kit, Dick Tarlton, and other dear friends I lost too early to the cruel hand of death, I penned the following poem.

When to the sessions of sweet silent thought
I summon up remembrance of things past,
I sigh the lack of many a thing I sought,
And with old woes new wail my dear time's waste;
Then can I drown an eye unus'd to flow,
For precious friends hid in death's dateless night,
And weep afresh love's long-since cancell'd woe,
And moan the expence of many a vanish'd sight;

Then can I grieve at grievances foregone,
And heavily from woe to woe tell o'er
The sad account of fore-bemoaned moan,
Which I new pay as if not paid before.
But if the while I think on thee, dear friend,
All losses are restor'd, and sorrows end.

Chapter XXXIX
Hamnet's Arrival

When I summon up remembrances of the cherished moments spent with my son, Hamnet, my heart is filled with love and regret. As I picture him, Hamnet forever remains a princely flower of youth. Innocent, yet always curious about the numerous mysteries of this world. It was my mission and my duty before God to see to Hamnet's proper upbringing and education. With the assistance of my wife, family and friends, I endeavored to do so.

One of the highlights of my life was the week ten-year-old Hamnet and I spent together in London during the summer of 1595. Hamnet traveled to the city with my brother Gil, who, at that time, was making a living as a peddler. Gil came to London twice a year to replenish his stock: silken bows and ribbons, toys, trinkets, cheap jewelry, and an item or two of the latest London fashions. Of course, most of the gloves and leather goods sold by Gil were made in my father's shop in our house on Henley Street.

Once in London, Gil would visit the best glovers' shops, purchasing a pair of gloves if they displayed a feature or design he had not seen before. He would bring those gloves back to Stratford where my father and my brother Richard used them as templates for the gloves we manufactured in our own shop. In this way, the fashion-conscious men and women of Stratford were able to keep pace with the ever-changing London fashion scene.

When Hamnet and Gil arrived at my lodgings, Hamnet regaled me with stories of the people, sights, and sounds he had experienced on his journey. As he did so, it brought back pleasant memories of my own first journey to London.

Like myself, Hamnet was especially impressed by the university town of Oxford, where he and Gil were entertained by family friends, Will and Jane Davenant, the owners of a substantial tavern and boarding house in the center of town.

In addition to enjoying the hospitality of the Davenants, and seeing the sights of Oxford, Gil and Hamnet conducted a little business along the way. They rented two post horses for the journey. Each of those horses carried trunks filled with goods to sell in the hamlets and villages they passed through. These trunks were works of art in themselves, both covered and lined with calfskin tanned in the pit in the back of our Henley Street home and applied to the wooden trunk frames in our family shop.

Gil, who was childless, was in many ways a second father to Hamnet. He welcomed Hamnet's assistance with the salesmanship and showmanship that was part of the peddlers' trade.

Gil's special talent was the magic he used to enhance his sales pitch. His sleight of hand attracted a crowd. On this trip, Gil taught Hamnet several card tricks. As Gil and I applauded Hamnet's newly learned skills, Hamnet enthusiastically said, "Father, Uncle Gil has taught me one of his jingles! Do you want to hear it?"

"Of course," I replied. "I've written a jingle or two for Uncle Gil?"

"Not this one. It's the best!"

I chuckled. "I can't wait. Take it away!"

Hamnet stood up and began singing.

Will you buy any tape,
Or lace for your cape,
My dainty duck, my dear-a?
Any silk, any thread,

Any toys for your head,
Of the new'st, and fin'st, fin' st ware-a?
Come to the pedlar;
Money's a medler,
That doth utter all men's ware-a.

As Hamnet finished singing, he smiled a wry smile of joy and satisfaction. Like any good player at the end of a well-received performance, Hamnet removed his cap and took a deep bow.

"Good show," Gil congratulated. "You'll make an excellent actor someday."

"God forbid!" I responded."Let him be a lawyer or doctor. Never a common player like myself. I'd like to see Hamnet go out into the world and be a mover and shaker, not someone who merely plays for the people who make a difference."

"Will! Don't disparage yourself. Your plays and performances bring joy to people from all walks of life!"

"Trifles and amusements," I countered. "Here today and gone tomorrow! Pribbles, prabbles, dribbles, drabbles, riddles, rattles, bubbles and babbles, vanishing in the air! Tinsel and toys submerged in your hair!"

"There' s the making of a jingle in that jumble," said Gil.

"Enough sparring for now," I remarked. "Let's get something to eat."

As I envision the three of us walking out the door of my lodgings together, the vision fades to gray, and then black, before another vision emerges and gradually comes into focus.

Chapter XL
The Golden Hind

It's a beautiful summer morning. The bright yellow orb of the sun is ascending above the olive green of the ocean waves. A brisk breeze buffets our cheeks and runs through the tasseled locks of our wind-blown hair.

Hamnet and I are standing together on the deck of the most famous ship in England — and the world. Originally christened, the Pelican, a symbol of longevity, but later renamed, and known throughout the globe, as the Golden Hind!

Francis Drake and his crew made their tremendous voyage around the world a few years before Hamnet was born. No one had attempted such a feat since the tattered remnants of Magellan's crew limped back into Lisbon over fifty years earlier. And Magellan never completed the circumnavigation, dying along the way in a fierce battle with the native people of an island in the Philippines.

Drake not only completed the circumnavigation, he arrived back after an almost three-year journey with a fabulous cargo of Spanish booty captured off the coasts of Chile and Peru. During his long privateering voyage, Drake had overtaken several Spanish treasure galleons loaded with tons of silver and other valuables. The cargo the Golden Hind brought home to England was worth over 600,000 English pounds.

The Queen, a not-so-secret investor in the voyage, received a substantial portion of the booty, as did several other aristocratic investors. Drake's share made him one of the richest men in England and earned him a knighthood. Queen Elizabeth knighted him here on the deck of this marvelous ship.

Now my son and I had the pleasure of standing in the very place history was made. As we moved inside the captain's cabin, we saw a magnificent portrait of the great mariner himself. Dressed in a scarlet doublet and breeches, he wore a matching cape with a black lining, stylishly draped over his left shoulder. He carried a black velvet hat with a cockade containing three slender fighting-cock feathers in his left hand, the base of which rested on the silver pommel of his long, slender rapier.

The sword was encased in a gold-tipped, black leather scabbard. His painstakingly crafted, multi-layered, beige satin sleeves were fringed by intricately laced cuffs. And his dark, closely trimmed beard was set off by a wide starched white ruff, whose hundred folds were made of the finest gossamer lawn fabric.

The outfit Francis Drake wore for the portrait before us was worth a small fortune. To top it all off, Drake's right hand rested on a marvelously crafted multi-colored globe showing all the continents and oceans of the earth. Drake's piercing eyes and resolute expression gave us a sense of the grit, determination, and courage enabling captain and crew to endure the hardships of his three-year odyssey to accomplish what many had considered an impossible feat.

What hardships they endured. As we walked the thick planks of the middle gun deck, the ceiling above was so low I had to walk with my back hunched over to keep my head from hitting the overhead beams. The former Drake sailor who served as our tour guide said the only person who had a bed to sleep in during that famous voyage was Francis Drake. The rank and file sailors had to sleep on deck. Although, at 300 tons displacement, the ship looked large floating in the water, it shrunk drastically when one considered it served as a home away from home for over seventy men for almost three years. Drake and his crew certainly deserved their reputation as iron men serving on wooden ships!

When Hamnet was five years old, just learning to read, I purchased a copy of the bestseller Richard Hakluyt wrote about the principal navigations, voyages, and discoveries of the English nation. Hamnet and I spent many a joyful hour perusing the stories and charts in that book, enjoying the narratives and adventures of the great explorers such as Sir Francis. Like all proud parents, I hoped my inquisitive and goodhearted son would be able to enjoy and participate in the opportunities presented by the new and exciting world opening-up before him.

After finishing our tour of the Golden Hind, we stopped for lunch in The White Unicorn tavern, a block from the Widow Bull's house where Christopher Marlowe was murdered a few years before. As we sat in the large dining room, enjoying our meals of baked flounder and cod, a balladeer stepped into the room dressed in somewhat tattered sailor's garb. His brown, wrinkled, prematurely aged face and hands were proof of the many years at sea he had spent earlier in his life.

While this Ancient Mariner tuned his instrument, he shared a few snippets of his life story. It turned out the man had the honor of serving with Francis Drake, although not on the circumnavigation. Had he done so, and received his share of the profits, he would have become wealthy. As luck would have it, he still had to sing for his supper.

When he finished tuning his lute, and entertaining us with his salty gift of gab, he began singing the following song in a raspy but appealing voice:

I was stuck in the crazy old doldrums,
Watching the way the wind blows.
The first watch was mending the rigging,
The crosswinds were chafing my nose.

I searched the empty horizon,
As I worked in my dirty old clothes.
We spliced our fancy sea stories,
With threads made of silver and gold.

The Captain, he said to the Boatswain,
"You must keep the men on their toes;
Give them the grog and the potion
That strips the gilt off the rose.

The Spanish ships are a-swaying,
With treasure laid down in their holds.
We've got to earn us some glory,
Before our bodies grow cold!

The dolphins are jumping beside us,
Swimming their way through the brine,
Like the beautiful mermaids,
Who grace the rocks of the Rhine.

They say that Davy Jones's locker
Is filled with jewels from the mines,
And bracelets discarded by ladies,
Who threw their pearls to the swine.

If we win us the battle,
I'll buy a new doublet and hose,
And give a kiss to my Sweetie,
That rings the bells off her toes!"

As the old man finished his song, all of us stood up and cheered. I gave Hamnet a penny to place in the Ancient Mariner's hat. Hamnet spoke to the sailor for a minute, returned to the table, and asked me for another penny to purchase a printed copy of the song for Gilbert. It was a request I could not refuse.

When we returned to my lodgings that evening, Hamnet entertained us with a rollicking rendition of the old sailor's song that left Gil and me in stitches.

"That's one talented boy you have there," said Gil, giving me a brotherly pat on the back.

It turned out the song proved to be so popular with Gil's clientele, he made it a permanent part of his repertoire.

CHAPTER XLI
LONDON BRIDGE

The day after returning from our outing to Deptford, I took Hamnet to see two of the can't miss sites of London Town, St. Paul's Cathedral and London Bridge. St. Paul's is still a glorious church, even though it's tremendous spire, whose tip was over 500 feet above street level, came crashing down years earlier in a great storm. Although our parish church in Stratford was the largest and most impressive building in our town, it was small compared with St. Paul's.

A highlight of our visit to St. Paul's was the time we spent browsing in the bookseller stalls close by the cathedral. One of the stalls belonged to our Stratford friend, Richard Field. During our visit, I surprised Hamnet by having Richard present him with his own leather-bound copy of Ovid's *Metamorphoses* — the creative and beautifully written tales of the gods and goddesses of Roman mythology.

Handing the book to Hamlet, Richard said, "I hope this work your father has purchased for you will bring many hours of enjoyment. It's been a source of inspiration for your father."

"It certainly has," I chimed in."It was so good, it kept me away from my Latin grammar and rhetoric lessons."

"I think it did you more good than harm," said Richard.

"I suppose you're right. But, it‘s still bantered about by those playwrights who have a university education, that I have "small Latine, and lesse Greeke."

"It's all Greek to me!" said Richard, causing me to laugh at his joke.

"Hamnet's going to change all that," I said. "He'll be able to have the education I was never able to obtain. He's more proficient at Latin than I was at his age. I think he'll follow one of the learned professions."

"Perhaps he'll study law at the Middle Temple," Richard said. Addressing Hamnet, he asked, "Would you like that? You would be here in London with your father and could see him every day if you want."

"I'd love that," answered Hamnet, holding the beautifully bound book in both hands. As he did so, Hamnet asked, "Do you have any of my father's books for sale?"

Before I could object, Richard said, "I do. I sell copies of both of his long poems, *Venus and Adonis* and *Lucrece*."

"Could you buy me one?" Hamnet asked, looking at me intently.

"I'm afraid your mother wouldn't be very pleased," I answered, "and neither would the Vicar. Those poems are written for an adult audience."

"I know Father," Hamnet answered. "But there are other students at school who have read them. I'm old enough to understand."

"The lad's got a point," Richard said, with a bit of a wry grin.

"True enough," I replied. Turning to Hamnet, I said: "If I buy one of the books of my poetry for you, it stays between us. Understood?"

"Yes sir!" Hamnet answered with a huge smile.

"Your Uncle Gil can provide us with cover. We'll say he brought it for himself. He can lend it to you when your mother's not around."

"Great," Hamnet said.

"Which of the two books would you like?" asked Richard.

"*Venus and Adonis*, that's the one everyone talks about," Hamnet replied.

"It figures," I chuckled, opening my purse, and extracting several coins.

"You truly are your father's son," said Richard, giving me a friendly wink as he took the book off the table and handed it to Hamnet, who immediately began to leaf through it.

After a few more minutes of small talk, we left the books for safekeeping with Richard, and set out on our leisurely walk to London Bridge. Along the way we stopped in at a reputable tavern, enjoying a meal of broiled cod, oysters, and small ale. Not long after resuming our trek, we found ourselves at the northern entrance to London Bridge.

If the visit to St. Paul's had been a mind-bending experience for Hamnet, seeing the vast 800 yards expanse of bridge, buildings, shops, people, carts, carriages and horses that was London Bridge must have been earth shattering. Back in Stratford we were all proud of the elegant stone, twelve-arch bridge over the Avon that was constructed by our illustrious native son, Hugh Clopton, in the 1480s. But London Bridge was built more than 250 years before that. Comparing Clopton Bridge to London Bridge was the equivalent of comparing a sardine to a leviathan.

Walking the length of the jam-packed spans, we arrived on the south side of the Thames. I asked Hamnet to look upward, pointing out what remained of the numerous rotting heads impaled upon the bridge gate.

Hamnet shivered, and asked: "Father, were all of those men bad persons?"

"For the most part, yes," I answered. "Several of the rotting skulls are of notorious highwaymen who robbed and killed innocent travelers. Others are those of men who plotted to steal the crown for themselves. But a few are of men who were merely practicing their faith. The sad truth is justice in this world is not always just. All we can do as common people is hope such things will be made right in the world to come."

We then spent several hours walking through the streets of Bankside, seeing the sights of Southwark, including its impressive cathedral. Finally, we stopped by the famous theater called the Rose. Here our rivals, The Lord Admiral's Men, entertained audiences with their plays.

After a short tour given by Philip Henslowe, the Rose's colorful owner, we returned to the banks of the Thames, and engaged one of the wherries that continuously crisscrossed the Thames to ferry us to the other side. This trip across the swiftly flowing river would be a great adventure for Hamnet. He had never before seen a body of water more impressive than the gently flowing Avon.

While the wherryman rowed us across, Hamnet enjoyed the impressive panorama, including the historic city landmarks, the dozens of other boats slicing through the water, and an unparalled view of the bridge itself.

The wherryman, a grizzled old salt, whose leathery skin was a result of both age and a lifetime of working in the sun, saw Hamnet admiring the bridge. Calling out, he said, "The boy's first time in London?"

"Yes," I answered. "After visiting St. Paul's this morning, we walked across the bridge."

"You show him the heads atop the gate?"asked the boatman.

"I did."

"Have you taken him to see the Tower?" he asked. "They say it was built by Julius Caesar. For the right price the Beefeaters will give you a tour. You can see the place where them that are noble lose their heads."

"I'm not sure we can fit it in," I answered. "I'm planning to take him to visit Westminster and Whitehall tomorrow."

"Sounds like the lad is having a great time! Hey!" he shouted to Hamnet, who momentarily diverted his attention to the boatman.

"You see the arches over there?"

"Yes sir," answered Hamnet politely.

"The water passing through them rushes as fast as the wind. Riding a boat through is like riding a sleigh. You'll never go faster on the water than you will passing under the arches of London Bridge!"

"Really?" Hamnet asked, a look of wonder in his eyes.

"Ay, but it's dangerous too! I've known several veteran wherry men who have lost their lives trying to shoot the rapids under those arches. It's not for the faint of heart!"

"Sounds so exciting!" said Hamnet. With an imploring look, he asked, "Father, can we do that?"

Giving the boatman a cynical grin, I answered, "Maybe someday. But not today. It's getting late. Uncle Gil's waiting for us. We have big things planned for tomorrow."

Chapter XLII
Westminster and Whitehall

The following day was special. After a hearty breakfast of sausages and eggs, made for us by my cheery, red-faced landlady, Gil proceeded on with his business for the day. Hamnet and I set forth on our journey to Westminster and Whitehall. On our way, I took him for a little tour of some of the well-known inns of the town. As we stood inside the busy courtyard of the Black Bull, I told Hamnet, "Son, you're now standing in the birthplace of the theaters we have here in London."

"Birthplace?'" Hamnet asked.

"This is where the putting-on of plays started. Before we had buildings like the Curtain, the Theater, and the Rose, players would set up a stage in the courtyard of a large inn such as this and give a performance for the guests and public willing to pay a penny admission. The guests watched from the galleries lining the three levels above us while the groundlings stood here in the courtyard."

"Now I understand why the Rose is designed the way it is, with multilevel galleries surrounding the stage, and the empty space for the penny-paying audience to stand in front of the stage."

"Correct," I answered. "Having our own building is such an improvement. We have a roof over the stage, a backstage area to store props, a tiring room for changing in and out of our costumes, and a box office to keep the receipts secure. We can also better police the audience to try to keep the cutpurses and pickpockets out."

Nodding his head, Hamnet asked, "Have you ever performed in an inn yard such as this one?"

"Sure. I've performed here. And at the Bell and the Cross Keys not far from here. I've also toured in a traveling troupe of actors on several occasions. We were constantly moving from town to town, performing wherever we were welcomed. That included large public buildings, like the Guildhall in Stratford, great houses of the nobles and gentry, and large inns such as this."

"Sounds like fun."

"Sometimes it was. Other times it was rough going. Although I was surrounded by the other players, I greatly missed your mother and you children. Add the fact there was not much money in it, I don't often miss those early days."

"What's it like to perform in front of so many people?" Hamnet asked.

"It's not something to worry about. Since your voice must carry a great distance, you shout your lines. Working to do so discharges a lot of nervous energy. You'll discover this in a few days when you perform with us. If you feel any fear, remember we are there with you. When necessary, maintain eye contact with me. Imagine we are merely having a private conversation, just as we're doing now. You'll do well. I'm certain of it," I said, giving Hamnet a friendly pat on the back.

"I hope so. I want to make you proud."

"You will!" I said. "Now, let's proceed to the resting place of kings and heroes!"

An hour later we found ourselves beneath the towering stone vaults of Westminster Abbey. After paying our respects to Geoffrey Chaucer, we visited the tomb of King Henry V, the author of our victory over the French at Agincourt. Suspended above his impressive stone effigy were his painted wooden shield, his saddle, his black and gold trimmed metal helmet, and his fierce, double-edged sword.

Like my son, my generation was raised upon the legends of chivalry and courtly love. During a wool brogging trip to London, my father bought me a copy of *Le Morte de Arthur*. I almost read it to pieces. The destruction I began was now being completed by Hamnet. The timeless tales of Arthur, Guinevere, Lancelot, and Sir Galahad's search for the Holy Grail will live forever in the hearts of every English boy.

Yearning for those bygone days, I began reciting an abridged version of the speech I had written for an inferior play about the reign of Henry V that I acted in some years ago. I would use it again in my own *Henry V* written several years later:

Once more unto the breach, dear friends, once
more;
Or close the wall up with our English dead!
In peace, there's nothing so becomes a man,
As modest stillness, and humility:
But when the blast of war blows in our ears,
Then imitate the action of the tiger;
Stiffen the sinews, summon up the blood,
Disguise fair nature with hard-favour'd rage:
And you, good yeoman,
Whose limbs were made in England, show us
here
The mettle of your pasture; let us swear
That you are worth your breeding: which I doubt
not;
For there is none of you so mean and base,
That hath not noble lustre in your eyes.
I see you stand like greyhounds in the slips,
Straining upon the start. The game's afoot;
Follow your spirit: and, upon this charge,
Cry — God for Harry! England! and St. George!

"Here lies a true hero," I remarked. Whether this statement was entirely true or not, let historians debate. It is to symbols and allusions that the child and artist in all of us relate.

After finishing our visit to Westminster Abbey, we walked over to Whitehall Palace. Fortunately, the Queen was not in residence. So, I was able to arrange a brief tour of some of the more public spaces. The most impressive part of the tour for Hamnet was our visit to what is known as the Map Room.

Painted on the wall of that room was a large mural of the globe, showing the path of the Golden Hind's circumnavigation. The mural consisted of two large circular paintings depicting the seas and the continents. The first painting contained Europe, Asia, and Africa. The second showed North and South America. The route of the Golden Hind's circumnavigation was traced by a series of dots, commencing and ending in Plymouth, England.

The dots traced the route through the North and South Atlantic, up the Pacific coasts of South and North America, across the Pacific and the Southern Indian oceans, around the African continent via the Cape of Good Hope, through the South and North Atlantic, back home to Plymouth.

Although the circumnavigation occurred sixteen years earlier, the mural was painted about five years ago. Until the defeat of the Spanish Armada, the English government kept the details of the circumnavigation secret, especially the fact Drake had found an alternate route around the tip of South America which did not require transit of the Straits of Magellan.

Hamnet was mesmerized by the mural and spent many minutes before each of the two circular globes absorbing the geographic information they contained. It was wonderful to live in an age when we knew what the world looked like in the eyes of the Supreme Being.

After our time in the Map Room, our guide took us for a tour of the tilt yard where the famous jousts were held. We then toured the armory where Hamnet marveled at the beautiful swords, pikes, halberds, cross bows, harquebuses, cavalier light rifles, and pistols.

Before leaving the palace, we had the opportunity to visit the huge kitchens where several of the cooks fixed us a quick lunch.

Leaving Whitehall, Hamnet and I made the long trek to the Theater on the outskirts of town. At that point in time, the Theater was the home of our acting company — The Lord Chamberlain's Men.

When we arrived, we went to the tiring room and donned our costumes. In a few days we would be performing a play of mine called *A Midsummer Night's Dream*. Although it was new to the actors in the company, it was not new to Hamnet. I had written the play while I was home in Stratford for the six weeks of Lent. I wrote half of my plays during these Lenten seasonal breaks.

Hamnet always took an interest in my play writing. Given the prevalence of the supernatural elements in this one, it was Hamnet's favorite. Before leaving Stratford for London, I hired a local scrivener to make a copy of the manuscript, and Hamnet and I practiced the roles of Oberon and Puck together. In the intervening months, Hamnet learned the role of Puck by heart, practicing with Susanna and Gil.

I was now going to put Hamnet through his paces using the boy actor who normally played the role of Puck as his guide. Over the last several nights, I had given Hamnet a refresher tutorial on the expressions, poses, gestures, and dances used in the role of Puck. This would be the opportunity for him to put everything he learned into practice. Though I had no desire to have Hamnet follow in my footsteps as a player, this experience would be a great confidence building exercise. Considering everything, the rehearsal went well.

Chapter XLIII
A Midsummer Night's Dream

Two nights later it was time for Hamnet's debut. As I stood offstage with the boy actor playing my fairy Queen, Titania, waiting for our cue, I watched another young actor, playing a member of Titania's fairy court, and my son, in his role as Puck, exchange the following playful dialogue I originally wrote for Hamnet's entertainment.

Fairy: Either I mistake your shape and making quite,
Or else you are that shrewd and knavish sprite,
Call'd Robin Good-fellow: are you not he,
That fright the maidens of the villagery;
Skim milk; and sometimes labour in the quern,
And bootless make the breathless housewife churn
And sometime make the drink to bear no barm;
Mislead night-wanderers, laughing at their harm
Those that Hobgoblin call you, and sweet Puck,
You do their work, and they shall have good luck.
Are not you he?

Puck: Thou speak'st aright;
I am that merry wanderer of the night.
I jest to Oberon, and make him smile,
When I a fat and bean-fed horse begile,
Neighing in likeness of a filly foal:

And sometimes lurk I in a gossip's bowl,
In very likeness of a roasted crab;
And, when she drinks, against her lips I bob,
And on her wither'd dew-lap pour the ale.
The wisest aunt, telling the saddest tale,
Sometime for three-foot stool mistaketh me:
Then slip I from her bum, down topples she,
And *tailor* cries, and falls into a cough;
And then the whole quire hold their hips, and loffe
And waxen in their mirth, and neeze, and swear
A merrier hour was never wasted there. —
But room, Faery! here comes Oberon.

Fairy: And here my mistress: —'Would that he were gone!

Hearing our cue, the actor playing Titania and I entered the scene. As I approached Hamnet, I smiled and winked before beginning to say my lines:

Oberon: Ill met by moon-light, proud Titania.
Titania: What, jealous Oberon? Fairy, skip hence;
I have forsworn his bed and company.
Oberon: Tarry, rash wanton; Am I not thy lord?
Titania: Then I must be thy lady....

As the play went on, Hamnet continued his excellent performance. In the final scene, after the rustics' skit telling the tragic love story of "Pyramus and Thisbe," Hamnet, as the mischief-loving Puck, comes out on stage setting up the entrance of the reconciled Oberon and Titania with the following lines.

Puck: Now the hungry lion roars,
And the wolf behowls the moon;
Whilst the heavy ploughman snores,
All with weary task fordone.
Now the wasted brands do glow,
Whilst the scritch-owl, scritching loud,
Puts the wretch, that lies in woe,
In remembrance of a shroud.
Now it is the time of night,
That the graves, all gaping wide,
Every one lets forth his sprite,
In the church-way paths to glide:
And we fairies, that do run
By the triple Hecate's team,
From the presence of the sun,
Following darkness like a dream;
Now are frolic; not a mouse
Shall disturb this hallow'd house:
I am sent with broom before,
To sweep the dust behind the door.

After Titania and Oberon bless the three sets of sleeping lovers, and their future offspring, I watched with pride as my son Hamnet joyfully delivered the play's closing lines.

Puck: If we shadows have offended,
Think but this (and all is mended,)
That you have but slumber'd here,
While these visions did appear.
And this weak and idle theme,
No more yielding but a dream,
Gentles, do not reprehend;
If you pardon, we will mend.
And, as I am an honest Puck,
If we have unearned luck
Now to 'scape the serpent's tongue,
We will make amends, ere long:
Else the Puck a liar call.
So, good night unto you all.
Give me your hands, if we be friends,
And Robin shall restore amends.

As Hamnet said his final lines, the crowd burst into applause and cheers. Shortly thereafter, he and I were happily dancing a jig together, all to the audience's delight. I had never felt closer to my brilliant young son.

At that moment, the world truly was Hamnet's oyster. If I could freeze time, I would freeze it then and there. But, sadly, all things of human origin cannot last, and that scintillating moment lies forever in the past.

For parting is such sweet sorrow. As surely as the sun travels from East to West, the time arrived for the paths of our lives to diverge again. And so, one fine and sunny morning, I said goodbye to Hamnet and Gil, as they set off on their journey back home to Stratford. After giving Gil my thanks and best wishes, I spoke to Hamnet.

"Son," I asked, "I hope you have enjoyed your time with me here in London?"

"This has been the best week of my life!" Hamnet replied, giving me a hug.

"I'm pleased," I responded. "These days have been special to me too. And I'd like you to have a unique gift to remember them by."

I opened my purse and removed the precious gift I had purchased from one of the proprietors of the Golden Hind. It was a shiny, silver commemorative medal of the Golden Hind's voyage around the world. It was as exact a copy of the mural displayed at Whitehall as could be produced by the engraver's art. As I handed it to Hamnet, his face lit up with joy as he first examined one side, and then the other, tracing the voyage in his mind's eye.

"Do you like it?" I asked.

"I love it!" Hamnet answered. "And I love you, Father!"

Those words shall live in my heart forever.

CHAPTER XLIV
GOOD NIGHT, SWEET PRINCE

And now to one of the darkest times in my life. It was the summer of 1596. Food was scarce as it normally was this pre-harvest time of year. Fortunately, we were now well-off enough so I did not have to worry about my family going through the "Starving Time." Many other families were not so lucky.

Sadly, there were plenty of other things my family did have to worry about. The most fearsome threat of all is the Black Death, which mysteriously comes and goes like the flickering light of the Will O' the Wisp.

Dancing beside the Black Knight of plague is its ugly faced partner, smallpox. If it does not kill you outright, then it often leaves you disfigured and unsightly for the remainder of your life. And our society is not kind to those who do not have a pretty face. The most conspicuous, high profile example of the damage smallpox can inflict upon a person's complexion was Queen Elizabeth. Although the Queen's pockmarked face was far from the worst I ever encountered, being a mercurial woman of some vanity, she strove mightily to conceal the scars. This never-ending struggle kept several frantic makeup artists in full employ.

The third performer in this Morris dance of death is the English flu. It returns like clockwork every year, and it is especially and mortally dangerous to the young and old. As it often leads to an infection of the lungs, it can also carry off those in the prime of life.

Then there is the whirling dervish called the ague. A fever brought on by infectious mists and miasmas especially prevalent in marshes and fens. Over a period of years, the fever comes and goes. Until there is one from which you do not recover.

Like the procession of Banquo's descendants in my play *Macbeth*, the ring of skeletal dancers continues with the sweating sickness. This is the illness which took the life of my fictitious Knight, Falstaff — sending him into a fit of delirium, causing him to murmur about green fields, and resting in Arthur's, or was it Abraham's, bosom? Perhaps dreaming the psychedelic preharvest dream that he was in the Kingdom of Cockaigne, the land of good and plenty, where food grows on trees, and there is enough to fill every peasant's pleading belly.

But even the sunny land of Cockaigne is not free from the empty-eyed skull, black robe and sickle of our constant companion, Signor Death. As Marlowe showed in Dr. Faustus, you cannot outwit or put off Death. There's no magic spell or incantation which allows you to escape your God-given rendezvous with Fate.

Like Christopher Marlowe, each of us is unconsciously sleepwalking towards our own reckoning in a little room in Deptford. Each of us will stand naked, stripped of all our titles, wealth and raiment, to give an account of our lives before the High Cross which stands between earthly life and eternity.

There the eternal judge of the living and the dead, the King of Divine Justice and Mercy, shall hear our case, and weigh in the balance all we have said and done, what we have believed and pretended to believe, those we have aided and injured, our good and bad intentions, speech, actions and inactions, and render the verdict from which there is no appeal

But then there is the case of the young and the innocent. Souls too young to bear the burden of Adam's sin or the mark of Cain. Ones too inexperienced in the tricks, ways, and whiles of this world to be called to account as thy brother's or thy sister's keeper. "God's ways are not man's ways," say the priest and the preacher. "Who are we to question the decrees of the Almighty?"

But, like Job, we all do question his ways. And, when it comes to the premature and untimely death of my eleven-year-old son Hamnet, I questioned the need and the purpose of it then, and I question it now.

In August of 1596 we were in the middle of a successful tour in Kent when my brother Gil, riding our fastest horse, Quicksilver, galloped into the courtyard of the Wild Hart Inn. We had just finished giving a performance of *Titus Andronicus* to a packed crowd. I happened to be leaning on the wainscoted half-wall of the first gallery above the courtyard, enjoying a pipe of the finest Trinidad Tobacco, when I saw my brother dismount from his exhausted horse, which had begun foaming at the mouth. In the glare of the blazing torchlight, I could see his ashen face wore the frown of tragedy.

As fear gripped my heart, I shouted, "Gil!" Rushing over to the nearest stairway, I started down, leaping two steps at a time.

Gil charged across the courtyard and bounded up the stairs, meeting me halfway.

"Mother? Father?" I asked impulsively.

Gil shook his head, looking at me with a face I shall never forget. "They're fine," he said.

"Then who?" I asked, a tense knot forming in my stomach.

Seizing me in a bear-hug, with tears streaming down his cheeks, Gil said: "It's Hamnet, Will! Hamnet! God forgive me for being the bearer of this news. He's got the sweating sickness."

"God! No! No! No! Not the sweating sickness! Is Anne with him?"

"Yes." Gil stated. "Mother too. They're at his bedside. Placing cool compresses on his forehead. Giving him water and cider to drink. Begging him to sip some chicken broth."

"Has the doctor been summoned?"

"Yes. It's a long ride. He hadn't arrived when I set out to find you."

"Have we sent for a priest?"

"No worries," Gil answered. "As I departed, Father left Stratford to summon the Marion priest who serves as a gardener on the Catesby estate."

"Father Underhill's a good man," I said. "And perhaps the doctor will administer an effective potion. The sweating sickness isn't always fatal. I came down with it after moving to London. It kept me in bed for three days. The fever eventually broke, and I recovered."

"Maybe it'll be the same for Hamnet." Gil said.

"Let's hope so," I replied. Then, as logical thinking began to dominate my emotions, I began formulating a plan of action to get to Stratford as soon as possible.

"Go downstairs. Find the ostler. Tell him we want to hire two of his fastest horses for the next ten days. While you're making arrangements for the horses, I'll explain the situation to my partners, Dick Burbage and Gus Phillips. They'll allow me to borrow enough to pay for rental of the horses and the trip to Stratford."

"What about Quicksilver?" Gil asked.

"Don't worry," I replied. "Ask the ostler if he can put him up until one of us returns. We'll make it worth his time and effort."

Under these emergent circumstances, Dick, Gus, the ostler, the innkeeper, and the other players, were all very helpful, making sure we had the food, money, and supplies necessary for our journey. Since we had to travel through darkness and light, down highways and byways frequented by highwaymen and brigands, the innkeeper was kind enough to lend us a pistol and cutlass, giving us additional protection to supplement the dirks we wore on our belts.

Twenty minutes later we were ready to begin our midnight ride. As Gil and I put spurs to our horses' flesh, and rode out of the torchlit inn yard, the innkeeper, the ostler, Dick, Gus, and many of my fellow players lined the covered galleries to wish us well. As we exited the gate, I heard Dick call out in the loud and penetrating voice he used on stage at the Theater: "God be with you, William Shakespeare!"

On and on we rode. Through the tree-lined roads and well-beaten paths — by night and by day. On towards Stratford and my sick son. Only stopping when necessary to water, feed, and rest our horses. As long as they could bear it, we pushed the poor beasts hard. As always in England, the weather was fickle, sometimes clear, cloudy, rainy, and a lot in-between.

After several days of brutally hard travel, we reached Stratford, riding our exhausted horses over Clopton Bridge. Reaching the far side, we rode down Bridge Street, veered right onto Henley Street, and made for home. Once there, we quickly dismounted. We tied the reins of our horses to one of the posts beside the backyard stables, rushing into the house via the door to the workshop.

We found my father and my brother Richard, dressed in their leather aprons, cutting the patterns for several pairs of stylish, high-end gloves.

"Hamnet?" I cried out.

Putting down his shears, my father said: "Not good. Awful sick. Sweating and vomiting. Can't keep food down. Growing weaker as time goes by."

"How about the doctor?" I asked.

"He cast Hamnet's waters," Richard answered. "Administered a potion, then a purge to rebalance the humors. They've done no good. Might even have made it worse. Bled him with leeches. To no avail."

"Doctors!" I exclaimed. "A bunch of quacks. Lots of talk, little action. What about the priest?"

"He's been here," my father replied. "Prayed a Rosary. Gave the anointing of the sick. So far, no improvement."

"Where's Hamnet now?" I asked.

"Upstairs in our bedroom. Your mother and Anne are with him. Getting him to drink when they can. Praying constantly."

"I'll see him now," I said.

"We assured him you would arrive soon. You're the greatest gift the poor boy can receive."

My father's use of the phrase "poor boy" sent a shiver down my spine. It signaled he had little hope Hamnet would survive this horrible affliction. Seized with fear, I bounded up the creaking stairs, and hurried to the master bedroom. There I found Anne and my mother seated on either side of the bed. Hamnet lay covered by a light blanket, a moist towel draped across his forehead. Seeing me, Hamnet's face lit up.

"Father!" he cried in a voice barely above a whisper.

"Son!" I responded.

I immediately went to Hamnet's side, kneeling, so my face was at his eye-level. Clasping his right hand, I said, "I hear the doctor and priest saw you. Are you feeling any better?"

"Now that you're here, I am," Hamnet answered.

"You'll get better. I feel it in my bones," I assured, half believing my own words.

"Thirsty?" I asked, observing numerous beads of sweat on Hamnet's face.

"Not now. Grandam just gave me some chicken broth."

"Rest best you can. I 'll stay here by your side. Tell you some stories about what's going on in London."

"I'd like that," Hamnet said.

Except for a brief respite to have a bowl of soup and see my daughters, I spent the remainder of the day with my son.

When evening drew on, Hamnet's fever intensified, as did his ceaseless sweating. Around ten o'clock in the evening, Hamnet went into convulsions. His stomach muscles continually contracted and released, causing him to crunch-up into a fetal position, moaning.

While I watched him writhe, complaining his stomach felt like it was being ripped apart, and feeling like an immense weight had been placed upon his chest, I felt hopeless.

If I could have switched places with my son, I would have gladly done so. But, I was incapable of carrying his burden. I could only stand by, praying feverishly. Sadly, Hamnet's pain lasted several hours before he lost consciousness.

As he lay sprawled on the bed, breathing shallowly, I realized my son was not going to live. Grief overwhelmed me. Grasping at straws, I fell back upon my childhood faith, reciting the Hail Mary, with its request for help at the doors of death.

Hail Mary, full of grace,
The Lord is with thee.
Blessed art thou, among women,
And blessed is the fruit of thy womb,
Jesus.
Holy Mary, Mother of God,
Pray for us sinners now,
And at the hour of our death,
Amen.

"'Pray for us sinners," I spoke the words emblazoned in my mind since before the time of my breeching. But, was this innocent boy of eleven lying before me a "sinner" in need of forgiveness? He seemed incapable of the necessary intent.

I prayed as intensely as I ever had that evening. To no avail. Hamnet's breathing grew shallower. An hour before dawn, he stopped breathing altogether.

When Anne realized Hamnet was gone, she wailed her heart out. Placing her head against my breast, she sobbed ceaselessly.

Wrapping my arms around her, I bowed my head, crying the cry of the brokenhearted.

This is the moment every person fears. The dark night of the soul. When the cries of one's heart seem to be answered with deafening silence, and life seems composed only of sound and fury.

Fortunately, our families were there to offer their support to help get us through this horror. Having buried three daughters, my parents were no strangers to grief. They were bulwarks of strength.

My mother and Anne, with the assistance of my sister Joan, took on the necessary task of preparing Hamnet's body for burial. Before Hamnet was placed in his linen winding sheet, there were several precious items I retrieved for burial with him. The first was a rosary, blessed and given to me by Edmund Campion. I carefully placed it in Hamnet's right-hand.

As I did so, the bizarre thought crossed my mind Hamnet no longer had to worry about the punishment he might receive for possessing Catholic "contraband" such as these simple prayer beads.

I placed the second item, the medal commemorating Sir Francis Drake's circumnavigation, in Hamnet's left hand. This medal symbolized everything Hamnet wished to be. If allowed the grace of a full life, I believe he could and would have achieved things as earth shattering as Francis Drake had done.

As I placed the medal in his cold hand, I kissed Hamnet on the forehead for the last time. Although I love my two daughters dearly, God gave me only one son. What God gave, God allowed to be taken away. Despite my prayers and entreaties, the miracle I prayed for did not occur. The sun did not stop. The seas did not part. A ladder of angels did not descend from the stars.

My once glorious "sun" had gone down. Nothing would ever be the same. I was thirty-two. But, for all extents and purposes, my life was over. In a very real sense, the hopes and dreams of my own youth lie buried with my son.

On the beautiful day Hamnet and Judith came into the world, they were carefully wrapped in swaddling. A few days later they were baptized with water from the baptismal font at Holy Trinity. Now, eleven years later, we were wrapping Hamnet in his winding sheet, preparing him for burial in the churchyard. His life's circle was far too short.

When Hamnet's illness intensified, my father foresaw it would likely be fatal. He made secret arrangements for a carpenter to construct a sturdy oak coffin.

As even most adults buried in Stratford are laid to rest in winding sheets and shrouds, my father was honoring Hamnet in a special manner. He was also kind enough to hire a stonemason to carve a handsome headstone.

It was imperative we bury Hamnet the following day. Around eleven the next morning, we carefully placed Hamnet's wrapped body in its casket. After nailing it securely shut, my father, Richard, Gil, myself, Hamnet Sadler, and the carpenter carried the coffin out of our house, placing it on the horse-drawn cart. Then the carpenter took the horse by the reins and led it down Henley Street, towards Holy Trinity.

Wearing black armbands, myself, Anne, my mother and father, Richard, Gil, Edmund, my sister Joan, her husband William Hart, Susanna, Judith, Hamnet and Judith Sadler, Bart Hathaway, and numerous other extended family members and friends, walked in the sad procession behind the cart carrying Hamnet's body. As we neared the churchyard, the bell in the tower began to toll for my son. Upon hearing it, Anne began weeping. No man can hope to understand the grief a mother experiences upon the death of her child.

While our sorrowful procession wove its way through our hometown streets, many people stopped what they were doing, took off their hats, and bowed their heads. Although our tragedy was not theirs, all suffered similar tragedies within their families. Too many children do not reach adulthood in our society.

The inevitability and commonplace nature of death from disease, famine, fire and war is certainly the Devil's most powerful weapon in the battle for our souls. It argues against the existence of a loving and caring God capable of intervening in the affairs of his children here on earth.

When it is one's own innocent children who are snatched by Death's claws, one often cannot avoid falling into a whirlpool of despair. The only hope of avoiding the consuming quicksand is the strength and solidarity one finds in the arms of one's family, friends, and fellow citizens.

After what seemed an eternity, we arrived at the grave site. The Vicar of Holy Trinity awaited. Two gravediggers, who had just finished digging the grave where the coffin would lie, stood leaning on their shovels at a respectful distance. To them, this was a common occurrence, one of the ways they made their living.

Although the Vicar was a member of the Church of England, he was a good man. By the time he was born, Queen Elizabeth was already in power. Before his birth, his parents pledged their allegiance to the Protestant cause, and dutifully raised him in the rubric of the new faith.

There was much in it that was acceptable. Its emphasis upon the Word of God was admirable. The English translations of the Bible it espoused allowed the Word to be read and understood by a wider audience. As the stories of Chaucer demonstrate, the Good Old Days were not all good. There was much corruption, serious abuses of power and position. There had been a need for reform in the Catholic church. But, in my opinion, the reformers went too far. As the old saying goes: "Two wrongs don't make a right."

We live in a fallen world. So, here we Roman Catholics stood around the grave of our dead son, enduring a service presided over by a clergyman, who, although a fine person, was not a member of our church. As I stood there listening to the Vicar reciting the burial service from The Book of Common Prayer, I took comfort in the fact Hamnet had received the last rites from a priest of our own church.

Being a good man, the Vicar allowed us to slightly modify the prescribed prayer service. At the conclusion, he led us all in a recitation of the Twenty-Third Psalm, Hamnet's favorite. As I sit here writing this memoir, I can still picture us all saying it through the depths of our tears.

As painful as it was to recite the words of this sublime psalm, it gave me some inner strength. As Gil, Richard, Edmund, my father, myself, and Hamnet Sadler, worked the ropes to lower Hamnet's coffin into the grave, I prayed fervently Hamnet was now in the arms of our Lord and Savior. If the repentant thief could have a place in Paradise, so could our child.

Jesus likened Paradise to a mansion with many rooms. There had to be a special class of rooms for those as young and pure as Hamnet. Jesus said one had to be like a child to be saved. He further requested children be allowed to come to Him. Surely, Hamnet must be among the elect.

These were my thoughts as I watched the gravediggers approach and begin shoveling dirt onto the coffin. As they did so, we all began to make our way back to a house which, for me, would be forever haunted by the vision of what happened there. On the walk home, I resolved it was high time Anne, Susanna, Judith, and myself had a home of our own. One free from the memories which haunted the house on Henley Street.

The love my father exhibited towards Hamnet made me appreciate him more than I ever had before. He was a kind, strong, honorable man who suffered unjustly. To me, he is a silent martyr who gave up much to persevere in his faith. It was his success and sacrifice that kept a roof over my head, and food in my belly, throughout my youth.

My father opened the door to my employment with the Burbages. He was the rock of our family. During the long periods of my absence in London, he served as second father to my children.

I resolved to repay some of the immense debt of gratitude I owed him by renewing his application for a family coat of arms with the Office of the Herald. I wanted my father to live the rest of his life with the title "gentleman." Given everything he accomplished and suffered, he most certainly deserved that honorable designation. Our proposed family motto, "Not without right," perfectly described my father's situation. The motto would appear on our coat of arms, along with a falcon, armor helmet, shield and spear.

During that walk home, I also resolved to throw myself back into my work. Although I wished with all my heart I had been taken rather than Hamnet, I still had a wife and two children to support, and two beloved parents not getting younger. My brother Edmund, sixteen years younger than I, only five years older than Hamnet, still had not found his way in life. So, on the sad day following Hamnet's funeral, we had a family meeting where it was decided Edmund would accompany me to London to begin an apprenticeship as a player in the theater business.

Anne and my parents felt Edmund's company would help me bear the pangs of loss I was presently feeling, and I would continue to feel for months and years to come. They hoped I could help Edmund find his bearings.

By this time, I was a shareholder in the Lord Chamberlain's Men. I was sure the Burbages would accommodate my request to have Edmund serve as my apprentice. After many years working as an actor and writer, I had honed my craft to a fine edge. The Burbages knew a significant portion of the future of the company rested on my shoulders.

As I lay in bed that night with Anne, who cried herself to sleep, I asked God to hold Hamnet close, and give us the strength I needed to continue to fulfill our many commitments. Anne, Susanna, Judith, my parents, Edmund, the Burbages, and my fellow players all depended upon me to one extent or the other. With the Lord's help, and my son looking down upon me, I resolved not to let them down.

Finishing my prayer, and closing my eyes, I whispered a salutation to my son which I continued to say before going to sleep for many years: "Good night, Sweet Prince; and flights of angels sing thee to thy rest!"

CHAPTER XLV
THE ELEGY

Several months after my return to London, I found myself browsing in the booksellers' stalls outside St. Paul's. This was my common practice when I had spare time. The physical exertion of walking to and from St. Paul's was good for the circulation, and the stimulation of the light, fresh air, and crowd of people going about their business helped clear the cobwebs from my mind after a long stretch of hours hunched over a manuscript.

Oh, how I sometimes envy the relatively mindless labor of a common scrivener. Or any common laborer for that matter. The worst they deal with after a long day of work is a sore hand, back or arm. To my way of thinking, it's preferable to dealing with the hazard of my profession, a burned-out mind.

I'm of the opinion the brain is a type of muscle. It can get as worn-out as any other. To keep it fit, we need variety and rest. One way I achieve this is through my daily walks.

My walk this day brought me to Richard Field's bookstall, where I purchased the books for Hamnet a year ago. To me, the time since then seemed an eternity. Where before, life went by in color, now it was black and white.

Looking through the many books and pamphlets in the stall, none piqued my interest. At last, I turned my attention to the half-penny ballads. I was looking for something I could incorporate into our plays, jigs and entertainments.

As I ran through the sheets for sale that day, one caught my eye. It was simply entitled "Elegy." Like many such broadsides, it was anonymous, written by a face in the madding crowd that flows through the streets of this great city. As I read the text, I knew the author was someone very special.

The piece struck a resonant chord in this bereaved father. It was a work too real and painful for me to ever use in one of our plays or jigs. But, it was one I needed to possess. It expressed my sorrow and grief in a way I could not do myself. The words are branded in my heart:

In his white winding sheet and shroud,
We laid him gently in the ground.
His life was in the spring of youth,
Full of beauty and of truth.

We thought that summertime would find
Him sound of body and of mind,
With a wife whose love would bring relief,
And his children playing by his feet.

That fall would bring its changing leaves,
The harvest and its gathered sheaves.
Winter would come late and mild,
And leave him with a bright grandchild.

But none of these dreams shall be,
For Death has felled our Greenwood Tree.
If one asks where my heart be found,
Tell him it's six feet underground.

CHAPTER XLVI
OLDCASTLE VS. FALSTAFF

For virtually all my career as an actor and playwright, I contended with the duel specters of government persecution and censorship.

Long before I began writing plays, the government enacted a statute forbidding them from containing content relating to religion or politics. Those violating these prohibitions were subject to severe penalties. A number of my colleagues, including Ben Johnson, were imprisoned for doing so.

I had my own close brush with the law when I named the character of a fat comic knight in a play about King Henry IV, Sir John Oldcastle. Many highly placed Protestants, including descendants of Sir John, took offense.

The historic Sir John Oldcastle was a Protestant Lombard leader who died well over a century before my play was written! The Lollards were a pre-Reformation religious sect which encouraged their members to pursue their own personal interpretations of the Bible. To allow their members to practice their private beliefs, the Lollards worked at translating the Bible from Latin into English, circulating their translations among their members.

The Roman Catholic Church feared the practices of the Lollards would lead to schism. Both the church and government fought to suppress the group, and executed certain of their leaders, including Sir John.

That was all a long time ago. The Master of the Revels, Sir Edmund Tilney, who had the Queen's warrant to review and supervise the content of our performances, reviewed the original manuscript of my first play concerning the reign of Henry IV, and did not raise any objection to the use of the name Oldcastle.

He pocketed his seven-shilling licensing fee and went about his business.

However, the popularity of the play and the character caused a problem to develop. As word made the rounds that the play's most popular character, a fat, lecherous, thieving knight, was named Sir John Oldcastle, powerful Protestant preachers claimed the character's name was an insult and mockery of their faith, and, by implication, the Queen's Protestant regime.

The growing firestorm of criticism quickly built up steam, resulting in angry hecklers disrupting a performance of the play. To calm the crowd, I took the stage. Improvising, I apologized in words similar to the following:

"Gentlemen and Gentlewomen, we humbly beg your pardon if what we have done here today offends. We are merely players — seeking to entertain. We mean no harm. Instead of succeeding, it appears we've fallen on our swords. To earn back your goodwill, we're willing to offer everyone a free round of ale at our expense, which you may obtain from the servers here in this theater."

The mention of free ale did much to calm the crowd, but there was still some disgruntled jeering. One of the groundlings, a large, flat-nosed, man, with the thick hands and muscular arms of a bricklayer, shouted: "You Popish ass! Oldcastle's a martyr! Not a drunken fool!"

His statements caused several other groundlings to start shouting: "Catholic lover! Traitor! Recusant!"

I realized this was turning very ugly very fast. Thinking on my feet, I said in a desperate fit of inspiration:

"You're right. Oldcastle was a martyr. We regret accidentally using his name for our comic knight. From this moment, the knight's name is Falstaff, not Oldcastle!"

Many in the crowd laughed at the new name of the character, catching the wordplay on my own name.

"Shakespeare's fallen on his spear!" someone shouted from the upper gallery, bringing on a wave of laughter that worked its way through the fickle audience.

As I left the stage, sweating profusely, Will Kemp and our other comics came on dancing, while our drummers and musicians played up a storm. Somehow, with the help of free food and drink, we got through the afternoon without the crowd burning the theater down.

The morning after this debacle, I received a summons to a private meeting with Sir Edmund Tilney. As I walked to that meeting, accompanied by two of Sir Edmund's sword carrying servants, I was very nervous. Given most of my family were Roman Catholics, and my livelihood depended upon manuscripts being approved by Sir Edmund, it was essential I stay in his good graces.

I knew the fact he had not realized the use of the name Oldcastle would offend such an influential segment of society was causing him as much political and social trouble as it was causing me. Since he held a position in the social order far above mine, if there was a lamb which needed to be sacrificed, it would be myself rather than Sir Edmund that was fed to the wolves.

While the guards led me through the historic stone building, up the stairs to Sir Edmund's office, I said a prayer to my protectress, the Blessed Virgin Mary, and mentally prepared myself for what could be a very dangerous conversation. When I entered the room, I found Sir Edmund sitting alone in a chair behind his large oak table, reviewing a page of my latest manuscript — the forthcoming sequel to the play causing so much trouble.

As I came into the room, I took off my cap and bowed.

"That was quite an incident at the Globe yesterday. I heard you almost had a riot on your hands."

"Yes sir," I answered. "It was rough for a while. But we managed to calm the crowd before it got out of hand."

"How did you accomplish that?" Sir Edmund asked.

"With free drink, and by renaming the offending character.

The name Sir John Oldcastle will no longer be used in that play, or in any other play I write."

"That's a step in the right direction," said Sir Edmund. "But, to please the clergy and pass muster, there has to be something more."

"Whatever's required," I responded, casting my eyes on the floor.

"You need to make a public and personal apology to the people of London who attend your theater. And your company will be fined a hundred pounds to ensure nothing as outrageous as this happens again," said Sir Edmund.

"One hundred pounds," I thought. Enough to purchase the largest house in Stratford, or any other town in England. This was going to be a painful hit to our bottom line.

"The apology must be a formal one approved by me," said Master Tilney. "You'll give it from the stage after every performance of this play I'm reviewing."

"Personally?" I asked, surprised.

"As the author of the offending piece, you must render

the apologies. When you stage the play at court, you'll also read it to the Queen, and the lords and ladies."

"To the Queen?"

"You heard me, Master Shakespeare. Your offense is great. You must do this well or I can't guarantee your safety. I need the draft of the written apology by noon tomorrow. I hope you can find the proper words to defuse the situation. We've worked together for quite a few years. I hope there'll be more to come."

Sir Edmund dismissed me with a wave of his hand. I trudged back to my lodging, mind reeling. I knew I had to come up with something good. It was clear my professional life, even my safety, depended upon it. I spent a long night burning the midnight oil, working and reworking the draft apology, delivering it to Sir Edmund before the clock struck twelve next morning.

Edmund Tilney had also been burning the midnight oil. While I was slaving over the text of the apology, he reviewed my entire new play, making only minor edits. When I handed the apology to him, I waited nervously while his eyes scanned it once, twice, and a third time.

Finally, he picked up his quill, made a few edits, and handed it back to me, saying, "Tomorrow afternoon you'll perform this before myself and your normal audience. At the conclusion, you'll give the apology. It better be convincing."

So, at the end of the following afternoon's performance, after the rejected John Falstaff is carried off to Fleet Prison, and Prince John of Lancaster and the Chief Justice speak of the likely invasion of France by the new king, I stepped out onto an empty stage in front of an expectant audience. Summoning up my strength, I began my penitential performance.

"First, my fear; then my court'sy; last, my speech. My fear is, your displeasure; my court'sy, my duty; and my speech, to beg your pardons.

"If you look for a good speech now, you undo me: for what I have to say, is of my own making; and what, indeed, I should say, will, I doubt, prove mine own marring.

"But to the purpose, and so to the venture. — Be it known to you, (as it is very well,) I was lately here in the end of a displeasing play, to pray your patience for it, and to promise you a better.

"I did mean, indeed, to pay you with this; which if, like an ill venture, it comes unluckily home, I break, and you, my gentle creditors, lose.

"Here, I promised you, I would be, and here I commit my body to your mercies: bate me some, and I will pay you some, and, as most debtors do, promise you infinitely.

"If my tongue cannot entreat you to acquit me, will you command me to use my legs? and yet that were but light payment, — to dance out of your debt.

"But a good conscience will make any possible satisfaction, and so will I. All the gentlewomen here have forgiven me; if the gentlemen will not, then the gentleman do not agree with the gentlewomen, which was never seen before in such an assembly.

"One word more, I beseech you. If you be not too much cloyed with fat meat, our humble author will continue the story, with Sir John in it, and make you merry with fair Katharine of France: where, for any thing I know, Falstaff shall die of a sweat, unless already he be killed with your hard opinions; for Oldcastle died a martyr, and this is not the man.

"My tongue is weary; when my legs are too, I will bid you good night: and so kneel down before you; — but, indeed, to pray for the queen."

As I ended this enforced speech, our musicians began playing a jig in quick time, and I began dancing in the high-stepping, antic manner I had been taught by Dick Tarlton and Will Kemp. Dressed as I was in my red and blue checkered fool's costume, coxcomb cap, and jangling bells, my parody of a frantic, country dance drew scattered laughs.

Soon Will Kemp, and several of our young boys, dressed as courtesans, joined me onstage. We all danced a merry galliard, Will Kemp throwing the boys up in the air in the manner we observed lords doing to the aristocratic ladies during our appearances at court. This brought roars of more general appreciation.

When our dance concluded, Will Kemp, myself, and the boys all kneeled and said a prayer dedicated to the Queen's health and long life. Fortunately, most of the crowd heeded my heartfelt apology, greeting us with applause. Mercy and forgiveness are beautiful things!

Chapter XLVII
Execution at Tyburn

Sadly, not everyone who ran afoul of the law in the reign of Queen Elizabeth was as lucky as myself. One of those poor souls was Elizabeth's own physician, the Portuguese former Jew, Dr. Roderigo Lopez. Not long before I had my own problem over use of the name Oldcastle, Dr. Lopez was arrested on the deadly serious charge he had conspired with the Spanish king to poison Queen Elizabeth. According to the allegations, Lopez was to receive the princely sum of 50,000 crowns in return for performing this traitorous deed.

Having met Dr. Lopez on several occasions when I was performing in plays at court, he did not seem like the type of man who would plot to assassinate the Queen in such a cowardly manner. He was warmhearted and friendly. His position as the Queen's physician already provided him with enough wealth, power, and position to satisfy most men. As a foreign-born person, and a Jew who, ostensibly at least, became a conforming member of the Protestant Church of England, he could not have expected Roman Catholic King Philip to ever provide him with a position equivalent to the one he already enjoyed with the Queen.

In my opinion, Dr. Lopez was a victim of circumstance. Like Christopher Marlowe, Dr. Lopez was caught between the warring factions of the Cecils and Lord Essex. The Essex faction wanted to again ignite the flames of war against Spain, and further ingratiate themselves with the Queen, by appearing to protect her from the heretical plot of Popish King Philip and an ungrateful and greedy Portuguese Jew.

The Cecils wished to steer a more moderate course, avoiding the vagaries and risks which accompany the tempests of war.

They were veterans of the days of the Armada. They knew, if God had not sent the stormy weather destroying the Spanish fleet, things might have turned out differently. It was best not to foolishly test the Lord's patience.

So, the adversaries' arguments ran, according to the court gossip filtering down from society's "upper crust" into our humble players' ears.

Unfortunately, like corrupt lobbyists of every age, Dr. Lopez's penchant for influence peddling did not help his case. Like virtually every other person at court who enjoyed close and regular access to the Queen, he accepted gifts from those who wanted him to plead their case.

The sometimes-disappointing results of those efforts, aided by the work of the Essex faction, led many seeking wealth and advancement to testify against him. The fact Dr. Lopez accepted a valuable jewel from the Spanish government in connection with his lobbying efforts sealed his death warrant.

As the sordid revelations of Dr. Lopez's influence peddling were revealed to the Queen and public, the Cecil faction's support evaporated. Large segments of the populace demanded his execution. The results of the trial were a foregone conclusion.

Under threat of torture, Dr. Lopez made a confession of sorts, claiming he was cozening the Spanish to obtain valuable information he intended to convey to the Queen. His explanation, and pleas for mercy, fell upon deaf ears. The fact Dr. Lopez's possessions, including the jewel, would revert to the crown weighed heavily against him.

Despite Dr. Lopez's desperate pleas, the Queen did not intervene, although she delayed signing his death warrant for several months. Like thousands of others, I followed the progress of the case closely. And, when Dr. Lopez's public execution was set for June 7th, 1594, I resolved to travel the short distance to the crossroads of Tyburn to hear any last words he might say on the scaffold.

Though executions in general nauseate me, this was not the only one I attended. As a closet Catholic, I went to a number of executions of captured Catholic priests and recusant Catholics as a secret source of support.I prayed for their souls as they paid the ultimate price for their faith.

Dr. Lopez was neither a Catholic nor a recusant. He was a conformist who regularly attended Church of England services I avoided like the plague. Whatever our differences, I felt a strange affinity for Dr. Lopez. We were both outsiders. Living within society, but never really accepted by it.

Neither of us was of noble birth. Our livelihood, our lives themselves, depended upon us maintaining the goodwill of those "stars" above us in the social firmament. For a time, Dr. Lopez flew within the close orbit of the "moon" itself — the Virgin Queen. I would now be a witness to his terrible plunge into the sea.

When I approached the crossroads of Tyburn, a human slaughterhouse in the manner Smithfield was a slaughterhouse for swine, a large crowd was gathering around the scaffold. Given the undercurrent of hatred for Jews which still existed in our country, even though all English Jews were forcibly deported and banished centuries ago, as well as the sensational allegations against Dr. Lopez, those who wanted to get a close view of the execution arrived at the crossroads long before me.

They were already enjoying picnic lunches — eating chicken drumsticks, apples, pears, and plums, and drinking wine, beer and ale.

Thirsty from the walk across town, I used my wineskin to slake my thirst. Then I moved into a position I hoped would be close enough to hear the dying man's last words.

Half an hour later, I began making out the roar of screaming voices accompanying the progress of the hurdle in which Dr. Lopez and his two convicted co-conspirators were bound. As it slowly progressed through the dirty streets of the city, the crowd shouted insults, threw rotten eggs and vegetables, and spit upon them. It was all part of a macabre ritual devised to dehumanize those condemned for treason against the state by appealing to the ageless prejudices lurking in the dark alleys and dungeons of the human psyche.

As the hurdle containing the condemned finally approached, the screams of the crowd rose to a fever pitch. The bloated face of the man next to me assumed an unnatural aspect. "Christ killer! Agent of the fiend!" he screamed with eyes bulging and a flaming bluster in his cheeks as he threw the half-eaten apple in his hand at Dr. Lopez.

A well-dressed man playfully elbowed me in the ribs. Pointing to the black draped executioner holding a large cleaver, he shouted: "Spanish treachery! Let King Philip and the Pope save them now!"

Looking me in the eyes, he said, "The executioner's a Smithfield butcher. Slices the choicest cuts of meat. He'll do his job equally well today. You can be sure of it!"

"I 'm certain you're right," I replied, hoping the disgust in my heart did not show.

When the hurdle arrived at the foot of the scaffold, the prisoners were quickly unfastened. They were pushed and bullied up the steps to the top of the platform, hands tied behind their backs. After Dr. Lopez's two alleged co-conspirators were bloodily dispatched, it came time for the main event in this gruesome theater of cruelty.

Dr. Lopez stood quietly beneath the scaffold as the hangman's noose was placed around his neck. An Anglican priest was quickly allowed to approach and say a last prayer for his soul. The burly man next to me said, "Some good that will do."

When the priest finished, Dr. Lopez prepared to say his last words to the blood thirsty crowd. Dr. Lopez, whose face remained calm and stoic, began speaking in a loud, steady voice:

"I wish everyone here today to know I did not commit treason. What I have done was for the protection of the Queen. I have always been loyal to her, and this my adopted country. I love the Queen as much as I love Our Savior, Jesus Christ."

During the first part of his short speech, the crowd remained relatively quiet. But, when he likened his love for the Queen to his love for Jesus Christ, many began laughing. As the laughter subsided, the jeering began again. Dr. Lopez reacted with a look of sadness and resignation I shall never forget.

While Dr. Lopez closed his eyes, the lead executioner raised his cleaver. The men holding the loose end of the rope strung around his neck pulled until the noose raised his struggling body several feet off the platform. Dr. Lopez's eyes bulged as his feet rapidly danced the skeleton jig. The hangmen held him high until the color of Dr. Lopez's face changed from white, to red, to purple. As death spasms began, the executioners' released him. His limp body crumpled back onto the platform.

The team of executioners quickly removed the light smock Dr. Lopez wore. They carried his now semi-unconscious body over to the blood-soaked table used for drawing and quartering.

The chief executioner castrated Dr. Lopez using a large butcher's knife. He then cut Dr. Lopez's torso open from just below the sternum down through the entire length of his stomach. Sticking his hands into Dr. Lopez's stomach cavity, he began removing Dr. Lopez's intestines and other internal organs. As he did so, he periodically placed handfuls into a shallow black cauldron heated by a roaring fire. It was difficult to tell exactly when Dr. Lopez died. It likely occurred after the hanging, during the initial portion of the butchery.

Before all the internal organs were removed, and the beheading and the cleaving of what remained of the body into quarters began, I made my way out of the crowd to begin my journey home. I had seen more than enough for one day.

Chapter XLVIII
The Merchant of Venice

On my way home from the horror show of Dr. Lopez's execution, I finished the wine remaining in my wineskin and stopped in at a local tavern. The vision of what I saw on the scaffold remained seared in my mind while I tried to drown the emotional pain I was feeling with some strong spirits.

In the weeks following, Dr. Lopez's execution haunted me like a ghostly specter, reappearing again and again in the dark and ghastly night. What especially bothered me was the heartless laughter of those surrounding the scaffold when Dr. Lopez told us his love for the Queen was as strong as his love for Jesus Christ.

Many in the crowd appeared to either flatly not believe this statement or take it as a sly Jewish joke. In the intervening days, some members of my company even were of the opinion Lopez had never really been a Christian and still secretly adhered to his former Jewish beliefs. Under their cynical interpretation, when Dr. Lopez expressed his love for the Queen, what he really meant was quite the opposite. But, having seen Dr. Lopez's utter devastation when the crowd mocked him, I knew his comments were not said in jest.

Whenever I experienced prolonged periods of insomnia over this incident, I would light a pair of candles. In the dim candlelight, I would write until I was tired enough to go back to sleep. What gradually began to take shape during these torturous sessions was a play I eventually named *The Merchant of Venice*.

One of the main characters in my play is a Jewish moneylender named Shylock. Unlike Dr. Lopez, Shylock is a practicing Jew at the beginning of the story. However, by the end of the play, Shylock is forced to convert to Christianity as part of his punishment for demanding his "pound of flesh" from the Christian merchant, Antonio.

Although the avaricious Jewish moneylender is a stock fictional character used in many of our English dramas, most recently by Christopher Marlowe in *The Jew of Malta*, after seeing Dr. Lopez's execution I found myself incorporating more humanity into Shylock than I might otherwise have done.

The idea of making Shylock an unrelenting, over-the-top villain like Marlowe's character, Barabbas, was something I could not do. Of course, given the government censorship I endured, not to mention the strong antisemitism existing within all segments of London society, I could not make Shylock the hero of the piece without inciting a backlash far more severe than the one I suffered for naming my comic knight Oldcastle.

The best I could do under the circumstances was to give Shylock a logical motivation for the revenge he seeks upon Antonio. That motivation has its genesis in the prejudice Antonio and Antonio's friends and colleagues in the Venetian business community exhibit towards Shylock. Just as certain members of the crowd at Dr. Lopez's execution had done, Antonio even goes as far as spitting upon Shylock.

To emphasize the effect such prejudicial conduct would have upon a person, I provided Shylock with the following dialogue in the middle of the play. Salarino, one of Antonio's colleagues on the Rialto, after discussing the loss of Antonio's ship with Shylock, questions Shylock about the consequences which will ensue if Antonio defaults upon his payment obligations to Shylock.

Salarino: Why, I am sure, if he forfeit, thou wilt not take his flesh; What's that good for?

Shylock: To bait fish withal: if it will feed nothing else, it will feed my revenge. He hath disgraced me, and hindered me of half a million; laughed at my losses, mocked at my gains, scorned

> my nation, thwarted my bargains, cooled my friends, heated mine enemies; and what's his reason? I am a Jew: Hath not a Jew eyes? hath not a Jew hands, organs, dimensions, senses, affections, passions? fed with the same food, hurt with the same weapons, subject to the same diseases, healed by the same means, warmed and cooled by the same winter and summer, as a Christian is? if you prick us, do we not bleed? if you tickle us, do we not laugh? if you poison us, do we not die? and if you wrong us, shall we not revenge? if we are like you in the rest, we will resemble you in that. If a Jew wrong a Christian, what is his humility? revenge; If a Christian wrong a Jew, what should his sufferance be by Christian example? why, revenge. The villany you teach me, I will execute; and it shall go hard, but I will better the instruction.

Although Shylock's motivation for revenge is understandable, it is his undoing. Portia, defending Antonio in the guise of a young male lawyer, urges Shylock to be merciful. But Shylock refuses, demanding his pound of flesh. Before Shylock can take his revenge, Portia prevents him from doing so, pointing out the penalty he is seeking to enforce allows him to take a pound of flesh, but not any blood. If he spills any of Antonio's blood, Shylock will be in violation of the law.

Before the dejected Shylock can leave the Duke's presence, Portia points out, when an alien such as Shylock seeks the life of any citizen of the state, the alien forfeits half his possessions to the citizen he conspired against, and half to the state.

When Antonio is offered the opportunity to show mercy to Shylock, Antonio does so in a manner which is also an act of cruelty. He permits Shylock to retain a portion of his possessions, providing he converts to Christianity, and agrees to deed what remains of his property to his daughter. Jessica has abandoned Shylock, married against his wishes, and has voluntarily converted to Christianity.

By dealing with Shylock's fate in this manner, I was able to make the play acceptable to government censors and the general public. It made a successful run, and I hope made some in the audience think a bit deeper about the treatment aliens, in matters of origin or religion, receive in our society.

Sometime after writing *The Merchant of Venice* I had another opportunity to write in favor of the tolerance and mercy I believe should be shown to persons outside the narrow bounds of acceptability in our society. The project was a collaboration with other playwrights upon a play recounting the life of Sir Thomas More. Sir Thomas is a hero to us Catholics because he gave his life to maintain his Catholic faith by refusing to acknowledge Queen Elizabeth's father, King Henry VIII, as the supreme head of the church on earth.

Henry needed More's support to legitimize his divorce of Queen Catherine of Aragon, and his marriage to Anne Boleyn, Queen Elizabeth's mother. More refused to give Henry the moral support and assistance Henry sought. More paid for it with his life.

Given the subject matter of this play, all of us involved knew it was a longshot to get it through the censorship of the Master of the Revels. However, it was at least worth the effort.

The portion of the play I wrote had to do with the fate of foreign immigrants who are resented for taking jobs which would otherwise go to English citizens. Sir Thomas quells a mob of citizens planning to instigate a riot against the foreigners with a speech that successfully allows the members of the mob to envision themselves in the immigrants' position –trudging to the seacoast ports with tattered luggage and babies strapped upon their backs. More warns the mob, if they go through with the attack, the same type of persecution may be visited upon them someday – and none may live to see old age in the dog-eat-dog world they will help create.

Tragically, *Thomas More* never made it past the censor. It was not acted upon the stage, either in the reign of Queen Elizabeth or King James.

My final word on the effects censorship and repression had upon my creative life occurs in a list of things I most despise clothed in a "sonnet" I wrote during one of my recurring bouts of insomnia.

> Tir'd with all these, for restful death I cry, —
> As, to behold desert a beggar born,
> And needy nothing trimm'd in jollity,
> And purest faith unhappily forsworn;
> And gilded honour shamefully misplac'd.
> And maiden virtue rudely strumpeted,
> And right perfection wrongly disgrac'd,
> And strength by limping sway disabled,
> And art made tongue-ty'd by authority,
> And folly (doctor-like) controlling skill,
> And simple truth miscall'd simplicity,
> And captive Good attending captain Ill:
> Tir'd with all these, from these I would be gone,
> Save that, to die, I leave my love alone.

Need I say more?

CHAPTER XLIX
EDMUND AND KEMP

One day, not long after the turn of the century, I stood above the stage of the recently built Globe theatre in the covered Lords' Gallery. Below, Will Kemp, and my brother, Edmund, were performing a comic jig concluding our popular history play, *Henry V*. Will was singing a song composed by a street balladeer we both admired. His beautiful voice was accompanied by the clashing twangs of a poorly tuned lute, intentionally misplayed by Edmund.

Dressed in the extravagant courtesan's clothing we recently purchased from a classy lady of the night, Edmund was playing the role of Will's dim-witted wife. The side-splitting nature of the ballad, and the "if looks could kill" faces Will and Edmund exchanged, worked brilliantly. The audience was in stitches.

Of course, with the copious ale and beer drinking that went on during our performances, it was easier to leave the crowd rolling in the aisles at the end of a show than it was at the beginning.

Once the laughter died down, Will and Edmund stepped forward, holding hands like young lovers, and sang a song Edmund recently composed.

A penny for your thoughts,
Or else our play is lost.

We lads of May will bloom,
And sing a merry tune,
If you but pay the groom,
Before our purse is ruined.

The price is worth the cost;
And your hour's not lost;
If we have made you smile,
With our wit and wile.

And, if we earned a laugh,
Our wage is worth the math.
So we humbly pray,
Good Fortune comes your way;

And brings you back again
To our Globe of men!

When the song ended, Edmund and Will bowed and left the stage, Edmund vigorously shaking the feather plumed fanny of his yellow dress. I couldn't help shouting: "Good show! Good show!"

At that instant, I was as proud of my younger brother as a father would be for his own son. Not only was Edmund's song a solid piece of showmanship, he performed it as only a master comedian could.

After paying my respects to the lords and ladies showing off their "plumage" in the three penny seats around me, I scrambled downstairs and went to the tiring room. Edmund and Will were already changing out of their costumes into street clothes.

Given the elaborate nature of Edmund's costume, including the blonde beehive wig, clay birds nestling within it, as well as the starched ruff, bright yellow farthingale dress and petticoat, and jet-black stomacher, narrowest at the waist, and widest just below the breasts, Edmund was having difficulty extricating himself from the domestic finery.

"I have no idea how women deal with these contraptions," Edmund whined as I approached.

"You only have to bear the burdens of the fairer sex a few hours at a time," I replied. "And your apprenticeship playing women's roles is nearly over. Soon you'll not have to shave every day."

"Thank God!" Edmund exclaimed. "To finally be released from this whalebone cage. And free my face from powder cake," Edmund went on, using a wet rag and well water from a wooden pail to wash it off.

"Now Edmund. We've all paid our dues coming up through the ranks," I said. "As I've reminded you on many occasions, I broke into the craft myself playing women's roles."

"So did I," Will Kemp added. "And if you don't mind my saying so, young lad, I think you cut a fine, hour-glass figure in that female get-up."

"Cut it out you two," Edmund objected. "Right now, I've got Will and will in over-plus; and Will plus Will equals — one too many Wills!"

Will Kemp chuckled. Looking at me, he said, "Your brother's really honing his wit. If you're not careful, he might outdo you someday."

"That will not bother me at all," I quipped. "The fairest star must soon decline. Even kings run out of time!"

"I don't think I'll be challenging my brother anytime soon," said Edmund. "He still beats me in a game of chess, though I came close to mating him recently."

"Even though that game was played in a tavern when we were in our cups, it's getting harder and harder to prevail against you," I said. "Perhaps it's best we call a truce. Though blood is thicker than water, it's best to avoid a civil war — even one taking place on a chessboard rather than a battlefield!"

"No civil wars needed here," said Will Kemp, before asking me, "What do you say we step out to the tavern next door and enjoy a drink together?"

Addressing Edmund, he said, "I'm sure this young lad here has better things to do than hang out with us gents. I bet there's at least one woman out there who likes you better than herself. So, here's a gift from me," he said, pulling a freshly minted shilling from the leather purse hanging from the belt around his waist and tossing it to Edmund.

"Thanks for your generosity!" said Edmund.

"You deserve it. And more!" Will replied. "That was a wonderful performance tonight. You made me look good. Enjoy your evening and leave your brother and me to our own devices," Will said, placing his hand on my shoulder as we left the tiring room.

Although Will and I went out for a drink quite often after performances, occasionally discussing how we might do better the next time around, I sensed there was something more significant to his invitation this evening.

A few minutes later, we were comfortably seated near a warm fire in the taphouse we built beside the Globe to cash in on some of the audiences' before and after show libations. Will was a man who wore his heart on his sleeve. Immediately after we took the first draughts from our tankards of ale, he got down to business.

"My dear friend," he began. "We've worked long and hard to earn our current success?"

"Certainly," I responded. "I remember touring together long before we formed the Lord Chamberlain's Men six years ago. How time flies."

"I've seen you grow from a fledgling actor and playwright to a fine actor and, in my opinion, the best playwright alive today."

"And I've seen you grow from a promising clown and comedian to the greatest of all. The true heir to Dick Tarlton. Without your genius, Falstaff wouldn't be the beloved figure he is."

"Without your brilliance, there would be no Falstaff. And many other wonderful characters, such as Dogberry in *Much Ado About Nothing*, Mercutio in *Romeo and Juliet*, and Christopher Sly in the *Taming of the Shrew*. But nothing lasts forever. I feel now's the time for me to end my relationship with the company, selling my interest to the other shareholders."

As the import of Will's words sank in, I blurted out: "Why now? Things are going so well. We're packing the house. And I've a new play I'm beginning; one in which I'm writing a role tailor-made for you. In many ways the comic spark you provide is the heart and soul of our operation. Edmund adores you. I know I speak for the other shareholders when I say we don't want to lose you. You're irreplaceable."

"I understand this comes as a surprise," said Will. "And I'm flattered you believe I'm irreplaceable. But you'll all survive. And thrive! The Lord Chamberlain's Men are the best in the business. I'm not the only star in the firmament.

"Now that Ned Alleyn's sun is past its zenith, Dick's considered the greatest leading actor on the stage. Given your phenomenal writing skills, people will come to see your plays regardless of who is acting in them."

"Thanks for your high opinion. But we're so much better as a team than as individuals," I argued. "You still haven't told me the reason you're leaving."

"It's personal," said Will. "After fifteen years as a theater performer, I'm burned out. I don't wake up motivated anymore. Despite our success, I need something new to stoke my passion for living. I've thought long and hard, so please don't try to talk me out of it. You're very persuasive, but don't waste your breath on a lost cause."

As Will spoke, I could see his mind was dead set on leaving us. Knowing him as I did, I realized there was only a slim possibility I could get him to reconsider. It certainly would not happen this evening.

"It seems, from what you're saying, you intend to leave the theater entirely," I stated, hoping my statement would prove true. If Will joined one of our rivals, it would be boom for them and bust for us.

"No worries," Will reassured. "After all we've been through, I wouldn't treat you and my other partners like that. I plan to strike out on my own. As you know, one of my specialties is Morris dancing."

"Yes," I said, relieved he was not going to be joining another acting company. "Your dances are always great hits in the theater."

"And I think they'll be great hits with people in the small towns and villages that rarely, if ever, can come to London and see a play."

"I believe you're right," I said. "How do you plan to reach them?"

"That's the beauty of it. Picture this. I 'm dressed in my Morris dancer's outfit, with bells sewn into the fabric of my clothes, so they announce my arrival. I'm accompanied by a musician playing the pipes and tabor drum. I dance, sing songs, and tell jokes, all the way from London to Norwich."

"From London to Norwich! That's got to be a hundred miles. Do you think you're in the physical condition to cover that distance?" I asked.

"That's why I want to do it now. The Lord's preserved my health. Things could be different in a year or two," said Will.

"How do you plan to make it pay?" I asked.

"We'll have our playbill printer do a run advertising this one-of-a-kind event, and we'll hire a messenger as an advance man, distributing the announcements in every hamlet, village and town along the way. There'll be major performances here in London and in Norwich, and less extensive performances in the larger villages."

"Sounds like it might work," I remarked. "I want to lend you my support. I have a new song I've written. I hope you'll like it. If you do, please feel free to use it in the entertainments you'll perform along the way."

"Thanks for your understanding and generosity," said Will.I felt you were the right person to address this issue. You've justified my trust," Will said, raising his tankard to his lips, taking a long draught of ale.

CHAPTER L
THE NINE DAYS' WONDER

After some relatively brief negotiations, Will Kemp sold his shares in the company. He was soon preparing for the one man traveling show he named "The Nine Days Wonder."

On February 11, 1600, Edmund and I, along with most of the other members of our company, and several thousand enthusiastic Londoners, attended the brilliant show Will gave in front of the London Lord Mayor's house at the beginning of his journey.

Will opened the performance with an inventive little song and dance I had seen him perform before at the end of my plays on the reign of Henry IV. Will had played the role of Falstaff and reveled in it. He recognized the similarities between Tarlton's and Falstaff's personalities and senses of humor. "Oh, if only Dick had been here to play that role!" Will had sighed on more than one occasion.

"So true! So true!" I replied. "I couldn't have written it without Dick's inspiration. I'm sure he's up there somewhere watching — and laughing!"

"I hope so," Will concluded.

Now, at the inception of the Nine Days Wonder, I realized I might be watching Will's own little tribute to Falstaff and Tarlton for the last time. As he performed several of Tarlton's signature gestures, bringing ripples of laughter and applause from the crowd, Will began to sing his own light-hearted homage to the Fat Knight.

> Jack Falstaff lives in sin;
> He knows where the ghostly skeleton's been.
> While drinking sack with a toothless grin,
> He fleeces even kith and kin.

He's searching for a widow's dower,
To stash inside his portly tower.
He's not afraid to act a coward,
To live and drink another hour.

He craves for gold, he lusts for power,
And when he's poor, he's mighty sour.
He's plucked the Rose, he's stripped the flower,
He jests and jigs in the witching hour!

As Will finished this energetic ditty, the crowd of rich and poor roared their approval.

Will next danced the high-stepping jig he learned from an itinerant Irish performer. Then he segued into another poetic takeoff on Falstaff he recently wrote:

In gardens where the primrose blooms,
Where nature paints its bright cartoons,
Water nymphs are humming tunes,
While the glowworm sparks in June.

Mistress Quickly shakes her tush,
Round about the burning bush.
As Doll Tearsheet whispers "hush,"
To the lad in such a rush.

They wash their dirty skirts in suds,
After swimming through the muck,

And throw the dice with Lady Luck,
Who laughs in bed with Friar Tuck!

Somewhere in the shadows lurks,
The Prince of Thieves, the great cutpurse,
Who steals our hearts, all their worth,
And masks his crimes in peals of mirth.

Raise your sword, but don't get hurt.
Roads to glory are paved with dirt.
And those who heed a call to battle,
End up bones that shake and rattle.

Give your ears to Justice Shallow,
While your soul still has its marrow,
So you may live to see tomorrow,
And taste the sack that's in the bottle!

When Will finished this performance, the audience broke into further cheers and enthusiastic applause.

Seizing on the high spirits, Will continued with a mime performance, mimicking the movements of a bellringing clock automaton. Finishing this segment, he told a series of bawdy jokes which had the audience shouting "Kemp! Kemp! Kemp!" while simultaneously stomping their feet.

At an appropriate moment towards the end of the show, Will stopped dancing. He shouted out: "I dedicate this next song to a great friend and former colleague, the Sweet Swan of Avon, Mr. William Shakespeare!"

To my surprise, many in the crowd started clapping. When the noise subsided, Will began singing in a clear tenor voice.

When that I was and a little tiny boy,
With hey, ho, the wind and the rain,
A foolish thing was but a toy,
For the rain it raineth every day.

But when I came to man's estate,
With hey, ho, the wind and the rain,
'Gainst knave and thief men shut their gate,
For the rain it raineth every day.

But when I came, alas! To wive,
With hey, ho, the wind and the rain,
By swaggering could I never thrive,
For the rain it raineth every day.

But when I came unto my bed,
With hey, ho, the wind and the rain,
With toss-pots still had drunken head,
For the rain it raineth every day.

A great while ago the world begun,
With hey, ho, the wind and the rain,
But that's all one, our play is done,
And we'll strive to please you every day.

Will's performance was excellent. As he descended from the temporary stage that had been constructed for him, accompanied by his drum and pipe player, Thomas Sly, his servant, William Bee, and a referee to ensure Will complied with the publicized rules, Will started dancing down the long road to Norwich.

While he danced, Will began chanting some of the endless series of improvised rhymes that used to effortlessly slip off the tip of his tongue while he was performing his famous jigs on stage.

Zany Janie
Went so crazy,
Dressed in rags,
She joined the Navy.

Little Davey,
He's so lazy,
Cries for milk,
Just like a baby!

Robbing Robert
Went to market,
Where a Cutpurse
Picked his pocket!

Annie Ryder
Slurps her cider,
Gets so mad,
She's like a tiger!

Like many others in the crowd, I listened attentively as long as I could still make out Will's voice and the sounds of the little jingling bells adorning his outfit. When I could no longer distinguish Will's bells and inventive rhymes above the noise of the dispersing crowd, I took my leave of Edmund and headed home to my lodgings with a heavy heart. I would miss Will greatly. He was a unique talent; one who could never be completely replaced.

As it turned out, Will Kemp's Nine Days Wonder was wildly successful and profitable to boot. The success of his feat here in England led him to undertake similar tours on the Continent. Given the language and cultural barriers those Continental tours presented, it still amazes me he successfully completed them. I saw Will a few times after his return, marveling at the stories he told about people and places I would never see.

Sadly, we never got to find out what Will might have accomplished in the years to come. For, not long after returning home, he had his life cut short by the terrible scourge of the plague — as have so many others I have loved. So ended the life of one of the greatest comedians to grace the English stage.

CHAPTER LI
THE WINTER OF DISCONTENT

The year 1601 was among the most difficult of my life. It was the year I lost my father, and I almost lost my own head as collateral damage of a failed plot to topple the aged Queen.

I well remember the bitter cold, grey February day when Lord Monteagle, Lord Essex's most influential Catholic ally, came knocking at the door of the Globe with several confederates in tow. Augustine Phillips, our business manager, hastily sent word to us shareholders there was an urgent matter of business to decide that morning. Along with Gus, myself, Richard and Cuthbert Burbage, John Heminges, and Henry Condell attended.

As we sat round the rough hewn table in the tiring room of the theater, which sometimes doubled as a prop of the famous roundtable of King Arthur, we each enjoyed a frothy mug of small ale. It was too early in the day to drink anything stronger. We needed to have our wits about us to perform our roles in our performance of *Twelfth Night* that afternoon.

I personally disliked attending winter meetings at the Globe because we did not have the warmth of a fire to take the bite out of the cold, wet mists that enveloped the neighborhoods bordering the Thames. Even seated within the tiring room, we could see vapor emerge from our mouths like jets of steam when we spoke.

Never one to keep his thoughts to himself, Dick remarked, "Well Gus, I hope it'll be worth our precious free time to have rousted us out of house and home this frosty, winter morning. I, for one, would rather be sleeping in my parlor's best bed than freezing my rump off at this little parlay."

John Heminges, whose chattering teeth made his slight but endearing stutter more pronounced than usual, said, "Na-na-nothing but the ba-ba-best bed for you!"

"You're right," Dick replied matter of factly. "Since I play kings and princes, and those of great renown, it's always the best for me!"

"A consumer of humble pie you're not," Dick's brother Bert cut in. "But a lawyer friend of mine recently told me a story of how you were once brought down to earth by our friend Will Shakespeare."

"Oh, that's excellent!" said Dick, looking my way, with a self-satisfied smile. "As Will himself wrote: 'let's kill all the lawyers.' Life would be such a carnival!"

"Be that as it may," Cuthbert responded, "this lawyer said, once upon a time, when you were acting in Will's play, *Richard the Third....*"

"I well remember it," interrupted Dick, winking at me, launching into a parody of *Richard the Third*'s opening line:

"Now is the winter of our discontent made glorious summer by the Sweet and Slippery Swan of Avon!"

"Enough of the Ned Alleyn impression," Bert interjected. "Back to my story. Apparently, your stage antics were enough to impress a sweet young courtesan attending the play that afternoon. So much so she invited you to visit her at her home that evening. When you showed up at her door ready to be entertained, you sent word, 'Richard the Third has arrived.' Meanwhile, Will had apparently overheard you and the young woman making arrangements for the rendezvous. He beat you to her, and was already at his merry game when you arrived. Rumor has it he sent word: 'William the Conqueror preceded Richard the Third!'"

As Bert delivered the punchline, everyone, including Dick, burst out laughing. When I recovered, I replied, "It's a nice tale. One worthy of our jolly friend, Falstaff!"

Just then, there was a knock at the door. A moment later, it opened to reveal a man dressed in a plush black velvet doublet and cloak. He wore a gentleman's rapier. The gilt tipped, black leather scabbard extended almost to the floor.

While his piercing blue eyes surveyed the motley group seated around the table, his bearded face broke into a toothy half grin. Carefully removing each of his white chevron gloves, he began:

"I don't know how much Mr. Phillips has told you about the purpose of this meeting…"

"Nothing at all, my Lord," interjected Dick, exuding a nonchalant air while taking a quick swig from his tankard.

"As most of you know, I'm Lord Monteagle. Myself, and my companions, Sir Charles Percy and Sir Jocelyn Percy, have been sent here by your honorable patrons, Lords Essex and Southhampton. They've asked me to request you players put on a command performance of *Richard II* in their honor at two o'clock tomorrow afternoon."

Bert, the only nonplayer in our group of shareholders, responded diffidently:

"With all due respect, my Lord, *Richard II* is an old, moldy play. It's unlikely such a moth-eaten offering will pack the house, especially on a cold February afternoon. Even if we agree, it's been a few years since we performed that one, so it'll take quite a few hours of rehearsal time for us to come up to speed."

"Be very careful," warned Lord Monteagle. "You wouldn't want me to report you rejected this request, would you? Lords Essex and Southhampton have been very good to your company over the years. You'll be well compensated for your time and effort. Forty shillings for just one performance of a ratty old play! Given the interest of your noble patrons in seeing it performed, I guarantee you'll have an appreciative audience."

Henry Condell asked, "Sir, if we agree to play the piece, could we have a few days to rehearse it?"

"I'm sorry, that's not possible. It must be performed tomorrow afternoon."

"That's a tall order," Gus said.

Sensing a potential crisis, I chimed in to defuse the situation: "While that's true, Gus, I'm sure we can pull it off."

"Easy for you to say," Dick rejoined. "You're not playing the leading role. Your prompt book is way shorter than mine. You've only got a few minor supporting roles."

"I hear you," I answered. "But I know what you can do when you put your mind to it!" hoping flattery would win the day.

Interrupting our conversation, Gus said to Lord Monteagle, "As you've seen, my Lord, we have a few things to work through before we can give a final answer. Can you return in a half hour?"

Lord Monteagle answered, "I'm surprised you've not immediately embraced this opportunity. If you realized how much the request means to your Lordships, you wouldn't delay. There'll be hell to pay if you refuse. That said, I'll be back in half an hour."

Ever the politician, Gus rejoined: "We're deeply sorry for the delay. But my partners and I need to talk this over. Are there any other important aspects of their Lordships' request we should know about?"

"The play has to be performed uncut, in its entirety."

Henry Condell, normally a quiet, thoughtful man, said, "Uncut? Including the scene showing the dethroning of the King prohibited by the Master of the Revels?"

"You've heard what I said," Lord Monteagle replied. "To receive payment, the play must be performed with the deposition scene. I'll be back soon to hear your response!" Lord Monteagle said impatiently, as he turned, lifted the door latch, and left the room.

Once he was safely gone, Dick angrily burst out: "Uncut! He's moonstruck! We'll all end up in the Clink or worse — ears and noses cut off!"

"You wouldn't make much of a leading man without your ears and pretty nose," said Bert with a wry smile Dick answered with an exaggerated frown.

"Why would Lords Monteagle, Southhampton, and Essex demand the play be performed with the banned scene involving the deposition of the King? That's the more troublesome question," Gus interjected.

"We've all heard rumors the Queen intensely dislikes this play. Especially the deposition scene.She sees it as an implied threat to her own grip on the Crown," said Henry Condell.

"With the cauldron Essex is already boiling in due to his conduct of the war in Ireland, and the unauthorized truce he entered with that Irish rogue, Tyrone, why in God's name would he want to further tick off the Queen and the Privy Council?" asked Dick.

"And why would we want to risk angering the Queen and the Privy Council?" Dick continued. "The court's patronage is our bread and butter. We've performed at court over a hundred times. The Queen's paid us tons more than the amount being offered to us for this performance! Even worse, Monteagle, Essex and Southhampton could deny they had a contract with us, leaving us high and dry to face the government's wrath. It could ruin the company."

"On the other hand, if we choose not to perform the play, we 'll face the anger of Monteagle, Essex and Southhampton," said Henry Condell. "Although not "shining stars" at court right now, they've been so in the past, and they may be in the ascendant again. Essex is the most popular person in the kingdom. Many feel he's been mistreated by the Queen, and the real Richard the Third, the head of her Privy Council, Lord Robert Cecil. Essex's defeat of the Spanish fleet at Cadiz is only surpassed in people's hearts by the defeat of the Armada in 1588."

"Will here has a special relationship with Southhampton, having dedicated his poems *Venus and Adonis*, and *Lucrece* to him. What are your thoughts about this bizarre request?" Bert asked.

I hesitated for a second before answering: "Damned if we do; damned if we don't. It's true the Queen's treated us well. So have Lord Southhampton, and his great friend, Lord Essex. The Queen isn't getting younger. When she dies, we might rue the day we refused them."

Pausing for a moment to let the import of my words sink in, I went on, "In the event the play comes to the Council's attention, we can plead it was done at the command of these great nobles. We were powerless to resist." Addressing Bert, I said, "we put great trust in your business judgment. Where do you come down on this?"

"It's a pickle," Bert answered. "Maybe we can play it both ways. Given the short notice, we can put on the performance without advertising. That'll reduce the attendance. We can hope word doesn't get back to the Master of the Revels the deposition scene was included. They only want a single performance. It's an old play, given on a cold day. Perhaps government spies will not be in the audience. The public doesn't know the scene concerning the king's deposition was censored."

"Perhaps pigs can fly," said Dick. "Walsingham, Lord Burghley, and now his son, the hump-backed Robert Cecil — nothing gets by the eyes and ears they've cozened, brought and bribed these twenty years. Remember our colleagues who ran afoul of them in the past. Kyd and Marlowe, to name but a few."

"Fools who couldn't bridle their tongues.Marlowe was a government agent and informer to boot," said Bert. "We haven't made their mistakes. We've powerful friends in current favor at court, including the Herberts. Will's close to William Herbert. If things go south, they should be able to protect us. Helping us plead our case to Queen and Privy Council. As much as the Puritans despise us, the Queen sees the value of providing entertainment to the groundlings. To deprive them of their bread and circus entertainments when things aren't going well in the war, amid the bad harvests, will make her more unpopular than she already is."

"I ha, ha, hope to God you're ra, ra, right," said John Hemmings.

"Does anyone else have something to say before we put it to a vote?" asked Gus.

The vote was taken. With the exception of Dick Burbage, all of us voted to accept the engagement. Gus was tasked with conveying the acceptance to Lord Monteagle and his companions.

With one hastily arranged rehearsal, we performed *Richard II t*o a half empty house on the afternoon of February 7, 1601. During the performance of the banned deposition scene, I stood backstage, listening to Dick Burbage passionately intone Richard II's lines, as he transfers the crown to his usurping successor.

After the victorious rebel, Henry Bolingbroke, asks: "Are you content to resign the crown?" King Richard responds:

> Ay, no; no, ay; — for I must nothing be,
> Therefore, no, for I resign to thee.
> Now mark me how I will undo myself: —
> I give this heavy weight from off my head,
> And this unwieldly sceptre from my hand,
> The pride of kingly sway from out my heart;
> With mine own tears I wash away my balm,
> With mine own hands I give away my crown,
> With my own tongue deny my sacred state,
> With mine own breath release all duteous oaths....

As I listened to Dick, I felt my hair begin to stand on end. A sense of foreboding came over me. I could feel winds of change blowing in the winter air, as a legion of snowflakes descended upon the shivering audience.

Chapter LII
The Essex Rebellion

The following morning I slept in. Like the other players in our company, I was tired from the rehearsal and the rushed performance of *Richard II* the previous day. At the time, I was renting a room in a Southwark boarding house, only a few hundred yards from the Globe.

Lord Monteagle and the Percys attended the performance of the play. At its conclusion, Monteagle delivered what Dick Burbage cynically called the "thirty pieces of silver." Dressing, I went down into the kitchen of the house to eat a late breakfast of rye bread, cheese, and small ale, served by my landlady's attractive young maid, Alice, a Warwickshire girl.

Having eaten, I went back to my room, placed my small, portable writing desk on the multi-purpose table, poured some black ink into the inkhorn, picked-up and recut the nub of my white, goose-quill pen, and continued working on the play *Hamlet*.

I spent the remainder of the morning working on the part of the play containing the exchange between Hamlet and Laertes in which Hamlet lamely asks Laertes's pardon for having inadvertently killed Laertes's father in a moment of passion.

Although Laertes ambiguously receives Hamlet's half apology, he is actively engaged in a conspiracy with Hamlet's stepfather — seeking to take Hamlet's life in revenge for Hamlet's taking of Laertes's father's life, and Hamlet's role in causing Laertes's sister Ophelia's madness and death.

While I finished writing, I could not help but reflect upon the parallels which existed between this scene and the stress in the relationship that had developed between the Queen and Lord Essex.

Like Hamlet's insensitive and ineffective apology to Laertes, Essex, since losing 12,000 of the 16,000 troops that went with him to Ireland, had been ineffectively apologizing and attempting to repair his severely damaged relationship with Queen Elizabeth. His apologies had fallen upon deaf ears.

As the stepson of Elizabeth's long favorite, Robert Dudley, the greatest love of Elizabeth's life, Elizabeth was naturally disposed to favor Essex. The fact he was also handsome, energetic, and an extremely devoted courtier during the early years of their relationship led to his rapid rise in favor.

Essex's earlier conquest of the Queen's heart was matched by his conquest of the hearts and minds of the people. His popularity was given a huge boost when he led the successful raid upon the Spanish fleet at Cadiz in 1596.

I had been acquainted with Lord Essex since well before 1596. Essex's closest friend, Lord Southhampton, had once been my artistic patron. I dedicated my two long poems to him when the London theaters closed because of the plague in 1593 and 1594.

Although he was still a young man in 1593, Lord Southhampton frequently attended our theater performances. Like many in their late teens and early twenties, he enjoyed projecting a liberal image, living on the wild side of life. He reputedly counted men and women among his amorous conquests. And he could well afford to do so. He was always impeccably dressed, and he had an arresting and unforgettable appearance.

In addition to wearing, and sometimes inaugurating, the latest fashion trends, Lord Southampton often draped a thick lock of his long auburn hair down the left side of his chest, giving him an androgynous appearance. This was accented by his slight, lanky frame, his soft, milk- white complexion, and his unusually long and narrow fingers — the envy of many a lady at court.

Lord Southhampton's unique appearance was complemented by his high pitched, lilting voice, his slow manner of speaking, and the feline way he moved. His unusual appearance, small voice, and graceful mannerisms made the young lord the master-mistress of many a young woman's and man's dreams.

In fact, during those plague years, I was a sometime guest at the country estate of Lord Southhampton's family. While living there, I wrote an aristocratic comedy of manners called *Love's Labor's Lost*. A glittering Lord Essex attended the first performance of the play our newly formed company gave at Southhampton's manor house.

It is often said opposites attract. The unusually strong and deep bond of friendship that developed between Lord Southhampton and Lord Essex was proof of the truth of that timeless adage. Essex was everything Southhampton was not. A natural, born leader, Essex was a masculine, powerful man, with a deep, commanding voice, and great charisma. His ego was gigantic, and he was ambitious to a fault.

In the ensuing years, Essex and Southhampton were present at many of the performances of the plays our company performed at court. They also frequently attended our plays at the Theater in Shoreditch, and, since the summer of 1599, at the Globe.

I distinctly remember the afternoon they attended our performance of *Henry V* before departing with the troops on their expedition to Ireland. The energy and patriotism of the soldiers in the audience was electrifying. When I spoke the following lines about Essex in the prologue to the final act, the performance was interrupted by cheers from the audience.

Go forth, and fetch their conquering Caesar in:
As, by a lower but by loving likelihood,
Were now the general of our gracious empress,

(As, in good time, he may,) from Ireland coming,
Bringing rebellion broached upon his sword,
How many would the peaceful city quit,
To welcome him?

The subsequent failure of Essex's and Southampton's venture in Ireland left me and many others greatly disheartened. But it was widely understood by the public; most English troops who died did so from disease, not from the conduct of Essex or Southhampton.

Essex's finger-pointing enemies on the Privy Council needed a scapegoat. The aging Queen sadly went along with them. They persuaded her to revoke Essex's monopoly on sweet wines. He was placed under house arrest. Rumor had it Essex's fall from grace, money and power drove him mad. His angry outbursts were unguarded, ill-advised, and he was once again being called before the Privy Council to explain his rash actions.

I had recently heard from others close to Southhampton "something important" would happen soon. The fact certain of Essex's supporters came to us to commission a performance of *Richard II* was further evidence rumors were often true.

Finishing my morning writing session, I decided to leave the house to take some air and find some dinner. As I was fastening my every day doublet, there was a knock at my chamber door. I opened it to find Alice, breathless from her climb up the stairs.

"Sorry to interrupt you, Mr. Shakespeare," she said, catching her breath, "but there's a gentleman named Gus downstairs. He urgently needs to speak with you."

"Show him up," I told Alice, a bit concerned. Gus usually sent the young apprentice lodging with him to convey his messages. While I waited, I took a pinch of tobacco from my pouch, tamped it into my long-stemmed clay pipe, and lit it with a piece of kindling from the fire lending some heat to an otherwise chilly room.

While I was puffing away a minute or so later, Gus came into the room flustered. Before shutting the door, he took a quick look down the stairwell, making sure Alice was not within hearing distance. Turning around, he asked, "Is there anyone in the room across the hall?"

"No," I said.

"Good," Gus replied. He blurted out: "Looks like we've got a serious problem!"

"What are you talking about?" I asked.

"You haven't heard?"

"No," I replied.

"Late this morning, Lords Essex, Southhampton, and a number of their followers, left Essex's town house on foot, heading for Whitehall Palace!

"In advance of their arrival within city precincts, the government sent heralds into the street shouting: 'Treason! Treason!'

"But Lord Essex was not in fighting attire. He professed he meant no harm to the Queen. He claimed he was trying to save her from a plot of Cecil and others to depose her and place Princess Isabella of Spain upon the throne!"

"That's insane!" I exclaimed. "Cecil would never put a Catholic monarch upon the throne. He and his father, Lord Burghley, have spent their entire lives working to prevent a Catholic monarchy here in England!"

"I know," Gus hurriedly assured me. "But that's his story. As they strode through the streets with their followers, Essex and Southhampton tried to get the people of the city to join with them. Few accepted the offer."

"Was there fighting?" I asked.

"Not much. There was armed government opposition at Ludgate, and a further skirmish with the Bishop's men. Lord Essex's page was killed."

"Sad. Is Essex still on the march?" I asked.

"No. Without the support of the citizens, and, in face of the government opposition, most of Essex's supporters have melted away. I heard he's abandoned his followers and is retreating back towards Essex House."

"Fortune's fool!" I remarked. "To rise so high, and fall so low, in such a short period of time. He can't survive. It'll be the last straw for the Queen. His enemies at court will draw and quarter what remains of his reputation. His head will end up food for ravens atop London Bridge."

"I only pray our heads don't end up there along with his," Gus joined- in. "I fear our agreement to perform *Richard II* yesterday could be the end of us."

"It's a valid concern," I replied. "But, remember, we didn't speak with Essex or Southhampton, only Lord Mounteagle. I pray none of us participated in the march. The Queen and her court enjoy our plays. We're mere players, not courtiers, soldiers, or governmental officials. We're not a threat to the government; the entertainments we provide help them stay in power."

"I hear what you're saying, Will. But I'm still concerned the taint of treason will extend to us," Gus replied. "Look at what happened to that attorney, John Haywood. Last year he writes a history of Henry IV which includes the fall of Richard II. This year the Queen throws him into the tower for merely mentioning it!"

"Hear, hear, Gus," I said, trying to comfort us both. "There's a bit more to that story. First, Haywood was of higher social status than we are. Second, he dedicated his book to Lord Essex. We never mentioned Lord Essex in our performance yesterday afternoon. Third, his book contains criticisms of Richard II's inept government and governing council that have many parallels to the way people feel today about the Queen's government and the Privy Council. Finally, I wrote *Richard II* years ago, well before this current crisis was on the horizon."

As I marshaled my thoughts, I hoped the arguments I was rehearsing with Gus would carry the day if I was ever called upon to make them before the powers that be.

During the fearful days that followed, I tried to work off some of the nervous energy and tension I felt by pouring myself into my work on *Hamlet.* Immersed in my reflections upon Essex, Southampton, and their failed rebellion, as well as the impact that failure might have upon the many clandestine Catholic supporters of Essex and Southampton, including myself, I made substantial revisions to the play. I included the following speech by Hamlet that I revised further on several occasions over the years:

> To be, or not to be, that is the question: —
> Whether 'tis nobler in the mind, to suffer
> The slings and arrows of outrageous fortune;
> Or to take arms against a sea of troubles,
> And, by opposing, end them? – To die, — to sleep, —
> No more; — and, by a sleep, to say we end
> The heart-ach, and the thousand natural shocks
> That flesh is heir to, — 'tis a consummation
> Devoutly to be wish'd. To die; — to sleep; —
> To sleep! perchance to dream; ay, there's the rub;
> For in that sleep of death what dreams may come,

When we have shuffled off this mortal coil,
Must give us pause: There's the respect,
That makes calamity of so long life:
For who would bear the whips and scorns of time,
The oppressor's wrong, the proud man's contumely,
The pangs of despis'd love, the law's delay,
The insolence of office, and the spurns
That patient merit of the unworthy takes,
When he himself might his quietus make
With a bare bodkin? who would fardels bear,
To grunt and sweat under a weary life;
But that the dread of something after death,
The undiscover'd country, from whose bourn
No traveller returns, — puzzles the will;
And makes us rather bear those ills we have,
Than fly to others that we know not of?
Thus conscience does make cowards of us all;
And thus the native hue of resolution
Is sicklied o'er with the pale cast of thought;
And enterprises of great pith and moment,
With this regard, their currents turn awry,
And lose the name of action.

This speech expresses the many fears, concerns, and doubts we Catholics experience daily in a country where we must live as ghostly outlaws hiding in plain sight. What we should or can do about the oppression that envelops us is indeed the most important *Question* of our lives.

As it turned out, it was Gus and not I who ended up having to testify before the Privy Council during their lightning fast investigation of the Essex Rebellion. Before that occurred, we shareholders were able to confirm, by the grace of God, none of the members of our company joined Essex to participate in the march upon Whitehall.

At the Privy Council hearing, Gus was able to state we never met with Essex or Southhampton concerning the performance. The fact it was a paid "command" performance helped, as did the fact there was little loss of life in the rebellion. We pled complete ignorance, and begged forgiveness. Many of our friends at court, including the Herbert brothers, put in a good word on our behalf.

Gus's performance before the Privy Council was the finest one he ever gave. It undoubtedly saved the company, our livelihood, and, quite possibly, our necks. None of us forgot it. When Gus died suddenly a few years later, our company paid his funeral expenses, and we all attended his funeral service.

Chapter LIII
The Virgin Queen

Even Gus's stellar performance did not enable us to completely avoid the Queen's censure. The Master of the Revels made us turn over the 40 shillings we received for the performance to the Crown. And, on February 24, 1601, the evening before Lord Essex's execution within the precincts of the Tower of London, we were summoned to give a command performance of *Richard II* before Queen Elizabeth and her court.

To say that performance was one of our most stressful is an understatement. At its conclusion, all of us actors in the company knelt down on stage, and penitentially said the customary prayer for the long life, health, and safety of the Queen.

The Queen appeared to watch me intently as we prayed for her. After the performance ended, and she retired to her private rooms, she gave orders for Robert Cecil to summon and escort me to a personal audience. As I walked down the hallway of the palace by Lord Cecil's side, my mind was reeling. In all the years I had appeared before her, the Queen had never summoned me to meet with her in private.

The closest she had ever come to doing so was after a performance at court of my second play on the reign of Henry IV a few years earlier. The Queen had asked me to come down off the stage and approach her. When I did, she asked me to write a play for her showing Sir John Falstaff in love, and to do so in time for the Knights of the Garter induction ceremony six weeks later. I wrote like a madman to meet that royal deadline, producing *The Merry Wives of Windsor* in time to perform it for her and the Knights of the Garter in conjunction with the ceremony at Windsor Castle.

This occasion, however, was much different. As we walked past the halberd wielding guards at the entrance to the Queen's private chambers, I could not help but think about Lords Essex and Southhampton, waiting in the cold stone Tower for the black clad executioner and his finely-honed axe. On numerous occasions, I had gazed up at the rotting, severed heads as I walked under the south entrance of London Bridge. I could not help thinking the woman I was about to speak with had it within her power to place my own head on a pike up there with the others.

The large carved-oak chamber door swung open to reveal a well-lit, richly appointed room. The smooth, dressed-stone floor was partly covered by a black and red Turkish carpet containing repetitive geometric designs. On two of the walls hung richly woven Flemish tapestries of biblical subjects. One was of Judith, holding a curved sword accompanied by a turbaned Moorish servant, carrying the bloody, glassy-eyed severed head of Holofernes on a golden platter. The other was that of a dark curly-haired Daniel, praying among a pride of saw-toothed lions in the Lions' Den.

A large part of the wall directly in front of me was occupied by a huge gray marble fireplace, with figures of carved dragons on either side of the mantle. Within that fireplace, a yule log burned fiercely, sporting numerous red, orange and yellow dancing tongues of fire. Above the fireplace hung an oil painting of an armor-clad St. George on horseback, thrusting the point of his lance into an enraged, green-scaled, fire-breathing dragon.

The Queen sat at the head of an ornately carved table. A silver, eight- wick candelabra rested in the center of the finely buffed and polished tabletop. She was still dressed in the elegant pearl and jewel encrusted outfit that graced her at the performance of the just completed play. She wore a richly brocaded red silk dress with white lace sleeves. Draped around her neck were several long strands of large white pearls. Within the radius of these strings of pearls, she wore a thick-chained gold necklace bearing her famous Phoenix pendant.

The Phoenix was made of solid gold and had diamonds for eyes. It stood upright, its feathered wings fully extended outward. Elizabeth was often known as the "Phoenix" by many of her admirers. The mythical Arabian bird symbolizes power, virginity and longevity. The legend holds, when an existing Phoenix consumes itself in fire, a new Phoenix rises from its ashes.

Elizabeth's red-wigged head was framed by an intricate and transparent semicircular halo of snowflake-like, starched lace.

The Queen's face was covered by a layer of white, egg-shell colored makeup. Her lips were accented by glistening cherry lipstick.

When I arrived at the other side of the table as directed by Lord Cecil, I stood still, removed my short brimmed felt hat, and bowed. As I raised my head, the Queen's eyes fixed upon mine. While she sized me up, her lips slowly wound themselves into a mysterious smile.

As she began speaking, I glimpsed her front teeth. They were blackened by decades of frequent consumption of sugared dishes.

"Master William Shakespeare of Stratford," she began. "I asked Lord Cecil to summon you here this evening because I have questions for you. You and your group of players have enjoyed the privilege of performing before the court on numerous occasions over the last seven years. True?"

"Yes, your Highness," I said, dropping my head, and lowering my eyes to the marble tiled floor.

"You've enjoyed great favor from myself, and the members of my court?"

"Yes, your Highness," I responded sheepishly. "We are most appreciative of the extraordinary graces you have bestowed upon us," I hastily added.

"If that's so, why would you agree to perform *Richard II*, with the forbidden scene showing the removal of the king's crown and power, on the afternoon before an attempt to depose me and possibly take my life?" she countered, as effectively as a skilled lawyer cross-examining a witness.

Looking into her icy stare, I responded with an air of earnest desperation: "I and our entire company apologize for this horrible mistake. We are merely players. It was a request from personages of much higher social status, made on behalf of Lords Southhampton and Essex. We had no ability to refuse."

"So Mr. Phillips testified," the Queen announced matter-of-factly. "But you, Mr. Shakespeare, are one of the most intelligent men of our age. I know this for a fact, having seen many of your plays. You're asking me to believe you're no more perceptive than Bottom the Weaver in your *A Midsummer Night's Dream*."

"While I am deeply flattered by your Highness's comments regarding my intelligence, I assure your Highness I am undeserving. I profess my utmost loyalty to you and your government. I knew nothing of the plot against you," I said trying to blunt her anger.

"Your father's a recusant; is he not?" she continued.

"My father was fined for recusancy some years ago, your Highness. I do not believe he has been fined in the recent past. I've never been."

"I see," said the Queen with a touch of sarcasm. "So, you're asking us to believe you're a horse of a different color." The Queen considered the point for a few seconds, before going on, "Like the Roman Catholic composer, William Byrd, I've been willing to tolerate your presence at court performances, whatever your beliefs, providing you're willing to keep them to yourself. But I will not tolerate disloyalty in any of my subjects. That includes you, Mr. Shakespeare," she said in a shrill voice. "Do we have an understanding?"

"We do, your Highness," I replied. "But I believe..."

"Hear! Hear! No more nonsense," she cut me off. "We're finished. Mark my words, if any hint of you or your company's disloyalty comes my way, your career, and that of the other players, is finished! You'll lose your patronage, your possessions will be forfeit to the Crown, and much worse. You'll regret the day you were born. Remove yourself from my presence!" she said with relish.

While I bowed low, before being escorted from the room by Lord Cecil, the Queen began calling out in a manner causing her words to echo off the walls in the stony chamber:

"You artists are such fools! Always building castles in the sands. Walls, turrets, draw bridges, all fashioned by hand. Only to see them besieged and washed away by the sea, careening in and out, endlessly. Idealists, harmless dreamers, you artists may sometimes be. Tread carefully, Mr. Shakespeare. All dreams someday wither and die. Tears of love and mercy don't always descend from the sky," she concluded, fire in her eyes.

Upon exiting the Queen's chamber, a grim-faced Lord Cecil led me back down the hall to where the other players were now preparing to leave the palace. Before parting company, Lord Cecil growled: "I hope you listened carefully to what Her Majesty said. You're fortunate to have been granted a second chance. Some at court wanted your head served up for supper on a silver platter."

"There will be no further problems, I assure you," I replied.

"Your life depends upon it," Lord Cecil warned, before striding off across the room to join in a conversation with two other courtiers.

On our way out of the palace, Gus asked, "What happened?"

"She gave us a warning," I replied.

"What type of warning," asked Gus, concern showing in his voice.

"She said, if we do anything she considers disloyal, our careers are over. We'll all die in disgrace."

"You're kidding," Gus said.

"Unfortunately, I'm not," I replied. "Before we parted, Lord Cecil intimated we could all lose our lives, not just our careers."

"We're not out of the woods yet!" Gus exclaimed.

"Let's call everyone together tomorrow morning," I replied. "We have to make sure they all understand the stakes, and immediately cut any ties they have with those who supported Essex or Southhampton."

"It's sad," said Gus.

"We've no choice. We have to think of our families," I replied with an air of grim determination.

CHAPTER LIV
THE PHOENIX & THE TURTLE

For the next two years, we all walked on eggshells. We knew the government had spies in the audience of each of our performances. There might even be paid informers within the company.

Regarding the fate of the "rebels," Lord Essex was beheaded the day after my meeting with the Queen. Several lesser co-conspirators were also executed. Due to the desperate entreaties of family and friends, including his mother and his wife, a former maid of honor to Queen Elizabeth, and the fact he was a "follower" rather than a "leader," Lord Southampton's death sentence was commuted. He remained imprisoned in the Tower for the remainder of Queen Elizabeth's reign. Lord Monteagle was imprisoned for approximately six months, and he was fined the astronomical sum of eight thousand pounds.

Several months after the executions, I was invited to contribute a poem to a collection being put together to honor a member of the aristocracy instrumental in helping to suppress the Essex Rebellion. It was a request I could not refuse. By contributing, I would be publicly demonstrating my loyalty to the Queen and her government.

But I knew the Queen would not live forever. Rumors were rampant the next ruler of England would be James VI of Scotland, son of the executed Mary Queen of Scots. Given a prime goal of the Essex Rebellion had allegedly been to place James VI on the throne, and there was a distinct possibility Lord Southhampton might soon again come into favor, writing the poem was going to be a tightrope act.

Under these circumstances, I needed to write a work seen as complementary to the Queen, but which also could be interpreted positively by what remained of the Essex faction. As I contemplated the matter more deeply, I eventually settled upon the Phoenix and the Turtle Dove as symbols which would bring my themes of love, loss, trust, and rebirth to life. Using this symbolism, I could construct a poem open to multiple interpretations.

I worked on the verses for days on end, going through a half-dozen drafts before I had a product with the right mix of imagery and themes to satisfy anyone's political persuasion. When it was complete, I brought it with me to the Globe. Meeting there with Gus and Bert, I recited it to them to ensure it would pass muster. Summoning up my best stage voice, I began:

Let the bird of loudest lay,
On the sole Arabian tree,
Herald sad and trumpet be,
To whose sound chaste wings obey.

But thou shrieking harbinger,
Foul pre-currer of the fiend,
Auger of the fever's end,
To this troop come thou not near.

From this session interdict
Every fowl of tyrant wing
Save the eagle, feather'd king:
Keep the obsequy so strict.

Let the priest in surplice white,
That defunctive music can,

Be the death-divining swan,
Lest the *requiem* lack his right.

And thou, treble-dated crow,
That thy sable gender mak'st
With the breath thou givest and talk'st,
'Mongst our mourners shalt thou go.

Here the anthem doth commence:
Love and constancy is dead;
Phoenix and the turtle fled
In a mutual flame from hence.

So they lov'd as love in twain
Had the essence but in one;
Two distincts, division none;
Number there in love was slain.

Hearts remote, yet not asunder:
Distance, and no space was seen
'Twixt the turtle and his queen:
But in them it were a wonder.

So between them did love shine,
That the turtle saw his right
Flaming in the phoenix' sight:
Either was the other's mine.

Property was thus appall'd,
That the self was not the same;
Single nature's double name
Neither two nor one was call'd

Reason, in itself confounded,
Saw division grow together;
To themselves yet either-neither,
Simple were so well compounded.

That it cried, how true a twain
Seemeth this concordant one!
Love hath reason, reason none,
If what parts can so remain.

Whereupon it made this threne
To the phoenix and the dove,
Co-supremes and stars of love;
As chorus to their tragic scene.

Threnos

Beauty, truth, and rarity,
Grace in all simplicity,
Here inclos'd in cinders lie.

Death is now the phoenix nest;
And the turtle's loyal breast
To eternity doth rest,

Leaving no posterity: —
'T was not their infirmity,
It was married chastity.

Truth may seem, but cannot be:
Beauty brag, but 'tis not she;
Truth and beauty buried be.

To this urn let those repair
That are either true or fair;
For these dead birds sigh a prayer.

When I finished, both Gus and Bert began clapping, and nodding their approval.

"Well done," Bert said.

"Great," Gus added. "Not only is it open to multiple interpretations concerning the Queen, Essex and others. It symbolizes the end of an era. The beginning of a world to come."

While I walked home, my boots leaving footprints in the freshly fallen snow, I realized Gus was right. The curtain was slowly falling on the last act of Elizabeth's reign. And the poem I had written was in one sense an elegy for the hopes and promises there had once been for us all.

What Gus and Bert would never know was there was an even deeper, hidden layer of meaning to the poem I had written. To the few closet Catholics who had the symbolic "keys" which could unlock its relic chest of meaning, the poem was also a eulogy for the recent Catholic martyr, Ann Line. She, along with two priests she was harboring, had been hung at Tyburn earlier that year.

Ann had married a Catholic husband who died in exile after being forcibly separated from her by the authorities years earlier. Upon their separation, and again after his subsequent death, Ann took a vow of chastity, dedicating her life to the service of the Lord.

Ann was a very important pillar of the underground Catholic community I belonged to in London. I first had the pleasure of her acquaintance when I attended a private reception she gave for the senior Jesuit priest, Henry Garnet, after his arrival in the city. Subsequently, I met her on numerous occasions when I went to Confession or received Communion from one of the priests staying with her.

For many years, Ann Line's boarding house served as the most important London safe house for Catholic priests in hiding. After numerous close calls, the mercenary priest hunters and paid informers finally caught up with their "prey."

Despite the risk and mortal danger constantly surrounding her, Ann always maintained a cheerful and positive disposition. Her soul possessed far more than its fair share of the milk of human kindness.

From what I've heard, Ann bore her imprisonment well. She persevered in her faith throughout her ordeal and martyrdom. She ran her race successfully, living a truly blessed life. Although I had never met Ann's husband, he also suffered greatly for his faith. By all accounts, they shared a deep and abiding love for each other and their Creator. Ann Line and her husband were the inner, spiritual "Phoenix" and "Turtle" of my poem.

The "treble dated crow" and "priest in surplice white" was father Henry Garnet, the chief priest of the Jesuit mission to England. "The bird of loudest lay" was my good friend, the Catholic musician and court composer, William Byrd.

I was privileged to attend the secret Requiem Mass said for the soul of Ann Line. It was celebrated by Henry Garnet, accompanied by the exquisite music of William Byrd.

As the character, Duke Thesus says in my play *Twelfth Night*, written about this time: "If music be the food of love, play on…."

Ann Line and her husband lived their lives in the presence of the music of the Celestial Sphere, which only the Choirs of Angels and Saints here on earth can hear. My poem is merely a faint echo of their glory!

Chapter LV
Southwell, Topcliffe & Forman

In those days, attendance at Church of England services was mandatory for all but a select few. If you did not attend, you were fined heavily and placed on a list of recusants which led to further repression and persecution. Attendance at a forbidden Roman Catholic Mass would result in imprisonment or worse. There were, however, Jesuit priests in the country and the city who held clandestine services despite the risk to life and limb.

If a priest was caught, there was a good chance he would be tortured, convicted as a traitor, and hung, drawn, and quartered. It happened to several persons I knew quite well, including an old friend, Robert Dibdale, from my days in Stratford, and a distant cousin, Robert Southwell, who was both a priest and a fine religious poet. Sadly, before being executed in 1595, Father Southwell was subjected to the rack and other unspeakable tortures by Queen Elizabeth's torturer in chief, the sadistic Richard Topcliffe.

Topcliffe specialized in the torture of priests. With the Queen's authorization, Topcliffe had Father Southwell transported to his home. There Topcliffe was able to torture Father Southwell in a personally designed chamber with torture devices of Topcliffe's own making. It is said Topcliffe even corresponded with the Queen regarding these torture sessions — sharing lurid details and the information he had extracted from his victims. If there was ever anyone possessed with aura of evil, it was Richard Topcliffe.

Father Southwell was a spiritual mystic. He believed a poet's highest calling was to give glory and praise to the Creator. His most well-known poem is "The Burning Babe" which recounts the narrator's wonderment at seeing a bright, flaming vision of the infant Christ child on Christmas day.

Father Southwell and I met on several occasions after I began working in the theater business. When he discovered I was writing a long poem about the unrequited love Venus had for Adonis, he expressed disappointment I was not directing my art to its highest calling — even going so far as penning an exhortation to me, as his cousin "W.S.," to take on more serious spiritual subjects and themes in my poetry and plays.

After Father Southwell's arrest and imprisonment, I did briefly turn my attention to what I hoped he would deem suitable subject matter — my long poem about the rape of Lucrece and sin of Tarquin.

But I was not in a position where I could afford to fully drink from the cup of sacrifice Father Southwell was offering. Given my family responsibilities, I could not take a public stand for my faith, as did my father, Robert Southwell, Robert Dibdale, and many others I admired. That being said, I did not meekly submit to being a conformist, betraying my faith like so many others. I devised quieter, less obvious ways to resist: writing poems and plays utilizing symbolism and espousing Christian virtues, attending clandestine Masses in the huge attic of a Blackfriars house I ended-up purchasing many years later, providing financial support to harried Catholic priests, and dodging mandatory Church of England services.

The fear and anger I experienced at having to live this double-life, including absenting myself at high-risk times from the rite of the Mass, and having to disguise the true messages of my artistic endeavors in oblique and sometimes obscure symbolism, found its best expression in a poem I wrote during the dark aftermath of the Essex Rebellion.

As an unperfect actor on the stage,
Who with his fear is put beside his part,
Or some fierce thing replete with too much rage,

Whose strength's abundance weakens his own heart,
So I, for fear of trust, forget to say
The perfect ceremony of love's rite,
And in my own love's strength seem to decay
O'ercharg'd with burthen of mine own love's might.
O let my books be then the eloquence
And dumb presages of my speaking breast;
Who plead for love, and look for recompense,
More than that tongue that more hath more express'd
O learn to read what silent love hath writ:
To hear with eyes belongs to love's fine wit.

Fortunately, around this time, a door opened allowing me to continue to avoid attending weekly government mandated services without coming to the attention of the authorities. Until this point, I avoided having to pay recusant fines through a combination of relying upon the power and influence of aristocratic Roman Catholic friends, moving frequently, and always renting rather than owning property in London. My rental arrangements were verbal rather than written, ensuring there was no paper trail for the investigators to follow. For the right price, one could always find a landlord willing to look the other way when it came to church attendance. It helps to have friends in both high and low places.

About a year prior to 1603, I found lodgings with a tavern owner, in the seedy neighborhood of the Clink on the south side of the Thames, near the Globe. As everyone in London knows, the Clink is one of the five notorious prisons in London, and the phrase "being thrown into the Clink" has come to mean being placed in the hades of a dank and dirty prison cell.

In any event, the Clink was an appropriate name for the neighborhood. It was filled with taverns, whorehouses called "stews," and gaming establishments. Families with resources did not live there. Drunks, pickpockets, cutpurses and common whores, also known as "punks," roamed the lanes and alleyways, robbing, stealing, seducing and waylaying those they could get their hands on.

Given the hazardous nature of my surroundings, I always carried my Scottish dirk with me when I left my room. Around the time of Queen Elizabeth's death, I decided I had experienced one too many close calls. It was time for a move. If the criminal element did not do me in, the taxman and the religious thought police would. My feet had again grown restless.

Luckily, around that time, I had the good fortune to discover a headdress maker we sometimes did business with had a room to let in a respectable business district within the city limits north of the Thames. The family I would be residing with was that of French Huguenot merchants, Christopher and Marie Mountjoy.

The Mountjoys lived in a spacious, two-story, half-timbered home located at the corner of Silver and Monkwell streets. Their daughter Mary, and their apprentice, Stephen Belott, lived with them. They all worked together in the portion of their home used as their workshop. There they manufactured the elaborate, delicate gold and silver wire headdresses, known as "tires," worn on special occasions by the wealthiest noble women at court.

In fact, after the reign of King James began, the Mountjoys were so proficient at their trade they were frequently tasked with manufacturing complex tires for Queen Anne.

In addition to providing a safe and relatively quiet place for me to live and work, residing with the Mountjoys gave me an additional asset I considered priceless — an exemption from the requirement of having to attend weekly Church of England services. As French Protestants, the Mountjoys, and all the members of their household, including lodgers like myself, enjoyed an exemption from the Church of England attendance requirement.

My relationship with the Mountjoys began quite some time before I became their tenant. My good friend, Richard Field, the printer from Stratford, who originally published *Venus and Adonis*, introduced me to them during a dinner he and his wife hosted for us.

Richard was one of those persons who appeared to have been born under a lucky star. His good fortune was so consistent he had no need for the services of astrologers or fortunetellers, such as Queen Elizabeth's astrologer, Dr. John Dee, or the satyr-like Simon Forman, a magus-like fortune teller who attended many of our plays and seemed to be as interested in seducing affection-starved housewives as he was in prognosticating upon their futures.

I remember being bored by Forman one evening, when, after attending a performance of our play *Julius Caesar*, he invited me out for a couple of drinks at a nearby tavern that turned out to be a thinly disguised stew.

When we walked through the open front door of the establishment, we were accosted by one of the resident punks who, like the other girls working at the bar, and entertaining customers at the tables, was bare–breasted, advertising her "wares" to male patrons such as ourselves.

The smoke-filled air of the main room was filled with an unpleasant aroma that was a mixture of human sweat, tobacco smoke, and the sickly-sweet smell of sour ale. The redhaired, freckle-faced punk, who looked to be about the age of my eldest daughter, Susanna, showed us to an empty table, and said with a smile, "Afternoon gentlemen. What'll you have?"

"I think I'll have you, my sweet little tart," said Simon Forman, his dark black eyes fixed upon her milk white breasts.

"Please draw me a pint of your best ale," I said. "The same for my friend," I added.

Having taken our order, the girl headed off to the bar. Simon watched her for a second, stroking his pointed goatee.

"A sight for sore eyes." he said, fixing his unsettling gaze upon me before changing the subject:

"I commend you for writing that Roman play. I enjoyed it immensely. I think it's one of your best."

"Thank you," I replied.

"I enjoy plays. I believe there's much that can be gleaned about human nature and motivations from them," Forman continued. "I often take notes upon the plots. This allows me to reflect upon their true meanings. Do you have hidden agendas, subtle messages you wish your audiences to take away?" he asked, leaning his swarthy face towards me.

Before I could answer, the young, freckle-faced girl returned with our pints. After Dr. Forman paid her, whispering something in her ear which brought a world-weary laugh, I answered his question cautiously:

"We players don't put much thought into the inner meaning of our plays. Theater is a business. We're all working to entertain the audience. If we don't please the public, we don't survive. It's as simple as that." I said, before taking a deep draught of the sweet, fermented ale.

"That might be what you say. But I have it on good authority that‘s not the way it is for certain other playwrights," Simon Forman responded.

"Who are you speaking of?" I asked with true concern, for I did construct many of my plays with a hidden pro-Catholic subtext. My most recent use of such a subtext was in my play

Twelfth Night. In that play, the sour-faced killjoy, Malvolio, represented the Puritan enemies of the theaters, and we players who make our living in them.

"Why that of your rival, the late, great Kit Marlowe," Dr. Forman responded. "I ate and drank with him right here in this tavern on many occasions when his plays were being performed on the stage — acted by the equally great Edward Alleyn. I can still hear Alleyn's booming voice speaking the moving lines of *Tamburlaine*, *The Jew of Malta*, *The Massacre at Paris*, and *Dr. Faustus*. I know *Faustus* by heart. Like Faustus, I've given up much to obtain the knowledge and power I possess. I sometimes wonder whether I'll have to pay a similar price."

"Marlowe was a great poet and playwright," I stated. "I learned how to write blank verse by studying the artistry of his line. We worked on *Titus Andronicus* together. I've also seen performances of each of the plays you've mentioned, and I shared more than a few pipes of tobacco with him before his untimely death in that boarding house in Deptford."

"A terrible tragedy," Dr. Forman remarked. "When I heard the news, it brought tears to my eyes."

"Mine too. So young. Such a promising future."

"You're right. The final chorus of *Dr. Faustus* is a fitting epitaph to Marlowe's life," Dr. Forman said. He began chanting from memory:

> Cut is the branch that might have grown full
> straight,
> And burned is Apollo's laurel-bough,
> That sometime grew within this learned man.
> Faustus is gone: regard his hellish fall,
> Whose fiendful fortune may exhort the wise,

Only to wonder at unlawful things,
Whose deepness doth entice such forward wits
To practise more than heavenly power permits.

Looking back these many years, much in Simon Forman's conversation was true. In many ways, he did resemble Dr. Faustus. The strange power he exercised over some of his women patients ruined the happiness of many a marriage. What price he may pay for it only God knows.

Chapter LVI
A River Transit

My conversation with Simon Forman occurred shortly before I began residing with the Mountjoys. As previously mentioned, I first met Christopher and Marie Mountjoy at the home of my printer and publisher friend, Richard Field. I had known Richard since childhood. We studied Latin together at the King Edward VI School. Richard left Stratford to come to London as a printer's apprentice a few years before me.

When Richard moved to London, he was only fourteen. Apprenticeship was a seven to ten year affair. Since a large percentage of books were printed in Latin, knowledge of Latin as well as English was necessary.

Although I don't use much Latin in my poetry and plays, the study of the Latin poets Ovid, Virgil, and Horace, and the plays of Terence and Platus, were of tremendous influence upon my development as a poet and playwright. In these ways, the expense of time and spirit Richard and I made studying Latin was well recompensed.

About the time Richard was completing his apprenticeship, his master died. Richard continued working with his master's widow, Jacqueline, for a time. One thing leading to another, Richard married Jackie a year or so after her former husband's death. This gave Richard the reins of a successful business early in life.

Richard's good fortune was also a lucky break for me. The printing press Richard and his wife ran published a wide variety of books. During the early years of my career, Richard often lent me copies of books I wanted to read. On occasion, he would even give me a copy of a book I especially liked as a gift.

In return, on several occasions, I arranged for Richard and Jackie to attend performances of our plays at the Globe as my guests, making sure they were able to view the performances from cushioned seating in the three-penny covered gallery.

My friendship with Richard was socially valuable. We both shared gossip we received from Stratford. We often reminisced about people we knew, and events we experienced growing up in that small town. Richard and Jacqueline also invited me into their circle of London friends, allowing me to become acquainted with numerous members of the French Huguenot community.

The Huguenots were Calvinistic Protestants who fled the Civil War of religion between the Catholic and Protestant factions fighting for control of the French government in the 1560s and 1570s. The greatest atrocity of that conflict, often termed "The Massacre at Paris," was the mass murder of Huguenots by members of the Catholic Guise faction on St. Bartholomew's Day, 1572. Thousands were stabbed, clubbed, and hacked to death. The violence that attack ignited spread throughout France.

Fearing for their lives, many Huguenots fled to Protestant England. England welcomed them. One of Elizabeth's most important advisors, Francis Walsingham, who ran the English government's network of foreign spies, was on government business in Paris the day of the massacre. He personally witnessed many of the atrocities.

Upon his safe return to England, Walsingham was a strong advocate for the Huguenots, as was Queen Elizabeth, the most important Protestant ruler of the time, and one considered a "bastard" by the Pope and many of her Catholic rivals. Jacqueline Field and her deceased husband had been among the Huguenot refugees, as were Christopher and Marie Mountjoy.

Now, to return to that memorable evening at the Fields. As a player my social position in society was not high. Most religiously zealous persons shunned us. Because acting involved role-playing, they considered it lying. In other words, to be an actor was to sin for a living.

Adding grease to the fire, the bawdy humor and wit, a necessary part of a successful play, was considered obscene by many religious people. Finally, zealots universally believed diversions like plays, bear-baiting, bull-baiting, and cock-fighting, kept people away from God, diverting them from prayer and proper worship of the Deity.

The fact theater audiences consisted of men and women from all walks and stations in life, including the criminal and sexually promiscuous, was cited as proof of Satan's presence in the playhouses by the Puritan preachers I often heard sermonizing on the raised platform of the Cross outside St. Paul's Cathedral.

So, the invitation I received to dine with Richard, Jackie, and their urbane, cosmopolitan friends was a welcome one. To look the part of a prosperous gent, I donned my best doublet jacket, black velvet britches, silken hose, and a pair of recently purchased silver-buckled black leather shoes I obtained from an ancient shoemaker whose shop was on the main thoroughfare of Cheapside.

Not wanting to attend dinner empty-handed, before proceeding to the nearest jetty on the muddy bank of the Thames, I ducked into a vinter's shop and purchased a flagon of white Spanish wine.

To reach the Fields' residence, I had to take one of the many wherries ferrying people across the river during the day and early evening. Fortunately, I was able to obtain a seat in the boat rowed and piloted by well-known wherryman, John Taylor. Like many boatmen, John fancied himself a jack of all trades and a sparkling wit to boot. As he rowed his customers from one side of the river to the other, he would often entertain them with tall tales of his adventures, and impromptu witticisms he invented on the fly.

Although I questioned the truth of much of what John said, I loved him as a man. And I enjoyed our gabbing banter during the journeys we shared.

Carefully stepping into John's wherry, I asked: "What zany thoughts are swimming in the millpond of your mind today?"

"Just minnows. It's been grueling," he answered. "Lots of rocks and rapids. Wife's giving me the business. Thinks I'm tight-fisted. Says I keep her on a short leash. Treat her no better than our pet spaniel. She stuck it to me last night. Acted like Katharina in your play about the shrew. I didn't sleep much. I'll tell you that!"

"So sorry. I hope it blows over this evening. Time heals all wounds," I added, in the most cheerful voice I could muster.

"I hope so. Whatever I do, I does it for her own good. Kate, I says, if you can't control yourself, your spending habits will get us thrown into Newgate. And we've no rich relations to bail us out!"

Before John could cast off, we were joined at the last minute by a passenger who leapt into the boat with the nimbleness of an acrobat. The late arrival was a fashionably dressed young man carrying a lute. As John pulled the oars, the young man began strumming the strings of his instrument while singing the lyrics of Kit Marlowe's most popular work, "The Passionate Shepherd to His Love."

Come live with me and be my love,
And we will all the pleasures prove,
That hills and valleys, dale and field,
And all the craggy mountains yield.

There will we sit upon the rocks,
And see the shepherds feed their flocks,

By shallow rivers, to whose falls
Melodious birds sing madrigals.

There will I make thee beds of roses
With a thousand fragrant posies,
A cap of flowers, and a kirtle
Embroidered all with leaves of myrtle;

A gown made of the finest wool
Which from our pretty lambs we pull;
Fair lined slippers for the cold
With buckles of the purest gold;

A belt of straw, and ivy buds,
With coral clasps and amber studs:
And, if these pleasures may thee move,
Than live with me and be my love.

The shepherd swains shall dance and sing
For thy delight each May morning;
If these delights thy mind may move,
Then live with me and be my love.

Listening to the young man's strong tenor resonate over the strokes of the oars, I once again found my thoughts pondering the mystery of Kit's death, as I have done many times before and since.

As the curtain of my wandering thoughts descended on the scene of Marlowe's demise, the singer sharing the wherry with me ended his rendition of the song with a flourish. The young man had a pleasant voice and had played his lute well.

Politely clapping, I said, "Well done."

"Appreciate the compliment, Master Shakespeare," he acknowledged with a smile.

"You know who I am?"

"I attend plays at the Globe when I can. I'm reading law at Gray's Inn."

"An aspiring young lawyer! I was once a scrivener in a lawyer's office back in Warwickshire," I shared, while John Taylor brought the bobbing wherry alongside the landing.

After paying John, I stepped off the boat onto the landing, saying goodbye to my young companion, "I wish you well, young friend."

"You too," he answered, briskly striding ahead of me and disappearing into the late afternoon crowd of city residents returning home after a hard day's work.

While making my way towards the Field's home on Silver Street, I began singing a song to myself which I had heard a strolling balladeer perform a few days before. The balladeer, who spoke and sang with a Scottish accent, began his street performance by playing a spirited tune on the bagpipes. Many of the onlookers danced. He then sang the song I now found myself singing.

Oh, when I was a lad of nine,
I learned to write and sing in rhyme,
And, when I was a boy of ten,
I used an inkhorn for my pen.

The papers flapped and blew away
Every word that I could say.

I loved to hug, kiss and play,
All the darling buds of May!

So, when I grew to be a man,
I danced my way through marriage banns,
Through petticoats and Spanish fans,
I plucked laced strings with my hands.

But when I heard the drums and fifes,
The footsteps of approaching night,
I played the pipes with all my might
To win back over my jealous wife!

Though I must go upon my way,
I'll make your love my daily pay,
We'll travel to the end of time,
While the bells of midnight chime!

Oh, when I was a lad of nine,
I loved to write and sing in rhyme!

Finishing this humorous trifle, I laughed to myself, drawing curious stares from passersby. "That lunatic!" "He's moonstruck!" "Belongs in Bedlam!" I imagined them saying to themselves. But the song was funny and catchy. Its words planted themselves in my memory.

My mind is strange that way. As a player, I had to memorize the lines of over thirty plays at a time. The public's appetite for plays is ravenous, fickle, and ever-changing. I was always on the lookout for new material.

It would not hurt the balladeer if we used this song in a performance at the Globe. Quite the contrary, it would be a compliment. Since he sang it better than any of us could, the popularity our use might engender could only be to his benefit.

When I next saw our current clown, Robert Armin, I would sing it for him. I was confident Robin would find it up to his high standards. The frantic nature of comedy demands constant interjection and juxtaposition of material. A humorous song like this, accompanied by the plucking of the lute in an antic manner, would make a nice interlude between the dancing and jokes concluding the afternoon play-going experience.

Nearing the Fields' home, I reflected upon the gift of comedy — the ability to make other people laugh was one of the greatest and rarest of gifts the Creator could give one of his creations. Comedians are one-of-a-kind. When God mints one, he breaks the mold.

Comedians are also notoriously hard people to get along with. They are perceptive enough to see through the masks and cloaks we use to conceal ourselves. Great comedians know we're all hypocrites at heart. Revealing our petty hypocrisies, they make us defensively laugh at ourselves.

Although not a comedian myself, I appreciate their art. And I wrote the best material I could for them to work their magic upon.

CHAPTER LVII
DINNER ON SILVER STREET

Finishing my thoughtful stroll through the city, I arrived at the home of my dear friends, Richard and Jacqueline. Within a few seconds of my knock, Jackie opened the door. Like many French women, her skin was darker than that of the English women filling the ranks of high society. Although Jackie was not considered a conventional beauty by aristocratic standards, I never shared that point of view.

I grew up in the country where women spend a lot of time working in the sun. The women I knew and admired had faces and hands with a healthy tan. Jackie had that glow year-round.

Handing the flagon of wine to Jackie, I kissed her on the lips. As interesting as it was, I often wondered about the origin of this English custom.

Jackie interrupted my momentary reverie. "Been awhile Will!"

"So it has! You're looking beautiful as always," I answered.

Jackie laughed coquettishly, showing her pearly white teeth.

"You know how to flatter us vain creatures. Being in the public eye, you're well-practiced singing the praises of Venus," she playfully said.

"Not as much as you suppose," I responded. "Between writing, acting, and helping to run the company, there's not time for much else. How's Richard?" I asked, changing the subject.

"Well," Jackie answered. "He's in the dining room with our guests, the Mountjoys. Shall we join them?"

"Lead on," I answered. "From the aroma, we're going to be sharing a wonderful supper."

"An aristocratic client gave the Mountjoys a shank of venison as a gift," Jackie explained. "There's also freshly killed hare, basted and buttered just the way you like it."

"Most impressive," I said, as we entered the well-appointed dining room — graced with fine French furniture.

Richard rose from his seat at the head of the polished table. Coming over and embracing me, he said, "So happy you could make it to our little repast."

"From what Jackie says, it's anything but little. Sounds like a feast for a king!"

"Thanks to the generosity of Christopher and Marie!"

While Richard spoke, he extended an outstretched arm towards the exquisitely dressed couple on the other side of the table.

"Glad to make your acquaintance," I said, assaying them for the first time.

Christopher Mountjoy appeared to be in his early forties. He was of average height and weight. He had a long, aquiline nose, small mouth, and slightly graying beard.

His wife Marie was a rare beauty. The type that causes men to write sonnets and carve names in the bark of trees. Her obsidian-colored eyes appeared to see straight into one's soul. Luxurious strands of black velvet hair lay loosely upon the low-cut portion of her pink taffeta dress. Her luminous face was framed by a halo of lace and sheer lawn fabric which rose in a semi-circle around her shapely head. As icing on the cake, Marie wore a diamond and ruby studded tiara.

Outside the circle of the royal court, I have not seen another woman as exquisitely attired as Marie Mountjoy that evening.

Bowing slightly, I said, "William Shakespeare, at your service."

I did so in a semi-humorous manner. For, while Marie certainly was dressed like someone of noble birth, her feet rested solidly upon the earth. She was the wife of a member of the merchant class.

Taking my deference in stride, Marie responded in a crystalline voice with a charming French accent, "Monsieur Shakespeare, there's no need to bow,"

"Someone of your grace and beauty deserves a bow. While many of those who rate a bow don't deserve one!" I quipped back.

"Your reputation as a wit is well deserved," remarked Christopher as we all sat down and the Fields' serving girls brought out the main dishes.

When the food was on the table, Richard said a quick grace. Then he carved the meat while one of the servants poured us each a glass of ruby-red Spanish wine.

Although the Fields could not afford silver plate, they possessed an exquisite set of wineglasses. As the servant poured the wine into Christopher's glass, he called out: "Nothing like sweet *vino* to go with fresh venison!"

"Verdad," I replied.

"This meat was a gift from one of our patrons. We provide her with tires and tiaras like the one Marie's wearing this evening."

"It's beautiful," I said.

"It should be. It would cost over three hundred pounds to purchase."

"Out of my league," I answered, spearing a piece of well-cooked meat. Between mouthfuls, I said, "Back in Stratford, you could buy four or five substantial homes for that price."

The rest of the meal was uneventful. Conversation revolved around the current events in the city, the scheduled public execution of a notorious highwayman at Tyburn, the latest court gossip, and numerous romantic liaisons between certain courtiers and Queen Elizabeth's "maids of honor."

Chapter LVIII
After-Dinner Entertainments

When the meal concluded, the Fields, the Mountjoys and I retired to the spacious parlor graced by a beautiful virginal they purchased several years earlier. Jackie asked if I would entertain them with a short excerpt from one of my plays. Although many people made similar requests, I rarely granted them. Acting in plays is what I did for a living. It was work, not something I enjoyed doing during my leisure time. But Jackie was not just anyone, so I asked her from which play she wished me to perform.

"Why not *The Taming of the Shrew*. Jackie's been acting like the headstrong Katharina lately," Richard cut-in.

"You've been mimicking that monkey man, Petruchio," Jacqueline replied with a toss of her head.

Not wanting to get caught in the marital crossfire between two friends, I suggested a compromise. "How about I perform something from the *Taming of the Shrew*, but from the induction, which features neither Katharina nor Petruchio."

Looking at Marie, now seated on a fireside bench beside her husband, I said, "Let's set the scene."

"A lord returns to an alehouse from the hunt. A drunken Warwickshire tinker, Christopher Sly, is passed out on a bench. A flight of fancy possesses the lord, and he decides to play a sly practical joke on our unsuspecting tinker. He has the tinker carried to his manor and placed in the lord's bedchamber. The lord further instructs his servants to do whatever is necessary to convince Christopher Sly he's master of the manor. When Sly awakes, the following ensues.

Sly: For God's sake, a pot of small ale.

First Servant: Will't please your honour drink a cup of sack?

Second Servant: Will't please your honour taste of these conserves?

Third Servant: What raiment will your honour wear today?

Sly: I am Christophero Sly; call not me — honour, nor lordship: I never drank sack in my life; and if you give me any conserves, give me conserves of beef: Ne'er ask me what raiment I'll wear; for I have no more doublets than backs, no more stockings than legs, nor no more shoes than feet; nay, sometimes, more feet than shoes, or such shoes as my toes look through the overleather.

Lord: Heaven cease this idle humour in your honour!
O, that a mighty man of such descent,
Of such possessions, and so high esteem,
Should be infused with so foul a spirit!

Sly: What, would you make me mad? Am not I Christopher Sly, old Sly's son of Burton-heath; by birth a pedlar, by education a card-maker, by transmutation a bear-herd, and now by present profession a tinker? Ask Marion Hacket, the fat ale wife of Wincot, if she know me not: if she say I am not fourteen pence on the score for sheer ale, score me up for the lyingest knave in Christendom.

At the end of my little performance, Richard laughed heartily.

"Ah Will, we had some fine times playing truant in that rickety Wincot alehouse. Marion Hacket was some character. Tough as nails! You were in to her for at least fourteen pence! I remember she took the cudgel down from above the fireplace threatening to beat the stuffing out of thee! I can still see you hightailing it out the door. And she waddling after you like a wounded duck. Those were great days!"

We all laughed at Richard's comic epilogue to my performance. Once the laughter subsided, Jackie stood up, went over to the virginal, and carefully sat down, trying not to wrinkle her dress.

"Will, in return for the entertainment you've just given us, I have something for you. A mutual friend has taught me a new galliard we all can all enjoy."

With that, Jackie's long fingers began to race along the keys, commonly known as "jacks," as we tapped to her quick, energetic performance. Finishing the galliard, Jacqueline continued, "Our same special friend also taught me a witty romantic song you authored."

Jacqueline began skillfully chanting with all the pacing and accented flair of an experienced chanteuse:

My mistress' eyes are nothing like the sun;
Coral is far more red than her lips' red:
If snow be white, why then her breasts are dun;
If hairs be wires, black wires grow on her head.
I have seen roses damask'd red and white,
But no such roses see I in her cheeks;
And in some perfumes is there more delight
Than in the breath that from my mistress reeks.
I love to hear her speak, — yet well I know
That music hath a far more pleasing sound;
I grant I never saw a goddess go, —
My mistress, when she walks, treads on the ground;
And yet by heaven, I think my love as rare
As any she bely'd with false compare.

As she finished, I clapped politely.

Richard said: "Well done! Encore!"

Acknowledging the applause, Jackie smiled. "Normally, I'd play another. But Marie has a surprise. Like me, she's studied for several years with our mutual friend — the brilliant Emilia Lanier of the Bassano family of court musicians. With Emilia's assistance, Marie has composed a piece of music in your honor."

"Really?" I asked, as Marie approached the virginal and changed places with Jackie.

While Marie's fingers passed over the keys, she said, "Mr. Shakespeare, while I respect you as one of the finest playwrights and actors on our stage, I most admire you as a poet. Although my first language is French, I've read and appreciated both your poems *Venus and Adonis* and *Lucrece*. So, when Emilia told me you've also written a series of unpublished sonnets which have circulated privately among your close friends, I begged her to share one with me, so I could set it to music and perform it for you. After some arm-twisting, she finally consented. That said, here's my gift to you this evening."

While I watched, Marie played a beautiful melody. She soon began singing in a clear, stage-worthy soprano:

> Shall I compare thee to a summer's day?
>
> Thou art more lovely and more temperate:
>
> Rough winds do shake the darling buds of May,
>
> And summer's lease hath all too short a date....

As Marie sang, her sweet voice and the languid tune she played carried me to another time and place. When she finished, I began steadily clapping. Fighting tears welling in my eyes, I said: "Thank you kindly." Gathering my composure, I continued:

"Mrs. Mountjoy, that is truly one of the greatest gifts anyone has given me. But now, I must ask a very great favor from you and my other friends in this room."

From her startled look, I sensed she could feel the pain leeching into my voice.

"Anything you desire," Marie instinctively assured. Richard, Jackie, and Christopher nodded their assent.

"Please don't sing that song to anyone else. It's a beautiful creation you have made, but certain sonnets I have written, especially that one, are not for mass consumption or performance. In many ways they're keys to my soul. They are too painful for me to recite. You can earn my gratitude by honoring my request. I don't think I could bear to hear common balladeers sing that one."

As I spoke, I could feel the atmosphere turn somber. But I also sensed their empathy. Each of us has our own crosses to bear. Whether those in the room understood it or not, although I had originally written the poem for Anne, the lines now seemed prophetic. Hearing them sung by Marie brought back sad memories of Hamnet.

To dispel the dark cloud that had come over an otherwise beautiful occasion, I quickly excused myself and slowly made my way back to my lodgings. It was difficult living alone here in London without my family. But it was safer for them to remain in Stratford. The pain of separation was one aspect of the personal cross I was called upon to bear in this veil of tears called life.

Arriving home with a dissatisfied mind, I purged my restless soul of its insomnia by penning the following lines to Anne.

O, never say that I was false of heart.
Though absence seem'd my flame to qualify.
As easy might I from my self depart,
As from my soul which in thy breast doth lie:

That is my home of love: if I have rang'd,
Like him that travels, I return again;
Just to the time, not with the time exchang'd, —
So that myself bring water for my stain.
Never believe, though in my nature reign'd
All frailties that besiege all kinds of blood,
That it could so preposterously be stain'd
To leave for nothing all thy sum of good;
For nothing this wide universe I call,
Save thou, my rose; in it thou art my all.

When I finished the poem, I said a prayer and journeyed off to sleep — dreaming of a long procession of gleaming starry-eyed goddesses, emerging from the zephyred winds and caressing foam of the Serene Sea of Tranquility.

CHAPTER LIX
CHANGE OF VENUE

Some years after that memorable dinner, my residence at the home of Christopher and Marie Mountjoy began. Edmund was now in his early twenties, well on his way towards establishing himself as an actor in his own right.

Although he still often performed with my own acting company, Edmund remained a journeyman player. Partnership was still several years over the horizon. As such, Edmund played with multiple acting companies while building his resume. So, when he had the opportunity to take a lucrative contract with Philip Henslowe, Edward Alleyn and the Admiral's Men, who were now playing at the newly built Fortune Theater, across the river and on the other side of town, Edmund jumped at the opportunity.

Our construction of the Globe in 1599, close by the older and smaller Rose, undoubtedly cut into the gate receipts at the always damp and shoddily built Rose. Philip Henslowe and the Lord Admirals Men wisely decided to build themselves a newer and larger theater in another part of town. This proved a win-win situation for all concerned.

Edmund was eager to strike out on his own. He now had a serious long-term girlfriend. Although I did not think she would make a good life partner for my brother, that was Edmund's business, not mine. He was now at an age where he could manage his own affairs without his older brother looking over his shoulder, second-guessing his decisions.

Given Edmund's impressive development as a character actor, I had no doubt he was well on his way to becoming a shareholder of our own company or another by the time he was thirty, the age at which I became a founding shareholder of the Lord Chamberlain's Men.

When Edmund moved out of the rooms we shared, I determined a change of venue would do me good. By this point, my business relationship with the Mountjoys was significant. As wig and tire makers, they provided us with both commodities on a much-needed basis.

Although Christopher rarely attended plays, Marie was a semi-regular. Given Marie had several servants, and a young adult daughter to assist with household chores, Marie had the time and financial resources to attend many of our performances with her favorite gossips.

To attract the widest audience possible, our plays strove to appeal to both men and women. I remember Marie telling me her favorite play was *The Merry Wives of Windsor* because it featured two intelligent housewives, Mistress Page and Mistress Ford, who outwit the aging knight, Sir John Falstaff, as well as their own husbands. It is clear who really runs the shows in their households.

Of course, all women enjoy a play which portrays women outwitting men, as much as men enjoy a play featuring men outwitting women. From a playwright's perspective, there is a great deal of money to be made in portraying spirited battles of the sexes.

I had certainly mined this golden vein many times over, in *The Taming of the Shrew*, *Much Ado About Nothing*, *The Merry Wives of Windsor*, and Portia's role in *The Merchant of Venice*.

After several performances she attended, Marie brought her gossips backstage to meet "my talented friend, Mr. William Shakespeare."

I heard rumors Marie formerly had several lovers, but I never saw any evidence of infidelity in her actions during the time I knew her. Gifted with an outgoing personality, she was an unusually good conversationalist. She had a fine wit and enjoyed a good joke.

From previous conversations with Christopher and Marie, I knew they occasionally had a room to rent in their large rambling residence and workshop at the corner of Monkwell and Silver streets. I was also aware, as nominal members of London's French Church, they, and all members of their household, including lodgers, were exempt from having to attend weekly Church of England services.

I have always been proud that, over the quarter century I spent working in London, I never once attended a service of the Church of England. This is a record rarely equaled by other recusants.

When one afternoon, after a spirited performance of *The Taming of the Shrew*, Marie and two of her friends stopped by, I decided to raise the issue of my desire to change lodgings. As Marie and her fashionably attired friends approached, I asked, "Hope you ladies enjoyed the performance?"

Marie answered, "We always enjoy your plays. They have interesting characters and excellent wit. Whenever I see the induction scene to this one, it brings back fond memories of the dinner at Richard's and Jackie's. But, while my friends and I thoroughly enjoyed this play, there's a way you can make one better!"

"How?" I asked, smiling.

"It would be nicer if you could write a sequel where Katherina tames Petruchio. I guarantee we women would love it!"

"Good idea," I answered. "Perhaps it could be called *The Shrew's Revenge*."

"Perhaps," Marie responded. "But I have an even better title in mind."

"What's that?" I asked.

"*The Tamer Tamed*," she suggested.

"Not bad!" I answered. Framing my chin between my thumb and forefinger, I said, "I can picture the victorious Katherina now. Dressed in men's attire, including high black leather boots, whip in hand!"

"And the half-drunk, hung-over Petruchio moaning before her in a cage!" one of Marie's friends interjected.

"It has possibilities," I responded. "There's much there worth considering."

Sadly, like most good ideas people come up with, this one never came to fruition during Marie's lifetime. But it served as the seed of a later play called *The Tamer Tamed* written by John Fletcher, my sometime collaborator and my successor as chief playwright of the King's Men.

Many years later, I discussed the idea of a sequel to *The Taming of the Shrew* with John. To make the storyline more believable, we decided the headstrong Petruchio would be "tamed" by his second wife, a woman even more shrewish, witty and shrewd than Katherina.

As Marie foresaw, *The Tamer Tamed* was even more popular than *The Taming of the Shrew*. Although John wrote the play without my assistance, he did graciously allow me to name Petruchio's new wife. I named her Maria.

During my meeting with Marie and her friends, I discovered Marie and Christopher had a large room to rent for a very reasonable rate. Marie assured me she'd talk the matter over with Christopher that evening.

As Marie and her two gossips exited the backstage area in their finery, I heard her say: "Imagine! I'll soon have the greatest playwright in the land living under my roof!"

Listening to Marie's and her friends' chatter, my lips formed a smile. If it was always so easy to please people, life would be simple.

The day after our conversation, Marie sent their apprentice, Stephen, over to the Globe to give me the good news — we had a deal! A week later, I was ready to move.

In the interim, I wrote a letter to Anne and the children, informing them of my change of address. After completing the letter, I folded the page, heated up some sealing wax, and affixed the seal upon it with the signet ring I purchased from a London goldsmith back in 1594 when I first became a shareholder in the Lord Chamberlain's Men.

The ring was the worldly emblem of this achievement. The face of the ring contained a simple but elegant design of my two initials, "W" and "S." A ribbon-like double-knotted design ran through the two prominent letters.

I treasured this ring. I brought it home when I retired to Stratford, only to lose it in Holy Trinity churchyard on the day of my brother Richard's funeral in 1613.

Sealing the letter to Anne, I hand carried it to the Stratford courier.

Then I arranged to move my furniture and other belongings to the Mountjoy home in Silver Street. Fortunately, my position as a shareholder gave me access to cheap acting apprentice labor. Within several days, I was happily ensconced in my new home on the other side of the Thames.

And a busy home it was, filled with motion and commotion, hustle and bustle, sweat and muscle, tossing and tussle, laughter and tears, love, hate, hopes and fears.

CHAPTER LX
THE MARVELOUS MOUNTJOYS

I thoroughly enjoyed my time living with the Mountjoys. The fast pace of their lives was a partial antidote to my loneliness. Their daughter, Mary, reminded me of my own daughter Susanna. Susanna and Mary both had entertaining laughs and fine senses of humor. Unlike most young woman, they were both literate. And they enjoyed reading my plays and poems.

Like all writers, I like having an audience. Although Susanna lived too far away, and Mary was not permitted to attend performances at the Globe, they devoured the manuscripts they could get their hands on. Fortunately for Susanna, she was the daughter of a playwright. She was a pretty good scrivener too.

Susanna spent many a happy hour in Stratford making our family's copies of the plays. Thank God she did. Many years later, Susanna's copies of the manuscripts prevented several works from being lost. I often thought of Susanna as my silent "collaborator." She has a special place in my heart for sharing the love of my work with me.

Although Mary did not copy any of my plays, I allowed her to read some of them. Like many a young woman, *Romeo and Juliet* was her favorite. I remember discussing that play with her while sitting by a warm fire one winter afternoon.

"Master Shakespeare," Mary began, as I watched the flickering light from the fire dance across her face.

"When you were creating Juliet, how did you capture the thoughts and feelings of a young girl of marriageable age?"

"It wasn't difficult," I answered. "After all, by the time I wrote those lines, I was the father of two daughters. Knowing my own daughters as well as I do allowed me to create an authentic Juliet.

"How about Romeo?"

"That was simpler. I was once a young man too."

"One in love?" Mary asked, with the hint of a smile.

"I once had a lover like Juliet. You know what her name was?"

"Pray tell!" Mary insisted.

"Anne — Anne Hathaway!" I answered. "Anne always has, and she always will, have her way with her Will!"

Mary burst out laughing. When we came to our senses, we enjoyed sipping the cups of spiced apple cider her mother, Marie, had provided.

As we continued our playful bantering, Marie came back into the room. "What are you two silly people up to?" she asked.

"Mr. Shakespeare's answering some questions I have about his plays — and his very interesting life," Mary replied.

"Mr. Shakespeare's well known for his wit, so you mustn't believe everything you hear," said Marie with an amused look. "For now, enough dueling of wits. Please bring the two cups of cider I left in the kitchen to your father and Stephen in the workshop."

"You're such a killjoy!" protested Mary.

"There'll be plenty of time later for jesting with Mr. Shakespeare," said Marie. "Now, please run along and do as I say," she commanded.

"All right," Mary petulantly answered with a slightly defiant shake of her head as she left the parlor to obtain the cups of cider.

After she had gone, Marie sat down and said, "Will, I appreciate your unique wit and humor. But Mary's still more a girl than a woman. And she adores you."

"I think she's more mature than you give her credit for. But I'll continue to be careful in my conversations with her," I reassured.

"I appreciate that," said Marie. "There's no need to remind you that you can give full reign to your wit with me."

"Brilliant," I answered,immediately taking her up on the offer and improvising a ditty in her honor:

There was a fair lady Marie,
Who was a fine friend to me.
She went to the playhouse to see
Players who played for a fee.

She had a large room to let,
She made the lodger her pet.
Once in a while she'd fret,
Her daughter had flown the nest.

Her life it was so blessed,
She looked as fine as she dressed.
Her ruff was neat and pressed,
Her fashion was always the best!

There was a fair lady Marie,
Who conjured her spell upon me,
When I fell under her powers,
Everything bloomed like the flowers.

Laughter rained down in showers,
And days flew by like hours.
There was a French lady Marie,
She was a good friend to me!

When I finished singing, Marie began clapping. As she did so, she said, "Bravo Will! Write that down so I can compose an arrangement for it on the virginal."

"Do you like it that much?" I asked. "It's only a trifle."

"But it's beautiful. And it's about me!"

"Putting it that way, I can't refuse. I'll write it down while the lyrics are still fresh in my mind."

Taking my leave, I went to my room and wrote down the lyrics from memory. Memorizing hundreds of lines at a time to make a living had its advantages.

Although the women of the Mountjoy household were my favorite conversationalists, I occasionally socialized with the men.

On one of my rare days off, the man of the house, Christopher Mountjoy, invited me for lunch at his favorite tavern, the Red Lion. There were over two hundred taverns in London. Every person had their personal favorites. I liked to frequent our company owned pub beside the Globe for after performance libations, and the Mermaid tavern in town for dinner and drinks with fellow actors and playwrights.

Because I was a "geographic bachelor," I spent more time in public houses than most married players in the Lord Chamberlain's Men. This suited me well. I consider my powers of observation key to my success as a playwright. To be popular, one has to feel the pulse of ever-changing times. What better way to live in the moment then to immerse oneself in the constant toil, struggle, and trouble of the public houses.

So, when Christopher Mountjoy invited me to go drinking with him at the Red Lion, I took him up on his offer. As everyone knows, pubs take on the personalities of their patrons. The patrons of the Red Lion were prosperous, on the make, upper-middle-class burghers like Christopher. They had little in common with the Bardolphs, Doll Tearsheets, and Sir John Falstaffs of this world.

Though some of the business schemes of the tire-makers, goldsmiths, silversmiths, and mercers who patronized the Red Lion might be akin to highway robbery, the lawyers at the Inns of Court go to great lengths to keep them legal.

Even though many a trip to the Red Lion was more about business than pleasure, this does not mean the burghers were above enjoying themselves. On the day in question, this meant participating in some time-honored drinking songs, popular at all levels of society.

To prepare for the boisterous singing, Chris and I ordered something a bit out of the ordinary for me, several small canikins of aquavite.

When the canikins arrived, Chris stood up to speak to those sitting on the simple wooden benches that lined the long plank tables. In his pronounced French accent, Chris said:

"Gentlemen, I'm here today with a special guest. My lodger and friend, the playwright and player, Mr. William Shakespeare. Mr. Shakespeare is rather familiar with taverns, especially the Boar's Head, where the mighty John Falstaff held court with Prince Hal before Hal became Henry V. Although the Red Lion is not the Boar's Head, I think we can all show Mr. Shakespeare we know how to have a good time!"

At this, there were shouts of "Hear! Hear!" with some of the patrons clinking their canakins and tankards together. After pausing, Chris continued with what I have to admit was turning into quite an admirable performance.

"Like many of us, Sir John Falstaff was a one-time soldier. Being a soldier is one of the seven ages of man described by Mr. Shakespeare in his play *As You Like It*. Well Mr. Shakespeare, we pretty much know how you like it. And now we have the chance to show you how those of us old soldiers here at the Red Lion like it. Boys, will you join me in 'The Canakin Song?'"

With that rousing invitation, everyone began singing:

And let me the canakin clink, clink;
And let me the canakin clink:
A soldier's a man;
A life's but a span;
Why then, let a soldier drink!

And let me the canakin clink, clink;
And let me the canakin clink:
My girl's with a man;
I don't give a damn;
Why then, let a soldier drink!

And let me the canakin clink, clink;
And let me the canakin clink:
The coins in my hands,
Flow like water in the sands;
Why then, let a soldier drink!

At the conclusion of this rollicking song, there was riotous laughter, drinking, and clinking of cannikin's and tankards. As I threw down one canakin after another of aquavite, I shouted out to Chris: "They don't call this the water of life for nothing!"

Chris sat there laughing. As I went on singing, he lit a pipe, silently observing us all, occasionally blowing smoke rings in the air!

CHAPTER LXI
THE DOWRY DILEMMA

Now the curtain rises on the most challenging chapter of my life with the Mountjoys. There's an old saying, true in all ages: "Nothing's certain except death and taxes." However, during our age, a third horseman rides with the other two. In our time, nothing's certain except death, taxes, and lawsuits!

In my humble opinion, the law is one of civilization's necessary evils. It sets a minimum standard of conduct and prevents society from descending into chaos. But laws are only as good as the persons making them. And some of the persons with the power to make laws are selfish and corrupt. They fashion laws for base purposes.

Over the course of my life, my family and I have felt the slings and arrows of the outrageous fortune of unjust laws and selective enforcement on many occasions.

Within the streets and alleyways near the Inns of Court, lurk certain Pharisees and Sadducees living by the letter of the law rather than its spirit. To me, the keystone of the law is mercy. That requires a heartfelt understanding of the Golden Rule: "whatsoever you would that men should do to you, do you also to them."

As Portia, in *The Merchant of Venice*, explains: "The quality of mercy is not strain'd; it droppeth, as the gentle rain from heaven upon the place beneath: it is twice bless'd; it blesseth him that gives, and him that takes."

Unfortunately, the domestic tale I am about to relate demonstrates the quality of mercy Portia describes is at times a rare commodity.

The story to come also illustrates the point I once made in the concluding couplet of a sonnet:

> For sweetest things turn sourest by their deeds;
> Lilies that fester smell far worse than weeds.

The family drama that would one day fester in a court of law all began innocently enough. I was finishing a hearty breakfast of scrambled eggs and bacon one fine fall day when Marie came into the kitchen and sat down across the table.

"I hope you slept well?" she asked.

"Yes, thank God. I haven't been sleeping as soundly as usual for the last several weeks. Part of getting older I guess. Last night was the exception to the rule. I slept like a baby."

"Like a baby! Babies often don't sleep through the night!"

"True," I said. "But when they do, they have less stress and worry to interrupt their sleep than we adults."

"You have a point," said Marie. "If you feel up to the task, I've a favor to ask,"

"What do you have in mind?"

"Mary's now of marriageable age?"

"Okay," I responded, wondering where this was going.

"Are you aware she's developed an affection for Christopher's apprentice, Stephen Belott."

"I know they enjoy each other's company," I carefully answered.

"You know Stephen's on the verge of completing his apprenticeship?"

"Yes," I responded. "He seems honest. From what Chris says, he's learned his trade well."

"I guess you'll not be surprised Chris and I have been thinking it might be best if Mary and Stephen were married."

"They'll make a fine couple."

"I'm glad you think so," said Marie. "But Chris and Stephen have never gotten along as well as I might have hoped, especially when it comes to the subject of money. We thought you might be able to assist us all by acting as the go-between during the dowry negotiations?"

Given my reluctance to come between a man and his money, as well as Chris's deserved reputation as a tightwad, I hesitated before answering.

As Marie hopefully looked at me, I tried to tactfully sidestep her request. "Although I respect you and Chris, and Mary's a fine young woman in all respects, I'm not cut out to be a marriage broker. Actors aren't the shrewdest men of business."

"I think you sell yourself short," Marie responded. "From what I've heard about your business from Dick and Bert, you've done quite well."

"You might think that," I answered. "But you know better than to believe everything you hear."

"You and your company have the favor of the King."

"You have the favor of the Queen," I retorted. "Given Queen Anne's fine taste in jewelry, I imagine you and Chris do well yourselves."

"We do okay. But, with changing tastes and fashions, who can see what the future holds?"

"That statement is true for us actors too. In times of plague, we must take to the roads. We're constantly at the mercy of the Crown, the Privy Council, the City, and the Church. We live from week to week, and month to month like tightrope acrobats."

Marie laughed. "Tightrope acrobats indeed. Your company's players' reputation among the town gossips is certainly acrobatic."

"I think you've been reading too much *Venus and Adonis*. The rumors of our escapades are greatly exaggerated."

"Really?" Marie questioned, throwing me a look of feigned disbelief. "You're trying to get me to believe the toast of the

London stage, an actor who has played hundreds of roles, a writer who has written dozens of plays, a part owner of the most successful theater in the country, and a shareholder in its most famous and profitable acting company, is incapable of successfully conducting a simple dowry negotiation for the daughter of close friends? Tell me it isn't so?"

As she launched this skillfully engineered attack upon my manly pride, Marie gave me a wide-eyed, mischievous smile. I involuntarily chuckled before answering, "It's not I couldn't do it if I put my mind to it. But, if I'm not successful, it could ruin my friendship with you all. I wouldn't want to risk that."

"You cannot lose. The man who wrote *Venus and Adonis*, *Romeo and Juliet*, and *A Midsummer Night's Dream*, is a master of the art of love and courtship!"

"Just because I write about it doesn't necessarily mean I can put it into practice," I answered.

Try thinking of it this way," she countered. "You've two daughters yourself. Helping us negotiate Mary's dowry will be good practice."

"I see the logic," I answered. "But no two dowry negotiations are the same."

"Stephen respects you. Mary adores you! She'll be devastated if you don't try! Discretion's not the better part of valour! It's to be, or not to be! Don't disappoint me!"

"You would've been an outstanding barrister," I said, as I tactfully conceded, "You know I'd find it very hard to say no to you and Mary!"

"So you'll help?" Marie asked, sporting a Cheshire cat smile.

"I'll try," I confirmed. "While I can guarantee the effort, I can't guarantee the result. To get down to business, what are you and Christopher willing to offer?"

"Chris is willing to provide a dowry of fifty pounds," Mary answered.

"Forgive me for saying so," I responded. "Since Mary's an only child, Stephen could find fifty pounds a bit stingy."

"It might seem low. Given the status of the business, Chris believes it's all he can afford. Of course, as his only heir, Mary stands to inherit our entire estate."

"Well, fifty pounds is certainly more than the average citizen can provide. And Mary's a special young woman. God willing, maybe love will win out," I said, trying to convince myself.

"I hope so," said Mary.

"Prayer can't hurt," I added, getting up from the table.

"Can you speak with Stephen today?" Mary asked.

"Not today. I've business at the Globe," I replied. "I'll ask him to join me for lunch at the Mermaid later this week. I'll see what I can do."

While I proceeded upstairs to my rented room, I could not help but reflect upon the concept of dowry. When and how did our society decide to institute it, and for what purpose? As a father of two daughters, it was something which concerned me greatly. I had done well enough. I could afford to provide attractive dowries for both Susanna and Judith. But there were so many less fortunate fathers who loved their daughters just as much as I love mine. They could not provide decent dowries for their children. Others could only afford to provide a dowry for their eldest daughter, leaving the younger ones to fend for themselves.

It was a tragedy played out thousands of times every year. At best, the dowryless daughters ended up servants or old maids. At worst, they ended up in stews such as Hollander's Leaguer, the Cardinal's Hat, or the Castle, well-known bawdy houses near the Globe.

In spite of my serious misgivings about the fairness of the dowry system, like every other member of our society, I was trapped in it. It was part of the fabric of our lives. Now, it was my turn to play the role of matchmaker.

Chapter LXII
A Sales Pitch

Several days later, I found myself at the Mermaid Tavern, having dinner with prospective bridegroom, Stephen Belott. My friend and colleague, Dick Burbage, moonlighting as a painter, had lent his artistic talents to the decorative scheme of the tavern. He had masterfully painted both the figure of the flaxen haired mermaid, swinging back and forth on the creaking sign hanging above the doorway, as well as the large mural of the school of mermaids gracing the wall behind the bar.

Despite having a limited amount of free time, Dick has become one of the best known and most skillful artists in the City. In addition to painting tavern signs and shield impresas used by the aristocracy at tilt yard jousts, Dick has become an outstanding portrait painter. Besides painting pictures of members of high society, he has painted many of us players. The portrait Dick painted of me is one of my prize possessions. It hangs prominently in the front parlor of New Place.

Upon receiving the portrait as a gift, I offered to write a poem for Dick, which he and his family could use as a eulogy when the time came. He pointedly asked me not to do so.

"I appreciate the offer," Dick said. "But I plan to go out of this world as simply as I came into it. I've told my wife and Bert that, when I go, I'd like the following engraved on my tombstone: 'Exit Burbage.'"

"It's simple, to the point, and brings a smile!" I chuckled.

"That's what I'm hoping for," Dick replied.

Now, in the presence of the playful mermaids painted by my good friend, I sat across the candlelit table from Stephen, enjoying the moist and tasty dish of baked cod, prepared for us by The Mermaid's proprietor, my friend and business associate, William Johnson.

In between savoring pieces of the tasty fish, I began "wooing"Stephen.

"As you know," I said, "I'm here today at the request of Mr. and Mrs. Mountjoy to discuss the issue of your potential marriage to Mary."

"Mary told me her parents requested you speak with me. When you invited me to dine here, I put two and two together."

"You're a smart young man, Stephen. Being so, you must know how difficult this is for me. I'm a player, not a marriage broker. But the Mountjoys are friends. And Mary is a special young woman: beautiful, smart, quick of wit, a good conversationalist, a fine sense of humor. You could do a lot worse."

"You need not waste any more words on that issue with me," Stephen answered. "I think the world of Mary. I look forward to the day she will wear my ring, and we call each other husband and wife."

"Great," I said enthusiastically. "It'll make the remainder of our conversation much easier." I raised my pewter tankard to my lips, taking a refreshing draught of ale.

As I did, Stephen continued, "One thing Mary and I are resolved upon is being treated fairly by her father. I've been employed with him seven years. Since you began lodging with the Mountjoys, I'm sure you've observed I've been honest, hard-working, faithful."

Finishing my ale, I said, "Of course. The Mountjoys know you possess these qualities, or they would never approve a match between you and their daughter."

"I know they want the match, Mr. Shakespeare. I'm afraid Mr. Mountjoy, knowing the great love Mary and I have for each other, will not provide a sufficient dowry to allow us a decent start to our lives."

As I listened, looking into Stephen's fiery eyes, I could feel storm clouds and thunder. This would not be easy.

Getting to the point, Stephen asked, "How much have they authorized?"

"Fifty pounds, some household furniture, and trade implements."

"Fifty pounds!" Stephen burst out. "That's how he treats his daughter! Look at the size of his house! He owns a substantial home in Brentford too. You pay him rent. What he collects from you and his house renters is only a drop in the bucket compared to what he makes on the jewel encrusted tires he manufactures for fashionable women at court. Just last week we delivered one that cost five-hundred pounds! There's a nice profit margin in that. Fifty pounds is insulting! Two-hundred pounds is reasonable."

"Calm down," I said. "I hear you. But fifty pounds is twice as much as my wife brought to our marriage. We've done well."

"With all due respect, you've been married twenty years. I doubt your father-in-law was as well off as Mr. Mountjoy."

"You have a point, Stephen. My father-in-law died before I married Anne. Fifty pounds is still a lot of money. Why, the house we own in Stratford only cost sixty pounds. It's the second largest in town."

"That may be," Stephen said. "But what would your house cost if it was in London rather than Stratford? The business of tire making requires substantial capital. You need equipment and inventory, gold and silver wire, pearls, jewels, precious stones. Mary and I need to secure our own lodging."

"Two-hundred pounds is a great deal of money. I doubt Mary's parents have the resources for such a sum. Even were they willing to pay it."

"I wouldn't be so sure," Stephen countered. "I will not say there's no flexibility upon our part. But fifty pounds will not do. I've given seven years of my life to Christopher to assist him in his business. My mother and stepfather had to send care packages to help me get by. They even paid the barber to cut my hair and pull an abscessed tooth!"

"I hear what you're saying," I told Stephen. "I'll be your advocate with Mary's parents. But you must adopt a spirit of compromise. After all, this is a love match, is it not?"

"Of course!" Stephen answered. "Mary and I are confident you'll do your best to protect our interest and help to open the door to our successful future."

CHAPTER LXIII
CHRIS BLOWS HIS TOP

As Stephen spoke, I felt my heart sink. He was seeking four times the amount Chris Mountjoy was willing to provide. I could see waves of great expectations breaking upon cliffs of cold reality. The marriage contract was in danger of wrecking upon the rocks due to the all-important issue of consideration. These were the legal terms my old attorney employer would have used to describe the problem I faced. How to convince a stubborn mule like Chris to cross a line in the sand.

After returning from dinner with Stephen, I found myself sitting with Chris and Marie at their dining table. When I relayed Stephen's two-hundred-pound demand, I was met with seconds of dead silence. Expressions spoke louder than words.

When Chris finally spoke, it was in a voice of fury. "That ungrateful, butt-kissing, finger-licking, donkey-kicking, idiot of a young man! I take him into my home, support him for seven years, teach him my trade, and offer him the hand of my daughter. This is how he pays me back! He's bumming, slumming trash! It's highway robbery — that's what it is. I've a good mind to take that blackthorn cudgel down from the mantle and beat the hell out of him! Let that bantam rooster step into this room. I'll show him who's the cock of the walk! I'll teach him a thing or two!"

As Christopher fell into the blistering rhythm of his tirade, his eyes took on the look of a Bedlam inmate. When he pushed back his chair, jumping-up with the intent of making good on his threat, Marie ran around the table placing herself between her husband and the fireplace.

Thrusting her palms out, Marie shouted: "Don't jump to conclusions! It's not the end of the world!"

"Not the end of the world?" Chris shouted back. "This whoreson sits at our table, eating us out of house and home. Now he wants to steal our savings. So he can traipse around in silks and ermine while doing the beast with two backs with our daughter — in a feather bed!"

"Chris!" Marie pleaded. "Don't say such things. These aren't enemies! Sit down! Let's discuss the situation with Mr. Shakespeare. He's seen everything under the sun. He's dealt with problems like this before. Haven't you?" she asked, with a hopeful glance.

"Right," I lied. "I'm sure there's a way this can be worked out to everyone's' satisfaction."

"Dammit!" said Chris. "Does he think our daughter's such a poor catch we'd pay a fortune to marry her off to a dumbass? What's he bring to the table? What security can he provide? He's no real father to speak of. His blowhard trumpeter of a stepfather pawned him off as my apprentice to get him out of the house. I 've a good mind to stick Humphrey Fludd's trumpet up his fat butt, blowing his worthless stepson to Kingdom Come!"

This last portion of Christopher's tirade was spoken with slightly less emotion. To survive this hurricane, we still had to chart a course through the reefs, shoals, and broiling water around us.

After much artful persuasion, Marie and I finally convinced Christopher to increase the amount of his offer to sixty pounds, and some additional equipment and furniture.

Having earned this concession, the tennis ball was back in my court. I needed to convince Stephen and Mary this was a reasonable offer.

Chapter LXIV
Sealing the Deal

The next afternoon, I met Mary and Stephen at the Mermaid. After settling into a booth that offered a modicum of privacy, and assessing their initial expressions and body language, I began:

"Let's just cut to the chase? Mary, you love Stephen?"

"Yes."

"Stephen, you Mary?"

"With all my heart."

"I assume you both realize marriage is not always a primrose path?"

"We know," said Stephen. "I think we see where you're going with this."

"Please bear with me."

"Hold on," Mary said to Stephen. "Before you gallop down the road like a headless horseman, let's hear him out."

"I like your attitude," I remarked, sensing a potential ally. "I imagine you're willing to sacrifice, taking each other in good or bad times, in health or sickness?"

"And wealth or poverty?" Stephen said, his voice laced with sarcasm.

"It will not be the end of the world if your marriage doesn't make you rich," I responded. "You're a talented young man."

"I'm not looking for instant wealth," he defended. "I just want what's due. Not for myself. For Mary. It's not right her father treats her this way. I want the best for her and our future children. I've done my time. I've worked for Mary's father seven years. But Mary's worked for him all her life. I'd hate to see her cheated!"

"I understand," I empathized. "Mary's parents want this to work out too. They're now offering sixty pounds."

"Only ten more!" Stephen grumbled, pounding his fist on the table.

Before he could launch into a diatribe, I quickly added, "And you'll have sufficient furniture and equipment to start a life together. You can stay at the Mountjoys' home, working at twenty pounds a year salary until you're ready to move out. Sixty pounds, room and board, furniture, tire-making equipment, salary. Sounds decent to me," I concluded with an air of hopeful confidence.

"What do you think, Mary?" I asked. I hated to put her in a dilemma. But, if I didn't press the point, it could be "game over."

Mary's eyes darted between Stephen's and mine before she answered: "You would have been a wonderful lawyer. The way you make it sound, we can't refuse. I 'm sure the effort you made with my father was significant."

"And painful!" added Stephen with a wry smile. His words caused Mary and me to laugh sympathetically.

"You're right," I rejoined, sensing the tide might be turning.

"I don't like the thought of prolonging your agony," Mary resumed. "As you've pointed out, although the dowry is not princely, I believe we should accept. My love is what I offer. Nothing more. Nothing less. I pray it's enough," she implored, gazing into Stephen's eyes.

Mary's speech was rendered beautifully. Its sincerity was something even the most heartless man would find difficult to resist.

Luckily for Mary and myself, Stephen had a heart. A few seconds after Mary finished her plea to his better angel, he pursed his lips in thought. Then, to our relief, he chuckled. Placing a hand on Mary's shoulder, he said: "Of course, your heart and soul has always been, and will always be, more than enough for me."

As he finished speaking, he pulled Mary closer to him, giving her a vigorous kiss on the lips.

I breathed a sigh of relief. The work of a marriage broker was tedious business. Before the spell could be broken, I hurriedly exclaimed:

"Wonderful! I can't wait to convey the good news to your mother. She'll be so happy."

"The skinflint will rejoice too," muttered Stephen.

Elbowing Stephen, Mary said, "Enough already! He's my father!"

Before Stephen could destroy what had been gained, I shouted, "Let's celebrate!" Signaling the bar maid, I called out, "Cups of sack for myself and my friends!"

Turning towards Stephen and Mary, I said, "Now that you're in agreement on the dowry, we can move on to the handfasting."

"Handfasting?" Asked Stephen.

"Surely you know what that is," I answered.

"I've heard about it," said Stephen. "It's a practice observed in the country."

"I'm not sure my parents will approve," added Mary.

"It's your decision," I reassured. "Worked well for Anne and myself. To my way of thinking, a marriage contract is a three-part agreement between both of you and God. The priest merely solemnizes the ritual. The glue that holds the marriage together is the vow you make to each other. If you're ready for that commitment, there's no need to wait upon the banns. As the old wives say: 'He's thy husband. She's thy wife. Get on with the married life. Light the fire, warm the bed, while the marriage banns are read!'"

Mary giggled. "I've never heard that. It's funny."

"Sounds nice," said Stephen.

"Let's get your parents to see things our way," I said, as the bar maid arrived with brimming cups of sack.

Several days later, in the festively decorated parlor of the Mountjoy home, I presided over a candlelit handfasting between

Stephen and Mary. Given all were finally in agreement on the terms of the dowry, it was easy to convince Chris and Marie to assent to the handfasting. The fact Stephen would continue to have a home and a job with the Mountjoys, as well as a sixty-pound dowry, meant there was no problem gaining Stephen's mother's and stepfather's consent. The Mountjoys were providing Stephen with a good start in life.

For an apprentice, marrying a successful master's daughter, and his only child, was an impressive feat. Although the dowry was not as generous as Stephen hoped, there was the inheritance to consider. That expectation probably sealed the deal.

Sadly, not all auspicious beginnings end happily. In this case, the wedded bliss of Stephen and Mary was soon overshadowed by daily clashes between Stephen and Chris. The two never were able to make the adjustment from being master and apprentice to being partners in the business of tire making. Although Marie and Mary tried — their efforts at mending the broken fences between their husbands ended in failure. After several cycles of leaving home, moving back, living and working together, volcanic disagreement, and moving out again, Stephen and Mary left for good. They moved into rented lodgings and started their own tire making business.

Throughout this process, I was stuck in the role of middleman. Both sides in this feud came to my lodgings to lean on my shoulders and cry in my ears. I tried to be a friend to all, consoling without taking sides, pressing on with my challenging work schedule.

Despite such domestic distractions, my time with the Mountjoys was one of my most artistically productive. I wrote *All's Well That Ends Well*, *Measure for Measure*, *King Lear*, and *Macbeth*, as well as several other plays.

This productivity is more surprising because some of it came in 1605, the year of the disastrous Gunpowder Plot.

For myself, the horror sparked by the unravelling of the Gunpowder Plot went on for several years. The plague came, bringing two additional great tragedies, the deaths of Marie Mountjoy and my younger brother Edmund. Then, within six months of Edmund's death, my mother died of a broken heart. Their deaths broke my own heart in so many ways I again wondered whether it was worthwhile to go on living. The dark and somber feelings I experienced at this juncture are passionately reflected in some of the plays I was writing.

With Marie's death, her daughter's leaving for good, Chris drinking heavily and showering his attentions upon a freckle-faced maid, it was time to find lodgings in a different part of town.

In the spring of 1607, I moved out of the Mountjoy residence, believing everything which occurred while I lived on Silver Street was safely locked away in my strong box of memories. The "bones" of my past on Silver Street remained buried five years. Then, Stephen and Mary, long frustrated by their fruitless demands upon Chris for payment of remaining dowry amounts, sued Chris in the Court of Requests.

Given my role as reluctant matchmaker, I was dragged into these senseless court proceedings, reawakening painful memories.

By this point, I was tired of conflicts.I wanted to get back to semi-retired life in Stratford. I knew Chris, Mary, and Stephen were aware of my Catholic "leanings." If I overtly favored one side or the other in a dispute which should have never made it to the courts, either side could use it to blackmail me or turn me in to government authorities.

Under these circumstances, I tailored my testimony. I gave everyone something, without destroying either party's case. Fortunately, I successfully walked that line. I came away unscathed, although the stretching of my conscience left my honor bruised and bandaged.

Chapter LXV
The Gunpowder Plot

When I think about the early years of the reign of King James, I can't help but ponder what might have been. With the death of Queen Elizabeth, and the ascension of the King to the throne, many in the kingdom, including myself, believed it was the dawning of a new age. When, within a year or so of his ascension, the King was able to bring the long-running war with Spain to a successful conclusion, many of us experienced a sense of relief. At last, we had a ruler who appeared to value peace more than war. Upon hearing the good news, I penned the following lines:

> The mortal moon hath her eclipse endur'd,
>
> And the sad augurs mock their own presage:
>
> Incertainties now crown themselves assur'd,
>
> And peace proclaims olives of endless age.

The above lines perfectly express my feelings during these early days. These positive feelings were bolstered by the occasional personal interactions I had with the King. From the beginning of his reign until now, I have always found him a decent and kind man at heart.

The King has been most appreciative and generous to many, including our company of players. Soon after taking the throne, he paid us a great honor — designating us "The King's Men." As a member of The King's Men, I got to wear a scarlet robe made of cloth provided by the Crown to myself and other company shareholders. We were given the honor of carrying a ceremonial canopy in the triumphal procession marking the King and the

Queen's formal arrival into the city. And our company was called upon to perform one of our plays for the King and the delegates to the peace conference resulting in the treaty with Spain.

When the Globe was closed due to a particularly virulent outbreak of the plague, the King gave our company an outright gift of thirty pounds to help us get through those tough times. But the greatest benefit of all was a tremendous increase in the number of performances we were invited to give at court. In short, the King's patronage and financial support has been life-changing for every member of our company.

The patronage we have received from the King has as much to do with Queen Anne's enthusiastic support and appreciation of the performing arts as it does with the King. Queen Anne is honest and open-hearted, possessing a keen sense of humor and genial nature. In addition to her love of the arts, including the masks of Ben Johnson, and the sets and costume designs of Inigo Jones, she is a fashion trend-setter.

During the numerous times we performed at court, I developed a friendship with the Queen. She enjoyed conversing with me about the themes, sources, and moral aspects of the plays I wrote. During the years she lived in Scotland, after leaving her home in Denmark and marrying King James at the age of fifteen, the Queen heard much about the plays we performed for Elizabeth, but she did not have the opportunity to see many. When she moved to London, she was thrilled to experience first-hand what she had admired from afar.

The friendship I enjoyed with the Queen was furthered by the friendship she shared with Marie Mountjoy. By the time Queen Anne arrived in London, Christopher's and Marie's reputation for superior workmanship and design in the fine art of tire-making was already well-established in court circles.

Some of the most powerful and beautiful women at court were already regular customers of Marie. Not long after the

Queen moved to London, she summoned Marie to meet with her and present some of her latest creations for the Queen's consideration.

I can still remember the excitement in the Mountjoy household the morning Marie was to first meet with Queen Anne. Marie incessantly, but charmingly, peppered me with questions. I freely shared what I knew about the Queen's likes and dislikes, assuring Marie I was confident they would get along. As predicted, they hit it off. Marie soon became the preferred "tire woman" to the Queen — enabling the Mountjoys' business to thrive at a level it had never done before.

My admiration for the Queen increased greatly when, as a result of underground Catholic community gossip, I became aware of the Queen's own sympathy for and acceptance of Roman Catholicism. Rumor had it, through the influence of a Roman Catholic friend, Henrietta Gordon, Queen Anne secretly converted to Roman Catholicism while she was Queen of Scots. What was mere rumor in English Court and Catholic circles was confirmed when Queen Anne refused to receive communion during her husband's Westminster Abbey coronation.

Unfortunately, despite Queen Anne's apparent sympathy for Catholics, and the rumors she was Catholic herself, it seemed to have little effect upon the King who, being separated from his Catholic mother Mary, was raised a staunch Protestant in theory, if not in practice. The King's strict adherence to his Protestant faith was part of the deal he struck with Robert Cecil and the Privy Council to obtain the English throne.

In retrospect, it was unreasonable for us English Catholics to expect a new birth of Roman Catholic toleration to emerge in the first few years of the King's reign. But, given the decades of persecution and repression we suffered through under the reign of Queen Elizabeth, it was natural for all of us Catholics to pray for a miracle. Perhaps this new King would be kind and merciful to those of us who followed the faith his mother gave her life for, and the one to which his wife had likely been converted.

Sadly, the high, if unreasonable hopes and expectations we Catholics had for this new age, were dealt a severe blow in an unlikely manner. The rumors of the Queen's possible allegiance to the Catholic faith had traveled over mountains, valleys, hills and dales, making their way to Pope Clement VIII in Rome. Trying to reach out to the Queen, the Pope arranged to have an English emissary, Sir Anthony Standen, carry a gift of a Rosary the Pope had blessed to Queen Anne in the hope it would encourage her to lobby her husband for Catholic toleration.

Just as the Catholics hoped for a new era of toleration with the ascension of King James, Robert Cecil and the Privy Council feared the new King would upset the status quo which had enabled them to amass an immense amount of wealth and live the lives of princes in their own fiefdoms. Although they had the assurance of King James he had no Catholic leanings, they saw the gift of the rosary as an opportunity to put his assurances to the test.

The foolish Anthony Standen, whose actions had unwittingly lit the fuse of an immense powder keg, was arrested and imprisoned. The King was urged by the Privy Council to banish Catholic priests from the realm, and to back the passage of a new set of anti-Catholic laws. The King, who had waited many years for the opportunity to govern the far richer Kingdom of England, and escape the strictures of the Scottish Kirk, was not about to jeopardize his position before he had an opportunity to consolidate his power.

So, much ado was made about something which could have been considered nothing, and the hopes we Catholics had for a new deal on the "Catholic Question" went up in smoke. Like a row of falling dominoes, with the advent and enforcement of the new anti-Catholic laws, a small group of young and frustrated

Catholic gentry decided to try to take fate into their own hands by forcing the change they desired using violence.

The misguided and marginalized souls who participated in this conspiracy included Thomas Percy, Robert Catesby, Thomas and Robert Wintour, John Grant, John and Christopher Wright, Sir Everard Digby, Ambrose Rookwood, Francis Tresham, and Guy Fawkes — a longtime ex-patriot Catholic soldier with a decade of experience fighting for the Catholic cause in the Low Countries.

The plan these desperate men came up with was to kill the King, Robert Cecil, the Privy Council, and many of the ruling Protestant aristocracy. Then, they would kidnap King James's daughter, the Princess Elizabeth, who was being raised and educated in the Warwick countryside, and install her as queen under the regency of a yet to be determined pro-Catholic noblemen.

To carry out the first stage of their plan, the conspirators would blow up the House of Lords when the King was convening the opening session of Parliament. With the King, the Privy Council, and many of the Protestant powerbrokers dead or injured, the conspirators would then join with their small group of supporters in the Midlands, kidnap the Princess, raise an army of pro-Catholic and disgruntled gentry and commoners, and take on whatever Protestant forces remained after the destruction of Parliament.

Before the specifics of their plan had been developed, certain of the conspirators sought the support of both the Spanish Crown and the Pope for an effort to overthrow the English government under King James. After decades of conflict with England, the Spanish had no interest in prolonging a war which had already cost them way too much in lives and treasure. The Pope did not believe such a revolt would be successful, and he feared for the safety of the remaining faithful Catholics and priests in England who would undoubtedly face reprisals if any attempt to overthrow the existing English government was unsuccessful.

Not dissuaded by their failure to secure the support of the Spanish government or the Pope, as their plan crystallized, the conspirators also unsuccessfully sought the support and blessing of the senior Jesuit priest remaining in England, Father Henry Garnet. Although they conveyed their general intent to Father Garnet, the conspirators never explicitly discussed the details of their plan to blow up the King and Parliament using barrels of gunpowder hidden in a large storeroom they rented underneath the chamber of the House of Lords in Whitehall — where Parliament was scheduled to convene on the fifth of November.

As the time for the ignition of the plot approached, Father Garnet learned some of the details which the conspirators had shared with a subordinate priest under the seal of Confession. Father Garnet then tried his best to convince the conspirators to abandon their plan. But, when his efforts proved unsuccessful, he did not believe he could break the seal of the confessional by revealing the plan to the government authorities.

What the Spanish King, the Pope, and Father Garnet understood, and the conspirators did not, is the diminishing number of practicing Catholics in England were largely confined to the wealthy but minor gentry. Only the wealthy could afford to bear the financial cost and risk of continued adherence to the Catholic faith. And those few who could still afford to host and hide a Catholic priest were not likely to invite rank-and-file commoners into their secret Masses and underground society. The risk of betrayal was too high.

Further, given the more than six decades since King Henry VIII first broke with the Roman Catholic Church, there were almost no remaining practicing Catholics at the highest level of the aristocracy. As a result of executions, imprisonment, denial of advancement and education, fines, and banishment, aristocratic practicing Catholics were relentlessly winnowed out of existence. Among the lower-level gentry, many of those who were still practicing Catholics had already been ruined, or their family's wealth significantly reduced, due to their continuing adherence to Roman Catholicism. This was certainly the case with many who became enmeshed in the Gunpowder Plot.

Changing the course and practice of a culture is much more effectively accomplished by financial coercion than by sheer violence. And, a combination of violence and financial coercion on the most powerful members of the opposition, with financial coercion applied to the middle and lower-class, is a lethal combination — providing it is consistently applied over multiple generations.

In this case, the Tudors, and their nouveau-riche Protestant confederates, had already applied a python-like stranglehold upon us English Catholics for more than two generations before King James came to the throne.

The Gunpowder Plot hatched by these ill-fated conspirators was a desperate and foolish act which never had a real chance of achieving its objectives. It only gave the anti-Catholic forces the upper hand in the propaganda war for the hearts and minds of the English people and provided the government with additional political capital to enact and strictly enforce anti-Catholic legislation.

It resulted in a vigorous round-up of the meager number of Catholic priests remaining in the country. And, along with Henry Garnet, who at least had some knowledge of the plotters' intentions, many others who had nothing at all to do with it were also imprisoned, banished, or executed.

Chapter LXVI
A Life Cut Short

Although I had no advance knowledge of the plot, being a member of the Catholic recusant community, I knew some of those involved to varying degrees. I had attended numerous secret Masses presided over by Father Garnet. He was a very intelligent, urbane man. Being the de facto leader of the Catholic Jesuits in England, Father Garnet had more than his share of courage and charisma. Unfortunately, no matter how courageous he was, he was constantly walking a tightrope, stuck between a rock and a hard place.

I also knew one of the other conspirators, John Grant, a Catholic who lived in a handsome manor house in the town of Northbrook, not far from Stratford. During the times I spent back home, I occasionally traveled to John Grant's house to attend Mass and go to Confession with one or another of the priests who often stayed there. Like many in the Stratford area, John and his family patronized our glove shop on Henley Street.

Another intersection of my life and the plot was geographic in nature. I leased some farmland outside of Stratford, next to an estate owned by Lord Carew. The manor house on Lord Carew's estate was known as Clopton house. While Lord Carew and his wife were away in London, that house was commandeered and used by the plotters for numerous purposes, including meetings, and the storage of Catholic religious items such as crucifixes, crosses, chalices and vestments.

The religious items were being held for delivery to the Catholic, George Badger. Mr. Badger owned the house next to ours on Henley Street and was a friend of my father. Like my father, Mr. Badger was forced to give up his position as a Stratford alderman because he refused to renounce his Catholic faith.

Though I was a secret Catholic myself, and I knew some of those who became involved with the plot, I was as horrified by it as were most Protestant residents of London. I realized, for all practical purposes, this Gunpowder Plot had blown the last best hope of Catholic toleration by the English Crown to Kingdom Come.

I knew the bonfires of celebration blazing in the streets of London were tolling the death knell for English Catholicism in the hearts and minds of all but a shattered fragment of the English population.

While I was living through the events of the plot and its aftermath at the end of 1605 and the beginning of 1606, I was concluding my work on *King Lear*, and writing *Macbeth*, the play about the murder of a Scottish king and the horrific aftermath which follows. To say the events of The Gunpowder Plot influenced the writing of *Macbeth* would be a gross understatement. *Macbeth* is drenched in the blood of the madness of murder, and the consequences of killing an anointed king. In the end, the murderers, Macbeth and Lady Macbeth, get their just and bloody desserts.

As I was working my way through the play, the Gunpowder Plot conspirators were being dragged on hurdles, hung, drawn, and quartered before huge crowds at their appointed places of execution — St. Paul's Cross and Westminster.

If attempted murder, conspiracy, and execution were not enough, when the clock of the year had not yet reached its eighth hour, the specter of plague emerged from the cesspool of its existence to indiscriminately rob and steal thousands of lives.

When the pestilence emerged and ravaged its way through town, creeping steadily towards my doorstep, the theaters closed. King, Queen and nobles fled town for safety. Ringed by ruth and rosemary, I slaved away at my Scottish play about murder, mayhem, and the blackness, darkness, spells, and curses which haunt the marshes and moors of our memories.

For, as I worked at my art, unseen daggers materialized, stabbing repeatedly at my heart. The first dagger took away my dream of practicing my faith without fear or danger. The second took the life of a dear friend. Then a year later, the third, cutting deepest of all, snuffed out the life of my brother Edmund.

In October, as the clock of 1606 struck ten, the scythe of the hooded horseman came for Marie Mountjoy. The death of Marie was a disaster for the entire household. Like many a wife, she was the glue holding the disparate sides of the family together. With her gone, there was little to no chance Mary, Stephen, and Christopher would ever be able to continue to live and work together. Further, with Marie's death, the tremendous prestige their business had come to enjoy from Marie being the Queen's designated "tire woman" abruptly ended. For no man could serve in such an intimate role as purveyor of tires to the Queen.

About a year after Marie's death, when I thought the scourge of the plague had receded, it came like the final shot, on the final day, of the final war, and took the life of my brother Edmund.

After the theaters closed in 1606, and I began work on *Macbeth*, Edmund and his theater troupe went on the road. Like all London based players, when the plague raged in London, they traveled from town to town, playing to smaller provincial audiences, trying to make ends meet. After making the rounds, they returned to London towards the end of the year, to participate in the lucrative court plays and performances given during the Christmas season.

When the Christmas season plays for 1606 concluded, Edmund's theatre troupe again found themselves on the road for a large part of 1607. A few months before Christmas that year, Edmund returned to London.

It was in the heart of the Christmas celebration of 1607 that Edmund first noticed the telltale tokens of plague sores erupting on his body. From that point forward, his brief season of hell on earth began. Within two days of the emergence of the first signs, my younger brother, the apple of my poor mother's eye, was no longer with us.

Sadly, because of his absence from London for a large part of the year, and the fact he was no longer residing with me, I only saw Edmund once during the six months leading up to his death. That was several weeks before he came down with the symptoms of the merciless disease.

While we enjoyed dinner at his favorite pub, Edmund told me about the quixotic adventures he experienced during the months touring with his company.

Although I had recently completed work on *Pericles* with tavern and brothel owner turned moonlighting playwright, George Wilkins, Edmund was far more interested in discussing *Macbeth* with me that evening.

The supernatural aspects of the work appealed to Edmund. He was especially interested in discussing the role the three witches played in determining Macbeth's fate. I explained I saw the witches as spiritual manifestations of Macbeth's morally blind ambition. Edmund saw them as the cause of Macbeth's downfall. I am always fascinated by the alternate interpretations given my works by other players and members of the audience. A play is like a child. We think we know our children's natures by heart. But, when it comes time to leave the nest, we are often surprised at the way others perceive them.

After discussing *Macbeth*, Edmund told me he recently crafted his own "Witch's Song" for a jig he performed in the aftermath of his company's rival play featuring a coven of witches that wreak havoc upon unsuspecting townsmen and townswomen.

I asked him whether he would perform it while we waited for dinner to be served.

With a characteristic shrug of his shoulders, Edmund dutifully obliged, assuming a serious look, while intoning:

Reds and greens and yellows and golds,
Bees and bats and frogs and toads,
Thimbles, needles, and broken threads,
Goblins and witches about your head.

Ghosts that cry out in rattling chains,
Moonstruck visions that haunt your brain,
Earthbound spirits which writhe in pain.
Star-crossed lovers who kiss in vain.

Devils and demons that walk the earth,
Stealing the children at their birth,
Robbing our lives of joy and mirth,
Leaving us only want and dearth.

Damning us all with hex and curse,
Stealing the coins out of our purse,
Flying their broomsticks into the sky,
Giving us all the Evil Eye!

"I love it," I exclaimed. "It plays into the King's interest in witchcraft and all things supernatural. Where a King's interests lie, his subjects' follow. Your work is getting better by the day. I'm going to talk to Dick, Bert and the other shareholders. I think it's time you completed your apprenticeship — and returned to the fold. I want to be able to call you 'partner.'"

"Being a shareholder of the King's Men would fulfill all my dreams!" said my youngest brother with an air of excitement.

But, alas, like many of the best laid plans of Man, it was not to be.

Only a fortnight later I stood among my colleagues and friends in the players' church of St. Savior's mourning the loss of my brother. As I listened to the great bell toll for Edmund, some of the final lines I wrote for *Macbeth* came back to haunt me.

> Out, out brief candle!
> Life's but a walking shadow; a poor player,
> That struts and frets his hour upon the stage,
> And then is heard no more: it is a tale
> Told by an idiot, full of sound and fury,
> Signifying nothing. —

In the inconsolable grief of the moment, it seemed I had prophetically written those lines for Edmund and myself rather than the ancient Scottish king I tried to conjure back to life. For it seemed to me then, by the pricking of guilt-ridden thumbs, the senseless Wheel of Fortune had spun, and something wicked this way had come!

CHAPTER LXVII
A MARRIAGE OF TRUE MINDS

In the year 1611 I wrote *The Tempest*, which turned out to be the final play I authored without a collaborator. I did not intend that to be the case. But unforeseen circumstances intervened to make it so.

Although *The Tempest* was not meant to be my final act as a solo writer, I did intend it to be my farewell to my life as an actor. At the time I wrote the play, I was 47 years old and I had been living the life of a geographic bachelor for well over 20 years. For the majority of each of those years, I had spent far more time away from my family than I had been able to spend with them.

Despite achieving fame and financial success, the cost to my personal life was immense. During these lonely years, I endured the loss of Hamnet, my father, my partner and friend Augustine Phillips, Marie Mountjoy, Edmund, and my mother, who died of a broken heart in 1608.

Amid the miserable tolls of the death knells, there were a few glimmering rays of light. In 1607, my eldest daughter, Susanna, married the eminent local doctor, John Hall. Although John was a dyed-in-the-black-wool Protestant, with Puritan leanings, I could not help but like him as a man. He was successful, intelligent, a good conversationalist with a sense of humor, and, most importantly, my daughter truly loved him. He knew of Susanna's and our family's Roman Catholic leanings, but he did not try to convert us to his own beliefs.

The fact Susanna had married a prominent Protestant physician also helped to provide our family with additional cover and protection. For, after the failure of the Gunpowder Plot, the persecution of Roman Catholics grew more intense than ever before. In fact, it appeared to many of us that God chose the

Protestant side. Over the course of the last eighty years, England had been gradually coerced and converted to the Protestant cause. Like most political revolutions, this religious revolution had lately trended towards its most radical and intolerant form — Puritanism.

So, being a practical citizen of this world, with only a poor sinner's hope of being granted a lease on a thatched cottage on the outskirts of the New Jerusalem of the next, I gave my blessing to the marriage of Susanna and John.

I remember their wedding day well. The air was brisk as we walked the short distance from the front of five-gabled New Place to Holy Trinity.

When Anne and I took our seats in the front pew of the church, my heart swelled with pride to see the beautiful woman my daughter Susanna had become.

While the Vicar recited the service, my thoughts wandered back to the joyful day of Susanna's birth. How wonderful it was to hold her in my arms for the first time. And what a marvelous child she turned out to be. Laughing, crying, singing, and bringing good cheer to everyone in our large household.

Now she was standing before me at the altar giving her heart and soul to the man she loved. As I listened to John and Susanna exchange their vows, I could feel my eyes tearing. As they did so, Anne handed me a soft linen handkerchief that she pulled from the sleeve of her taffeta dress.

As I took the handkerchief Anne offered, our eyes met. I saw tears running down her face too. She was the true hero of our story. Because my work required me to be on the road as much as it did, it is Anne who deserves most of the credit for helping Susanna become the magnificent person she is.

When the service concluded, we all made our way back home to host the wedding reception for Susanna and John in the walled garden behind our home. This garden was my pride and joy. I loved to sit on the bench within it, soaking up the rays of the early morning sun, surrounded by my carefully tended roses and the green mulberry sapling that was a gift from King James.

Mulberry trees were tremendously expensive. For King James to have presented me with one, was a great honor. He had imported them to establish a domestic silk industry in England. Unfortunately, the captain sent to purchase the trees was hoodwinked into bringing back the wrong type of mulberry tree — one not a source of food for the precious silk worms.

Given the embarrassing situation, the King managed to find a use for those trees, giving the seedlings as ornamental gifts to his court favorites. I was fortunate enough to receive mine as a present after our company entertained him with my modern reworking of the old play, *King Lear*.

The theme of *King Lear* is the chaos which ensues when a kingdom is unwisely divided into competing factions. Its performance was especially relevant because, at that time, King James was engaged in an unsuccessful political struggle with Parliament to turn the Kingdoms of England, Wales, and Scotland into a United Kingdom. As he watched the play, his face lit up as he came to understand the underlying political message.

So there we were, gathered with family, friends and guests in the fine back garden of our home in Stratford, among the mulberry tree and the roses, framed by the orchard with its apple, pear and plum trees.

Along with the sumptuous feast of roast suckling pig, beef, chicken, pheasant, and hare, our servants busily filled glasses and tankards with beer, ale, hard cider, and wine. The beer and ale were made in our two barns, from malt and hops harvested on farmland Anne and I owned outside of Stratford. The cider was made in our cider press, using the apples gathered from trees in our orchard. The expensive Spanish and Rhenish wines were purchased from the Quineys, a prominent local family with a vinter son named Thomas.

Before the meal began, the Vicar led us all in prayer. When it was time for the toast, I stood up. Raising my glass, I began:

"Family, guests, and friends. We are here today to celebrate the marriage of my daughter, Susanna, to Dr. John Hall. Like many a proud and protective father, I was somewhat nervous and skeptical when John began courting Susanna — taking her for long walks in the garden and orchard behind us.

"However, as I got to know John better, those fears vanished. I'm happy to say John Hall is someone I believe will be a wonderful husband to my daughter. And I look forward to the day Susanna and John provide us with grandchildren to dote upon!"

Hearing this comment, many in the crowd laughed. My friend, Hamnet Sadler, called out, "Hear! Hear!"

Acknowledging him, I continued, "To further commemorate this special occasion, I've written a poem for Susanna and John best expressing my feelings about their sacred union."

With that, I began reciting the following lines:

> Let me not to the marriage of true minds
> Admit impediments. Love is not love
> Which alters when it alteration finds,
> Or bends with the remover to remove:
> O no! It is an ever-fixed mark,
> That looks on tempests, and is never shaken;
> It is the star to every wand'ring bark,
> Whose worth's unknown, although his height be
> taken.
> Love's not Time's fool, though rosy lips and cheeks

Within his bending sickle's compass come;
Love alters not with his brief hours and weeks,
But bears it out even to the edge of doom.
If this be error, and upon me prov'd,
I never writ, nor no man ever lov'd.

When I finished, the crowd of guests began clapping. Extending the glass of wine I held up in the air, I said:

"To Susanna and John. May the good Lord give you long life, and may He bless your marriage with happiness and children who will be a comfort to you in the years to come!"

Concluding my toast, I turned to face Susanna and John while sipping the sweet wine in one of the clear Venetian glasses we paid so dearly for. After I settled back down into my seat at the head of the table, John stood-up.

Straightening his jacket, and clearing his throat, John said:

"Thank you, Father. I call you Father because, by virtue of today's ceremony, I've become a new member of your family. Most of all, I'm proud and honored to be the husband of this beautiful woman sitting beside me — your daughter Susanna!"

I smiled as I took in John's speech.

"As your poem implies, it was no easy task to win your consent. However, I think all will agree the prize was worth the cost!"

If John had not pursued the study of medicine, he would have been a superb actor. He had the charisma and presence necessary to bring an audience to its feet.

With the skill of a master harpist plucking a Psalm, John went on:

"Courting the daughter of a famous poet and playwright requires great skill. Trying to match the natural air and wit of her father, as well as the wisdom and common sense of her equally beautiful mother, is next to impossible."

At these words, Anne's face beamed with pride.

"To successfully woo Susanna, I would have to do something special. Something which would allow me the pleasure of a *Love's Labor's Won* rather than the sorrow of a *Love's Labor's Lost*," John quipped, working the titles of two of my early plays into his speech, and bringing roars of laughter.

When the laughter died down, John continued: "I spent many nights trying to come up with a poem worthy of Susanna's wit and beauty. When I finally had something I thought worthy, I came to New Place one sunny afternoon. And, with Mrs. Shakespeare's consent, walked with Susanna in this beautiful garden and the orchard over there.

"As the sun set, I gathered up my courage and recited this poem, which no one has heard except Susanna."

> Precious the night, when together,
> Alone in the mist of a fruited grove,
> We sealed ourselves beneath an orange sky,
> Marveling at the pearl, which hung,
> Mysterious, among unknown worlds above.
> Like a vine, which twists around its branch,
> Reaching for the sun, I shall always cling to you,
> Offering my ripened fruit.
> Even time, with its flaming two-edged sword,
> Shall not bar the path between my Love and I.

When John finished, we all applauded. As the applause receded, John raised his wineglass. Turning to Susanna, he said: "Thank you for consenting to become my wife. You have fulfilled my dreams. I will love you until all days have passed and the seas go dry!"

As John sat down, Susanna surprised us all by standing. Smoothing out the wrinkled folds of her dress, she gave me a mischievous wink, as she often did when she had the upper hand in our games of chess.

After I winked back, she began, "Gentlemen and Gentlewomen, I've heard the excellent verse and wit of both my honored father and my honorable husband. But, less they think we of the weaker sex do not possess wits to rival theirs in creativity and ingenuity, I offer you this little piece I've written in honor of my marriage to this eminent man."

While Susanna looked at John, she began:

Your blood and my blood flow together,
Red and white, thick and thin,
Through the stem and branches,
Straight to the Heart of the Vine.

Your song and my song are sung together,
High and low, fast and slow,
Their harmonious melodies intertwine.

Your heart and my heart beat together,
Drummers marching off to Wars of Love,
Swords crossed and bows pulled taut.

Let fly the arrows and pierce our hearts;
Surgeons will sow our souls together,
With ties that bind and strings which never part.

As she finished, both John and I stood up clapping. "Good show, Susanna!" I shouted over the applause as Susanna and John embraced. Caught up in this special moment, Anne and I embraced and kissed, something we had not done for quite some time.

When the meal was over, the music and dancing began. I had hired a group of singers and musicians from London to perform at the reception. While the men played their lutes, citterns and pipes, the trio of women singers sang the haunting lyrics of a new song by Thomas Campion. I can still hear the words echoing – from time out of mind.

> Thrice toss these oaken ashes in the air,
> Thrice sit thou mute in this enchanted chair,
> Then thrice-three times tie up this true love's knot,
> And murmur soft "She will or she will not."
>
> Then come, you Fairies! dance with me a round!
> Melt her hard heart with your melodious sound!
> In vain are all the charms I can devise:
> She hath an art to break them with her eyes.

CHAPTER LXVIII
BIRTH OF AN ANGEL

The wedding of John and Susanna was followed within the year by an even greater miracle, the birth of our granddaughter, Elizabeth. I was fortunate to be able to travel home to Stratford to be present when she came into the world in February 1608. At the time, Susanna and John were residing with us at New Place. By the grace of God, my mother lived long enough to see her great granddaughter. My mother, Anne, and Judith served as midwives, assisting Susanna through a prolonged labor of over twelve hours.

John and I awaited news of the birth in the parlor. Even though John was a physician, the women of our family were in charge of this great event. John visited the bedroom on several occasions that day. He took Susanna's pulse and brought her a cup of a special herbal potion he brewed to provide strength during the ordeal. While John tended to Susanna, I stepped outside into the cold winter air to enjoy a pipe of tobacco.

Anne did not permit me to smoke in the house. Like most men, I bragged I was king of my own castle. But I knew who buttered my bread and brewed my ale, not to mention ran the household staff, and kept the accounts during my long periods of absence.

As I enjoyed a pipe of tobacco, leaning against the wall beside the front door, I noticed a row of small, gradually melting icicles hanging from the roof entrance-way that was almost identical to the entrance-way of our family home on Henley Street.

Seeing the melting icicles brought back childhood memories of our family sitting around the fireplace while my father entertained us with one of the many Winter's Tales he had picked up at the fireside of his parents' farm in Snitterfield.

Early in my career, I incorporated a song I had written when still a teenager into the last scene of *Love's Labor's Lost*. It was inspired by my own family's winter storytelling sessions. Between puffs of smoke, I now found myself reciting it into the icy winter wind.

When icicles hang by the wall,
And Dick the shepherd blows his nail,
And Tom bears logs into the hall,
And milk comes frozen home in pail,
When blood is nipp'd, and ways be foul,
Then nightly sings the staring owl,
To-who;
Tu-whit, to-who, a merry note,
While greasy Joan doth keel the pot.

When all aloud the wind doth blow,
And coughing drowns the parson's saw
And birds sit brooding in the snow,
And Marian's nose looks red and raw,
When roasted crabs hiss in the bowl,
Then nightly sings the staring owl,
To-who;
Tu-whit, to-who, a merry note,
While greasy Joan doth keel the pot.

As I finished my pipe, the front door opened. John stepped out for a breather.

"How goes it?"

"So far, so good. Susanna's pulse is strong."

"I 'm praying for a safe delivery. It's sad one's entry into this world is filled with such risk."

"We must trust in the Lord," John said.

"I guess so," I replied, as we re-entered the hall, and heard Susanna crying out in the final throes of her labor.

Hearing those cries made my heart bleed.

When Susanna's cries subsided, we heard the shrill cry of a newborn. John and I bounded up the stairs. Reaching the top first, John rushed across the small landing, knocking forcefully on the bedroom door.

"A minute please," Anne's firm voice responded.

After what seemed an eternity, she opened the door. My mother, Anne and Judith allowed us to approach the bed where Susanna lay covered by a blanket, holding the swaddled baby.

Before John could get a word in, Susanna said, "You're the father of a beautiful girl."

Looking at me, she said, "Say hello to Elizabeth!"

"She's wonderful!" John exclaimed, kissing Susanna on the forehead. Addressing the little one, John said, "Elizabeth, you gave your mother a hard time. But we're glad you're here!"

Admiring Elizabeth's cherubim-like features, I felt an immediate and powerful connection. I sensed this child could prove to be the silver lining of the cloud of grief overshadowing my life for the last several years. I am happy to say my intuition proved correct.

Elizabeth's heart was true. And her mind proved both playful and mischievous. Her smile and spontaneous laugh were irresistible. Just being around her put me in a good mood. As weeks passed, and I found myself back in London performing and writing for long stretches of time, I came to miss my family in Stratford more than ever.

CHAPTER LXIX
TEMPEST GENESIS

By the grace of God, I no longer had to work to keep food on the table and a roof over our heads. The success of our acting company brought me enough wealth to allow myself and my family to live comfortably for the remainder of our lives. We owned the second largest home in Stratford, as well as the Henley Street property I inherited from my father — part of which we converted into a tavern called the Maidenhead. We also owned a substantial interest in Holy Trinity's parish tithes. And we owned sufficient farmland to allow us to brew a great deal of malt ale to sell to local taverns including the Maidenhead.

Further, I had now become the owner of an interest in two theaters rather than one. After many delays, in 1608, the King's Men were finally able to open the indoor Blackfriars Theater, located in a posh section of London. Although the Blackfriars contained far fewer seats than the Globe, the cheapest seats in the Blackfriars cost as much as the most expensive in The Globe. Just as importantly, plays could be performed year-round, without regard to weather. This made the Blackfriars more profitable than the Globe.

As I considered these facts, I decided I did not want to continue working full-time. I spoke with the other shareholders about my decision. They reluctantly agreed to allow me to step out of the limelight. Provided I agreed to serve as a mentor to my successor as the company's leading playwright, John Fletcher, I would be allowed to stop performing as an actor.

In preparation for my stage retirement, I began working on what would turn out to be the last play I would author alone. That play was *The Tempest*. In many ways, like Michaelangelo's painting of the *Last Judgment* in Rome's Sistine Chapel, it is the summation of my work as an artist.

My life has certainly been a tempest of sorts. The personal tragedies which occurred on the private stage of my own life have been heartrending.

From childhood I have possessed the firm conviction I was not destined to live a long life. I received my fair share of gifts from the Creator. But the gift of living to ripe old age is not one of them. I felt the best use I could make of the final act of my life was to return to Stratford and be the husband, father and grandfather I had not been able to be up until this point.

I tried to work these thoughts into *The Tempest*. In many ways my character, Prospero, echoes my thoughts and feelings. Just as the magic he performs comes from books, my writing would not be possible without the "magical" books that fired my imagination and provided the basis of many plots for my plays.

Like myself, Prospero has a daughter dear to his heart. Miranda is a beautiful vision. Their relationship is a mirror of my relationship with Susanna.

The spirit Ariel is the lighthearted side of my art, seen in comedies such as *A Midsummer's Night's Dream*, *Much Ado About Nothing*, *Twelfth Night*, *The Taming of the Shrew*, *The Merry Wives of Windsor*, *As You Like It*, and *Love's Labour's Lost*.

The monster Caliban is the grasping, earthy side of my art, most evident in plays like *Othello*, *King Lear*, *Macbeth*, and *Richard III*.

To Prospero's initial consternation, the beautiful, pure, and innocent Miranda falls in love with Ferdinand, the son of a co-conspirator who helped oust Prospero from his Dukedom.

In some ways, the handsome and sincerely smitten Ferdinand is an image of my son-in law, John Hall. A good man in the service of a not so good cause.

Like Prospero, long years of exile in London as a servant of my enemies gradually led me to the font of wisdom and mercy. As the old saying goes: "To err is human; to forgive is divine." In the end, Prospero chooses the wiser course of forgiveness and reconciliation over the base instincts of hatred and revenge. Prospero reconciles with his brother, gives his blessing to Ferdinand and Miranda, abjures his books of wisdom and magic, and returns home.

CHAPTER LXX
A TURN IN THE ROAD

Upon completing *The Tempest*, I delivered the manuscript to the King's Men. They offered me the singular honor of playing Prospero in its first performance at The Blackfriars. I had only played supporting roles for quite a few years before undertaking the role of Prospero. As it would be my final performance, I rehearsed intensely. Since I had written the work with the Blackfriars in mind, I included special effects suited to that indoor venue.

The periodic need to tend to the candles within the theater necessitated the performance be delivered in five acts, rather than one seamless performance. Although the division of the play into acts did break up the flow of the action, it provided time for more elaborate changes to set and costumes. Finally, the sophistication of the Blackfriars well-heeled audience allowed me to write a play of great complexity and nuance with a reasonable expectation it would be appreciated.

Because this was my final stage performance, I wanted as many of my family to attend as possible. Since Elizabeth was now a delightfully rambunctious three-year-old, Susanna and John were able to leave her in the care of my sister, Joan and her husband, the hatter William Hart. Along with Susanna and John, Anne, Gil, Richard and Judith also made the long journey from Stratford to London.

I arranged for everyone except Anne to stay at the Green Dragon, one of the best inns in town. Anne stayed with me in the humble but clean lodgings that had served as my home-away-from-home for several years. Even though she got the worst part of the deal, Anne bore it cheerily. She knew this was an important milestone.

While Anne and I comfortably rested in bed the evening before my performance, I told her how much I appreciated and loved her for always standing by my side. Anne told me she appreciated the sacrifices I had made to provide her and the children with a safe and comfortable home. Then she surprised me.

"Will," she said, "I know you sometimes like to think you're the only poet in this family. But, during the weeks leading up to this trip, I've been reflecting upon our relationship over the years. I 've put pen to paper to create something I hope you'll like."

"I can't wait to hear it!" I replied.

"So you shall," Anne said, reaching over and removing a folded sheet of paper from the jewelry box she had placed on the small stool beside the bed. Unfolding it, she began reading with an energy and vigor in her face and voice that brought back pleasant memories of the vibrant young woman I once courted.

We have walked a road together,
Filled with both pain and pleasure.
Through the roses, through the heather,
Came sunshine and storm-filled weather.

We have seen the bright sunrise,
And sailed on high and ebbing tides.
We have heard the bells and chimes,
Ring in best and worst of times.

Through it all, our love endured,
Remaining true of heart and pure.
It brings a smile to my face,
To feel your strong and sweet embrace.

Love's Labour's Won

I know our road is ending soon,
The harvest's in, the leaves have turned.
But, as the fire's embers burn,
We reminisce, and then return,

To the life we share together,
Full of love that lasts forever.

"Wow!" I exclaimed. "That really says it all. It's a gift I shall always cherish." I meant it. The words Anne said to me that day are etched in my heart.

Chapter LXXI
Curtain Call

The next morning Anne and I had breakfast. Then I headed over to the Blackfriars to make final preparations for that afternoon's performance. Walking through the bustling streets, I noticed numerous handbills tacked on tavern doors and walls:

"See the farewell performance of the Sweet Swan of Avon! The most famous player and playwright, Mr. William Shakespeare, in his magical production of *The Tempest*!"

Excitement was in the air. I was happy to be part of it.

Arriving at the theater around ten, I ran into our business managers, John Hemmings and Bert Burbage. They were supervising the construction of the set. After paying my respects to them, I went to the tiring room to run through the script one more time. When I completed my solo "rehearsal," I inspected the costumes and properties.

To become Prospero, I would wear a long, midnight-blue satin robe decorated with esoteric embroidered signs and symbols. These included a large yellow sun surrounded by a circle of red tongues of fire, numerous white crescent moons, and seven silver spangled stars. In addition to wearing this Magus robe, I also would carry a carved wooden staff depicting a hissing serpent. Finally, I checked out the silver-haired periwig and the crown of laurel I would wear to give Prospero the look of maturity and wisdom I desired.

As I finished my inventory of the costumes and props, Nathan Field, the talented young actor playing my daughter Miranda, came into the tiring room and began the tedious process of applying the make-up necessary to transform his appearance into that of a young woman. Nathan was now about fifteen, but he still had the face and figure shared by girls and boys before reaching puberty.

Although his voice had gone through "the change" from the high pitch of a boy to the deeper tone of a man, Nathan had learned to speak and sing in a falsetto convincingly imitating the higher pitch and tone of a grown woman's voice.

Nathan began his career as a member of the company of boys that performed in this theater before that company went out of business. As one of the leading actors of the boys' company, Nathan had developed a significant reputation and following. We were fortunate to acquire him. When not on stage, he was a quiet and respectful person, who, given our age difference, usually addressed me as "Mr. Shakespeare."

"Good to see you, Nathan," I welcomed.

"You too, Mr. Shakespeare," he replied in his soft-spoken manner. "Sir, I want you to know it's an honor to be by your side today. You're an inspiration to us young actors. A legend really!"

"A legend in my own mind, maybe," I replied. "But, as you already know, the public's taste is fickle. What's up today, is down tomorrow. One minute it's laughter, the next sorrow. Sometimes a plethora of riches, other times one begs or borrows."

Nathan laughed. Using the falsetto he would employ to play Miranda, he said, "All good lines. You should write them down for the future."

"Probably should," I said. "The writing doesn't come as easily these days, especially the verse."

"I wouldn't have guessed that," said Nathan. "Personally, I think *The Tempest* is the best play you've written."

"I appreciate the compliment. I put my heart and soul into it, and it took a lot out of me. I hope some of the enthusiasm I have for it will be shared by the audience."

"They'll love it," Nathan assured.

"Flattery will get you nowhere," I remarked, patting him on the shoulder and addressing the other actors who had entered the room to begin their preparations: "Enough with the small talk. Let's get cracking!"

"Cracking indeed!" said a deep baritone voice behind me. I immediately recognized it as belonging to my competitor and oftentimes friend, Ben Johnson. I turned around just in time to receive a huge hug from this bear of a man.

By any stretch of imagination, Ben could not be called handsome. His features were the plain, thick and hearty ones of the common tradesman stock from which he came. He had worked for a time with his stepfather, a bricklayer. Ben had the thick, stubby fingers, muscular forearms and large biceps customary to the men of that profession.

He had the additional advantage of being able to hold his liquor far better than the average man. Ben consistently drank me under the table during the many meals we shared at the Mermaid, imbibing, eating, and engaging in friendly argument until the proprietor, our friend, Will Johnson, shut us down and sent us home.

Although Ben might look and sometimes act the part of the common laborer, he possesses one of the finest intellects I have known. Despite good-naturedly ribbing me for having "small Latine and less Greeke," for the most part we get along famously.

Although Ben did not act on stage often, he did so for special occasions. He was quite good when he put his heart into it. Even though he was not a shareholder in an acting company, he had no trouble selling his own high-quality plays. But, for him, play-writing had become more passion than necessity. Most of Ben's substantial income was derived from the elaborate court "masks" he collaborated on with fellow innovative genius, Inigo Jones.

The masks were more pageants than plays. The costumes and props often cost thousands of pounds. Women at court loved them. They got to dress up in the most elaborate fashions and jewelry, as well as being featured performers. Despite the money that could be made writing the affected highfalutin verse the ladies of the court enjoyed, that form of society art held no attraction for me. Ben, on the other hand, loved it. His proficient scripts made him rich. Unfortunately, money runs through his hands like quicksilver.

Tonight, Ben was doing me the great honor of playing Caliban, the monstrous son of the witch who has earned Prospero's enmity for attempting to rape his daughter. Ben volunteered to play the role after hearing this was to be my final performance. Ben said, "Caliban's the role for me. You've always been more of an Ariel. I've got animal magnetism in my soul."

As the curtain opened, I stood in the wings, awaiting my cue to step into the glow of the footlights one last time. When it arrived, I stepped out on stage cloaked in my magical robe carrying my wizard's staff. For a fleeting moment, I felt I really was a Merlin, conjuring my own vision of Avalon. Through the glare of flickering lights, I could see my family seated in the front row. To my surprise, I also saw our dearest friends, Hamnet and Judith Sadler. Not far away sat my old friends, Richard and Jacqueline Field, and my Oxford friends, William and Jane Davenant.

On either side of the stage sat my great aristocratic patrons, Lord Southhampton, and the Herbert brothers, whose support had been so essential to my success throughout my career. As the performance continued, I noticed many other familiar faces in the crowd, including the great Edward Alleyn, who smiled a greeting.

All our actors performed their roles flawlessly. When the curtain closed, tears of joy and relief welled in my eyes.

While fellow actors Dick Burbage, John Heminges, Henry Condell, Ben Johnson, Nathan Field, and Robert Armin offered their congratulations, applause and cheers arose from the audience. Slowly but surely the cheering began to organize itself into a chant of "Shakespeare! Shakespeare! Shakespeare!" If only my parents and son Hamnet could have been there to experience that moment with me, it would have been perfect.

As the chanting of my name continued, it came time to step in front of the curtain and deliver the epilogue I composed for this occasion. I stepped out from behind the curtain basking in the warm applause. When the noise died down, I began speaking in the loudest and deepest voice I could muster:

> Now my charms are all o'erthrown,
> And what strength I have's my own;
> Which is most faint: now, 'tis true,
> I must be here confin'd by you,
> Or sent to Naples: Let me not,
> Since I have my dukedom got,
> And pardon'd the deceiver, dwell
> In this bare island, by your spell;
> But release me from my bands,
> With the help of your good hands.
> Gentle breath of yours my sails
> Must fill, or else my project fails,
> Which was to please: now I want
> Spirits to enforce, art to enchant;
> And my ending is despair,
> Unless I be reliev'd by prayer;
> Which pierces so, that it assaults
> Mercy itself, and frees all faults.
> As you from crimes would pardon'd be,
> Let your indulgence set me free.

Chapter LXXII
Global Conflagration

Although my last performance on the stage was in *The Tempest*, my departure from the players ranks did not end my business and professional relationship with The King's Men. I continued as a shareholder in the company of players, as well as being a part owner of the Globe and the Blackfriars. My dual shareholder and ownership status paid good dividends. To maintain my shareholder status, I still wrote plays. But, rather than penning them on my own, I now collaborated as I had during the beginning of my writing career.

The three most recent plays I've written were co-authored with a very talented playwright named John Fletcher. Before John began to work with me, he wrote a significant number of successful plays with his longtime writing partner, Francis Beaumont. The names "Beaumont and Fletcher" were synonymous with box office success during the first decade of this century.

As all things must come to an end, Francis eventually fell in love and married. Since his bride had enough wealth to comfortably support them both, he decided to leave the theater business. This left John looking for a partner at the same time I was looking for someone to share in the playwriting responsibilities for the company.

Though our collaboration was primarily a long distance one, my scenes written at my home in Stratford, while John wrote his in London, we still managed to produce three reasonably good shows, *The Two Noble Kinsman*, based on Chaucer's "The Knight's Tale," *Cardenio*, based on a character and incidents from Miguel Cervantes's *Don Quixote*, and our most commercially successful collaboration, *All Is True*, the retelling of the tale of Henry VIII's breakup with his wife and the Roman Catholic Church, and his subsequent marriage to Anne Boleyn.

Of course, a play about this subject could not be written while Queen Elizabeth was alive. Even if it presented her birth as a sign of hope, as my Protestant collaborator, John Fletcher, made sure it did.

Ten years into the reign of King James, John and I decided to see if we could get the Master of the Revels to go along with the idea. The Master of the Revels consulted with the Crown. The Crown gave its assent providing the play presented the former monarchy in the "proper light."

To gain the censor's and the Government's blessing, we made the play heavy on pomp and circumstance. Henry was portrayed with sympathy, and the birth of Elizabeth was seen as a bright ray of hope. The events depicted were so far in the past they were beyond living memory. For most, what they saw depicted was the only "truth" they would ever know. That is why, when John was searching for a title, I suggested *All is True*.

In response, John burst into a gregarious laugh, saying, "That's perfect."

"It's a double entendre," I stated. "It'll appeal to everyone."

Those who buy the Crown's whitewashed story of Henry the Eighth's reign will take it at face value," said John.

"And those who haven't brought into it will see the irony in the title," I added.

"So, it'll appeal to both our core audiences."

"I hope so," I said. "With the concluding panegyric you've written about King James, it will, hopefully, be acceptable to the Master of the Revels."

"I think it will. What nut would ban a play that says this of the King:

> Wherever the bright sun of heaven shall shine,
> His honour and the greatness of his name
> Shall be, and make new nations: He shall flourish,

And, like a mountain cedar, reach his branches
To all the plains about him: — Our children's
children
Shall see this, and bless Heaven.

"I'm glad you wrote that piece," I said. "After seeing what I've seen, it's difficult to write anything like that about the government."

"One does what one must do to get by in this world," said John.

Sure enough, the abject flattery enabled our play to receive the Master of the Revel's seal of approval.

The King's Men were soon purchasing the costumes and props necessary to put on the elaborate show. In addition to the gowns, tires, baubles, crowns, and Beefeater's uniforms, we even went to the expense of procuring ceremonial cannons to bring the house to its feet with their bellowing roar!

Given the hard work and risks John and I undertook in writing this play, I wanted to be there for the opening performance. So, in mid- June 1613, I once again journeyed from Stratford to London to spend a week or so assisting my old friends and colleagues and to watch what I had written on the page brought to life by an immensely talented cast of players.

As is true with most plays, the first two performances were a bit rough. John Heminges, Richard Burbage, John Fletcher, and I worked very hard ironing out the kinks. By the June 29th third performance, I was comfortable enough to take a seat in the players' box.

What a fateful show it turned out to be. At the point where King Henry participates in a mask at the mansion of Cardinal Wolsey, several cannon shots were fired by the stagehands to accent the action. Liven up the performance they did. Several pieces of smoking cannon fodder landed on a segment of the thatched roof. After a few smoldering moments, the dry, fourteen-year-old reeds burst into flames which streaked around the circular roofline of the Globe like a fleeting Mercury.

While I momentarily sat frozen in my box watching the growing conflagration, the groundlings on the lowest level of the theater let out a tremendous hue and cry. Fortunately, the fire burned towards the ground level more slowly, leaving enough time for the terrified groundlings to rush out of the theater in a jumble of arms, legs and torsos, while those in the covered galleries rapidly made our way down stairs and out the theater doors in the wake of the scrambling groundlings.

Amid the chaos, I made my way to the box office to help Bert ensure the precious manuscripts of our plays were safely loaded into a chest. A few minutes later, as stagehands assisted us with carrying the large chest out of the theater, we saw the white-hot flames had already spread to the highest gallery level — engulfing the wooden seating and supporting timbers.

Suddenly, a section of flaming roof thatch fell to the ground nearby, managing to ignite the breeches of one of the bottled-ale sellers.

Luckily, the man was carrying a large basket full of ale bottles, which he dropped when his breeches caught on fire. As he rolled around in the sawdust squawking, those of us nearby sprang into action. Together, we doused him with ale from the bottles he had been carrying. The man survived his dance with the fire devil, suffering only minor injuries.

As Bert, the stagehands and I exited the blazing theater carrying the chest of manuscripts and assisting the injured ale seller, we encountered a bewildered John Heminges rapidly clenching and unclenching his raised fists as if he was trying to squeeze the life out of the fire while shouting in his characteristic stutter, "Wa-wa-Will! Wa-wa-we're ruined!"

I grabbed him with my free hand shouting: "Let's get the hell out of here!" as I dragged him away from the burning building which had served as our world of imagination.

As I watched our precious Globe burn to the ground over the course of the next hour, I came to the realization it was more than just a building perishing in the flames. The theater business had provided a good living for myself and my family. But, perhaps this event was a sign from Providence. I was now approaching the ripe old age of fifty. It was time to let the young bloods make a go of it.

Not long after the fire I sold my shares in the company and headed home to Stratford for good. I knew my former colleagues would rebuild the Globe, but my time to bask in the rays of the sun had come and gone. I would not be a part of that venture.

Chapter LXXIII
Back to Stratford

As all things in this world must come to an end, I feel my time of departure fast approaching. I thank God, the Lord and Creator of us all, for watching over and protecting me in this life, and granting me the singular opportunity and the ability to create the plays and poetry I was able to write and perform upon the stage. I further thank the Lord for the gift of a loyal and faithful wife, two worthy daughters, and a granddaughter who holds within her bright eyes and agile mind the hope of things to come.

I look forward to reuniting with my grandparents, parents, son, brothers, sisters, and friends who wait for me on the other side of this mortal coil which binds us to this earth. As St. Paul said: "I have fought a good fight, I have finished my course, I have kept the faith."

While I write these lines on the bed Anne brought with her from her family home in Shottery, the marriage bed which will soon be my portal to the undiscovered country to which we all must journey, I look back with gratitude upon the many persons who had a hand in weaving the unique tapestry of my life.

In some ways, my story is one which has been told a million times and shall be told a million times again. Whatever view we may have of ourselves and the significance of our lives, our time of reckoning will come. But, before I go to meet my maker, there are a few pieces of unfinished business that must be attended to, the most important of which is the making of my will.

So, when the consumption I suffered from these last few years took a turn for the worse in January, I turned my attention to the wrapping up of my affairs. Anne had urged me to have a will prepared since my diagnosis several years ago. I found excuses to put it off. But, time and tide wait for no man.

One morning, as the sun shone through the expensive pane glass window, spreading its welcoming rays upon the burgundy curtains enclosing our four poster bed, I turned to Anne, who insisted on remaining by my side throughout the ups and downs of this chronic illness, and said: "I'd appreciate it if you would make arrangements to have Francis Collins come to see me today or tomorrow — if he has the time."

Anne, who had been sleeping on her side to protect her from my periodic coughing fits, rolled over. Lying flat on her back, she said, "Certainly. I'll have Robert go see Francis this morning." Then she asked: "Are you feeling okay?"

"Not really," I answered. "I had several fits last night. Brought up some blood. Plus, the fire went out. I didn't have the energy to restart it."

"I told that lazy maid to check the fire periodically during the night. You being sick and all! I've a good mind to send her back to her family."

"There's no need to go that far. She's Hamnet's niece. With his Judith gone, the last thing Hamnet needs is another problem."

"Will, you know how close I was to Judith. That doesn't mean we have to accept such performance."

"Okay. Okay," I answered, as I sat up and began to get out of bed.

Settling onto the commode, I continued, "I don't like Mary's poor performance any more than you. But, for Hamnet's sake, let's settle for a good chewing out and a warning. We have more serious things to focus upon."

"All right," Anne answered, as she got up out of her side of the bed and began to get dressed. "I'll give that lazy girl a piece of my mind she'll not forget. I don't want her further jeopardizing your health."

"Thanks," I said, as I stood up, walked over to my clothes chest, took off my nightshirt, and began getting dressed.

After putting on my undergarments, I proceeded over to the small walnut table where my towel, razor, and washbasin were laid out. I rinsed my hands in the ice-cold water. Creating a lather with a bar of homemade soap, I spread it across my face and neck. I picked up my razor and carefully began to scrape the stubble off my face.

I used a small mirror that sat on the washbasin stand to aid my placement of the razor against the skin, and to try to keep from cutting myself. Like most men, I don't enjoy shaving. It's a necessary evil.

What people think of us is important. Certainly, obtaining a coat of arms for our family is one of my most important achievements. As I thought of the gentleman's sword I proudly wore on special occasions, I realized I had no male heir to leave it too. With my father, Hamnet, Gil, Richard and Edmund gone, I was the sole remaining male in the Shakespeare bloodline. Given the amount of work my father and I put into obtaining the title of "gentlemen," it is ironic it will all end soon.

As I thought about the whole situation, I began laughing. Out of the corner of my eyes, I saw Anne looking at me with an air of concern.

"What's wrong?" She earnestly asked.

"Nothing. Just your crazy husband laughing at himself again!"

"Sometimes I worry about you," Anne said, shaking her head.

To my way of thinking at that moment, the absence of a male heir to carry on my name was one more example of God's sense of humor. It is senseless for us to try to store up treasures upon this earth. Maybe this is God's way of keeping me humble — preventing me from flying too close to the heat of the sun.

Like many other Greek and Roman myths, the story of Icarus impressed itself upon my mind at an early age. Thanks to the unique friendship that developed between myself and Lord Southhampton, I was able to visit his library quite often. Within that impressive room was a copy of a small Dutch painting featuring the legend of Icarus. Lord Southhampton obtained it as a gift from one of his aristocratic friends in the Low Countries.

I spent numerous afternoons admiring this exquisitely detailed picture. Rather than focusing on the tiny figure of the falling Icarus, only his thrashing legs are visible. His head, torso and melted wings have already splashed into the sea. Much of the painting depicts a seaside landscape, filled with everyday people going about their daily business; a farmhand works cropland, a shepherd tends his flock. Sailors sail their ships. An angler casts for fish. Icarus meets his fate. Shakespeare writes his plays. One person's tragedy is another's joy. One's victory is another's defeat.

Studying this painting, I came to understand an individual's life is but one cog in the gears of the eternal clock whose minutes sound off, tick- tock, tick-tock! The man who painted that slice of life had remarkable insight. Soon my own role in our collective passion play will be finished. The next scene will be played by others. Another "actor" will step out onto the stage and steal the scene with little or no knowledge of what has come before!

As I finished shaving, I splashed some water onto my face, and began dabbing it with a towel. As I did, I noticed my wife had already left the room. "Daydreaming Will" was one of her playful nicknames for me. What I consider deep thought, she often considers idleness. I guess the truth as God sees it is somewhere between.

When I finished dressing, I carefully went downstairs using the handrail that my son-in-law John Hall and prospective son-in-law, Thomas Quiney recently installed for me. If I became any weaker than I was today, I would probably have to abandon sleeping in our second-best marital bed and begin sleeping in the showy best bed in the first story parlor of our home.

After reaching the bottom of the stairs, I turned left and walked down the hallway to the dining room. Anne, Susanna, Judith and Elizabeth were already seated around the table.

"Where's John?" I asked, as I took my customary seat at the head of the table.

"Already visiting a patient who has come down with a fever. A bad cold's making the rounds," said Susanna.

"Vomiting too!" added Elizabeth.

"Remember we're at breakfast," said Anne.

"Vomiting too!" I said to Elizabeth, winking playfully.

"You're in top form today," Anne said, with a touch of sarcasm.

"I'm glad to see you're your old self Father! Busy corrupting the youth," Susanna said, tongue in cheek.

"Maybe so," I responded. "But I trust I didn't do too much damage to you and your sister. Seems you both turned out just fine!"

"It's all in the eyes of the beholder. One person's jewel is another's trifle," Judith chimed in, demonstrating she had not fallen off the turnip cart when it came to the gift of wit.

"What all this makes clear is both you girls take after your father and his peculiar sense of humor. How I've managed to live among you all is beyond me," said Anne.

"If any of us make it into the gates of Paradise, it will be because of your efforts," I said. "As for myself, I only hope your prayers will get me through the Gates of Heaven before the devil knows I'm dead."

"Spoken like the verbal acrobat you are!" Anne replied.

"With that said, let's see what the kitchen staff have rustled up for this historic repast," I offered, changing the topic.

"Some porridge, curds, and your favorite cured ham," said Judith.

"A fine meal for a fine morning," I said, as our kitchen serving girls brought the food to the table. We each removed our personal eating knives from their sheaths to cut our servings of the salted ham, while one of the girls poured me a large cup of near frozen milk from a pitcher.

Cold, creamy milk was one of the few pleasures of winter — my least favorite season. As I took a long, cold draught, I felt the invigorating liquid coursing through my body. Our milk cows, Bessie and Tessie, were two of the finest in Stratford.

After drinking half a cup, I used a prized possession, one of the French two-pronged forks I purchased at a renowned silversmith's shop in London, to spear the ham, while I used my knife to cut the meat into bite-size pieces. Though most of our family still ate their slices of meat with their knives, Anne and I preferred to eat ours in the new French fashion — with forks.

When we finished breakfast, I asked everyone to join me in my study for a few minutes before we each went our separate ways.

Chapter LXXIV
An Impromptu Concert

Upon arriving in the study, I picked up the lute I was given by Mr. Hoghton those many years ago and took a seat in my favorite chair. Addressing Susanna and Judith, I said, "I wanted you both to accompany me here to hear a new song I've written for the most important person in my life — your mother!" Looking at Elizabeth, I added, "And your granddam!"

"Ah Will," Anne spoke up. "Don't you be pulling my leg once again with one of your comic little songs to get the girls laughing at my expense!"

"Now Anne, do you really think I would do that after all our years together? Listen-up before you render judgment."

I began playing the strings of the time-honored instrument. At the proper point, I began:

I don't have much to offer
Except this silver pen.
From this amber sundown
One doesn't come back again.

I've seen the blazing sunrise
And welcomed in the dawn.
I know that Heaven smiled
On the morning you were born.

You are a ray of sunshine
That brightens up my life.

I love to see you laughing
In the pale moonlight.

Your voice is like an Angel's,
So clear and pure and true.
It reveals all the beauty
That is inside of you.

Dark hair frames the portrait
Of your pretty face.
With an air of mystery
You shine in silk and lace.

The gates of Heaven opened
To bring your soul to life;
And I am blessed to know you
In this earthly life.

As I finished, Susanna, Judith and Elizabeth were all clapping. I looked at Anne, who wore a broad smile, and asked, "What's your opinion, my toughest critic?"

"Not bad. You might have some talent after all," she answered.

"It was wonderful," said Elizabeth. "Can you do an encore?"

"I'm afraid I can't today," I gently replied. "But, as you know, I'm not the only lute-playing songwriter in this house. Your grandmother wrote quite a few songs over these last few years. We use several in our plays. There's one which has a special place in my heart. I'd like to hear it again today."

"Which one's that Grandfather?" asked Elizabeth.

"It's a song called 'The Southern Wind.' I play it for myself on cold and lonely nights."

Switching her attention to Anne, Elizabeth asked, "Grandmother, will you play that song for grandfather and me?"

"I'd love to," Anne answered. "But I don't remember all the words. Given the stiffness in my fingers, I don't believe I can bend the strings anymore."

"Fine objection," I said, walking over to my desk and lifting the sheet of paper which lay upon it. "But you're not getting off that easily. I happen to have a copy of the lyrics right here. I'd be happy to do the honors of accompanying you on the lute."

"Oh Grandmother, sing it for me!" Elizabeth pleaded.

"All right. You and your grandfather have painted me into a corner. Let's see those lyrics. I'll give it a try. Although my voice is far from what it once was."

Striking while the iron was hot, I brought the lyric sheet to Anne, resumed my seat, and picked up the lute. After a brief false start, I resumed playing. Anne began singing in her beautiful voice.

Sleeping in the Southern Wind
Causes us to dream again
Of all the things we have done
Sailing underneath the sun.

The friendships that have come and gone,
The faces we did dote upon,
The castles swirling in the air,
The visions of the here and there,

The games we lost, the games we won,
The things we did that came undone,
The pains in life, the joys and fun,
The laughs we shared with everyone,

The gifts we gave to those we love,
The blessings sent from God above.
They all gather in our minds
And weave the tapestry of time.

Floating in the Southern Wind
Is all we need to live again,
The first and last of our desires,
The sparks rising from our fires!

As I listened, I couldn't help thinking about how good a stage singer Anne could be. No matter how hard the young men in our acting company tried, their falsettos were only a pale imitation of a true woman's voice.

When Anne finished, Susanna, Judith and Elizabeth clapped even more enthusiastically than for my performance.

Elizabeth shouted, "That's great, Grandmother. It's the best!"

"Hush child! I don't like my song the best. I like the song your grandfather wrote for me. It's a wonderful gift."

"Both songs were wonderful in their own way," said Susanna, playing her role as family mediator.

"I agree," said Judith.

"Thank you all," I said, "especially your mother."

CHAPTER LXXV
SEEDS OF INSPIRATION

Having finished our impromptu concert, we each went our separate ways. I remained in my study to prepare for the arrival of my attorney and friend, Francis Collins. The study was my favorite room at New Place. It was my sanctuary, my oasis, my El Dorado, my world within a world.

The room was graced with a large stone fireplace, providing warmth on even the coldest days. It had several comfortable sitting chairs, a rare Turkish carpet that was a gift from Lord Pembroke, and a custom-made writing desk and chair I used for the business of writing plays for The King's Men.

But the most valuable possessions contained in this room were the leather-bound books lining the bookshelves we specially constructed to house them. Among these treasures of the mind were numerous plays by Seneca and Platus, Plutarch's *Lives of the Noble Romans*, Holingshed's *Chronicles of England*, the two volumes of Richard Halkyut's *Voyages of Discovery*, the copy of Ovid's *Metamorphoses* I purchased as agift for my son Hamnet, a worn copy of Sir Thomas Mallory's *Le Morte de Arthur*, which my own father gave me when I was a child, *The Iliad* and *The Odyssey* of Homer, The *Aenied* of Virgil, Cervantes's *Don Quixote*, Chaucer's *The Canterbury Tales*, Sir Thomas More's *Utopia*, Erasmus's *In Praise of Folly*, as well as one of the most recent volumes in my collection, the magnificent English translation of *The Bible* commissioned by King James, and published in 1611, only five years ago.

This book had been a multi-year labor of love and scholarship which was both a spiritual and linguistic triumph. The magnificent *Bible* had been a special gift to Anne and me from Susanna and John. We have spent many an evening beside the fire reading passages to each other, glorying in both the language and spirituality infusing it.

So many of these books have provided me with material to use, shape, and build upon when composing my own plays and poems. A play by Platus provided me with the foundation of the plot for my own play, *The Comedy of Errors*. I simply enhanced a work of a genius written over 1300 years ago by adding to the mayhem caused by a set of twins, whose presence in the city is unknown to each other and other characters in the play, by adding a second set of twins, thereby causing further instances of mistaken identity and multiplying the comic possibilities.

Plutarch's *Lives of the Noble Grecians and Romans* gave me the raw material for many of my Roman plays, including *Julius Caesar*, and *Anthony and Cleopatra*.

Hollingshead's Chronicles gave me historical material for my history plays including *Richard II*, *Richard III*, the two plays concerning the reign of Henry IV, *Henry V*, and the three plays concerning the reign of Henry VI.

The books on the shelves of my little library have been one of my most important touchstones. Another essential touchstone, which made the writing of my plays possible, was the rich tradition of folk tales I mined to enliven my plays.

Examples, which come to mind as I sit here writing, include Mercutio's Queen Mab speech in *Romeo and Juliet*, the story of Hearn the Hunter in *The Merry Wives of Windsor*, and the characters and going-ons of Puck, Oberon, and Titania in *A Midsummer Night's Dream*.

A third touchstone which made my plays possible was the huge cast of personalities I encountered over the course of my life. These real characters allowed me to create an equally large cast of fictional characters in my plays. Suffice it to say Falstaff would not have been possible without Dick Tarlton, Mercutio would not have existed without Christopher Marlowe, and

Prospero would not have worked his stage magic without the essence of my own personality and spirit.

Like a talented portrait artist, a great playwright paints many pictures. The artist uses tempura and oil while the playwright paints with words. Just as the artist distorts and enhances what he sees to please his patron and earn his commission, the playwright distorts and enhances what he sees to create a vision he hopes the audience finds worth the price of admission.

Writing a successful play requires a great deal of faith, hope, research, and luck. Oftentimes, the greatest of these ingredients is luck. A successful play is like a many faceted gem, reflecting and refracting the light appearing to the subjective viewer's eye. It is a complex dish requiring just the right mix of temperature, salt and seasoning. Some of those dramatic ingredients include: high and low humor, suspense, drama, plot twists, action, and pathos. The audience's psyches need to be tuned and plucked like the strings of fine instruments. If a false note is sounded, the harmony is destroyed.

In sum, the small library of my home in Stratford is my own version of Prospero's enchanted isle in *The Tempest*. These books were the tomes which allowed me to cast my spells over the audience.

But the days of my stage magic are over. It is now the eleventh hour, time to prepare for my voyage to a New World. Given the time I have been granted, I believe it is one's duty to do what is necessary to protect one's family and to prepare one's soul to meet its Maker. For me, that means it is time to make my last will and testament, and to receive the Sacrament of the Last Rites.

The arrangements necessary for the making of my will are simple compared to the arrangements required to locate and bring a priest to Stratford to administer the Last Rites. The priests ordained during Queen Mary's reign are either dead or in their dotage. And the relentless hunting of missionary Catholic priests occurring in the aftermath of the Gunpowder Plot resulted in the martyrdom of most of the remaining Jesuit missionaries, including my good friend, Henry Garnet, and saintly Father Edward Oldcorne. The few brave souls who survived operate under deep cover.

For myself, I had not been able to attend Mass since I moved back to Stratford. But I knew the tenant of the London gatehouse I purchased in 1613 had a brother who is a Catholic priest. As both my brothers, Richard and Gilbert, are now deceased, and it is not safe to post a letter seeking the assistance of a priest, there is only one person I could trust with undertaking such a mission to London — my lifelong friend, Hamnet Sadler.

Fortunately, Hamnet's bakery is very successful. He agreed to take a few weeks off from work to journey to London. While in London, Hamnet stayed with my gatehouse tenant, John Robinson. Through the efforts of Mr. Robinson, they eventually found a priest willing to undertake the dangerous journey.

Hamnet returned to Stratford three days later with the news Mr. Robinson and the courageous priest were expected within the month.

On the way to and from London, Hamnet stayed in Oxford with my close friends, William and Jane Davenant. During Hamnet's return journey, Jane gave Hamnet a small silver flask of spiced wine. The wine was a French home remedy Jane hoped would "warm the heart and soothe the soul of our mutual friend, William." As I uncorked the flask and poured the rich, red ambrosia into a short-stemmed goblet, I thought about what a remarkable friend Jane had become.

Jane was one of those women whose outer beauty was matched, and even exceeded, by her inner beauty. As I savored the flavor of the spiced wine, I thought what a pity it was that I would not get to thank her in person for this final, exquisite gift.

Given the circumstances, all I could do is write a short thank you note. I sent it via the courrier who carries mail between Stratford and London several times a month.

After writing the note to Jane, it was time to get down to the business of assembling the documents I would need to show Francis Collins during our meeting. Those included the copies of the deed to New Place and the cottage nearby, which we purchased to provide a residence for one of our long-time family servants, as well as the deeds to the Henley Street home, the farmland we owned outside of Stratford, the contract pertaining to my interest in the Stratford Parish Tithes, and the deed of trust concerning the ownership of the Blackfriars London gatehouse.

The documents, as well as the most precious items I own, including my father's agate alderman's ring, my spiritual will and testament, my Mother's rosary and crucifix, and a catch of gold coins we had socked away for a rainy day, were all locked in a hidden compartment below the bottom shelf of the built-in bookcase.

After retrieving the key, removing the books and the false bottom shelf, I opened the compartment, took out the documents I needed, and put everything back in place. Inventorying these documents, I stacked them on the left corner of my desk, sat down in my chair, and resumed working on this manuscript.

While I worked, I could hear the clock which sat on the far wall of the room ticking away the minutes. Like the mulberry tree in the garden behind New Place, the clock was one of my prize possessions. The mulberry tree was a gift from King James. The clock was a gift from Queen Anne.

Although the King often attended the plays we put on at court, he sometimes would yawn and even fall asleep during performances. Unlike the King, Queen Anne always paid close attention. She also enjoyed participating in the court masks.

Sometime after the coronation of King James, Queen Anne began living separately from the King at her sumptuous town home, Somerset House. The rumored reason for their separation was the excessive affection King James showered upon a series of young male favorites. For a very short period, one of those favorites was Philip Herbert, the First Earl of Montgomery. Philip and his brother, William Herbert, have been very important patrons and friends of mine for most of my professional life.

I first met Will when he arrived at court in 1597. He was one of the most beautiful young men I ever set eyes upon. His singular good looks were equally attractive to men and women. Wherever he travelled, he was surrounded by an entourage of both sexes. In many ways, Will resembled and reminded me of my recently deceased son Hamnet. Unfortunately, like many beautiful young people, Will tended to reciprocate the affections of too many of those who directed their attentions towards him.

To try to cure him of these tendencies, Will's mother, the Countess Pembroke, hired me to write a series of sonnets encouraging Will to settle down and marry. Although I fulfilled my commission and more, it did not immediately have its desired effect. Despite it all, Will and his brother Phillip have remained great patrons of mine throughout my life.

The King's special favorite during the first ten years of his reign was his former page, Robert Carr. King James successfully elevated Carr through a series of ever-increasing offices, culminating in his appointment as Earl of Somerset in 1613.

After the disappointments of Carr's marriage to the former wife of the Earl of Essex, Carr's and his new wife's conviction for conspiracy to murder Sir Thomas Overby, and their subsequent imprisonment in The Tower, James found a new favorite, George Villiers. Current gossip says the king is about to appoint Villiers to the coveted position of Master of the Horse.

Before her untimely death, Marie Mountjoy confided that the Queen no longer felt it necessary to compete for the King's affections with the "Old Goat's boy toys." With the King's permission, she set up her own household. As absence sometimes does make the heart grow fonder, the arrangement seems to work well. When the royal couple get together for formal state affairs and informal entertainments, they get along famously.

When they are apart, they each pursue their own interests. In Queen Anne's case, she is passionate about the arts. She surrounds herself with writers, musicians, and architects. My friend, Ben Johnson, the set designer and architect, Inigo Jones, and composer and musician, William Byrd, are her favorites. Although I have never been in the Queen's inner artistic circle, I have occasionally visited Somerset House, enjoying the company and conversation of the Queen and the other artists who grace her "salon."

On one occasion, after I entertained the Queen and others present with an impromptu performance of well-known soliloquies, Ben Johnson and I got into a friendly argument about use of the concept of time in our plays. Ben is a traditionalist, believing in the classical "unities." That concept holds all action in a play should occur in one geographical location, over the course of one day.

At the time our conversation occurred, Ben was a Roman Catholic. He was converted to Catholicism by a Catholic priest while he was imprisoned, awaiting trial for killing fellow actor, Gabriel Spencer, in a sword fight. Fortunately, Ben was able to escape the gallows by taking advantage of a legal loophole called "benefit of clergy." By reading Psalm 50, commonly called the "neck verse," in Latin, he escaped his date with the hangman.

Ben is not the type of man you want for an enemy. Despite his tough outer shell, he is a brilliant poet, playwright, and the author of numerous, entertaining, fabulously expensive masks. Although effervescent soap bubbles, they are beautiful to behold!

Chapter LXXVI
A Bear of a Man

The more I thought about Ben, the more I missed him. I decided to interrupt the work on this manuscript to write him a letter. I told him my illness had taken a turn for the worse and invited him for a visit. For my family's sake, I hoped he would accept. The only time Anne, Susanna, John, and Judith had seen Ben was at my farewell performance of *The Tempest* over four years ago. Elizabeth had never had the opportunity to meet this larger-than-life, one-of-a-kind character.

My admiration for Ben extends to the courage shown in his art. Ben does not shy away from addressing contemporary issues and controversies — sometimes to his great detriment. The most infamous example of governmental ire caused by Ben's work was the retribution visited upon him and several other actors because of his co-authorship of a satiric play called *The Isle of Dogs*. There is a real Isle of Dogs. It lies in the Thames, across from the Royal Palace at Greenwich. The play viciously attacked the corruption and mocked the vanity of fawning courtiers.

While the greed, corruption and vanity inherent in our society are always a target of Ben's art and wit, they are the driving themes of what I consider to be the best of Ben's work, the plays *Volpone* and *The Alchemist*.

Volpone is an aging con artist who, with the help of his toady, Mosca, relieves their victims of coin and jewels by feigning Volpone's terminal illness. Since Volpone has no wife or legitimate children (he has an alleged bevy of illegitimate ones), the competition among the prospective heirs is intense and darkly comic.

In *The Alchemist*, another group of grifters, including a butler, a prostitute, and a confidence man, set the con man up as an alchemist who possesses the philosopher's stone. A procession of victims, made vulnerable by their own faults and vices, march through the house the grifters have taken possession of during the absence of its owner.

Although *Volpone* and *The Alchemist* are great works of social criticism, the *Isle of Dogs* was far more radical in nature, as it was aimed at those in power — the political establishment. Because of the firestorm ignited by its performance, Ben, and two other actors in the Lord Admiral's Men, were imprisoned for six weeks. The angry Privy Council issued an order that all existing freestanding playhouses, including the Theater and the Curtain, be torn down! Thankfully, that did not come to pass. Cooler heads prevailed. Ben and the other offending actors were released, and the theaters were allowed to reopen.

It was several months later when Ben, and one of the actors imprisoned with him, had a violent disagreement. One challenged the other to duel by sword.

Ben was wounded. But Ben killed his opponent. This led to his further imprisonment, his conversion to Catholicism, his dodging the hangman's noose through benefit of clergy, and Ben's being branded on the thumb with a "T." The "T" is a symbol for Tyburn, the place of Ben's execution if he is again convicted of a capital crime. Despite the sword hanging over his head, Ben remains a brilliant and biting satirist. His contemporary farces are the best the English stage has to offer.

For the last decade, Ben's plays have populated the stage, much as mine had for the decade before. But, the laurel of premier London playwright is now resting on the ambitious and talented head of John Fletcher, the current writer-in-chief for

The King's Men, and my collaborator on my three most recent plays. Ben is now discovering, as I have, that:

Taste and fashion are forever fleeting;
They defy logic, confound reason.
What's all the rage today
Will soon fade into yesterday.

Where once the audience swooned,
Now they sing a different tune.
When once they laughed and cried,
Now they yawn and shuffle by.

While once they praised your skill and
rhyme,
They crave no more your mighty line.
The precious Muse once brought to life
Has now become a widowed wife.

Like my own plays, Ben's are an acquired taste. And the public's taste is changing to one of ever more fevered, convoluted plots. I spent the better part of seven years trying to adapt my style to accommodate the change. But I always felt out of my element in doing so, which is why I brought in younger collaborators, like George Wilkins, Thomas Middleton and John Fletcher, to try and make the adjustment to changing times and tastes.

Having written over thirty plays, I was beginning to run out of new ideas and stories. The fires of ambition no longer burned brightly in the furnace of my mind. It was time to reminisce upon things past and gone. To recall the chimes at midnight. To increase the odds of Ben's acceptance of my invitation, I ended my epistle to him thus: "I earnestly and prayerfully await your response."

I no sooner finished placing my signature on this letter then I heard a knock at the door. Unlocking it, I found myself face to face with my lawyer and friend, Francis Collins.

Chapter LXXVII
Testamentary Considerations

Francis is a cherubim-faced, portly man of average height. His full head of curly red hair makes him stand out in a crowd. He has crystal blue eyes, and a flush, freckle-faced complexion that go well together and make him look like he is in perpetually good spirits. He occasionally drinks too much, and he has a unique high-pitched laugh that sounds like a bevy of little bells.

All in all, Francis is a jovial, happy man. Besides being good company, he has a reasonably good head on his shoulders. Although only a country solicitor, Francis has a reputation for honesty and skill in drawing up wills. As we walked across the room, I said to Francis: "Take a seat. Make yourself comfortable. I'm afraid we'll be here for a while."

"It's not going to be all that bad. I suspect it'll be over before you know it," said Francis, in his characteristically upbeat manner.

"You sound like Tommy the barber surgeon. He speaks so sweetly before he uses his pliers to yank out your teeth," I replied.

"Think of it this way. At least you get to drown the pain with a bottle of strong spirits."

"Always on the bright side, aren't you?" I asked.

"Why not? All the worry in the world isn't going to grow another lock of hair on your head!" Francis responded.

"Really? Bet you can't quote me chapter and verse on that," I said, breaking into an amused grin.

"I admit you've got me there," said Francis.

"Enough gibberish, you fox. Let's get down to business."

"Business it is," said Francis. "Can you pass me quill and inkhorn so I can take some notes?"

While I fulfilled his request, Francis continued, "So, you're finally ready to make your will. If you don't mind my saying, it's high time. A man who has done as well as you have needs to protect his family. Make sure his estate is distributed as he desires."

The change in Francis's face and demeanor as he spoke these lines was remarkable. In a blink of an eye he went from frothy frivolity to studied earnestness. As I watched him, our eyes met.

He raised his thick red eyebrows, and asked, "I assume you want to leave the bulk of your estate to Anne?"

"Nice guess, but incorrect," I responded.

"Incorrect?" asked Francis. "You realize she has a dower right?"

"Of course," I answered. "It's nothing to do with the status of our marriage. It's always been strong. But, there's no sense in leaving the bulk of my estate to Anne. She's eight years older than I."

"How about your father and mother," Francis interrupted. "They lived to be more than ten years older than Anne is now. And Anne's in good health."

Giving Francis an icy stare, I replied: "I've discussed this with Anne. We implicitly trust Susanna and John. Anne's going to stay in the house. John, Susanna and Elizabeth will move in with her. Anne can help with Elizabeth and any other children John and Susanna are blessed with. When Anne passes on, there'll be no need for probate. The property will already be distributed as we desire."

"If that's what you want, I'll draw it up. I admit, from what you've explained, it seems to make sense," said Francis. "I assume you want Susanna and John to be the executors?"

"Yes," I replied. "And I want them to inherit all of the properties except for the Rowington Manor cottage Judith currently occupies. I've got the deeds to the properties right here on my desk."

"What about Judith and her fiancé, Thomas Quiney? "Francis asked.

"As you know, Judith and Thomas will be married in a few weeks. I want to leave them a substantial gift of one hundred pounds as a wedding present, and an additional one hundred fifty pounds inheritance. I also want to leave Judith a further fifty pounds if, after her marriage, she chooses to deed the Rowington Manor property over to Susanna."

"Given Judith is the younger daughter, that seems a reasonable settlement," said Francis.

"I hope so," I said. "I've had a lot of time to think it over. I confess I have my reservations about leaving Judith so large a sum without protective strings attached. Frankly, I don't yet have the same level of faith in Thomas I have in John. John's been a member of our family for eight years. He's extremely successful in his own right. He doesn't need my money. To top it all off, he's honest and devout. He's been a loyal husband to Susanna, a wonderful father to Elizabeth, and a good friend."

"Although Thomas comes from a good family, he sometimes samples his wares to excess. He also has the reputation of being a ladies' man — which doesn't bode well for a future of marital bliss. Despite my warnings, Judith is headstrong. She's convinced she can keep him from running roughshod over her. I'm afraid it may turn into a case of the tamer being tamed! I only pray it works out well."

I paused, and then continued, "Oh, I neglected to mention my sister Joan and her husband, William Hart. They currently occupy a portion of the house in Henley street where we both grew up. I would like to put a provision in the will which allows them to stay in the house for a nominal rent for the remainder of her life. I'd also like to leave my clothes to Joan to sell or do with as she likes. Some items could bring a good price."

"That's most generous. I know you and Joan have always been close," said Francis.

"She's my surviving sibling. I can't let her down. Her husband is ill. He acts a bit crazy at times. His haberdashery business hasn't done well these last few years."

"Have you thought about your personal property? It's customary to prepare a list of your important belongings, indicating the person you would like to leave a particular item," Francis pointed out.

"I've given it some thought," I answered. "I want Judith to have the silver gilt bowl that sits on the shelf over there. It's an important gift presented to me by the Queen after my last performance at court as an actor. I also want Elizabeth to have some of my silver plate when she's old enough to have a household of her own. Regarding my rapier, John Hall has one of his own. Neither of the girls are interested; so I've decided to leave it to my friend Thomas Combe. We've entertained each other quite a bit over the years. I think he'd appreciate it."

"I'm glad you've already thought it out. My recommendation is you prepare the list and send it over within the next couple of days."

"I'll do that, but I have some further small but special bequests I'd like to make," I went on, "including, leaving enough money to my fellow players, Richard Burbage, John Heminges, and Henry Condell, to buy them each a remembrance ring. They've been both my friends and business partners for many years. Over the course of that time, we've all shared the ups and downs of life. They've made the characters I 've written come alive on the stage. To think it all started here at Burbage's Tavern, a short distance from our family home in Henley Street. I 've my father to thank for making that connection. Finally, I want to leave a bequest to my godson, and some of my longtime friends."

"What about the poor?" asked Francis.

"Thanks for reminding me," I said. "I've no intention of forgetting my Christian obligation to assist those less fortunate. As you know, my purchase of a portion of the Parish Tithes for the princely sum of four-hundred-forty pounds was not only to provide my family with an income. It was also to provide the church with enough funds to make necessary repairs to Holy Trinity and to give relief to the poor of the parish. Given these circumstances, I believe a bequest of ten pounds is appropriate."

"That's logical," said Francis. "Your purchase of the tithes has certainly made a difference for the church and the community."

"It's the church I was baptized in many years ago. And it's the church I will be buried in. Most of those I loved are buried there. When my time comes, I want to rest beside them."

"I and many others believe you could have a more prestigious resting place, if you desire," Francis interjected.

"Ah, yes. Westminster Abbey?"

"Chaucer's there, and Spencer too!" Francis said. "Your patrons, Lord Southhampton and Lord Pembroke, are powerful people. You've enjoyed the favor of the King and Queen. The company for which you wrote and acted is the finest and most influential in the land. I think it could be arranged."

"Thanks for saying that, Francis. Perhaps you're right. But tastes are changing. Right now, I'm a rose whose bloom is beginning to fade. More importantly, I've no desire to be enshrined among kings and queens. They have their place in the Divine Plan, and I have mine. Much like ships passing in the night, never the twain should meet. Each of us has our proper sphere of influence. Mine is here in Stratford, among my family and friends. In fact, I feel so strongly about this, I've composed an epitaph, more of a warning really, that tries to make this point clear."

As I finished speaking, I picked up a sheet of paper containing a copy of the epitaph and began reading it in a voice designed to imitate that of a swashbuckling seafarer.

> Good Friend, for Jesus sake, forbear
> To dig the Dust inclosed here.
> Blest be the Man that spares these Stones,
> And Curst be he that moves my Bones.

When I finished reading it, Francis gave a good-natured chuckle and said: "It's good! Tailored perfectly to accomplish your goal. It appeals to both faith and superstition. But you need have no fear of being moved to Westminster or anywhere else if you don't desire it. You're a well-loved favorite son of Stratford. There are so many of us who value the great contributions you and your family, particularly your father, yourself, and John Hall, have made to our town. Given your wishes, we would never allow you to be moved out of Holy Trinity!"

"That's nice to hear," I replied.

With that, Francis and I discussed his fees. Pursuant to the customary practice, we agreed he would put them into the will as bequests, so they could be paid out of the estate's assets by Susanna and John in their capacity as executors.

Once our business was concluded, Francis accepted my invitation to join Anne and me in the dining room for a glass of Canary wine. As we sat around the table, Francis said: "During our meeting, Will read the epitaph he's written. It has the special touch of his great wit."

Turning from Anne to myself, Francis winked and said, "Will's talent for epitaphs lends credence to the rumors I've heard that, one afternoon at the Maidenhead, being in a mischievous mood, he composed an epitaph on the money lending practices of our departed friend, John Combe."

"I 've heard that fish tale too," I said. "It must be the one which goes as follows:

> Ten in the Hundred lies here ingrav'd,
> 'Tis a Hundred to Ten, his Soul is not sav'd:
> If any Man ask, Who lies in this Tomb?
> Oh! ho! quoth the Devil, 'tis my John-a- Combe.'

As I finished, Anne giggled.

Francis said with a flourish, "Yes! That's the one. Is it true you actually said that?"

"Now Francis! You know the Combes are our special friends," I cautioned.

"More yours than mine," Anne countered.

"Be that as it may," I said, raising my eyebrows and glancing Anne's way. "One cannot believe every rumor one hears. As you know, we purchased some land north of town from the Combes in 1602. Given the Combes' ongoing attempt to fence-in and enclose the arable land they own to convert it to sheep pasturage, and the intense opposition of many here in Stratford, including my partner in land ownership, Town Clerk Thomas Greene, there are many here with axes to grind against the Combes. This is not surprising, given they're the richest family in town. And they own the largest and most expensive home. But they've been wonderful to me. I've spent many an evening drinking and conversing with them on every issue under the sun."

"I agree with you, Will. The Combe home is quite remarkable," said Francis in his lawyerly manner. "There's a fireplace in virtually every room."

"That's true," I said, taking the bait. "If I remember right, they have fifteen hearths to our ten. And, I've thoroughly enjoyed my fencing matches with Thomas Combe, which is one reason I'm leaving him my sword. Given my friendship with the Combes, I've tried to maintain my neutrality in the land enclosure dispute."

"That, and the fact that one of the Combes' allies promised to compensate you in the event the attempt to enclose their lands affects the value of our land holdings," interjected Anne.

"Now Anne," I said. "I know how you feel. But the tithes are our biggest investment. What I've done has been essential for the future well-being of you and the girls."

"Maybe so. But this dispute has caused a rift between you and Thomas Greene. That's sad. The Greenes were great company for me and the girls during the years they lodged with us while you were still working in London. They thought so much of you they named their son William."

"Don't worry Anne. I've also secured indemnification for Thomas in the event of a worst-case scenario. As I told Thomas when he came to visit John and me while we were in London some time ago, I don't believe the Combes will succeed. The opposition Thomas leads is much too strong. And that opposition includes the Quiney family — which we are aligning ourselves with through Judith's marriage.

"I've invited Thomas and his wife to Judith's wedding, and they've accepted our invitation. While he may be disappointed I didn't strongly support him, I did not publicly oppose his efforts to block the land enclosures. He knows my friendship with the Combes has put me in a tight spot. Given the Greene's acceptance of the wedding invitation, I believe the adage "time heals all wounds" will apply."

"Hope springs eternal," Anne said. "I'll believe it when I see it."

"You will, Anne. As surely as my name's Will, the sun will rise on a new day of friendship with the Greenes," I assured her, despite the doubt harbored in my own heart.

CHAPTER LXXVIII
TWO OLD FRIENDS

Perhaps the highlight of these last three months was the visit my friends, Ben Johnson and Michael Drayton, paid me in early April. They arrived quite unexpectedly on a breezy Saturday afternoon. Given the poor condition of the roads, it had taken Ben and Michael three days to make the journey from London. When they arrived, I was sitting in the back garden taking in the early afternoon sun beside the still leafless mulberry tree. In just a few more months the leaves would reappear. The grasses would turn green and a carpet of wildflowers would fill the nearby meadows with their rainbow of colors.

It was with a tinge of sadness I realized, given the advanced state of my illness, I probably would not see the miraculous transformation of nature coming back to life once again. There was nothing I could do about that; the length of each of our lives is in the Lord's hands. So, I enjoyed each day and every moment to the best of my ability. During the rustle, hustle, and bustle of our workaday lives, we too often take for granted the everyday beauty that lies at our fingertips. Each moment is unique, never to be repeated.

These deep thoughts were swept away when Ben Johnson burst out the back door to our home shouting: "Will Shakespeare! Where's my long-lost comrade! The Bard of Avon! Light of the London stage! Master of the Globe! And Master of the Revels!"

As I watched his burly frame bounding down the stairs and virtually bouncing across the lawn, I could not help but return the smile he extended.

"Ben Johnson! You're a sight for sore eyes!" I called out to him in a most jovial voice. "Why don't you take a seat, and let me pour you a glass of Canary?"

"Sounds delightful. I need a little vino to help me get over this dreary journey. You know what they say: The fruit of the vine strengthens the body and sharpens the mind."

"Yes indeed," I replied.

"A little touch of spirits helps the fox catch the vixen, and the buck tame the hind," Ben completed the thought, as I poured him a cup of wine from the pitcher Anne had left on the table beside me.

Taking a seat, Ben took off the simple black wool cap he was wearing. He looked around at the two barns, the garden plot where we were seated, and the orchard extending out behind our home, and said:

"I understand why you spend so much time here in Stratford. It's beautiful. I'm sure it's a great refuge from the grit, grime and politics of the city and the court. Out here in the fresh air, among the common people, away from the soot of ten thousand sea-coal fires, you live a simple, uncomplicated life. There's much to be said for it."

I raised my cup to toast him and said: "Two old friends! Like the finest of wines, they get better with time."

"Hear! Hear!" said Ben, clinking his cup with mine and quaffing his drink in one extended draught while I carefully savored a small portion of mine.

As I put my cup down, and poured Ben a second, I said, "With respect to life being simple in a country town like Stratford, don't believe everything you hear. Different? Yes. Simple? No. Persons are similar wherever you find them."

"It's better to be a big fish in a small pond like Stratford then it is to be a minnow swimming among the sharks in London. At least you'll give me that?" Ben asked, as he raised his cup and took another substantial draught.

"I'll concede that much," I answered. "And I don't miss the constant presence of drabs, cut-purses, government censors, and coney-catchers!"

"Really?" said Ben with a playful look. "Seems I remember one evening years ago when I coaxed you into having dinner with me at Hollander's Leaguer."

I took another sip from my wine glass, before warily looking over my shoulder, and replying: "That was a memorable evening."

"As I recall, we dined with two of the young women who make their living there. If my memory is correct, you chose the strawberry blonde, and I chose a dark-haired raven, who turned out to be a splendid maven, once we were hugger-mugger, behind the latched door of her safe-haven."

"What happens behind a latched door is often better left there." I said. "But, to tell the truth, I chose not to drink from the cup I was offered. Turns out the girl was a product of tragedy. She was sending money back to Yorkshire to help support her aged parents and a daughter born out of wedlock."

"You've always had a soft spot for the fairer sex, Will. I can hear the violas playing that sad song now. There's more than one way a woman can separate a man from his crowns, or give him a "French crown" for that matter!"

"You're right," I replied. "Even without the tug at the heart strings that girl's story produced, the clap is the kiss of death in our business. One can't have a successful career on the stage if, like the Earl of Oxford, one no longer has a nose!"

"In the Earl's case, he deserves it," said Ben. "From all accounts, he's cruel and heartless. I heard a story that, while still a young man, he and William Cecil ruined the family of a poor servant in Cecil's employ. Oxford was, at a minimum, grossly negligent while fencing at Cecil's great house. He stabbed Cecil's servant, an innocent bystander, in the thigh. The poor man died, leaving a wife and child without husband or father."

"So sad," I said.

"That's only half the story," Ben said. "I regret to say it's the better half. The worst part is, during the coroner's inquest, Cecil and Oxford pressured those involved into producing an official report that found the servant committed 'suicide.'"

"Terrible!" I commented.

"Of course," Ben went on in the impassioned voice used when he became emotional, "it doesn't end there. As a suicide, he couldn't be buried in consecrated ground. By law, his possessions were forfeit to the Crown!"

"I've heard similar stories about many of those in positions of power— particularly the Cecil's and their ilk," I said. "As you know, it's politically incorrect and dangerous to say these things in public. Like most of us, I try to keep my head down, and get on with my work and family life."

"I know exactly what you mean," said Ben, finishing his second cup of wine. As I poured him a third cup, draining the pitcher, he continued:

"As you know, I converted to Catholicism while imprisoned ten years ago. But, after the unveiling of the Gunpowder Plot, and the government's renewed crackdown, Catholicism has become a lost cause in this country. There really appears to be no option other than martyrdom or conformity. I know I can speak freely with you about this because of your own sympathies."

"I hear everything you're saying," I replied. "I don't disagree." It's not our place to judge each other. Like you, my family and I have had to make our peace with the way things are rather than the way we wish them to be."

"It really makes one wonder what God's purpose is in all of this," Ben said. "Why have those who have perverted and persecuted the Old Religion been allowed to prosper? Why have those who turned apostate, and fought against those they once loved, been allowed to succeed?"

"There are no easy answers," I remarked. "I seem to remember we touched upon the issue of "sunshine patriots" and "turncoats" during one of our marathon sessions at the Mermaid a few years ago. In between cups of wine and tankards of ale, we each composed a poem on the subject. Do you remember how yours went?"

"Are you kidding?" Ben said. "Us old actors never forget anything. As I've suffered the pain of betrayal so many times in my life, I've had many opportunities to recite it to myself these last few years."

"I'd like to hear it again. If I remember, you titled it 'Chanticleers.'"

"Right, as always. To show you my memory is as reliable as ever, here it goes."

And with that, Ben launched into an energetic recital, enlivening it with unique intonations, gestures, and facial expressions that could only be pulled off successfully by an actor with many years of experience.

Yes, I've seen fair weather friends
Raise wet fingers in the wind;
Cloaking hearts with masks so thin,
You can see the fear within.

Where they've gone, and where they've
been,
Is way beyond the river's bend;
And, though they greet you with a grin,
They leave you in the lions' den.

All roads diverge, and then they wend,
They simply don't come back again.
And, while these friends can tax and
spend,
They never do hold up their end.

So, when the cock crows for the hen,
We must all remember then:
The foxes hidden in the fields
Will kill before they show their heels.

"Bravo! Good show Ben! You've still got your stage presence. That was a performance to bring the house down. On point to boot!"

"Fine, fine, Will. I appreciate the compliment. Having hooked me, you're not getting away so easily. Having put my memory to the test, I'll return the favor. Just as you remembered my poem 'Chanticleers,' I remember your entry on the subject of those who betray us for greed, money, or base instincts. Do you?"

"Of course," I said. "I believe I called it 'Dog and Bone.'"

"Right," said Ben with a mischievous smile. "Given most people, seem to consider you the better actor, I expect your performance to be at least as entertaining as mine."

"You're really putting me in a bind," I replied. "It's been a long time, but I'll take my best shot to try to make you happy."

With that, I began reciting the poem in my best Edward Alleyn voice, illustrating it with facial expressions and gestures I hoped would add a humorous twist to the mix.

Every dog must have its bone,
I've heard the painted ladies moan:
They find the scraps, and drag them home,
And throw them where the wind has blown.

The world is wide; it's filled with foam,
And mongrel mutts that bark alone.
Having raided honeycombs,
They feel the slinging stings of stone.

"Every dog will have its day!"
I've heard the lords and ladies say;
Throw the dice, and watch them play,
In the dirty laundry way.

The sun is like a fiery ray:
It sizzles up the doggie day;
And makes the keepers say "Hey, Hey!
Keep those hounds of Hell at bay!"

Well, every dog will bark and groan,
Crying for its doggie bone;
And every mutt must dig its hole,
To hide the treasure that it stole!

When I finished, Ben raised his cup, saying, "Cheers! I think you one-upped me with that performance."

"I don't think so," I replied. "They each have their virtues and their vices, like stars in the constellations of Gemini and Pisces!"

"Well said," Ben remarked, as I went on, finishing the thoughts we had been discussing when we forayed into our poetic contest of wits.

"In the end, if we wish to survive, we must be realists rather than idealists. I personally take solace in the thought that, whatever our doctrinal differences, we all worship the same God. Whether God sees it as I do, I cannot say. I pray a great deal for all of us who have been placed in this difficult position. That's all I can do at this point," I concluded.

CHAPTER LXXIX
A PIPE OF TOBACCO

While Ben nodded, and continued drinking his wine, I inquired, "In the letter you sent regarding your travel plans, you mentioned Michael Drayton might join you?"

"He's here," Ben answered to my surprise. "He's been good company. I left him in the house being entertained and offered some cheese and freshly baked bread by your beautiful wife. The last time I saw her was at your final performance of *The Tempest*. It's good to have the opportunity to see Anne again. You're a lucky man to have had a woman like that at your side all these years!"

"I know that better than anyone," I responded. "When comparing Anne to myself, she's a dove. I'm just a poor crow."

"An apt and well-chosen analogy," Ben commented. "You must know, it brings to mind the song I wrote after seeing your play *Othello*. Your clown, Robert Armin, nicked it from me. I've heard he's performed it on several occasions."

"Maybe that's true," I said. "Perhaps you can sing it for us later today. Since we've finished off the wine, let's go back inside, get a refill, and catch up with Michael and Anne. Then I'll show you my library — my pride and joy!"

"Sounds like a plan," said Ben. "I'm always ready for a refill. And I look forward to seeing your collection of books. Given the variety of sources you draw upon in your writing, it should be a good one. Like you, I pride myself on the collection I have in my home in London."

Ben and I got up and went inside the house. When we entered the dining room, Anne and Michael Drayton were sitting across from each other at the table. Michael was using his knife to cut generous wedges of cheese out of the hard cheese round Anne had placed in a large platter. Beside it was a partially consumed loaf of white manchet bread.

Seeing us, Michael got up and shook my hand. "Glad to see you Will. It's been a long time."

"It has. But some things never change. You still have a hearty appetite!"

"Your wife is taking good care of me. Helping me recuperate."

"Thanks for undertaking this trek this time of year. Seeing you does my heart good. After you've rested a bit, I hope you'll join Anne and me for a couple of drinks at our family's pub, the Maidenhead."

"Do you mean to say you own it?" asked Ben, pouring himself a cup of ale from the pitcher Anne had provided for Michael.

"Not exactly," I replied. "But we own the property. The pub is in a portion of our former family home on Henley Street. The remainder is occupied by my sister Joan, my brother-in-law, Will Hart, and their children. Anne and I lived there quite a few years. The current proprietor is not just a tenant. He's a business partner. Together, we own the land which grows the corn that makes the ale for the pub."

"Brilliant! The way you've explained it, it really is your pub," said Ben. "I tip my hat to you. I wish I had a shilling for every ten I spent in the Mermaid tavern over the years. I'd be a very rich man!"

"Wherever the truth may lie, there's one thing I'm certain of," I said.

"What's that?" Ben asked.

"Although your purse may not be the largest, your heart and soul surely are!"

"Well said," Ben answered.

"Since that's settled, let's adjourn to my study. While I show you my collection of books, you can enjoy a pipe of Trinidad Tobacco if you're so inclined."

"Trinidad Tobacco! That's mighty good stuff!" interjected Michael.

"I have a three-month supply shipped to me from my tobacconist in London," I explained.

"Well then, let's get to it," Michael said enthusiastically.

As we got up, Ben momentarily excused himself to retrieve "something important" from his guest room. Michael and I went to my study, while Anne attended to household business.

Arriving in the study, I went to my desk, opened the top drawer, and withdrew my embossed leather pouch of tobacco and several clay pipes. As Michael filled his pipe, I said: "You don't know how lucky you are. Until recently, Anne didn't allow me to smoke at all within the house. She's finally given a little ground, allowing me to enjoy an occasional pipe here in the study. The rest of the house is off-limits."

"I'm glad she's relented," Michael said, handing the pouch back to me so I could fill my own pipe. As I did so, Michael said, "Tobacco is miraculous. It soothes the mind and soul. The American Indians use it to seal peace treaties."

"I've heard that," I said, walking over to the fireplace and using a small stick of kindling as a lighter. "Sir Walter Raleigh was an early tobacco devotee. I met him when he attended our play, *Julius Caesar*."

"Raleigh's fascinating. Marrying Queen Elizabeth's lady-in-waiting, Frances Throckmorton, got him in hot water."

"There's nothing the Virgin Queen hated more than having one of her maids lose her virginity without permission," I said.

"Especially when the man was fancied by the Queen herself," said Michael.

"I agree."

"Raleigh paid the price for having plucked one of the pearls from the royal oyster bed," Michael said.

"Imprisonment in the Tower is a heavy price to pay for a tumble in the hay," I remarked.

"Raleigh's second imprisonment hasn't been for love. It's for plotting against the life of the King."

"If you believe the show trial the prosecutor, Mr. Coke, put on. Coke alleged Raleigh plotted to put Arabella Stuart on the throne. Raleigh has always contended he was framed by Cecil and his cohorts," I explained.

"At least he's put some of that time in the Tower to good use, siring a child with his wife during conjugal visits, and writing an impressive volume on the history of the world."

"I've a copy on the shelves over there," I said, pointing to my book collection.

"Have you read it?" asked Michael.

"Some. It's quite good."

"I hear Raleigh's trying to wiggle his way out of The Tower again. He wants to lead a second expedition to Guiana – to find the fabled El Dorado!"

"The glitter of riches pulls down one's britches. It makes even kings feel the sting of switches!" I remarked.

"That's good Will. Like a cat with nine lives, Raleigh's managed to survive. Someday his luck will run out. One can tempt fate too often."

As Michael finished speaking, the door to the study swung open. Ben came bustling through in his usually hurried manner. As he approached the desk, I saw he carried a rectangular leather packet in his huge bricklayer hands. Giving it to me, he said, "I've got something I want you to see."

Opening the packet, I extracted a thick sheaf of folio sized pages. Examining the first page, I recognized the opening lines of Ben's finest play, *Volpone*.

"Proofs of your play?" I asked.

"More than that," said Ben. They're proofs for a soon to be published leather-bound edition of my best works. I'm carefully editing a chosen selection of my plays, masks, and poems."

"Imagine that," I said, with a touch of envy. "A full-sized edition rather than the quarto sized, often pirated, editions of our plays we've had to settle for up until now. Leather bound! Suitable for the finest libraries. Something that will outlast us. It's almost enough to make life worth living by itself, isn't it?" I asked, looking from Michael to Ben in earnest.

"It's a special thing for us writers. Something I knew you would appreciate," said Ben.

"How on earth are you paying for it?" I asked.

"With assistance from friends, as well as my own money. Of course, we hope to recoup the costs and make a little profit on the sales," said Ben.

"When do you expect to have it published?" asked Michael.

"By the end of the year," Ben said.

"Will there be sufficient demand to make it worthwhile?" I asked.

"Hope so," Ben answered. "Only time will tell."

"It's a bold venture. If successful, it'll open the door for many others," I said.

"Such as yourself, Will?" asked Michael Drayton. "You've written well over thirty plays. Collecting them in one volume would be something."

"True. But remember, I 'm not the owner of my plays. They belong to the King's Men. I sold my shares when the Globe burned down in 1613. I still do some work with them, but I no longer have an ownership interest. I doubt the other shareholders would agree to publish the plays while they're still a profitable part of the repertory."

"Perhaps there will come a time where it will be advantageous for them to do so," Ben suggested.

"Maybe," I replied. "For the sake of my posterity, it would be nice to be able to have a handsome volume of the plays to pass down as an heirloom. It's something I'll suggest to my colleagues,

Burbage, Hemmings, and Condell. Enough of this idle talk for now. I invited you here to have some fun while I'm still able to do so. I hope you're ready for some hearty food, music, and strong drink over at the Maiden."

"I've never been known to pass up a good time!" Ben exclaimed.

"You on board?" I asked Michael.

"I can feel my appetite building again."

"Well then, the ayes have it. I'll get Anne."

Chapter LXXX
The Dove and the Crow

An hour later, Anne, Ben, Michael and I were all ensconced in the great room of the Maidenhead. The proprietor was roasting four freshly killed chickens for our repast. My sister Joan joined us, making excuses for her husband who was not feeling well.

Anne and Joan were sitting by the roaring fire, toasting cheese. Ben was already on his second tankard of ale when he slammed it down and said: "It's time for a song to liven things up! Will, you're a fine lute player. Do you know 'The Poor Girl's Dowry?'"

"I do," I replied. "It's a great song."

"I suppose it is," said Ben, a devilish gleam in his eyes. "But I've written a set of lyrics for it I think you and Anne will enjoy even more!"

"Is that so, Ben Johnson!" said Anne.

"Yes Ma'am, very much so."

"Then I'd like to hear it. But, beware Ben. If I don't care for it, I've got a hot iron poker simmering here in the fire that's just begging to kiss your behind!"

"I'd be very careful if I were you," Michael warned. "From the look of it, she means business!"

Ben responded to Anne with characteristic bravado: "My darling lady don't be unkind. I value highly the place where the sun doesn't shine. I know Hell hath no fury like a woman scorned. I believe my song is sweet and leaves you unwronged. But, as to your husband, he might be suborned."

"I'll be the judge of that. Let's hear it first," I chimed in playfully as I picked up my lute from the chair beside me. While

Love's Labour's Won

I began to strum the popular song melody, Ben cleared his throat with a swig of strong ale and began singing.

The Dove and the Crow
Watch affection grow;
One black as ink;
The Other white as snow.

Who in the world knows
Why the West Wind blows,
Or what brought together
The Dove and the Crow?

One comes from Heaven,
The Other's from Hell.
One's draped in blossoms,
The other just smells.

One's in the palace,
The Other he dwells,
Down by the river
In the muddy swells.

Singing in the plum tree
On the castle grounds,
The Dove cries to Heaven
With the sweetest sounds.

Hidden in the brambles
At the fringe of town,
The Crow hunts and pecks
On the burial mound.

The Dove will someday
Wear a golden crown,
Dress the Crow in ermine,
And warm goose down.

Until then, the Scarecrow
Must wear a frown,
As Crow strips the seeds
From the fertile ground!

As Ben concluded, I called out, "At least you know where your bread is buttered!"

"And where his toast is burned!" Anne added with a smile, causing Michael and Joan to burst out laughing.

"Would you care to take up the challenge with a song of your own?" Ben asked me.

"For once, I'll give you the last word," I replied, putting the lute down, and taking a generous swig from my tankard.

"It's about time you finally acknowledge my superiority at something," said Ben, resuming his place at the table.

"Consider yourself lucky. There's a first time for everything," I answered.

Ben finished his tankard and called for another. Joan and Anne joined us at table while the barmaids began serving a memorable dinner.

CHAPTER LXXXI
THE LAST CONFESSION

It was not long after Ben and Michael began their return trip to London, Mr. John Robinson, my tenant at the London Blackfriars Gatehouse, arrived in Stratford. He was accompanied by another very special guest, Father Robert Chandler. Like the other Catholic priests remaining in England, Father Robert operates under deep cover. By day a tailor. By night, Sundays, and special occasions, a priest.

Father Robert received his calling to the priesthood after completing an apprenticeship in Norwich. He left England some years ago to undertake his seminary studies among the English Catholic exiles in Rome. Five years after being ordained he managed to slip back into England incognito, assuming a position as an employee of an established London tailor who is a member of the remaining secret Catholic community.

How and why that small community continues to exist, and why a select few devout and intrepid souls remain willing to assume the risk of harboring a Catholic priest in the aftermath of the Gunpowder Plot, is beyond my level of understanding. All one can do is be grateful there are still a few spiritual heroes left in this world.

In my book, Hamnet Sadler's and John Robinson's actions in arranging and bringing Father Robert to minister to me are also heroic. Had Father Robert been apprehended, it is likely all of us would face imprisonment, torture and possible execution. As the Good Book says: "Greater love than this no man hath, that a man lay down his life for his friends." I am one of the fortunate souls that has friends like these, willing to risk life and limb for the salvation of my soul.

That Hamnet and John were willing to undertake this risk on my behalf is not surprising. They are both very courageous. Hamnet has stood up for his faith on numerous occasions. And he has been fined as a recusant for doing so.

Although I did not meet John Robinson until near the end of my London working life, he is an upstanding and God-fearing man with a brother who is a Catholic priest. I first met John when I attended one of the rare secret Masses held in the attic of a house adjacent to my house in Blackfriars. How we all managed to cram ourselves into that small space, I will never know.

The beauty of this visit was that Father Robert would not only minister to me, he would also minister to Anne, Susanna, Judith, and our granddaughter Elizabeth. The very thought thrilled me. We each could experience the Sacraments of Confession and the Holy Eucharist, and I could receive the Anointing of the Sick.

On the day of his arrival, Father Robert successively heard my Confession and those of Anne, Susanna, Judith, and Elizabeth. As it was her first Confession, this was a very special day for Elizabeth. Given the dismal status of Catholics in England, it might be the only Confession she ever receives!

While this was Elizabeth's first Confession, I knew it would be my last. During the days preceding Father Robert's arrival, I carefully examined my soul, making a mental list of the sins I committed against God and man since my last Confession in London several years ago. For us Catholics, Confession is a rare and precious gift from God to us his children. Because we are imperfect beings, we are all sinners in need of forgiveness.

After finishing our Confessions, we assembled together in the study. Using my work desk as a private altar, our best pewter goblet as a chalice, and unleavened bread provided by Hamnet for the Eucharist, Father Robert said a Mass for us all.

The Mass was yet another special occasion for my granddaughter Elizabeth. During this Mass, Elizabeth received her First Communion. Following Mass, we all adjourned to the dining room. There we had a small feast in honor of Elizabeth and Father Robert's visit.

After the meal, Susanna and Elizabeth left to return to the beautiful new home recently built for them. It was smaller than New Place, but it incorporated the latest in design trends, including a complete set of removable glass windows.

Once we saw Elizabeth and Susanna off, Father Robert, Anne, Judith and I went to the study where Father Robert gave me the Last Rites, also known in the Catholic Church has "Extreme Unction." As Father Robert said the prayers in Latin, and anointed my head with oil, a deep sense of serenity came over me. I knew it would not be long until I would join many of those I love at a place and with a body far better than the one I inhabit here on earth.

Within my heart of hearts, I uttered the words: "I am ready to meet you Lord when you are ready to take me." I prayed the Lord's response would be the same one he gave the repentant thief hanging beside him on Golgotha: "This day thou shalt be with me in paradise."

Chapter LXXXII
A Fond Farewell

The wedding of Judith and Thomas Quiney was eloquent and understated. It was a bittersweet experience to give my youngest daughter away, especially knowing it was probably my last public social event. Like most parents, Anne and I strove not to play favorites. I was every bit as committed to protecting and providing for Judith as I was for Susanna. As my youngest daughter, Judith has an irreplaceable place in my heart. This is especially so given how much our son, Hamnet, loved her. As twins, Hamnet and Judith had a special connection those of us not twins can never understand. The closest I came to describe it in my plays was the relationship Sebastian and Viola have in *Twelfth Night*.

Although *Twelfth Night*, like all good comedies, ends with a scene of reunification and rebirth for Sebastian and Viola, the dramas of real life rarely end as happily. I sense Hamnet's early death left a wound in Judith's psyche that will never heal. It is a wound equal to or even greater than my own.

It was Judith's vulnerability that left me with a certain sense of foreboding regarding this marriage. As I observed Judith and Thomas exchanging their vows in Holy Trinity and enjoyed their toast at the sumptuous reception we put on at New Place, I determined to take extra steps to protect Judith through a more careful structuring of my estate.

My reservations were sadly and painfully confirmed when, only a few weeks after the wedding, it became public knowledge Thomas Quiney had impregnated a young unmarried woman named Margaret Wheeler. Tragically, Margaret and her child died in the ordeal of childbirth. In the tumultuous wake of this scandal, it became imperative I make certain changes to my will while I still could.

It was tough enough doing my part to console my daughter Judith, whose heart was broken by the shame and embarrassment resulting from Thomas's disgraceful actions, but now I had to quickly take steps to prevent Thomas from having the capability to destroy our family's financial future with the same type of reckless conduct that has damaged Judith's and our family's good name.

As a family, we have endured the treacherous winds of scandal before. Like most families who have earned a modicum of success in this world, we have our detractors. Out of jealousy and envy, they seek to bring us down and "teach us a lesson" any way they can. One of our family's detractors, a former frustrated suitor of Susanna's named John Lane, sought to ruin Susanna's reputation by accusing her, a married woman, of having a sexually transmitted disease called "the running of the reins" stemming from a purported liaison with Rafe Smith, one of Stratford's reputable haberdashers.

The allegations were patently and viciously false. They were designed to injure my eldest daughter, her husband, John Hall, and the innocent Rafe Smith, in the worst way possible. For, one of the most important possessions we have on this earth is our good name.

To protect her reputation, with the full support of John and I, Susanna brought a defamation suit in the Ecclesiastical Consistory Court in Warwick. Typical of the Judas-like character he is, John Lane defaulted by failing to appear in court to answer the charges against him. So, like the biblical heroine she was named for, Susanna was, by the grace of God, able to clear her name and reputation.

Although the satisfaction we received in court left much to be desired, the townspeople of Stratford have their ways of making things right. Justice in this case was more appropriately served in the form of an anonymous ditty about John Lane that is making the rounds in the taverns of Stratford. It goes like this:

John Lane's a dirty waste of shame.
His head's filled with dung hills
And lies that feed his brain.
He's brown-nosed and he's butt-kissed
To sniff a whiff of fame,
But all he tastes is failure
And running of the raines!

No one knows for sure where this popular ditty comes from. But, I must confess I laugh every time I hear it!

Sadly, the disgrace Thomas Quiney is bringing upon my daughter Judith and our family is not that occasioned by unjust calumny. Instead, it is a tale of dishonorable conduct firmly rooted in truth. For the protection of Judith and the rest of our family it was necessary for me to again seek the counsel of Francis Collins.

By the time Francis came to see me, the circumstances of my health had changed significantly. Within the last few days, I had come down with the symptoms of a very bad cold. It began, as most colds do, with a nagging and persistent sore throat which made it hard for me to swallow. Over the years, I had experienced these symptoms at least a dozen times before. I knew what would inevitably follow: fever, congestion, and cough.

During my younger days, my body had the strength to shake such symptoms off within five or six days. But, given my consumption and difficulty breathing, I knew I might not be so lucky this time.Before the cold entered its worst phase, I needed to get my estate in order.

Anne, loyal through thick and thin, was doing everything she could to help me survive this latest trial. She made sure our bedroom was kept warm with a steady fire burning, fed me hot, lightly-salted chicken broth, and covered me with several thick woolen blankets. John Hall stopped by to administer an herbal concoction he devised to restore my strength.

After John left, I sat propped up in bed, working on this manuscript, occasionally dipping my goose quill into the inkwell, scribbling away on the paper that lay flat on the small smooth board I was using as a homemade writing desk. Anne was seated in a comfortable chair beside me, knitting a shawl she was making for our granddaughter Elizabeth.

A short time later, there was a knock at the door. "Come in," I called out in a hoarse voice. The door opened, revealing Francis Collins and his scrivener. Francis was carrying a packet under his arm which I assumed contained an executed copy of the will I had made several months earlier. Stopping halfway between the door and the bed, Francis said, "I understand you wanted to speak with me regarding some changes."

"I'm sure you've heard the news about my son-in-law Thomas Quiney."

"It's unfortunate," said Francis.

"And sad," said Anne, continuing with her knitting.

"I can't tell you what a disappointment Thomas is," I said to Francis. "That's something we can't change now. But we need your help to revise the will to better protect Judith."

I then detailed the changes I desired, including providing for certain contingencies and restrictions upon half of the three-hundred pounds I had originally intended to give Judith outright. I hope this will ensure Thomas will not have the ability to quickly run through Judith's inheritance.

As an afterthought, I told Francis I also wanted a provision that made it clear Anne maintains complete ownership of this bed I am in, including all its furnishings.

"Oh Will, that's not necessary!" Anne protested. "Susanna and John would never interfere with my rights regarding this bedroom's furniture."

"I know that Anne," I replied. "But humor me regarding this request. I don't feel right without mentioning you somewhere in the will. And, as this bed came with you into our marriage, I want you to be able to leave it to whomever you desire when it comes time."

"It's a beautiful gesture," Anne said, tears welling in her eyes.

At that moment, her tears meant the world to me.

Proceeding down to the dining room with Anne, Francis and his scrivener expeditiously made the will revisions I requested. After scouring the house and neighborhood, they returned to the bedroom with the appropriate number of witnesses, including Hamnet Sadler and John Robinson. After reviewing the changes, I signed the revised will on the writing board which rested on my lap. My hand shook mildly as I wrote my signature for what would likely be the final time.

After I thanked Francis, his scrivener, Hamnet, John, and the others they left the room in Anne's company. When they were gone and I resumed writing, I could not help but feel the last page of the book of my life was being written. I have done what I could to best protect and assist my family as they journey forth into a future I cannot see.

That brings me to this current moment, lying here in bed, contemplating the waning fire gently burning in the fireplace. Like the remnants of that fire, I have not much time left before the flame of my life burns no more. As the Catholic priest asks us to remember on Ash Wednesday, the beginning of the season of repentance and reflection: "For dust thou art, and into dust thou shalt return."

While I feel my body begin to heat up with fever, and the fluid dripping down into my throat brings on a fit of coughing, I realize it is time to put down this pen. For, like the beating of the hearts in our breasts, all our lives end sooner or later.

Looking back, I have been luckier than most. By the grace of God, I achieved a modicum of success in a business I, for the most part, enjoyed. Anne and I had a successful marriage, raising two beautiful children to adulthood. I have a beautiful grandchild, Elizabeth, and every hope of additional grandchildren to come. Susanna's husband, John Hall, is a good man, successful in his own right. I am confident he and Susanna will care for and protect the other members of our family after I am gone.

I conclude my story with a prayer and my best wishes for those who come after me and have the benefit of reading this manuscript. Within its pages, I have sought to impart some of the joy, love, and heartbreak that was my life. And give you, the reader, a sense of who I was, and the values held dear to my heart.

However, as every honest writer must admit, you can never capture the complete essence of a person or a moment on the page. Words are a poor substitute for the sound and fury of life. At this point in our history, they are all we have to leave a lasting legacy of who we are and what we experienced: the things we saw and did, and what we thought about it all, the unique way our minds worked, our lives and our hearts, our joys and sufferings, laughter and tears, successes and failures, the applause, and the jeers.

The best we can hope to capture with our words are fleeting images, flashing shadows glimpsed in the flickering candlelight. For, after all is said and done, the rising tides, the setting suns, the peaceful pipes, the warlike drums, love's labour's lost, love's labour's won, we are such stuff as dreams are made on!

Chapter LXXXIII
Recalling the Past

While the coach rumbled on, and Elizabeth Barnard finished reading the final words on the last page of the faded manuscript she held in her hands, tears were welling in her eyes. She had now finished the last "visit" she would ever have with the kindly grandfather who had been such an important part of her early life. The bundle of pages she held in her hands were more than a historical chronicle of her grandfather's life. They were a window into his heart and soul. They contained the essence of her grandfather's emotions, passions, and feelings, as well as his thoughts and opinions on the myriad of persons, places, and things he had encountered during his pilgrimage on earth.

As to whether his life had been a comedy, a tragedy, or a tragi-comedy, she thought the best answer to the question her grandfather posed at the beginning of the manuscript he had left them was "all of the above!" For "comedy," "tragedy," and "tragi-comedy" were terms of art. And, to Elizabeth's way of thinking, life does not imitate art, and art cannot recreate the truth, complexity, and endless variations of life. Even the best artistic works are only pale shadows of what is concrete and real.

Despite these limitations, what Elizabeth's grandfather had achieved in the best of his plays and poems was an accomplishment that would, in Elizabeth's opinion, stand the test of time. For many of the qualities, perspectives, and personalities he created in his characters resonated and touched a common nerve in every reader and member of his audience. If William Shakespeare's characters were only fleeting shadows, they were shadows that left a deep and indelible impression upon one's mind.

Fortunately, Elizabeth's feelings concerning the high quality of her grandfather's works were shared by all members of her family, her grandfather's business associates, and his wealthy and powerful patrons and admirers. For, although all her grandfather's poetry of note had been published in his lifetime, many of his plays had not been published by the time of his death. And, some of the plays which had made it into print, were earlier, inferior, or pirated versions of the final works the actors and his audiences had come to know and love.

To rectify this situation and honor a man who had served and honored them, they pooled their resources in a labor of love to create a beautiful, folio-sized edition of all her grandfather's plays for which they had been able to obtain a manuscript or good previously printed version. Unfortunately, they had not been able to locate manuscripts or copies of every play written by William Shakespeare.

The missing plays included *Cardenio*, co-written with John Fletcher, *Love's Labor's Won*, the sequel to the very successful *Love's Labor's Lost*, and *Pericles*, the adventurous, experimental play co-written with the controversial tavern owner and brothel keeper, George Wilkins. Sadly, the only version of *Macbeth* that could be found was a condensed version that had been edited by the playwright and acquaintance of William Shakespeare, Thomas Middleton.

Creating this first edition of Elizabeth's grandfather's plays was a multi-year project, primarily orchestrated by two of his fellow actors and shareholders in The King's Men and the old Globe theater, John Heminges and Henry Condell. Originally, Dick Burbage, the leading actor of The King's Men, and Elizabeth's grandfather's collaborator on numerous creative projects, including the painted shields and impresas they made for members of the aristocracy for use at jousting tournaments, was also involved. But Dick died unexpectedly in 1619, four years before the first edition of Elizabeth's grandfather's works was published.

When the project to publish that folio edition neared completion in 1623, seven years after Elizabeth's grandfather's death, several of his literary friends and admirers contributed dedicatory poems to the introductory section. The longest and most important of these was by Ben Johnson. Elizabeth believed Ben's poem most effectively described her grandfather's precious gifts of artistic versatility and creative imagination.

Elizabeth and her family were deeply grateful to the many talented friends and associates of her grandfather who contributed their time, effort, and money to make the preservation of her grandfather's dramatic legacy possible. Elizabeth fondly remembered the moment her family received their precious copy of the first folio from the hands of Henry Condell and John Heminges. Given the high labor and material costs involved with printing a huge collection of thirty-six plays, the price of this first folio was one pound, far more than a majority of the English population could afford. Despite the limited market, it sold hundreds of copies — making it a break-even proposition.

Subsequent history had proved kind to her grandfather. There were enough persons of means interested in the plays to allow for a second folio edition to be printed in the 1640s, ensuring their survival into yet another generation. The substantial level of wealth enjoyed by Elizabeth and her husband made it possible for them to possess not only the heirloom copy of the first folio passed down to Elizabeth by her mother, but also a copy of the second folio.

Elizabeth's family's devotion and love for her grandfather extended much further than what could be accomplished on the printed page. Not long after his elaborate and honorable burial in the chancel of his beloved Holy Trinity church, Elizabeth's father and mother had commissioned the well-known sculptor, Gerard

Janssen, to make a suitable monument to her grandfather for installation upon the upper north wall of Holy Trinity's chancel.

The well-executed monument included a painted likeness of her grandfather engaged in the act of writing. It got rave reviews from his colleagues in The King's Men who came to see it while they were on tour some years later.

Although the Puritan-dominated Stratford Town Council had paid her grandfather's acting troupe for agreeing not to give an "ungodly" performance of one of her grandfather's plays in Stratford, Elizabeth treasured the visit of The King's Men as one of her precious memories. After viewing her grandfather's monument, the players descended upon New Place for cakes and ale provided by Elizabeth's parents.

Players being players, the actors thoroughly enjoyed the party, singing, dancing, and regaling Elizabeth, her grandmother, and her parents, with many humorous stories and anecdotes about the Will Shakespeare they knew and loved.

Elizabeth knew the humorous stories told by her grandfather's actor friends and colleagues were the way her grandfather wished to be remembered. He had not wanted his family to wear customary black mourning clothes during the year after his death.

To make sure he got his point across, he had Francis Collins read his Sonnet LXXI during the formal reading of the will that occurred a few days after her grandfather's funeral. As they sat around the dining room table, Elizabeth remembered Francis Collins reciting the words of the poem she subsequently learned by heart.

> No longer mourn for me when I am dead
> Then you shall hear the surly sullen bell
> Give warning to the world that I am fled

From this vile world, with vilest worms to dwell;
Nay, if you read this line, remember not
The hand that writ it; for I love you so,
That I in your sweet thoughts would be forgot,
If thinking on me then should make you woe.
O if (I say) you look upon this verse,
When I perhaps compounded am with clay,
Do not so much as my poor name rehearse;
But let your love even with my life decay:
Lest the wise world should look into your moan,
And mock you with me after I am gone.

Of course, this was a request which neither Elizabeth nor anyone else in the family honored. They all wore mourning "weeds" for a full year. Elizabeth's grandmother dressed in black for the remaining seven years of her life. Elizabeth remembered her grandmother sobbing as Mr. Collins read the poem, blurting out at its conclusion: "I'll be damned if I'm not going to mourn for you, Will Shakespeare! You're the light of my life!" Despite her grandfather's wishes, his death hit her grandmother hard. Her health and mental acuity began a gradual decline.

In the last few months of his illness, Elizabeth's grandfather experienced some periods of melancholy wistfulness, which is undoubtedly true of everyone who comes to the realization they are not long for this earth.

As Elizabeth sat in the bouncing coach, inching its way closer to her hometown, she recollected chancing upon her grandfather seated behind his desk reading from the slim volume of his sonnets he kept in one of the desk drawers. When Elizabeth entered the room, she said, "Grandfather, can you read me a story?" Looking up, he replied, "Not today, Angel. But, would you like me to read you one of my poems?"

"Yes," she had replied, taking a seat in one of the chairs that sat in front of his desk.

"I'm going to read you one that has been on my mind quite a bit lately," he said. Looking her straight in the eyes, he continued, "I want you to listen closely. When I'm finished reading, let me know what you think the poem is about. Fair enough?"

"Yes," Elizabeth dutifully replied, not really wanting to tax her eight-year-old mind too much, as everything her grandfather wrote seemed to be written for adults.

Taking her simple answer in stride, her grandfather began speaking in a slightly slower than usual voice:

> That time of year thou may'st in me behold
> When yellow leaves, or none, or few do hang
> Upon those boughs which shake against the cold,
> Bare ruin'd choirs, where late the sweet birds sang,
> In me thou seest the twilight of such day,
> As after sun-set fadeth in the west,
> Which by and by black night doth take away,
> Death's second self, that seals up all in rest.
> In me thou seest the glowing of such fire,
> That on the ashes of his youth doth lie,
> As the death-bed whereon it must expire,
> Consum'd with that which it was nourish'd by.
> This thou perceiv'st, which makes thy love more
> strong,
> To love that well which thou must leave ere long.

When he finished reading, Elizabeth's grandfather looked over and asked, "Now, what do you think of that?"

"I think it's nice, but a bit sad," she answered, showing wisdom far beyond her years.

"What causes you to say that?" he asked.

"Because I love you. And I don't want to lose you so soon!"

As soon as those words left her lips, she saw her grandfather's eyes light-up. With a warm smile, he said, "And I'm not ready to leave you either. Now, come around that desk, and give me a big hug!"

Hearing his words, Elizabeth jumped to her feet, ran around the desk, and embraced him. As she placed her head on his breast, she could hear his heart steadily beating its soothing rhythm. At that moment, she wished she could remain securely in her grandfather's arms forever.

But, like the soap bubbles she enjoyed creating with the little wand her grandfather carved for her, nothing on earth lasts forever. Eventually, her grandfather placed his hands on her shoulders. As she looked up into his watery eyes, he said, "I love you dearly Elizabeth. Let's go see if your grandmother is making us something good for dinner." With that, they went off merrily together.

As the warm glow of that vision enveloped her, bringing her back in time to bask once again in the sunshine of her childhood, Elizabeth drifted off into a deep and peaceful sleep, a rare blessing at her age.

She was awakened from her slumber by the knock of the dismounted coachman at the carriage door. Looking out the window, she could see the light waning. It was close to nightfall.

When her eyes adjusted to the light, she was pleasantly surprised to see the house her grandmother had grown up in. As she opened the carriage door and allowed the coachman to help her navigate the portable steps he had put in place for her, she complimented him, saying, "Thank you Tom. I see you found the place without any problem."

"Yes, my Lady," he responded. "The directions and map you drew served their purpose."

"Wonderful," Elizabeth remarked. "Please be careful bringing my things into the house. Most importantly, my grandfather's chair and the box on the seat inside the carriage." While she spoke, Elizabeth opened her purse and extracted two shillings.

As Tom took the shillings, Elizabeth said, "There's a little something extra for each of you. There will be more once we complete the journey. When you both have unloaded the carriage and seen to the horses, please join us in the house. I'm sure there will be meat, cakes and ale for all. As you know, we sent Robin here last week to provide the Hathaways with our schedule and funds in advance for our provision these next few nights. I'm sure they'll host us in style."

CHAPTER LXXXIV
HATHAWAY HOSPITALITY

True to form, the Hathaway family rolled out the red carpet for their illustrious relative. Cousin John was a consummate master of ceremonies. He arranged a lavish feast and entertainment for the evening, featuring an exotic roast turkey with all the fixings. The hearty meal was followed by a series of reels and jigs performed by John and several of his friends who often moonlighted as musical performers for local wedding feasts, barn raisings, and other community events.

The arthritis Elizabeth now suffered from prevented her from joining- in with the other players on the lute, a skill she had begun learning with her grandfather. But she tapped her toes and hummed along as John energetically played the strings on his fiddle with a horsehair bow, while his friend Jack nimbly played the flute, and Joseph kept time on a small tabor drum.

At the end of a wonderful evening, Elizabeth said goodnight. She made her way upstairs, stopping by the master bedroom to pay her respects to the newest member of the Hathaway family. Baby Jenny, lying half-awake in her cradle, sensed Elizabeth's presence. She began sobbing softly. Elizabeth took a seat in a comfortable walnut rocking chair. As she reached over and gently rocked the cradle, Elizabeth sang a song from her grandfather's play *The Tempest*, which she had modified for her own purposes.

Where the bee sucks, there suck I;
In a cowslip's bell I lie:
There I couch when owls do cry.
On the bat's back I do fly.

From the ground up to the sky,
Winging through the way-up high,
Viewing wonders with my eyes,
Seeing Angels laugh and sigh.

Calling out: Oh me! Oh my!
While tomorrow drifts on by,
Gliding home to everything
That my loving family brings!

Ding ding! Ding ding! Ding ding!
Merrily, merrily, shall I live now,
Under the blossom that hangs on the bough.

While Elizabeth sang, the little one gradually stopped sobbing, and settled into a comfortable sleep. Getting up to make her way to her bedroom, Elizabeth noticed Mary Hathaway standing in the doorway.

"That's a beautiful song, Aunt Elizabeth."

"It's just an old tune from days gone by."

"I hope you'll write it down. I can add it to the repertoire of songs I sing to Jenny."

"I'd be glad to," said Elizabeth, following Mary down the hallway to the bedroom.

Entering the room, she immediately recognized the bed as the one belonging to her grandparents. Her grandmother brought it into her marriage as part of her dowry.

Elizabeth, who had inherited it from her grandmother, gifted it back to the Hathaways when she and her second husband left Stratford to take up residence in the ancestral home he inherited when his older brother passed away.

After she wished Mary good night, and she sat down on the bed to rest for a moment before beginning to get undressed, Elizabeth contemplated the three androgynous figures on the headboard. According to her grandmother, they were carved by an itinerant woodworker who lost his employment when King Henry VIII dissolved the religious orders.

As Elizabeth lay in bed after saying her evening prayers, the thought came into her head that the figures carved into the headboard might just be Muses. Perhaps they helped fire-up her grandfather's imagination all those years ago.

Chapter LXXXV
Holy Trinity

When she awoke the next morning, Elizabeth freshened-up and went downstairs. After breakfasting with cousin John, they set out for Stratford in her coach, passing several of their hired hands driving a cart filled with tools, paint and supplies.

Arriving at Holy Trinity, they made their way into the churchyard, stopping to walk among the weathered tombstones — paying their respects to the many members of the Shakespeare and Hathaway families buried there, including Elizabeth's great grandparents, John and Mary Shakespeare, her great uncles, Richard and Gilbert, as well as her uncle Hamnet, who died while still a boy. Then they walked through the remainder of the churchyard to the entrance of the church.

As far as small-town parish churches go, Stratford's was more beautiful than most. Although its colorful stained-glass windows had been destroyed in the desecration of the churches and altars which occurred during the convulsions of the English Reformation, Holy Trinity was fortunate enough to have the hand-carved misericord seats the monks once used to support themselves during the long hours of evening and morning prayer.

While she walked down the central aisle, between wooden rows of pews where the good people of Stratford spent hours every Sunday listening to what seemed like interminable sermons of the long-winded Vicar, her heart was filled with a strange mixture of sadness and anticipation. Beneath stone slabs at the foot of the chancel lay the mortal remains of many of those she held most dear, including those of her grandparents, father, mother, and first husband, Thomas Nash.

Inscribed on the tomb of her mother was a poem Elizabeth had written to try to give those who came upon it an inkling of the kind, intelligent, pious and generous person Susanna Shakespeare was:

Witty above her sexe, but that's not all,
Wise to salvation was good Mistress Hall:
Something of Shakespeare was in that; but this
Wholly of him with whom she's now in blisse.

Then passenger, hast ne're a tear
To weep with her that wept with all;
That wept, yet set herselfe to cheere
Them up with comforts cordial?
Her love shall live, her mercy spread,
When thou hast ne're a tear to shed.

When Elizabeth read this heartfelt inscription, she could not stop the tears. Seeing them, her cousin John impulsively wrapped his arms around her.

While John comforted his cousin, the current Vicar of Holy Trinity approached. He waited at a respectful distance while Elizabeth gathered her composure. When she had recovered, Elizabeth said: "It's nice to see you again."

"You too, Lady Elizabeth. I hope Sir John is well."

"He sends his warm regards."

"As I was walking-over, I saw what appears to be your workmen and cart at the church entrance," said the Vicar.

"We passed them on the way here," John chimed-in.

"Are you sure you can get the work you need to perform on the monument completed in one day?" the Vicar asked.

"No worries," assured John. "That's why we had the scaffolding put in place over the last several days."

"I took the liberty of climbing up there myself early this morning. I can see why you want to clean and touch it up," said the Vicar. "Forty years of dust, dirt, grime, and several floods of the Avon have taken their toll."

"Thank you for allowing us access," said Elizabeth. "It's important to our family to keep my grandfather's memory alive."

"It's I who should thank you," said the Vicar. "Through the tithes your grandfather purchased, and the generous contributions of your father, Dr. Hall, your family has done more to support this church and its ministry than just about any other family here in Stratford. So, if there is anything you need from me today, just let me know."

"I don't believe that will be necessary. But we'll contact you if the need arises," said John Hathaway.

"Lady Elizabeth, will you at least do me the honor of joining me for mid-day supper," asked the Vicar in a manner which made it difficult for Elizabeth to refuse.

"I will in an hour or so," said Elizabeth, not wanting to offend the man who, consciously and unconsciously, would be the custodian of her grandfather's legacy in more ways than one.

"Great. I'll let you get to it, and stay out of your way," said the Vicar, as he departed and walked down the aisle on his way back to the vicarage.

Chapter LXXXVI
A Hidden Legacy

While John went his own way to meet up with the laborers and friends of the family he selected to perform this important work, Elizabeth sat down in the pew which once belonged to her family. In honor of her father, mother, and the other loved ones whose earthly remains lay here in the church chancel and the churchyard outside, she began to silently say the forbidden prayers of the Rosary.

About the time Elizabeth finished the first decade of her Rosary, John, and the men who would be working upon this first and most critical phase of the monument restoration, arrived with their toolboxes, buckets of water, and paint. They climbed up the short ladder to begin their most important and delicate work — removing the bust of Elizabeth's grandfather to create an opening in the box-like foundation of the monument. This would allow Elizabeth to place the package containing her grandfather's manuscript in its new resting place.

For, once her husband decided the manuscript must "disappear forever," Elizabeth had given the method of its disappearance much thought. She finally decided "burying it" here in her family's ancestral church was preferable to consigning it to the flames of the voracious stone fireplaces in her husband's family home.

Although Elizabeth loved Sir John dearly, he was a second husband, and she was a second wife. The fiery passions of their youths burned elsewhere. Sir John was a practical man who lived the politics of reality rather than dreams of artistic immortality. He had no intention of jeopardizing the futures of his children by his first wife with the skeletons of scandal which might lurk within the "closets" of his second wife's family.

That simply was the way it was. As Elizabeth sighed, returning to her Hail Marys, she could hear the tap, tap, tap of the hammer John was holding with one hand as it struck the top of the chisel he held with the other.

Elizabeth's next several prayers were for the success of the delicate operation John was performing. He could not afford to damage the monument in a manner noticeable after the "restoration" work. That is why John was doing this part of the job himself.

Although every blow of the hammer filled Elizabeth with trepidation, it was not long before she heard John exclaim: "Thank God!"

Looking up, Elizabeth asked in the loudest voice she could muster, "Are we okay?"

With a confident smile, John said: "We're good. Head-on over. We'll be ready in a few minutes."

"Praise the Lord!" Elizabeth remarked, as she made the sign of the cross and headed towards the scaffolding below the monument. John and his assistants carefully removed the bust of her grandfather from the monument's base, revealing the box-like space below.

When Elizabeth reached the ladder underneath the scaffolding, she began climbing, stopping momentarily on the third rung to hand the package containing the manuscript to John, who reached over and took it out of her hands.

Once John assisted Elizabeth up onto the scaffold platform, she sat down to catch her breath, contemplating both the lifelike bust of her illustrious grandfather, and the now more apt than ever inscription which her parents had jointly composed for the monument. She remembered sitting at the dinner table with her parents as they pooled intellects to come up with the enigmatic inscription that now seemed to read like a prophecy fulfilled:

> Stay, passenger, why goest thou by so fast?
> Read, if thou canst, who envious Death hath plast
> Within this monument, Shakspeare; with whome
> Quick nature dide, whose name doth deck this tombe
> Far more than cost; sieh (sith) all that he hath writt
> Leaves living art but page to serve his witt.

And now, what Elizabeth was about to do would give another and deeper meaning to her parents' words. An act which Elizabeth hoped would bring a smile to her parents and her grandparents as they looked down upon her from the Kingdom of Heaven.

Having caught her breath, Elizabeth received the manuscript package from John. Rising onto her knees, she moved over, carefully placing it in the monument's base. As she did so, she felt tears streaming down her face. To her way of thinking, this was every bit as much the burial of her grandfather as the funeral she attended four decades earlier.

In keeping with this thought, before allowing John and his trusted colleagues to go to work putting the bust back in place, Elizabeth asked John and the two workers to join her in reciting the Twenty-Third Psalm, her grandfather's favorite.

When they finished, Elizabeth watched while John and the workers placed the statue back upon its base and re-secured it.

After it was safely in place, Elizabeth descended to floor level, telling John she was leaving to take the Vicar up on his kind invitation.

As she slowly walked down the aisle of this venerable church, out the front door, down the steps, and along the tree-lined pathway that led through the churchyard to the Vicar's residence, Elizabeth thought of all that had been and what was to come. She was sure the future held great promise. It would see tremendous achievements. Subsequent generations would continue to build upon the foundations of those who went before them.

But, for Elizabeth and the Shakespeare family, their days of glory had now faded into the realm of legend. Fortunately, most of her grandfather's plays and poems had been published, as had her father's notes on his most memorable medical cases.

And there was at least a glimmer of hope the manuscript might, like Lazarus, be resurrected from its "tomb" in the distant future. Whether that day would ever come was in the Lord's hands. It was not something to worry about.

To ease her mind, Elizabeth began humming the tune of one of the old folk songs her mother learned from Elizabeth's great-grandmother, Mary Arden Shakespeare. As she walked along the path, Elizabeth sang the words she recently wrote to accompany that tune.

It was an Age of Rhyme;
It was an Age of Reason.
True Wit and Love
Were both in season.

The Sun and Moon,
Now in decline,
Shone their light
On better times.

They walked the stage;
They strode the earth,
And gave to Art
A new rebirth.

The Orchard's trees
Were all in bloom
And we enjoyed
A Harvest Moon.

Love's Labour's Lost,
Love's Labour's Won,
Joined together
And became One.

Shakespeare Monument: Holy Trinity Church

Afterword: All Things Shakespeare

I. Separating Fact From Fiction

Congratulations on finishing the fictional biography *Love's Labour's Won*. You now know a great deal about the life of William Shakespeare. This essay is written to assist the reader interested in sorting out the historically verifiable portions of Shakespeare's life from the fictional characters and details added to the novel to flesh it out and make it a more entertaining read.

As a preliminary matter, there is much we will never know about Shakespeare's life. We do not have any surviving letters written by him, and only one addressed to him by a fellow Stratford Townsman. We also do not have Shakespeare's diary. Since very few people kept diaries in those times, it is doubtful he kept one.

Although there is a great deal of circumstantial evidence that supports my belief Shakespeare was born into a devout Roman Catholic family, and remained a secret practicing Catholic throughout his adult life, we do not have any direct autobiographical evidence of Shakespeare's religious beliefs. Given the lack of direct evidence, interpreting the circumstantial evidence which exists is a bit like trying to divine the future by reading signs in tea leaves. As a result, there are Shakespearean scholars who have passionately and convincingly argued Shakespeare was an Anglican, a Puritan, a Catholic, an agnostic, and an atheist.

As a novelist, I chose to make my fictional Shakespeare a Catholic because it allowed me to portray him as an outsider.

It also permitted me to explore the darker aspects and prejudices of English government and society during the Elizabethan and Early Jacobian Ages,

Despite a lack of autobiographical material, there is a great deal we do know about Shakespeare's life. He was born in April of 1564 in or around Stratford-upon-Avon. He was baptized in Holy Trinity Church on April 26th of that year. His father, John Shakespeare, was a glover who held various municipal offices (including that of town Bailiff) during Shakespeare's youth. Shakespeare's mother, Mary Arden Shakespeare, was a member of the historically important, Roman Catholic, Arden family.

William Shakespeare was his parents' first child to live to adulthood. Two older daughters, Margaret and Joan, died while still infants. In addition to William, John and Mary had five other children that survived infancy: Gilbert, Richard, Joan, Anne, and Edmund. Unfortunately, Anne died when she was only 7 years old (William was almost 15 at the time) which must have been a devastating blow to the family.

We do not know with certainty that Shakespeare went to Stratford's King Edward VI's school because the records from the time Shakespeare would have been enrolled were destroyed long ago. But, it is almost certain he attended the school as it was a free school located only a few blocks from his home. This circumstantial evidence is bolstered by the fact Shakespeare became a playwright, and he possessed a passable knowledge of Latin and Greek. Where would he have learned to read and write, and study Latin and Greek (which were part of school curriculums of the time), if not in school?

Unfortunately, it is unlikely Shakespeare attended Oxford or Cambridge Universities. During the latter part of Shakespeare's youth, his father suffered a series of financial reverses. Some of these financial problems are attributable to fines he incurred for illegally dealing in wool and lending money at interest. Others were likely related to his recusancy — his failure to attend weekly Church of England services. Another possible reason for Shakespeare's non-attendance at university is related to the probable religious faith of his parents. Roman Catholics were prohibited from attending university. Shakespeare may have fallen victim to this prohibition.

Given the financial difficulties experienced by his family, it would have been natural for Shakespeare to seek employment outside the home. With his level of education and intelligence, becoming a tutor would have been a logical choice.

We do not know whether Shakespeare travelled to Lancashire and worked as a tutor for the Hoghtons and Hesketh. But a William Shakeshafte is mentioned in Alexander Hoghton's will. There is a long-standing tradition in the Hoghton and Hesketh families that Shakespeare worked among them. The son of one of Shakespeare's fellow players informed antiquarian John Aubrey Shakespeare told his father he taught school in the country during his youth.

John Cottam was the schoolmaster at King Edward VI's school around the time Shakespeare would have finished his studies. The Cottam family was from Lancashire and had significant ties to the Hoghton family. And John Cottam's brother, Thomas, was a Catholic priest who was part of Edmund Campion's 1580 mission to England (although the historical Father Cottam was already in government custody by the time the Lancashire events involving the "Father Tom" of the novel would have occurred).

Prior to being captured in the Summer of 1581, Father Campion resided for some time with Alexander Hoghton's brother Thomas. In fact, Father Campion was on his way back to Thomas Hoghton's home to retrieve important books and papers when he was apprehended. Although Father Campion revealed some of the names of those Catholics who harbored him under extreme torture, there is no way to completely recreate Father Campion's travels while he was on his mission to tend to English Catholics. When Father Campion visited with a Catholic host family, he would say Mass and hear confessions. The sermon Edmund Campion gives in the novel is crafted to mirror the concerns and Catholic theological issues of the time.

The Shakespeare family had at least indirect contact with a priest or priests involved with the Jesuit Mission to English Catholics. John Shakespeare's hand-written Catholic Spiritual Testament was found wedged in between the roof rafters and tiles by workmen performing repairs to the former Shakespeare family home on Henley Street in 1757. Campion and other members of the English Mission distributed printed versions of these testaments to English Catholics during their travels.

Although the vast majority of the characters in the novel are historical personages, Geoffrey the cook and Shakespeare's first love, Sylvia, are fictional ones created to give the novel local color, humor, and an early romantic interest for Shakespeare. The number and names of the children Shakespeare teaches in the novel are also fictional, as are the names given to the pets and other animals.

Whether or not Shakespeare travelled to Lancashire, he was back in Stratford in time to court local farm girl, Anne Hathaway, by the summer of 1582. Anne was 8 years older than the 18-year-old Shakespeare. Anne soon became pregnant. To avoid the prohibition of weddings during the season of Advent, a hasty marriage was arranged and performed by Father Frith (an elderly priest who had been ordained many years earlier during the short Roman Catholic restoration under Queen Mary). Shakespeare was soon the father of a daughter (Susanna). Twins Hamnet and Judith followed two years later in 1585.

What Shakespeare did during the seven-year period between 1585 and 1592 (often called the "Lost Years") is unknown. He may have helped run the family glove shop and wool dealing business. Some have speculated, given the abundance and correct use of numerous legal terms and concepts in Shakespeare's plays and poems, he might have been employed as a lawyer's clerk or legal copyist. What is certain is, sometime during that seven-year period, Shakespeare moved to London without his family.

Why Shakespeare relocated to London is not known with certainty. Within a generation or two of his passing, an oral tradition arose that Shakespeare left Stratford to avoid continued persecution by local aristocrat, Sir Thomas Lucy. Lucy was one of Queen Elizabeth's Protestant anti-Catholic enforcers. The tradition, which comes from multiple sources, holds that Shakespeare was persecuted and/or whipped by Lucy for poaching deer on Lucy's land. Some historians believe the poaching never occurred. Others believe the story was created to conceal the real source of the persecution — religious intolerance. Several years earlier, in 1583, the head of the Arden family, Edward Arden, was hung, drawn and quartered for allegedly conspiring to take the life of Queen Elizabeth with his son-in-law, the mentally disturbed John Somerville.

In the wake of the "Somerville Plot," Lucy was empowered to ferret out any other plotters. Many Arden related homes were searched for Popish relics and evidence of disloyalty. Though Shakespeare's mother, Mary Arden, was a minor member of the family, the Shakespeare home may have been searched. If it was not, they probably were in constant fear of what might occur.

A second strand of the legendary conflict between Shakespeare and Thomas Lucy is also portrayed in the novel. This part of the tradition holds, as a result of Lucy's persecution of Shakespeare, Shakespeare wrote a scathing ballad about Lucy — who then increased his persecution. In his famous *Sketch Book*, the great American writer, Washington Irving, recounts the highlights of a journey he took to Stratford in the first decades of the nineteenth century. In that chapter, Irving includes the one still-existing, alleged stanza of the reputed lampoon. Following that tradition, I have included it in the novel.

We are not sure how Shakespeare first came to London or how he got his start in the theater. There are numerous theories. One holds, when the Protestant troupe of actors, The Queen's Men, came to town they needed a new player to fill their ranks because one of their best actors was recently killed in a fight. Shakespeare may have joined them, becoming an itinerant player who eventually made his way to London. Another theory holds Shakespeare went to London to work with theatrical impresario James Burbage. There was a family of Burbages in Stratford (John Burbage was Stratford's Bailiff in 1555-56), but we are not sure if they were related to the theatrical Burbages. As Burbage is not an extremely common name, there is a reasonable possibility they were related — and may have facilitated Shakespeare's connection with the London Burbages.

James Burbage was the owner of the first successful stand-alone theater in the London area. His sons, leading man Dick Burbage, and businessman Cuthbert Burbage, became business partners with Shakespeare from 1594 until at least 1613 (when Shakespeare stopped writing plays), first in the Lord Chamberlain's Men, and then, after the accession of King James I, in the King's Men. Over time, Shakespeare became known as both a player and a writer. By 1592, he was enough of a threat to be criticized by competing playwright Robert Greene.

It is likely Shakespeare acted in plays before he began writing them. There has been much debate about the identity of the first complete play written by Shakespeare. My personal choice is *The Two Gentleman of Verona* because of its relative brevity and less than sophisticated handling of the plot. Other common candidates are *The Comedy of Errors* (largely based upon a comedy by Roman playwright Platus whom Shakespeare studied in school), *The Taming of the Shrew*, and the three plays concerning the reign of Henry VI (probably written with collaborating playwrights — a common practice at the time).

Although *The Taming of the Shrew* is not my choice for Shakespeare's first play (in my opinion, it is too good to be the first one), I believe the induction scenes (which were probably revised several times over the years before being published in the First Folio seven years after Shakespeare's death), featuring the drunken Warwickshire Tinker, Christopher Sly, are among Shakespeare's earliest dramatic works.

My belief is based upon the assumption that an actor learning the playwrighting trade would not begin by writing a complete play. He would start honing his craft by play-doctoring and writing short scenes like the ones which open *The Taming of the Shrew*. The induction scenes are not related to the main plot of *Shrew* and could be used to open any comedy or history. It is the only induction appearing in any of Shakespeare's surviving plays. And Scene II mentions a character, the fat ale-wife, Marion Hacket, from Shakespeare's mother's home village of Wilmcote, a few miles outside Stratford. Was Marion Hacket a real ale-wife to whom Shakespeare once owed money? In the scene in the novel where the Stratford-born printer Richard Field and Shakespeare are reminiscing about their lives in Stratford, I treat her as one.

During part of 1593 and 1594, Shakespeare's stage work was interrupted when the London theaters were closed because of a severe outbreak of the plague. Shakespeare and his major competitor, Christopher Marlowe (who very likely was a part-time anti-Catholic spy for Elizabeth's government), turned their attention to writing poetry. Shakespeare was writing his long poem *Venus and Adonis* at the same time Christopher Marlowe was writing his *Hero and Leander*. Before his poem could be completed, Christopher Marlowe lay dead in the Widow Bull's house in Deptford under suspicious circumstances — killed by a knife thrust to the eye after attending a feast with government agents and informants connected to the powerful Essex and Cecil factions at Court. At the time of his death, Marlowe was awaiting trial before the all-powerful Privy Council on apparent charges he was an atheist who may have been involved with a libelous, riot inciting diatribe against Protestant "Dutch" refugees living in the City of London.

The relationship between Shakespeare and Christopher Marlowe is a mysterious one. Given the size of the London Theater community, they knew each other. They were the same age. Marlowe was born just a few months before Shakespeare. Their fathers were common tradesmen. Marlowe achieved fame first. He was undoubtedly an influence upon some of Shakespeare's earliest plays.

Marlowe's *Tamburlaine* was one of the first plays to show the potential of unrhymed blank verse — an artistic form of expression Shakespeare used to perfection. There are obvious similarities between Marlowe's *Edward II* and Shakespeare's later *Richard II*, and Marlowe's *The Jew of Malta* and Shakespeare's later *The Merchant of Venice*. And there appears to be a great affinity of sensibility between Marlowe's plays and Shakespeare's *Titus Andronicus* — which is why, in the novel, I fictionally had Shakespeare and Christopher Marlowe collaborate on the writing of this shocking, nihilistic play.

Some critics and scholars have seen an element of black comedy in Marlowe's plays – and, and as other critics and scholars have observed, perhaps there is more than a trace of black comedy running through the over-the-top violence, irrationality and cannibalism present in *Titus Andronicus*. Or perhaps Shakespeare was just trying to drive home the point that violence begets violence to an extreme degree by raising the curtain upon this seminal example of the theater of the absurd.

With Marlowe's death, Shakespeare lost his greatest competitor. Had Marlowe survived, who knows what heights of artistic achievement they might have driven each other to achieve. However, neither would have enjoyed the freedom of expression we take for granted today. For both Marlowe and Shakespeare lived in an early modern police state where censorship was the norm. Before Shakespeare or Marlowe wrote their first plays, a statute was enacted prohibiting the discussion of politics or religion in theatrical performances. A breach could result in imprisonment or worse — as playwright Ben Johnson discovered when he was imprisoned, and the London theaters were temporarily closed, due to the performance of his co-authored play *The Isle of Dogs* — a work critical of Queen Elizabeth's fawning courtiers. Unsurprisingly, it was never licensed to be printed.

The Crown's censorship of plays was enforced through the office of The Master of the Revels (Sir Edmund Tilney). No play could be performed unless it obtained Sir Edmund's approval. Shakespeare had several run-ins with Sir Edmund's office. The deposition scene in *King Richard II* was likely censored because depicting a King losing his crown to a usurper cut too close to home for Elizabeth (who lived in fear something similar might happen to her — especially as she entered old age). The collaborative *Sir Thomas More*, a play for which Shakespeare wrote a scene or two, was never licensed to be performed. What is most remarkable about *Sir Thomas More*, a commoner who dared to defy a king on religious grounds of conscience, is that it was written at all.

Most strikingly, Shakespeare was forced to change the name of the shrewd, fat knight, in his plays concerning the reign of Henry IV, from Sir John Oldcastle to Sir John Falstaff. Sir John Oldcastle, a member of a pre-Reformation sect called the Lollards, was recognized as an early Protestant martyr. Descendants of Sir

John Oldcastle and certain Protestant preachers of the time were offended by Shakespeare's application of the name to a dissolute comedic character.

To mitigate the uproar in the Protestant community, Shakespeare changed the name of the offending character to Sir John Falstaff (a possible play upon Shakespeare's own name) and wrote an apology to be delivered on stage. That apology has been preserved as the epilogue to *Henry IV, Part II.* Although the apology is purportedly given by a "Dancer," it is written in the first person. I believe it was originally performed by Shakespeare himself as part of the penance for his offense. We do not have any letters written by Shakespeare, but we have this apology — and its language (which appears word for word in the novel) is one of the key pieces of documentary evidence I used to create Shakespeare's fictional "voice." Additionally, I believe the fact Shakespeare originally named his character Oldcastle is further evidence of Shakespeare's Catholicism. It is doubtful a Protestant would have done so.

According to scholar Clare Asquith (see the Recommended Reading section which follows), evidence of Shakespeare's secret Catholicism can be found in the coded language he used in many of his plays and poems. She contends that coded language was designed to convey messages to the other Catholics in Shakespeare's audience. Given the prohibition against higher education Catholics faced, many of the actors, as well as those in the audience, were underground Catholics.

In my opinion, the strongest evidence of Shakespeare's use of coded language to reach a Catholic audience appears in his enigmatic poem known today as *The Phoenix and The Turtle.* As further described in the novel, this poem, Shakespeare's contribution to a volume of verse dedicated to an aristocrat instrumental in suppressing The Essex Rebellion against Queen Elizabeth, is ostensibly about the romance between A Phoenix (a mythical bird symbolizing eternal life and new birth) and a Turtle Dove (a symbol of innocence and the Holy Spirit).

Since Queen Elizabeth was often likened to a Phoenix, and she had recently had to order the execution of one of her former favorites, Lord Essex, it was easy to read the poem as a reflection upon the recent events in Queen Elizabeth's life. But, as John T. Noonan, Jr. (see the Recommended Reading section) and other scholars have posited, there is an even deeper symbolic meaning to the poem. As recounted in the novel, at its deepest level Shakespeare's most cryptic poem can be seen as a eulogy to the Catholic Martyr Ann Line (a widow executed for harboring Catholic Priests whose husband was banished for his adherence to Catholicism). Perhaps it is more than coincidental that the volume of verse Shakespeare's poem appears in was titled *Love's Martyr*.

When the plague subsided in 1594, Kit Marlowe was dead, and William Shakespeare was back at work acting and writing plays. The long length of the plague outbreak caused many of the existing acting companies to fail. The survivors formed the two great companies of the Elizabethan Age: The Lord Admiral's Men and the Lord Chamberlain's Men. The Lord Admiral's Men, featuring leading man, Edward Alleyn, performed for proprietor Philip Henslowe at the Rose theater south of the Thames in Southwark. The Lord Chamberlain's Men, featuring leading man Richard Burbage and actor/writer William Shakespeare, performed at the Theater north of the City of London for proprietor James Burbage.

In the summer of 1596, Shakespeare suffered what was the greatest tragedy of his life, the death of his only son Hamnet. The Lord Chamberlain's Men were on tour at the time. Some scholars have expressed the opinion it is unlikely Shakespeare was able to reach his son's bedside before his death. This may well be the case. But it is possible Hamnet was able to cling to life long enough for his father to be there. That is the path I chose to portray in the novel.

Although deaths of children were much more common in Shakespeare's time, it is certain he grieved for Hamnet. Hamnet was the only son Shakespeare would have. Even a cursory reading of Shakespeare's plays and poems demonstrate how important it was to men in Elizabethan society to have a male heir to carry on their name. Shakespeare was no exception. Within several months of Hamnet's death, Shakespeare renewed his father's application for a Shakespeare family coat of arms.

Along with many others, I suspect the application renewal was part of the family reaction to the death of Shakespeare's son. Shakespeare's brothers Gilbert, Richard and Edmund were still living. Even if Shakespeare did not produce another male heir, there was a chance his brothers would — and the Shakespeare name and coat of arms would live on. Edmund was about 16 years younger than Shakespeare. Following in his older brother's footsteps, Edmund moved to London and began his practical apprenticeship as an actor. In the novel, the death of Hamnet serves as catalyst for Edmund's move to London.

I believe it is only with the passage of time that the finality and full significance of Hamnet's death was realized by Shakespeare. As that realization occurred, it had a profound effect upon Shakespeare's life and art. His plays grew darker in content and tone. So did the sonnet sequence he likely wrote in the years following Hamnet's death.

In a body of work filled with enigmas, the sonnets are the greatest riddle of all. Why and for whom were they written? Are the Beautiful Young Man, the Rival Poet and the Dark Lady mere literary conceits or real persons? When were the poems written, and did Shakespeare have a hand in publishing them? Reams of paper have been covered with ink trying to answer these questions. I chose not to make them the central issues of the novel. They are not topics Shakespeare would have written about in an heirloom manuscript he prepared for his Stratford family. But, like everyone who has read the sonnets, I have my own opinions.

Some of the sonnets likely contain autobiographical information. Those that do contain it to varying degrees. Given their number (154), and wide variety of themes and experiences, they were most likely composed over a period of years — 3 to 5 years (averaging 30 to 50 poems per year) would be reasonable given Shakespeare's work and family obligations. We know at least some were in existence by 1598, when two concerning the Dark Lady appeared in a volume of verse titled *The Passionate Pilgrim,* and a literary commentator noted Shakespeare's "sugared sonnets" were privately circulating in manuscript among his friends.

With respect to the question of whether Shakespeare was involved with and oversaw the printing of the sonnets, I believe he was for the following reasons. The two poems appearing in *The Passionate Pilgrim* were revised prior to the publication of the sonnets in 1609. There is a logical thematic order to the sonnets. It is not perfect and never could be because the poems were not written with the intent that they be published as one cohesive work. But someone took the time to put them into a sensible sequence. Finally, the sonnets were published with another long poem of Shakespeare's, *The Lover's Complaint*. Who but Shakespeare would have done such a good job sequencing the sonnets and providing the publisher with as extensive a companion poem as *The Lover's Complaint*? All authors like to see their work in print. It makes sense that, as Shakespeare neared the end of his writing career, he would want to see his sonnets and his remaining long poem published.

As to the Beautiful Young Man to whom many of the sonnets are addressed, there are two leading candidates: Lord

Southampton (Henry Wriothesley) and Lord Pembroke (William Herbert). I side with those who believe the young man of the sonnets is William Herbert. William Herbert was the right age, had the right name, and he had the sexual proclivities of the young man in the sonnets.

The publisher of the sonnets dedicated them to their only begetter, Mr. "W.H." Lord Southampton's initials were H.W. William Herbert was 17 in 1597 (the year after Hamnet's death). Henry Wriothesley was 24. More importantly, the sonnets concerning the Dark Lady speak of her having two lovers named Will. And William Herbert was a ladies' man. He impregnated maid of honour, Mary Fitton, and refused to marry her. Some years after the period the sonnets were written, he engaged in a scandalous affair with his younger cousin, Lady Mary Wroth — a liaison which produced two illegitimate children.

Additionally, Mary Sidney, William Herbert's mother and Philip Sydney's sister, was a great beauty, a renowned poetess, and a patron of the arts. The reference in sonnet 3 to the young man being his mother's "glass," and his causing her to recall the "lovely April of her prime," takes on additional significance when one considers William Herbert was born in April 1580— when his mother was 18 years old.

Finally, there is evidence of a continuing relationship between Shakespeare and William Herbert. In the prologue to the First Folio of Shakespeare's plays, published seven years after Shakespeare's death, Shakespeare's partners in the King's Men, John Heminges and Henry Condell, thank the Herbert Brothers (Philip and William) for the support they gave to Shakespeare during his life and after his death. Not only does this show a continuing closeness to Shakespeare, but it probably is evidence that the Herbert Brothers provided some financing for the expensive and time-consuming project of editing and printing the First Folio of Shakespeare's plays.

Although Shakespeare admired and was infatuated with the Beautiful Young Man, I do not believe there was a consummated sexual relationship between them. Friendships between heterosexual men were far more intimate than today. And both "Wills" in the sonnets are sexual partners of the Dark Lady. Further, the sonnets evidence the author's guilt at the breaking of their "bed vow" (s) by the author and the Dark Lady. One would expect to see similar feelings of guilt if there was a sexually consummated relationship between the sonnets' author and the Beautiful Young Man.

Regarding the identity of the Dark Lady, numerous candidates have been proposed. Building upon the research of historian, A.L. Rouse, Michael Wood, in his book *Shakespeare*, makes a good case for Emilia Bassano Lanier. She came from the Bassano family of Venetian Jews who were renowned musicians. There is a sonnet which features the Dark Lady skillfully playing the jacks (keys) of a virginal. Additionally, Shakespeare wrote *The Merchant of Venice* around the time the affair would have occurred. Interestingly, The Merchant of Venice has a character named Bassanio. And *Othello*, Shakespeare's other Venetian play, has a character named Emilia.

Given the sonnet about the mutual breaking of bed vows, the sonnet protagonist's mistress was a married woman. Emilia Lanier had formerly been the mistress of the Lord Chamberlain (Lord Hundson) — who was until his death the patron of Shakespeare's company. When Emilia became pregnant, she was married off to one of Lord Hundson's subordinates.

Around the time the events described in the sonnets would have occurred, Emilia was a patient of the lusty, fortune-telling magus, Simon Forman. From his cryptic notebooks, we know Emilia had social ambitions and believed she might again be pregnant during a period her husband was away on an extended military expedition. It appears plausible she could have been the type of person willing to betray a man of lower social standing to be with one of far greater standing and wealth.

The sonnets reveal Shakespeare was acutely aware of his social inferiority. Not only was he born without a title, he was a mere "player." To many respectable members of society, players were among the lowest of the low. They were immoral people who lied for a living, little better than the prostitutes and pickpockets that comprised much of their audience. But they were earning substantial sums of money. This allowed many of the leading actors to apply for that all-important badge of social respectability — a family coat of arms — and the right to be called a "gentleman." Shakespeare's social sensitivity (including the fact he may have been denied a university education due to his family's Catholicism) would help explain the depth of the hurt and anger present in the sonnets' author over the Dark Lady's betrayal.

Whatever wounds Shakespeare suffered after the death of his son, he was able to continue on with the business of working and living. In 1597, Shakespeare purchased the second largest home in Stratford (called New Place) as a residence for his family. The Lord Chamberlain's Men tore down the Theater and used many of the timbers to build the Globe theater in 1599. The building of the Globe allowed Shakespeare to buy a share in this new theater, which brought him income to supplement what he already received as a shareholder of The Lord Chamberlain's Men. The years following Hamnet's death also saw some of his greatest dramatic achievements: *Henry V*, *Hamlet, Twelfth Night* and *Othello*, to name but a few.

However, in 1601 Shakespeare and The Lord Chamberlain's Men came close to losing everything they had worked to achieve. In early February of that year, they were visited by representatives of Lord Essex and Lord Southampton and asked to perform *Richard II* on short notice. *Richard II* was an older play in the Shakespeare cannon. Because it portrayed a weak and ineffective monarch who loses his crown to a usurper, it was a controversial one. In fact, the deposition scene involving the transfer of the crown from *Richard II* to usurper Henry Bolingbroke had been censored.

Ominously, the representatives of Essex and Southampton demanded the deposition scene be performed. The Lord Chamberlain's Men agreed to do it as requested in return for a supplemental payment of forty shillings. The day after the play was performed, Lord Essex, with the assistance of Lord Southampton and others, launched what has come to be known as the Essex Rebellion.

As far as rebellions go, this one was an ill-organized act of desperation. Lord Essex's star at court had fallen as a result of the severe setbacks suffered by the Crown's army in Ireland, which Essex had commanded. Returning to England without authorization, he angered the Queen by storming into her private chambers unannounced. Essex became a convenient scapegoat for the failure of the Crown's Irish policy — and his enemies at court and on the Privy Council moved in for the kill. The Queen had already revoked his lucrative monopoly on sweet wines, cutting off a major source of his revenue.

With the walls closing in, Essex led about 300 of his followers on a march from Essex House to the Palace of Whitehall. Ostensibly, they were on a mission to rescue the Queen from her bad advisors, including Robert Cecil. But they were intercepted by several groups of pro-government forces. Essex hoped his group would swell with sympathetic supporters from the City of London, but that did not occur. After several skirmishes, what support he had evaporated. He and Lord Southampton retreated back to Essex House. After a several hour stand-off, they were surrounded and taken into custody.

Essex, Southampton and certain of their supporters were tried for treason and sentenced to death. The Lord Chamberlain's

Men were swept into the investigation. Their representative, Augustine Phillips, was called before The Privy Council. He swore that the Lord Chamberlain's Men were not part of the plot. They were lowly players. The arrangement for putting on Richard II was a mere financial transaction. The members of the Council appear to have bought the story.

Essex was beheaded, but Southampton's sentence was commuted in response to the pleas of his family.On the evening before Essex's execution, the Lord Chamberlain's Men were summoned to give a performance before the Queen. Was she sending them a message she knew more than she let on? And was the play they performed *Richard II*? In the novel, I have the Queen summon Shakespeare to a private audience after the play's performance where she lets him know his company has not pulled the wool over her eyes.

Although Lord Southampton may not have been the Beautiful Young Man of the sonnets, he was a significant patron of Shakespeare. Shakespeare dedicated his two early long poems *Venus and Adonis* and *The Rape of Lucrece* to Southampton. Southampton was rumored to be a secret Catholic. At a minimum, he had significant Roman Catholic connections. Many Catholic gentry sympathized with Essex and Southampton. Given the repression the Catholic gentry had suffered for decades, what did they have to lose if a change of regime occurred?

In the aftermath of The Essex Rebellion, Shakespeare published *The Phoenix and the Turtle* in the collection of poems titled *Love's Martyr*. If this work is a coded poem celebrating the martyrdom of Catholic widow Ann Line as John T. Noonan, Jr. and others have argued, one can only admire Shakespeare's courage in taking such a risk so soon after the failed Essex Rebellion. But, if Shakespeare and the Lord Chamberlain's men were complicit in the Essex Rebellion, it may have paid huge dividends a few years later.

Essex was in secret communication with James VI in Scotland. When Elizabeth died in 1603, and King James assumed the English throne, he took action to reward some of those who had supported him. Lord Southampton was released from the Tower. And The Lord Chamberlain's men became The King's Men. As The King's Men, they were privileged to perform at court many more times than they were during the reign of Queen Elizabeth. Whether their elevated status and privileges had anything to do with a witting or unwitting role in the Essex Rebellion is not known.

Around the time of Queen Elizabeth's death, and the accession of King James, Shakespeare began residing with the Mountjoys, a family of French Huguenots who owned a home on the corner of Silver and Monkwell Streets in the City of London. One reason he may have lived with them is to avoid having to attend weekly Church of England services. Despite extensive review of the surviving Church records, no evidence of Shakespeare's attendance at a London church service has ever been found. French Huguenots, and everyone in their household, including lodgers, were exempt from the weekly church attendance requirement. The Mountjoys made elaborate gold, silver, pearl and jeweled headdresses (called tires) worn by the Queen and other aristocratic women at court. During the time Shakespeare resided with them, Marie Mountjoy became tiremaker to Queen Anne (the wife of King James I). While in their household, Shakespeare wrote some of his best plays, including *Measure for Measure*, *King Lear*, and *Macbeth*.

The most significant historical event which occurred while Shakespeare was living with the Mountjoys was the unravelling of the Gunpowder Plot in November of 1605. Although Shakespeare was likely a Catholic or Catholic sympathizer, he was probably repulsed by the desperate terrorist acts of the disaffected Catholic gentry responsible for the Gunpowder Plot.

Given his and his Company's position as servants of the King, and the patronage and support he received from various members of the aristocracy, it is extremely unlikely Shakespeare would have been involved with a plot to blow up the King, the King's family, and Parliament. But he had significant contacts with some of those who were involved. And he probably understood the frustrations and repression that led the disaffected Catholic gentry involved to take the actions they did.

After Shakespeare had lived with the Mountjoys for a time, they asked for his assistance in negotiating a dowry for the marriage of their daughter, Mary, to their apprentice, Stephen Belott. Shakespeare's negotiations were successful. Years later, long after Shakespeare moved out and Marie Mountjoy had died, he was called upon to testify in a lawsuit brought by the apprentice against Christopher Mountjoy to enforce the terms of the dowry agreement. Although, from the records we have, the results of the lawsuit were inconclusive, those records include a written deposition of Shakespeare — which shows he was careful not to favor either side.

At some point in time, Shakespeare moved out of the Mountjoy household. By now, Shakespeare was entering the final phase of his career, writing his late plays *Cymbeline*, *The Winter's Tale* and his final masterpiece, *The Tempest* (1611). Over the years, Shakespeare had lost his father (1601), his brother Edmund (1607) and his Mother (1608). His oldest daughter had married local Stratford Doctor John Hall in 1607, and they had given Shakespeare a granddaughter in 1608, just before his mother's death.

The King's Men had done extremely well, and Shakespeare's share in the Globe theater proved so profitable that he, the Burbages and their other shareholders had even been able to open London's first indoor theater (The Blackfriars) in 1608. As the oldest son, Shakespeare had inherited the Henley Street home at his father's death in 1601. In addition to New Place, he had made additional real estate investments in and around Stratford. In sum, Shakespeare was in good financial shape. It is likely that, around the time he wrote *The Tempest* (his last solo-authored play), he was looking to take a step back from the hectic business schedule that had occupied him for over two decades.

For these reasons, I believe *The Tempest* was his farewell to the stage. Although he would write three plays (*The Two Noble Kinsmen*, the lost play *Cardenio*, and *Henry VIII*) in collaboration with his successor (John Fletcher) as chief playwright of The King's Men, I do not believe Shakespeare continued to act on stage. Numerous others have proposed the epilogue in *The Tempest*, one in which the Magus, Prospero, asks for the audiences' prayers and goodwill as he returns home, is Shakespeare's farewell to his audience. I agree with that position. In the novel, I have Shakespeare play the role of Prospero and deliver the epilogue in his final performance at the intimate Blackfriars theater.

By 1612, I believe Shakespeare had semi-permanently relocated to Stratford. When he testified in the Mountjoy lawsuit in 1612 he identified himself as a gentleman of Stratford. He was probably working with John Fletcher on a part time basis, coming to London now and then on business. It was at this time (1613) he purchased a substantial home in the Blackfriars district of London. The home was obviously close by the Blackfriars theater, which makes sense, but it also had a history as a Roman Catholic safe house for priests. Shakespeare's tenant in the Gatehouse was a man named John Robinson. His brother became a Catholic priest. And he is likely the John Robinson who witnessed Shakespeare's will in Stratford in 1616. Why he happened to be in Stratford (several days journey from London) at that particular time, is anyone's guess. But it might have had something to do with the recorded report by a member of the clergy that Shakespeare died a Papist. In the novel, I have John

Robinson bring a priest to Stratford to administer the Last Rites to Shakespeare.

I believe Shakespeare likely ended his association with The King's Men in 1613 when the Globe Theater burned down during a performance of *Henry VIII*. The rebuilding of the Globe required a great investment of capital by the shareholders. Given that Shakespeare was already semi-retired, and may have had chronic health issues, it is doubtful he would have wanted to make such a significant investment at that point in his life.

If Shakespeare did end his relationship with The King's Men in 1613, he did so on good terms. For he left his partners, Richard Burbage, Henry Condell and John Heminges, funds to purchase remembrance rings in his will. Additionally, in 1623, seven years after Shakespeare's death, Heminges and Condell were instrumental in publishing the collected volume of William Shakespeare's plays known as the First Folio (Richard Burbage died in 1619).

One would like to think Shakespeare's final years in Stratford were idyllic. But life rarely works out the way we plan. Shakespeare's brothers, Gilbert and Richard, died in 1612 and 1613. And his sister's husband, William Hart, died just shortly before Shakespeare's own death in 1616. Two months before Shakespeare's death, his younger daughter Judith married a vinter (Thomas Quiney) who brought scandal upon the family when it was discovered he had impregnated an unmarried woman (who died in childbirth) in the months leading up to his marriage to Judith. Shakespeare had to make last minute changes to his will to better protect Judith and the rest of the family.

Regarding Shakespeare's will, much has been written about the fact Shakespeare only left the second best-bed to his wife Anne. Given Anne was about 60 at the time of Shakespeare wrote his will, I do not find this to be unusual. Sixty was a ripe old age in Shakespeare's time. Anne was undoubtedly living in

New Place at the time of Shakespeare's death. New Place was huge, and there was plenty of room for what today would be called a mother-in-law suite.

By all accounts, Shakespeare had a good relationship with his son-in-law, Dr. John Hall, who, along with Shakespeare's daughter, Susanna, and his grand-daughter, Elizabeth, moved from the elegant Hall's Croft into New Place after Shakespeare's death. It defies logic to believe the care of Anne during her last years would not have been part of the understanding Shakespeare had with John and Susanna regarding the inheritance and obligations they were to receive and undertake.

Additionally, structuring the will in the manner Shakespeare did avoided the expense and subsequent legal proceedings of another will-making and estate distribution when Anne died. Finally, in the extremely unlikely event of a falling-out between Anne, John and Susanna, Anne may have had an enforceable dower right upon a portion of the estate. Everyone, including Shakespeare, John, and Susanna, may have been aware of this.

Respecting the best bed, according to common custom, it would have been displayed in the parlor of New Place, reserved for the use of special guests. The second-best bed would be the one shared by the master and mistress of the household. It is also possible the second-best bed was part of the dowry Anne brought into the marriage with Shakespeare. In leaving the second-best bed to Anne, Shakespeare was ensuring it remained for Anne's use and disposition.

There is a long-standing tradition Shakespeare died after a bout of drinking with his friends, playwright Ben Johnson and poet Michael Drayton. I have integrated some of that tradition into the novel. However, I believe the most likely cause of Shakespeare's death was a chronic illness. In the novel I chose consumption but it could have been diabetes (the Elizabethans loved sweets), cancer, alcoholism (due to the lack of safe drinking water, the Elizabethans drank alcohol at every meal), gout or other disease (some have even suggested syphilis, as his two final sonnets appear to reference treatments of the time for venereal disease).

Given the damage to the organs and immune system caused by such chronic conditions, it would not take a severe sudden illness to end the life of the greatest dramatic poet who ever lived. Unfortunately, unless Dr. John Hall's missing casebook for this time-period is ever found, we will never know the cause of Shakespeare's death.

II. RECOMMENDED READING

For those readers who want to deepen their knowledge on topics and characters in the novel they have found interesting, I recommend the following:

Stratford, Shakespeare Family Homes, and Origins: The best book to begin further study of Shakespeare's life with is the official guide of The Shakespeare Birthplace Trust, *Shakespeare Work, Life and Times* (The Shakespeare Birthplace Trust and Jigsaw Design and Publishing, 2016). The photographs, illustrations and charts in this book are all excellent, and the text takes you on an armchair tour through the Stratford of Shakespeare's day, and the properties that played important roles in his life story, including: Shakespeare's Birthplace, New Place, Hall's Croft, Anne Hathaway's Cottage, and Mary Arden's Farm. If you cannot make the trip to Stratford, or want to do some advance planning for such a trip, the guide is available (along with other interesting books and unique gifts) at **shop.shakespeare.org.uk**

Nicholas Fogg's *Stratford Upon Avon: Portrait of a Town* (Phillimore 1986) is a well-written history of Shakespeare's beloved hometown. The text, illustrations and photographs all work together to tell Stratford's unique story. The section of the book discussing Shakespeare's origins and life is excellent and thought provoking, and so are the portions of the book discussing Stratford's role in the English Civil War and Stratford's history in the subsequent centuries leading up to the First World War. The photographs of the Birthplace before and after its "restoration" in the mid-nineteenth century are a revelation.

Shakespeare Biographies: In my opinion, the best entry level biography for the Shakespeare "fan" is Michael Wood's *Shakespeare* (first published in the United States by Basic Books, 2003). *Shakespeare is* the companion book to Mr. Wood's outstanding *In Search of Shakespeare* television series. The Basic Books edition is invaluable because of its wealth of photographs, portraits, drawings, and maps. This gives you a good sense of how London and Londoners looked and dressed in the Elizabethan and early Jacobean Ages.

The Chapters of this fast-reading book are broken down into numerous, well-constructed subchapters, allowing for better absorption of the essential information they contain. When used in conjunction with the television series, the book and series create an immersive and enjoyable educational experience. With respect to Shakespeare's possible Catholicism, Wood believes that Shakespeare was born into a solidly Roman Catholic family, but, as with many, over the course of his professional life the practice of his Catholicism and fervor of his faith became less pronounced, although Wood acknowledges Shakespeare may have had a resurgence of faith during the last years of his life.

Stephen Greenblatt's *Will in the World: How Shakespeare Became Shakespeare* (W.W. Norton &Co., 2016) is a deep, well thought-out biography that takes you inside the mind of the world's greatest playwright and attempts to explain why he wrote his great works. One of the many highlights is the chapter possibly linking the writing of *The Merchant of Venice* with the execution of Queen Elizabeth's physician, Dr. Roderigo Lopez.

A fine summary of the evidence supporting the argument Shakespeare was born into a Catholic family, and he remained a practicing Roman Catholic throughout his relatively short life, is made in Joseph Pearce's captivating biography, *The Quest for Shakespeare: The Bard of Avon and the Church of Rome* (Ignatius Press, 2008). Given its premise, the book contains interesting discussions of Shakespeare's Catholic family roots, his possible stay in Lancashire, the probable persecution by Sir Thomas Lucy, John Shakespeare's recusancy, the Gunpowder Plot, the purchase of the Blackfriars Gatehouse in 1613, and the Catholic spiritual will and testament of Shakespeare's father, John, found hidden in the roof of the Shakespeare family home in 1757.

Although not a traditional historical biography, Harold Bloom's *Shakespeare: The Invention of the Human* (Riverhead Books, 1998) is a creative and insightful analysis of the growth and influence upon society Shakespeare's intellect had over the course of his life and afterwards.It also contains critical analyses of each of Shakespeare's plays. In essence, it is a biography of Shakespeare's intellectual development from Bloom's unique perspective. Bloom postulates that Shakespeare is a transformative figure who invented the way those of us in modern society think and feel about the common existential issues in our lives. Mr. Bloom's *Falstaff: Give Me Life* (Scribner, 2017) is a thoughtful exploration of many aspects of one of Shakespeare's most innovative, entertaining, and influential creations, Sir John Falstaff.

Bill Bryson's *Shakespeare* (Harper*Press*, 2007) is a concise, quick-reading biography presenting the essentials of Shakespeare's life story in an entertaining manner. The discussion of Shakespeare's many contributions to the English language is elucidating.

William Shakespeare, A Very Short Introduction (Oxford University Press, 2015) by dean of Shakespearian scholars, Stanley Wells, is even briefer than Bryson's book. Its small pocket size makes it an excellent companion to bring along and dip into when you are taking a tour of Shakespeare related historical sites or during down time while you are attending one of Shakespeare's plays.

John Aubrey's *Brief Lives* consists of short biographical notes on significant historical personages which were unpublished at the time of Aubrey's death in 1697. *Lives of Eminent Men* (Hesperus Classics, 2007) consists of a selection of those biographies, including Aubrey's notes upon Shakespeare, Ben Johnson, Francis Bacon, Edmund Spencer and Michael Drayton. Aubrey's notes recount that there was another tradesman's son in Stratford who also had a great natural wit, but that boy did not live to adulthood. We also read that Shakespeare travelled to London, and he went on to become an excellent actor at one of the city's theaters. Aubrey further notes that Shakespeare's plays, while not considered high art, drew a good audience. He notes Shakespeare was a handsome man, possessed a smooth and enjoyable wit, and was a fine companion. He also states that Shakespeare made a yearly trip to Stratford, he composed an epitaph upon John Coombe, and he had a decent knowledge of Latin which served him well during his employment as a country schoolmaster during his youth. Aubrey further claims that Shakespeare based the constable Dogberry upon a constable he met in Grendon, Buckinghamshire — which is on the road between London and Stratford.

Aubrey's information about Shakespeare is hearsay. But it is hearsay that was recorded within a generation or two of Shakespeare's death. I have incorporated certain portions of Aubrey's early hearsay into the novel's storyline.

Nicholas Rowe's *The Life of Shakespeare* (Introduction by Charles Nicholl, Pallas Athene, 2009) contains a slightly edited reprint of Rowe's preface to his six volume 1709 Edition of Shakespeare's plays. Rowe's preface was the first attempt at a biography of Shakespeare. Among other significant contributions to Shakespearean scholarship, it contains the first print reference to Shakespeare being "prosecuted" by Sir Thomas Lucy for poaching deer. It further relates, as a result of the initial prosecution, Shakespeare wrote a "bitter" ballad about Lucy causing increased prosecution of Shakespeare. According to Rowe, this caused Shakespeare to seek "shelter" in London.

As Charles Nicholl notes in his illuminating introduction, Rowe's preface is not the only source for the poaching story. A hand-written manuscript of Richard Davies, a parson of the latter 1600's, says Lucy often had Shakespeare whipped for poaching both deer and rabbits.

Rowe's and Davies's early versions of the poaching story serve as background sources for the run-ins Shakespeare has with Sir Thomas Lucy in the novel.

Interestingly, Rowe asserts Shakespeare's father was a wool dealer (Aubrey heard Shakespeare was a butcher's son) which subsequent scholarship has proven true. Rowe further passes on a story that Shakespeare's patron, Lord Southampton, once gave Shakespeare one thousand pounds in connection with a purchase Shakespeare was making. Rowe is also the source for the assertion that Shakespeare played the Ghost in *Hamlet*.

Another highlight of this book are its period illustrations. Most are from Rowe's 1709 edition of the plays.

Shakespeare's Family, Friends Colleagues, Patrons and Neighbors: The most comprehensive book on these subjects I have encountered is *The Shakespeare Circle: An Alternative*

Biography, edited by Paul Edmondson and Stanley Wells (Cambridge University Press, 2015). This unique book features short chapters written on many of the characters in this novel. Each chapter is authored by a separate distinguished Shakespearean scholar. A quick internet search will lead you to that author's works.

Germaine Greer's *Shakespeare's Wife* (Bloomsbury, 2007) assembles a wealth of facts, customs and practices to paint a convincing picture of the great contributions made to the Shakespeare family and William Shakespeare's legacy by his necessarily resourceful and capable wife, Anne Hathaway.

Actors, Playwrights and Collaborators: Stanley Wells's *Shakespeare and Co.* (First Vintage Books edition, March 2008) is not only a great source of information on the other theater professionals Shakespeare interacted with during his working life, it is also an enjoyable read. If you want to know more about Dick Tarlton, Will Kemp, Dick Burbage, Kit Marlowe, Ben Johnson and John Fletcher, this is the book for you.

Catherine Arnold's *Globe: Life in Shakespeare's London* (Simon & Schuster, 2015) is a well-researched book which contains an excellent account of James Burbage's career and the many sacrifices, trials and tribulations he and his sons, Cuthbert and Richard, made to build the theatrical dynasty which gave rise to the Theatre, the Globe, and the Blackfriars.

The Death of Christopher Marlowe: The best and most intriguing book about Kit Marlowe's death is Charles Nicholl's *The Reckoning, The Murder of Christopher Marlowe (University of Chicago Press Edition, 1995).* With the skill of a master sleuth, Nicholls uncovers the many layers of mystery and deception surrounding what really happened to the "Dead Shepherd" in that little room in Deptford on May 30, 1593.

Queen Elizabeth I: Historical novelist Alison Weir's *The Life of Elizabeth I* (Ballantine Books, 1998) is an excellent and complete biography of the enigmatic and sometimes unpredictable Virgin Queen. The story of Lord Essex's execution is a highlight. As Queen Elizabeth was the most important personage in the age which bears her name, this is essential reading.

Mary Queen of Scots and King James I: Allan Massie's well-written chronicle, *The Royal Stuarts, A History of the Family That Shaped Britain* (Thomas Dunne Books, 2010), contains excellent chapters on Mary, Queen of Scots, and her son, King James I.

Peter Ackroyd's *Rebellion, The History of England From James I to the Glorious Revolution* (Thomas Dunne Books, 2014) is an excellent telling of the history of the English Stuart dynasty and the Cromwell Interregnum. It also contains a succinct description of the Gunpowder Plot. Mr. Ackroyd's *Shakespeare: The Biography* (Anchor Books, 2006) is an extremely well-written, comprehensive, and extensively researched life of the Bard.

The Gunpowder Plot: James Shapiro's admirable year in the life biography, *The Year of Lear: Shakespeare* in 1606 (Simon & Shuster, 2015), contains a detailed narrative of the events surrounding The Gunpowder Plot and its effect upon Shakespeare's work during one of the most creative artistic periods in his life. Professor Shapiro's *A Year in the Life of William Shakespeare: 1599* (Harper Collins, 2005) (the year the Globe was built) is also highly recommended.

John Gerard, S. J.'s *The Autobiography of a Hunted Priest* (see the recommended reading on "Edmund Campion and the Jesuit Mission to England") contains a fascinating discussion of the Gunpowder Plot written by one of the Jesuit priests enmeshed in its aftermath.

The English Reformation: Professor Eamon Duffy's *Saints, Sacrilege & Sedition* (Bloomsbury Publishing, 2012), which builds upon his seminal work, *The Stripping of the Altars: Traditional Religion in England, 1400-1580* (Yale University Press, 1992), is a broad-ranging exploration of the ways successive waves of Protestant reformation under Henry VIII, Edward VI and Elizabeth I tore apart the rich social tapestry of later Renaissance Roman Catholicism.

Roger Rosewell's *Saint's Shrines and Pilgrims* (Bloomsbury Shire, 2017) is a short, beautifully written book containing well over 70 pictures/illustrations allowing you to visualize some of the rich religious cultural and artistic heritage which was severely damaged in the English Reformation. If this is what survives, we can only imagine what was lost. The book contains a picture of St. Winefride's Well at Holywell, the site of John Shakespeare's fictional pilgrimages for the well-being of his wife and children depicted in the novel. Saint Winefride was the patron Saint chosen by John Shakespeare in his now missing Spiritual Will and Testament.

The Cathedrals of Britain by David L. Edwards (Pitkin Guides Limited, 1992) is a marvelous journey through some of the most impressive and admired houses of worship ever built. The creativity and beauty of the architecture of these magnificent structures was not marred by the Reformation, but much of the interior stained glass, carvings, statuary, wall paintings, and colorful decoration were. In fact, Shakespeare's father, in his role as a Stratford town official, may have authorized the whitewashing of the painting of the Last Judgment that graced the Stratford Guild Chapel, across the street from Shakespeare's eventual home at New Place.

Even if Shakespeare was a Catholic recusant, churches and cathedrals built during the Middle Ages, including Stratford's

Holy Trinity, London's Old St. Paul's, Westminster Abbey, and Southwark's St. Saviour's (present day Southwark Cathedral) were an ever-present and important part of his life. We can imagine Shakespeare, during a brief respite from his labors at the Globe, climbing the steps of one of the towers of St. Savior's to take in the same breathtaking view of London captured a generation later by engraver Wenceslas Hollar in his justly famous bird's-eye view of the London cityscape. A cityscape that was dominated by the massive edifice of Old St. Paul's Cathedral.

Peter Marshall's *The Reformation: A Very Short Introduction* (Oxford University Press, 2009), provides a broad factual, thematic and doctrinal overview of the tremendous religious changes which rocked European culture and society in the sixteenth and seventeenth centuries.

No study of the English Reformation would be complete without considering the impact *Foxe's Book of Martyrs* (Spire Edition, 1998) had upon Elizabethan and post-Elizabethan society. John Foxe's compelling, beautifully written book is inspirational, devotional, and, at the same time, a work of sophisticated anti-Catholic propaganda. Its influence upon the hearts and minds of its large number of readers was significant. Given the censorship practiced by Elizabeth's government, no comparable Catholic response was possible. One of the heroic martyrs prominently featured in Foxe's book is the Lollard leader, Sir John Oldcastle. Given the ubiquitous presence of Foxe's Book in Elizabethan society, Shakespeare's original choice of Sir John Oldcastle as the name for his fat, lecherous, drunken, dissolute knight takes on additional significance.

A beneficial result of The English Reformation was the translation and publishing of the King James version of *The Holy Bible* (1611). This great work was a collaboration of the greatest

Biblical scholars of the time. Along with Shakespeare's works, it is one of the true glories of the English language. Shakespeare was certainly very familiar with prior English translations of The Bible, and numerous references to them appear in his plays. But the King James version exceeds them in accuracy and literary merit. Along with Shakespeare's works, it had a tremendous influence upon the evolution of modern English.

Arguably the greatest writer of all time, I believe Shakespeare would have admired and appreciated the sublime beauty of the King James Version. Holy Trinity church at Stratford possesses a copy of this great work (which was stolen but returned to its rightful place some years ago). It is possible that readings from that book would have been part of Shakespeare's own burial service, and those of his wife, daughters, and son-in law, Dr. John Hall. In the novel, Dr. Hall and Susanna give Shakespeare and his wife Anne a King James Bible as a gift, and it becomes a cherished part of their private library.

Edmund Campion and the Jesuit Mission to England: Evelyn Waugh's succinctly written biography of the Jesuit martyr *Edmund Campion* (Hollis and Carter, 1935) reads like an exciting novel. In telling the story of this charismatic Saint, it paints a grim picture of a religiously intolerant police state and the heroic priests and parishioners who defied the many agents and informers deployed to destroy them.

John Gerard's memoir, *The Autobiography of a Hunted Priest* (Philip Caraman, S.J., translator, Ignatius Press, 2012) is a primary source account of the adventures and dangers that were part of the daily lives of Catholic priests participating in the English mission. Gerard's service to his flock was the stuff of legend within the English Catholic community at home and abroad. He arrived in England in 1588, shortly after the defeat of the Spanish Armada. He remained there for 17 years, escaping to the continent in the aftermath of the Gunpowder Plot as part of the entourage of the Spanish Ambassador.

During his mission, Gerard was arrested by the London authorities in 1594. He was eventually moved to the Tower of London and endured severe torture without being broken. Along with several others, he was able to escape from the Tower in 1597, despite the injuries he received as a result of the torture. He became the most wanted man in England. But, with the assistance of the remaining English Catholic aristocracy and gentry, Gerard managed to evade the clutches of the priest and bounty hunters for eight additional years before safely returning to the continent in the aftermath of the Gunpowder Plot. At the behest of his superiors, he wrote his extraordinary narrative in Latin to serve as inspiration for other priests preparing to undertake hazardous missions.

Shakespeare's Coded Language: Although still somewhat controversial, former British intelligence agent and Shakespearian scholar Clare Asquith has advanced the theory that Shakespeare may have been an underground Roman Catholic dissident (or dissident sympathizer) who used coded language to discreetly convey pro-Catholic messages in his plays and poems. Her brilliant book elucidating her argument is *Shadowplay: The Hidden Beliefs and Coded Politics of William Shakespeare* (Public Affairs/ Perseus Books Group, 2005). She has recently written a second book, *Shakespeare and The Resistance: The Earl of Southampton, The Essex Rebellion, and The Poems That Challenged Tudor Tyranny* (Public Affairs, 2018) which extends her argument to the use of allegedly coded language and allegory in Shakespeare's early long poems *Venus and Adonis* and *The Rape of Lucrece*.

John T. Noonan Jr.'s *Shakespeare's Spiritual Sonnets (John T. Noonan, Jr. 2011)* contains an excellent summary of the argument several scholars have made that Shakespeare's enigmatic poem, commonly known as *The Phoenix and the Turtle,* is a work which uses obscure Catholic imagery and symbolism to honor Catholic martyr Anne Line (a widow executed for harboring priests just before the poem's composition in the aftermath of the Essex Rebellion).

The arguments advanced by Asquith and Noonan were instrumental in my decision to include a section on Shakespeare's composition of *The Phoenix and The Turtle* in the novel.

Christopher and Marie Mountjoy: The definitive book on William Shakespeare's life with the Mountjoy family is Charles Nicholl's *The Lodger Shakespeare: His Life on Silver Street* (Penguin, 2008). In addition to telling the dowry story dramatized in the novel, the book contains transcriptions of many of the legal documents (including a signed deposition of Shakespeare) that were part of the eventual lawsuit over the dowry.

The Mountjoy legal documents provide a great deal of insight into the personalities of the participants. Shakespeare is clearly steering as much of a neutral course as possible — trying not to give too much offense to either Christopher Mountjoy or his former apprentice and son-in-law Stephen Belott.

Interestingly, what we know about the Mountjoy family and their dowry dispute is due to the work of two American Shakespeare sleuths. Dr. Charles William Wallace, an English Professor of the University of Nebraska, and his wife, Hulda, journeyed to London in the early 20th Century. They spent years combing through dusty, dingy records of Elizabeth's and James's bureaucracies, eventually uncovering the documents relating to the dowry lawsuit.

The Strange Case of Simon Forman: Every age has its frauds, cads and mountebanks. Some of them, however, are intelligent and fascinating. This is the case with the Elizabethan fortune telling astrologer Simon Forman. In addition to purporting to see into his clients' futures, he was a serial seducer of women — sometimes accepting sexual favors in lieu of money for the services he provided. In his own biographical notes, Forman admitted to beating a maid and physically abusing his master's wife when he was still an apprentice (his master beat him as a result of the latter incident). For a significant portion of his adult life, Forman's mistress was a married recusant Catholic. Their many squabbles, and on-again, off-again affair, would provide more than enough material for a soap opera.

Forman did not marry until his late 40's. His bride was nineteen. He once had sexual relations with two women patients on the same day he bedded his young wife. He was often in litigation with the Doctors of the day — who considered him a quack. Yet, in the superstitious early-modern age in which he lived, he not only survived, he thrived. Among his "patients" from all walks of life and levels of society, were friends and business associates of Shakespeare, including his landlady, Marie Mountjoy, and his possible mistress, Emilia Bassano Lanier.

Forman was also a regular playgoer, and he made notes containing plot synopses on a number of Shakespeare's plays he attended, including *Macbeth*, *Cymbeline*, *Richard II*, and *The Winter's Tale*. The notes on *Richard II* and *The Winter's Tale* attempt to derive proverb-like lessons from the shows. Given his shadowy presence in Shakespeare's social and business circles, he appears in a chapter of the novel discussing Marlowe's Dr. Faustus, and intently questions Shakespeare regarding hidden messages and meanings within his plays.

How do we know as much as we do about Forman? It is thanks to the work of historian A.L. Rouse, who spent years studying Forman's personal papers and published a book about the information he uncovered entitled: *The Case Books of Simon Forman: Sex and Society in Shakespeare's Age* (Picador, 1976).

Rouse's book not only sheds light upon the passions and motivations of certain people within Shakespeare's circle. Given the diversity of Forman's large client base, it sheds light upon the common hopes, fears, beliefs and desires of those living in the later Elizabethan and early Jacobean Ages.

The Elizabethan Age: A. N. Wilson's *The Elizabethans* (First American Edition, Farrar, Straus and Girox, 2012) is a sweeping, comprehensive tour through the age of Elizabeth, its world-changing events, and its colorful, eccentric cast of characters. Among many interesting chapters, the book contains ones on the St. Bartholomew's Day Massacre, Ireland, Drake's Circumnavigation, Mary Stuart, the Spanish Armada, London theatre, and the Essex Rebellion.

Daily Life in Elizabethan Times: There are a wealth of good books on this topic. Those I have found particularly useful include Liza Picard's *Elizabeth's London: Everyday Life in Elizabethan London* (St. Martin's Griffin, 2003), Ian Mortimer's *The Time Traveler's Guide to Elizabethan England* (Penguin Books, 2014), Ruth Goodman's *How To Be A Tudor: A Dawn to Dusk Guide To Tudor Life* (Liveright Publishing Corporation, 2016), and Maggie Secara's *A Compendium of Common Knowledge 1558-1603: Elizabethan Commonplaces for Writers, Actors & Re-enactors* (Popinjay Press).

A Picture is Worth A Thousand Words: *Shakespeare and His Contemporaries* (National Portrait Gallery Publications, 2015) contains portraits of Shakespeare and many of his fellow actors, playwrights, poets, and the courtiers and patrons who supported their work. The text by renowned Shakespearean scholar Charles Nicholl provides useful background on the persons depicted. Taken together, the portraits themselves are a cornucopia of Elizabethan and Jacobean high fashion.

Although there was no known English artist that specialized in painting peasant's and small villagers during Shakespeare's lifetime, Pieter Bruegel the Elder (about 1525-1569) was doing so in the Low Countries during the early days of Shakespeare's youth. *Bruegel: The Complete Paintings* (Taschen 2005), with text by Rose-Marie and Rainer Hagen, allows one to see what it was like to live as an agrarian peasant or small village commoner in the Low Countries during Shakespeare's time. It was not an easy life.

In addition to painting peasant and small village life, Bruegel also painted scenes of war, demons, and apocalyptic violence. Towards the end of Bruegel's life, the Low Countries were occupied by the Spanish forces of the Duke of Alba, and repression, warfare and persecution became rampant. As with Shakespeare, we do not know with certainty whether Bruegel favored the Catholic or Protestant side. From the well-written analysis of the Hagens, it is likely he favored the Protestant. Looking at the body of his work, it is evident that he is a spiritual and God-fearing man who abhors mankind's capacity for inhumanity towards its fellow man. Like Shakespeare, he appears to be advocating for religious tolerance in an age full of intolerance.

It is extremely doubtful Shakespeare ever had the privilege of viewing any of Bruegel's paintings. But, in the novel, as Shakespeare is going through the process of mentally preparing himself for death, I have Shakespeare recall studying a copy of Bruegel's painting of Icarus plunging into the sea during Shakespeare's stay at Lord Southampton's mansion. Many aristocrats of Shakespeare's time kept cabinets of curiosities which would have included paintings like Bruegel's.

What is remarkable about Bruegel's painting is that its subject matter, the fall of Icarus into the sea, is only one of many events simultaneously occurring in the painting. Only the bottom half of Icarus's legs remain visible above the ocean surface, and no one else in the painting takes particular notice of the momentous event. This theme is present in other Bruegel paintings, including one depicting the arrival of the Holy Family into a snow-covered low country Bethlehem. Given the historic, Catholic-crushing events Shakespeare had lived through, his love of Classical Myths, and the world-wise sensibility and irony present in many of Shakespeare's later plays, I believe a painting such as Bruegel's would have struck a strong chord of recognition in the fellow artist.

Shakespeare's Restless World: Portrait of An Era (Penguin Books, Ltd. 2012) tells the story of the constantly changing world Shakespeare lived in through many Elizabethan and Jacobean objects, portraits, and prints, including: Henry V's shield, helmet, sword and saddle, a rapier and dagger, a fork, a theater money-box, a Church of England Communion chalice, The Drake circumnavigation medal, an apprentice cap, Dr. John Dee's magical mirror, a Venetian glass goblet, Moroccan gold items from a shipwreck, a peddler's trunk containing Catholic religious items, a musical clock, and many other objects.

Shakespeare and the Stuff of Life: Treasures from the Shakespeare Birthplace Trust (Bloomsbury Arden Shakespeare, 2016) features fifty items from the Trust's collection — which help illustrate Elizabethan and Jacobean beliefs about the seven ages of man as described by Shakespeare's character Jaques in *As You Like It*.

The Plays and Poems: Although there are numerous good, economical one volume collections of Shakespeare's poems and plays, I prefer to read them one play at a time in single paperback editions. My favorite portable paperback editions of his plays and poems are the Dover Thrift Editions published by Dover Publications, Inc. The comparatively large size of the books allows them to be thin and flexible. The page layouts are generous. The texts used are generally from good, easy-to-read standard editions. These reasonably priced books are available at **doverpublications.com**.

Dover also publishes similar editions of works by Christopher Marlowe (including *Dr. Faustus*, *Tamburlaine*, and *The Jew of Malta*), Ben Johnson (including *The Alchemist* and *Volpone*) and John Webster (*The Duchess of Malfi*).Among their poetry offerings are *Shakespeare's Sonnets* and his *Long Poems*, *Christopher Marlowe Complete Poems*, *John Donne Selected Poems*, and the generous and excellent *Elizabethan Poetry: An Anthology* (edited by Bob Blaisdell). Viewing Shakespeare's work in the context of that of his fellow contemporary poets and playwrights allows for a better understanding and appreciation of his achievements.

The New Folger Shakespeare Library edition of Shakespeare's individual plays, published by Simon & Schuster Paperbacks, are also excellent and draw on the extensive collection of early editions of the plays held by the Folger to compile superior texts. They also contain well researched notes opposite the text of the play, as well as a scholarly essay on each play.

Shakespeare's Cultural Influence In the United States: *Shakespeare in America: An Anthology From The Revolution To Now* (The Library of America, 2014), edited by James Shapiro, contains a wide ranging selection of thoughts, essays, letters, stories and articles about Shakespeare and his works by American literary and political figures as diverse as John Adams, Washington Irving, Ralph Waldo Emerson, Abraham Lincoln, Walt Whitman, Mark Twain, and many others. Washington Irving's essay *Stratford-on-Avon*, published as part of his *The Sketch Book,* which recounts Irving's visit to Shakespeare's Birthplace in the summer of 1815, is a time capsule allowing us to experience what it was like to visit Stratford over two centuries ago.

Shakespeare Trivia, Facts, and Play Summaries: Jane Armstrong's *The Arden Shakespeare Miscellany (Methuen Drama, 2011)* assembles and summarizes a wealth of information, facts and theories about Shakespeare the man, and his plays and poems. Among other highlights, it contains pithy, well-written synopses of each of the plays.

Marchette Chute's *Stories From Shakespeare* (Meridian, 1987) contains excellent summaries, in story form, of the plots of the First Folio's thirty-six plays.

Charles and Mary Lambs' *Tales From Shakespeare* (Fall River Press, 2018), originally written in the early 1800's, contain well-written summaries of twenty of Shakespeare's most important plays in family-friendly, storybook form. It is a great book to read before the fire on a cold winter evening.

III. Great and Good Shakespearian Movies

1. ***Othello*** (1952), directed by Orson Welles. Orson Welles does a brilliant job portraying Othello, but what makes the movie unique in the Shakespearian film canon is its innovative use of light, shadow and camera angles to tell this timeless story of jealousy, obsession and murder. As a result, the film is a collaboration between two geniuses —Shakespeare and Welles.As *Citizen Kane* is my favorite movie, it is only natural I would be drawn to the Shakespearean films of this great director. In addition to filming Othello, Welles also filmed *Macbeth* (including recording a soundtrack in which the actors speak with Scottish accents!) and *Chimes at Midnight*. *Chimes at Midnight* combines the story Shakespeare tells in *Henry IV, parts I and II* into a cohesive film. If you cannot find the Welles version of *Othello*, the version directed by Oliver Parker, and starring Laurence Fishburne, Irene Jacob and Kenneth Branagh (1995) is a reasonably good substitute.

2. ***Macbeth*** (1971), directed by Roman Polanski. Polanski has directed many excellent movies, including *Chinatown*, *Oliver Twist* and *Tess* (his version of Thomas Hardy's *Tess of the d'Urbervilles*). His version of *Macbeth* ranks right up there with the best of them. Unlike some modern films of this play, this is a period piece set in the Scotland of the original. Given its subject matter, the wind and rain, jagged, rocky terrain, and the cold castle setting of much of the action creates an atmosphere that enhances the film's impact. The cinematic experience created by Polanski makes you believe what you are seeing on the screen could really occur. Polanski's handling of the witches and other supernatural scenes are also very well done. He made this film not long after the murder of his wife, Sharon Tate, by members of the Charles Manson family. What impact that may have had upon the making of this film has been the subject of much speculation.

3. ***Henry V*** (1989), directed by Kenneth Branagh. This choice was a close call because the version of *Henry V* made by Laurence Olivier during World War II (1944) is also a great movie. I gave first position to Branagh's film because of its excellent cinematic storytelling technique — especially the handling of the chorus scenes that propel the narrative. Obviously, comparing a film made in 1989 to one made in the 1940's is a bit unfair, but for those born in the television age, I give the Branagh film the edge. Both Branagh's and Oliver's films are superb action adventures. Given the time in which it was made, Olivier's version is more nationalistic than Branagh's. But they are both "must sees" for any Shakespeare film fan.

4. ***Romeo and Juliet*** (1968), directed by Franco Ziffirelli. No list of favorite Shakespearean films would be complete without this gem. The beauty of the young actors playing the main roles, as well as the bright colors of the costumes, and the quality of the sets, are stand-outs. They are matched by the hauntingly romantic

musical score. Like all the movies on this list, Shakespeare would have been thrilled to see how cinematic art has enhanced his dramatic works. Another more recent version of *Romeo & Juliet* (2013), one starring Hailee Steinfeld and Douglas Booth, deserves honorable mention. It is a well-done, visually attractive film for the post-millennial audience.

5. **Richard III** (1955), directed by Laurence Olivier. Olivier's portrayal of the villain everyone loves to hate is brilliant and definitive. His performance is the one by which every other actor who takes on this role is measured. Shakespeare was a master at painting the many psychological faces of evil. No one has created more memorable villains: Aaron the Moor, Richard III, Iago, King Lear's Edmund, to name but a few. Like Alfred Hitchcock, Shakespeare was able to reveal the darker sides of our human nature. While we may outwardly hate his villains, we are fascinated by them.

6. ***Chimes at Midnight*** (1965), directed by Orson Welles. Welles's portrayal of Falstaff is also definitive. By this time in his life, Welles was a perfect fit for the role. He made the most of it. The most amazing thing about Welles is he created such high-quality films with a fraction of the budgets other directors had available. *Othello* is a case in point. Because of funding issues, Welles had to film the movie in fits and starts over a period of years. When costumes were unavailable for an important scene, he changed the setting to a steam bath. And he had his actors wear towels in place of costumes! Welles believed the Earl of Oxford was the real author of Shakespeare's plays (a belief I do not share). Regardless, I believe he was the greatest American Shakespearian actor of his age. In the 1950's he returned to the United States to play King Lear in a television production. Although the production did not include the subplot, Welles's performance as Lear is the best I have ever seen.

7. ***The Taming of the Shrew*** (1967), directed by Franco Zeffirelli and starring Richard Burton and Elizabeth Taylor. This is a beautifully filmed, colorful, well-acted movie which set the stage for Zeffirelli's film of *Romeo and Juliet* a few years later. Given their fiery, on again-off again relationship, the casting of Elizabeth Taylor and Richard Burton in the roles of Katherina and Petruchio is perfect. The demanding nature of the role makes it one of Elizabeth Taylor's greatest film performances. Richard Burton demonstrates that his reputation as a fine Shakespearean actor was well deserved. The soundtrack enhances the action and the supporting cast is outstanding. As is true of most modern productions of the play, the movie omits the induction scene featuring the drunken and deceived tinker, Christopher Sly.

8. ***The Merchant of Venice*** (2004), directed by Michael Radford and starring Al Pacino, Jeremy Irons, Joseph Fiennes, and Lynn Collins (2004). This is a very well- done version of the controversial play. It is graced by a stellar cast performing at the top of their game. The courtroom scenes are particularly notable.

9. ***A Midsummer Night's Dream*** (1935), directed by Max Reinhardt and William Dieterle. This is the oldest film on the list. It deserves to be here for several reasons. The dream sequences involving the king and queen of the fairies and their minions have never been equaled. The film is very entertaining and family friendly. It has other attractions. A young Mickey Rooney is marvelous in the role of Puck. And, despite being criticized at the time, James Cagney does a good job playing Bottom the Weaver. Olivia de Havilland appears in her first screen role. The movie's score features the music of Felix Mendelssohn. Honorable mention goes to the film version of the play directed by Adrian Noble (1996) and featuring The Royal Shakespeare Company. The version of *A Midsummer's Night Dream* (1999) directed by Michael Hoffman and starring Michelle Pfeiffer,

Calista Flockhart, and Rupert Everett is lush, colorful, and mildly entertaining,

10. ***Hamlet*** (1990), directed by Franco Zeffirelli. This is a beautifully filmed version of Shakespeare's most important play featuring an A-list cast, including Mel Gibson, Glenn Close, Alan Bates, Ian Holm and Helena Bonham Carter. However, no cast can completely do Shakespeare's masterwork justice. Part of the problem is to fully perform all the lines of dialog would result in a movie that was over four hours long. For that reason, it is doubtful Shakespeare's own audiences ever saw the play performed in all its glory. Zefirelli's cinematic version is quite entertaining. Laurence Olivier also filmed an award winning and critically acclaimed version of this play in the late 1940's. Olivier's version is another must-see for the Shakespeare fan.

11. ***Much Ado About Nothing*** (1993), directed by Kenneth Branagh and starring Kenneth Branagh, Michael Keating, Keanu Reeves, Emma Thompson and Denzel Washington. The battle of wits portrayed in this comedy is less physical than the one portrayed in the *Taming of the Shrew*, but it is every bit as spirited. This is a very watchable comedic romp with a stellar cast. The bright and optimistic nature of the play is matched by the sunny locations where it was filmed.

12. ***Twelfth Night*** (1996), directed by Trevor Nunn, starring Helena Bonham Carter and Ben Kingsley. Another good version of a Shakespeare comedy from the mini-Shakespeare film boom of the 1990's. Ben Kingsley's performance as Malvolio is a stand-out. This is Shakespeare's only play featuring twins of opposite sexes. His son Hamnet died several years before the play was written. One can only wonder what influence that might have had upon him as he wrote this comedy's happy ending — with both twins saved from shipwreck, peril, and happily married to someone they love.

13. ***The Tempest*** (2010), directed by Julie Taymor, starring Helen Mirren. Perhaps the summation of Shakespeare's work as an artist, *The Tempest* is a difficult play to film because it is more about the inner workings of the artist's mind and spirit than it is about the physical action occurring on the stage or set. Its placement by Shakespeare's partners, Heminges and Condell, as the opening play in the First Folio of Shakespeare's works did not likely occur by accident. The contents of the epilogue make it probable it was Shakespeare's farewell to the stage, and that Shakespeare probably played the role of Prospero. Julie Taymor and Helen Mirren do an admirable job bringing this sublime play to the screen. The film is ethereal and visually arresting. Helen Mirren successfully portrays Prospera's gravitas and spiritual dilemma.

14. ***Titus*** (1999), directed by Julie Taymor, starring Anthony Hopkins and Jessica Lange. Although this is a very violent and somewhat sexually explicit movie, containing jarring and shocking images, *Titus Andronicus* is a violent and sexually explicit play. In my opinion, it is the darkest of all Shakespeare's works Over the centuries, its brutal nature has made some question whether Shakespeare even wrote it. I believe he did, although he probably worked with one or more collaborators. In the novel, I chose to have Shakespeare collaborate on this play with Kit Marlowe. It is unlikely that occurred. But Shakespeare was influenced by Marlowe during the early part of his career, and, if their two creative spirits ever collaborated on a play, the result would have been something like *Titus Andronicus*. If you choose to view this film, be forewarned — its subject matter, and visionary but disturbing images, may stay with you for some time.

15. ***As You Like It*** (2006), directed by Kenneth Branagh. This is a nicely done rendition of this important Shakespearian comedy, justly famous for its seven ages of man speech and for one of Shakespeare's greatest female heroines, the courageous and witty

Rosalind. As he did on many occasions, Shakespeare mines the sexual ambiguity and comic possibilities of having a young male actor, playing a young woman, playing a young man, for all that it's worth.

16. ***Anthony and Cleopatra** (1972)*, directed by Charlton Heston. Heston believed Shakespeare's dramas were the measuring stick by which an actor's abilities should be judged. His first role on Broadway was as a supporting character in *Anthony and Cleopatra*. Years later, after the successes he had in such iconic films as *The Ten Commandments*, *Ben-Hur*, *The Agony and The Ecstasy* and *Touch of Evil*, he acted in, adapted, and directed his own version of this late Shakespearian play. He certainly was up to the task of playing Mark Antony. This film, which was a work of love, is well worth a look.

17. ***Julius Caesar*** (1953), directed by Joseph L. Mankiewicz, starring Marlon Brando, James Mason and John Gielgud. If you ever wondered what it would be like to see method actor Marlon Brando take on a Shakespearian role, then look no further. He plays Mark Antony in this award-winning film. I'll let you be the judge as to whether he takes home the laurels!

18. ***Shakespeare in Love*** (1998), directed by John Madden, starring Gwyneth Paltrow, Joseph Fiennes, Geoffrey Rush, Colin Firth, Ben Affleck and Judi Dench. This popular and critically acclaimed film centers upon a fictional romance between Shakespeare and a young woman aristocrat who secretly and dangerously moonlights as a male actor playing Juliet in the Lord Chamberlin Men's production of *Romeo and Juliet*. It is a suspenseful comedic romp which deftly illuminates some of the social challenges facing those living in the later Elizabethan Age.

19. ***The Hollow Crown*** (Series I and II), Universal Home Entertainment—executive producer Sam Mendes. This is

a recent series of well-done films based upon Shakespeare's ground-breaking histories. Series I (*The Complete* Series) includes *Richard II*, *Henry IV, Part I*, *Henry IV, Part II*, and *Henry V*. Series II (*The Wars of the Roses*) includes *Henry VI, Part I*, *Henry VI, Part II*, and *Richard III*.

IV. Essential Documentaries

*1. **In Search of Shakespeare*** (2003), hosted by Michael Wood, distributed by PBS. Michael Wood's four-hour, four-part, cradle-to-the-grave documentary on Shakespeare's life is superb. It takes you to Stratford, Hoghton Tower, Old Rufford Hall, the replica of the Globe Theatre, Holy Trinity Church, and many other places essential to Shakespeare's story. It is filled with interviews and stories told by scholars, and actors performing illuminating portions of many of Shakespeare's plays. This is the best film biography of Shakespeare's life ever made. It is essential viewing for everyone interested in Shakespeare and his world-changing works. It is available at **pbs.org**.

*2. **Shakespeare's Stratford: An In-Depth look at the City & its Illustrious Native Son*** (2008), is an Artsmagic DVD available for purchase in the United States at **mvdshop.com**. This excellent DVD contains an armchair video tour of The Shakespeare Birthplace Trust Properties, Holy Trinity church, the King Edward VI school Shakespeare likely attended, and other sites of interest in and around Stratford. The three-hour video features narration by experienced Stratford guide and Shakespearean actress, Sue Sutton, and presentations and explanations of what is being seen at the various properties by Birthplace Trust staff.

*3. **Shakespeare Uncovered*** (Series I, II, and III): This is an excellent series of films in which significant Shakespearean directors and actors investigate, analyze, and tell the story of a

Shakespearian or plays they have been associated with and its fascinating literary and historical background. The series are available at **pbs.org**.

V. Shakespearean Vacations and Day Trips

For those readers wishing to integrate Shakespearian sites and events into an English vacation, I make the following suggestions:

London Sights and Sounds: London offers a wealth of Shakespearian attractions including:

The Globe Theater: The most important Shakespearian attraction in London is the replica of the Globe and Blackfriar's theaters which sits on the South Bank of the Thames in Southwark, not far from where the original Globe stood from 1599 until it burned down during a performance of Henry VIII in June 1613. As described in the novel and "Separating Fact From Fiction" section of this afterword, Shakespeare may have sold his shares in the King's Men and the Globe as a result of the fire. At this late point in his career, Shakespeare might not have wanted to participate in the significant capital investment which would have been involved with building the new version of the Globe that opened a few years later.

Somewhat surprisingly, the current replica of the Globe would not have been built without the tireless efforts and fundraising of American actor and philanthropist Sam Wanamaker. Unfortunately, Mr. Wanamaker did not live to see the completion of his labor of love in 1997.

As a general rule, plays are put on in the outdoor theater during the months of April through October. Performances are given at the indoor theater during the months of October through April. Whether or not you are able to attend a play, do not miss the reasonably priced tour of the Globe and the basement exhibition of historical artifacts and information uncovered during the theater excavations. The tour I attended was given by one of the actors who performs regularly in the theaters. It was filled with a treasure trove of stories and fascinating information about the Globe and its history.

The Globe complex also contains a good-sized gift shop where you can stock-up on Shakespeare themed gifts for friends and family. You can visit the gift shop online at **shop.shakespearesglobe.com**. There you can purchase *Shakespeare's Globe Guide Book* and use the information it contains to help plan your trip. There is also a "Globe 360 App" which allows you to make a virtual tour of the theater.

There are several good restaurants nearby for before and after tour/performance food and drink. The Globe is located on the waterfront and there are plenty of opportunities for sightseeing and picture taking of the Globe and the panoramic view of the cityscape on the other side of the Thames.

Information regarding theater performances and tours of the Globe and the indoor theater (known as the Sam Wanamaker Playhouse) is available on the Globe website at **shakespearesglobe.com**.

Southwark Cathedral: Southwark Cathedral (formerly St. Saviour's) was known as the actors' church because of its proximity to what we might today call the Southwark Theater District. At various times during the latter part of the sixteenth and early seventeenth centuries, the Swan, the Rose, a bear-baiting garden, and the two Globe theaters were located within easy walking distance of this venerable church. The church was frequented by many players. Shakespeare's collaborator and successor as chief playwright of the King's Men, John Fletcher, was buried inside the church, as was the fourteenth century poet, John Gower. Gower serves as the chorus in Shakespeare's *Pericles* (co-authored with tavern and brothel owner George Wilkins). *Pericles* uses a

Gower poem as its primary source. Gower's polychrome memorial monument is contained within the church.

Although there is no existing record showing that Shakespeare ever attended a service in Southwark Cathedral (or any other London church), it nonetheless has a strong connection to his life. For it is here within the interior of the church that Shakespeare's brother Edmund was buried in December of 1607. There is a plaque memorializing Edmund, a reclining statue of Shakespeare, and a stained-glass window commemorating some of his best-known characters and plays. As recounted in the novel, Edmund was Shakespeare's youngest brother. There was about a sixteen-year difference between them. Given their nearness in age, Edmund was probably more like a brother than an uncle to Shakespeare's son Hamnet.

At some point in time, Edmund moved to London and, following in his older brother's footsteps, became a player. In the novel I theorize Edmund's move occurred immediately after Hamnet's death. Whether Edmund acted with Shakespeare's company (then known as the Lord Chamberlin's Men) is unknown. He is not among the list of principal players named by Shakespeare's partners, Heminges and Condell, in the 1623 First Folio of Shakespeare's plays. But, unless he was a company shareholder, one would not expect him to be there.

Southwark Cathedral's website (**cathedral.southwark.anglican.org**) is user friendly and well designed. It contains some interesting historical information, and it will be invaluable in making the most of your visit. While you are there, make sure to stop by the Gift Shop. The *Southwark Cathedral* guide is colorful and well designed. It makes a great souvenir that will enhance your tour of the Cathedral.

The Golden Hinde: In a drydock virtually in the shadow of Southwark Cathedral is an accurate reconstruction of one of the most famous ship's in world history — Francis Drake's Golden Hind. This replica, built in Devon England in the early 1970's, has completed its own circumnavigation. Although Shakespeare possessed a remarkable knowledge of seafaring jargon, and London was a port city, we do not know if he was ever a passenger or crew member on a sailing vessel. During his lifetime, England began its ascent as a maritime power. It is safe to assume, like most English people of his time, Shakespeare was proud of his country's maritime achievements. The fact Shakespeare's company chose the Globe as the name for their theater evidences their awareness of the new horizons maritime exploration opened for them.

Francis Drake is undoubtedly the greatest of the English Sea Dogs. His many exploits were critical to Queen Elizabeth's successful defense of her throne in the face of Spanish hostility. His raid on the Spanish fleet at Cadiz (in which 30 Spanish ships were destroyed) brought the English valuable time and weakened the Armada before it ever set sail. He was one of the leaders of the English seafarers who harried, disrupted, and scattered the Armada as it made its way up the English Channel. But, at the same time, he was a brutal and ruthless privateer, a one-time slave trader the Spanish called "The Dragon."

Perhaps Drake's most historically notable achievement was the circumnavigation (1577-1580) on board his flagship the Golden Hind (formerly known as the Pelican, a bird famous for its mythical longevity, until Drake renamed the ship mid-voyage for the deer which appeared on his patron Christopher Hatton's family coat of arms). The circumnavigation occurred as a result of a privateering voyage secretly authorized and financially backed by Queen Elizabeth and some of her favorites at Court. During the voyage, Drake captured and plundered numerous Spanish ships carrying precious metals and other valuable cargo. The fabulous booty he amassed vastly enriched not only himself but Queen Elizabeth and the other secret investors.

To celebrate the successful voyage, Queen Elizabeth ordered the Golden Hind moved from Plymouth to Deptford. It was given a new coat of paint and otherwise made ship-shape. Then Drake hosted a sumptuous dinner for the Queen onboard the ship. She knighted him then and there.

As one explores the replica of this historic ship, one cannot help but marvel at its comparatively small size. It is incredible that a crew of 60 men or more called this creaking wooden vessel home during their record setting three-year odyssey. The Captain (Francis Drake) was the only person onboard to have a bed to sleep in. The remainder of the crew had to sleep on the decks of the ship. The gun deck, situated between the main deck and the cargo hold, is so tight-fitting a person of average height today must walk hunched over to avoid striking the overhead beams. And, in addition to its crew, the ship carried cannon, ammunition, powder, food, beer, rope and sail material. One comes away from a tour of this vessel with a new respect and appreciation for the iron men who manned the wooden ships of the Age of Sail.

The Golden Hinde has a simple but informative website (**goldenhinde.co.uk**) which contains information about Drake, the Circumnavigation, The Spanish Armada and the history of the current ship.

The National Portrait Gallery: It is said that a picture is worth a thousand words. And, if you want to put a face to a name, and get a sense of the flamboyance, variety and eccentricity of Elizabethan and Jacobean fashions, there is no better place to do it than at the National Portrait Gallery.

The most important Shakespearian portrait in the Gallery is acquisition number 1 (donated by the Duke of Chandros in 1856, and displayed in Room 4), commonly known as the "Chandos Portrait" of Shakespeare. Although, like many things concerning Shakespeare, we cannot be absolutely sure the portrait is of him, considering it is over 400 years old, the provenance of this portrait is very good.

Although some have speculated that the portrait was painted by Shakespeare's friend and partner, Richard Burbage, an early owner identified the painter as John Taylor, a contemporary of Shakespeare who was a member of the painter's guild and a possible former boy actor in the children's acting company of St. Paul's Cathedral. Analysis of the simple black jacket and wide white collar of the sitter reveals the sitter's dress correlates with that which would have been worn between 1600 and 1610.

Another early owner of the portrait was poet and playwright William Davenant (1606-1668) who became poet laureate after the death of Ben Johnson. William Davenant was the son of Shakespeare's Oxford friends, tavern owners John and Jane Davenant. Shakespeare used to stay at the Davenants' tavern on his journeys between Stratford and London. William Davenant's older brother, Robert, told antiquarian John Aubrey that Shakespeare had bestowed numerous kisses upon him during the course of those visits.

Jane Davenant was an uncommonly pretty woman. A rumor arose that her son William, who was apparently named for Shakespeare, and may have been his godson, was Shakespeare's illegitimate son. According to John Aubrey, William Davenant liked to believe he wrote with the spirit of Shakespeare and, when he had a bit to drink, told close friends he was content to be considered Shakespeare's son. Although the Davenants are only bit players in the novel, Jane Davenant forwards spiced wine to Shakespeare to refresh and give Shakespeare strength during his final illness.

What is clear from all this is the Davenant family had a close relationship with Shakespeare, and William Davenant greatly admired Shakespeare. William Davenant and his brother, Robert, personally knew Shakespeare in their youth. It is highly unlikely he would acquire a false portrait of Shakespeare as an adult.

What makes the Chandros portrait so special is the elegance, intelligence and vitality of the portrait's subject. This comports with the Shakespeare we expect to see. Although his hairline has receded to the middle of his scalp, the swept back mane of hair that remains is thick. He sports a light beard and mustache. He is dressed in understated elegance with no lace or ruff. Most surprisingly, his left earlobe sports a simple gold earring.

The portrait sitter's eyes have a dark intensity, and, combined with his noncommittal closed lips, give the viewer an impression of well-considered but wary thought. These aspects of the portrait make it highly likely the painting was done from life. One can only wish one was present to hear the conversation that occurred between dramatic artist and painter as the portrait was being made.

Viewing the Chandros portrait is enough to make a visit worthwhile for any Shakespeare fan, but it is only the tip of the iceberg of this unrivalled collection. The many Eilzabethan and Jacobian portraits in the collection include those of: Queen Elizabeth I, Robert Cecil, Lord Essex, King James I, The Duke of Buckingham, Sir Francis Drake, Francis Walsingham, Ben Johnson, John Fletcher, Sir Philip Sidney, Michael Drayton, John Donne, the Earl of Oxford, Francis Bacon, William Herbert (Earl of Pembroke) and Sir Walter Raleigh!

The Gallery's Portrait Restaurant and Bar has high quality food and a beautiful skyline view including Nelson's Column in

Trafalgar Square, Big Ben, The Houses of Parliament, the London Eye and more. The Gallery also contains a well-stocked Gift Shop, a Bookshop and an Exhibition Shop. Many items carried in the shops can be purchased on line at **npgshop.org.uk**.

The Gallery's website (**npg.org.uk**) contains a wealth of information. It gives you the hours of operation, allows you to examine the layout and subject matter of the Gallery exhibition rooms, and permits you to search the Gallery's collection of over 11,000 holdings by the name of the person portrayed.

For those Shakespeare fans wanting to make the most of their visit, as well as those who wish to make an armchair visit, I highly recommend purchasing (available on the website) the small drawing and portrait-packed volume by Charles Nicholl entitled *Shakespeare and his Contemporaries* (National Portrait Gallery Publications, 2015). Along with reproductions of some of the portraits you will see in the Gallery (and numerous others from private collections and other sources you will not see), It features valuable background information on Shakespeare and his contemporaries in the aristocracy, the arts, and otherwise.

Other London Sites with Shakespearian Connections: Most of the day-to- day London Shakespeare knew has fallen victim to the Civil War, the Great Fire of 1666, the Blitz, subsequent development, and many other ravages of time. Old London Bridge, Old St. Paul's, much of Whitehall Palace, Greenwich Palace, the Bell, the Green Dragon, and other galleried inns, Shakespeare's home in the Blackfriars District, the Mountjoy residence at the corner of Silver and Monkwell (Muggle) Streets, the Theater, the original Globe, the Curtain, Rose, Swan, Fortune, and Blackfriars theaters are no longer with us. Despite this fact, there are a few places Shakespeare was familiar with that do survive, including Westminster Abbey and the Tower of London.

Westminster Abbey is one of the sites Shakespeare visits with his son in the novel (along with Old St. Paul's, London Bridge, the Rose theater, the Bell inn, the Theater, Whitehall Palace, and the Golden Hind (then in Deptford)). In the Abbey, they stop at the tomb of Henry V and view Henry's sword, shield and saddle while Shakespeare recites Henry V's most famous speech from Shakespeare's play of the same name. Many of Shakespeare's contemporaries, including Edmund Spencer, Francis Beaumont, and Ben Johnson are buried in the Abbey, as are many Kings and Queens, including Henry V, Queen Mary I, Mary Queen of Scots, Queen Elizabeth I and King James I. It is likely Shakespeare could have been buried there among them if he so desired. But he preferred to be buried in his home town of Stratford among his family and friends. He even wrote a poem to place upon his tomb warning anyone who moves his bones that they would be cursed.

I believe the purpose of the curse in the poem on Shakespeare's tomb may have been in part to make sure no one would move his remains to Westminster Abbey. He worked in London, but his family resided in Stratford. He always identified himself as a citizen of Stratford. His wife Anne, both his daughters, their husbands, his sister and his granddaughter all resided in Stratford. His parents, his son, his sister Anne, and his brothers Gilbert and Richard were buried in Holy Trinity's Churchyard. If Shakespeare was at heart a family man (which I believe he was), then why would he want to be buried alone one hundred miles away in London? Additionally, if Shakespeare was still a practicing Roman Catholic, he would not have wanted to be buried by and with members of a Protestant Establishment he did not spiritually support

Although Shakespeare did not attend regular church services in Westminster Abbey, as a member of The King's

Men, he participated in the ceremonies surrounding the coronation of King James I at the Abbey. He and some of the other principal shareholders were issued special scarlet fabric to have their ceremonial outfits made. And they carried a canopy during the King's procession through the city and under a series of ostentatious ceremonial arches and monuments specially constructed for the occasion. Shakespeare's ambivalent feelings about participating in the coronation ceremony are recorded for posterity in sonnet 125. The sonnet questions the inner worth of those who elevate form over substance in pursuit of worldly honors, wealth and preferment. It stresses the true worth of one whose offering of self is "poor but free."

The Tower of London: In Shakespeare's day, many believed Julius Caesar was responsible for building the Tower. The portion known as the White Tower was actually built by William the Counqueror.It had been a part of London life since time out of mind. A one-time palace, it was now a prison, a torture chamber, a fortress and an armory. Many illustrious historical and contemporary figures were imprisoned and/or lost their heads there. Elizabeth's mother, Anne Boleyn, Catherine Howard (Henry VIII's fifth wife), Thomas More, Lord Essex, and Walter Raleigh all were beheaded there or on nearby Tower Hill.

Elizabeth I was temporarily imprisoned there by her sister Mary I — under suspicion of seeking the throne. It likely psychologically scarred her for life. Richard III imprisoned his brother's children in the Tower, and he might have had them murdered and buried within its precincts. Shakespeare's patron, Lord Southampton, was imprisoned there for several years due to his role in the Essex Rebellion. Priests imprisoned or tortured in the Tower included Edmund Campion and John Gerard. With underground Catholic assistance, John Gerard escaped from the Tower during the evening of October 4, 1597.

During Shakespeare's time, the Beefeaters defending The Tower and guarding the prisoners were already giving guided tours to Elizabethan tourists. In the novel, I have a wherryman discuss the legendary Julius Caesar connection and the availability of Beefeater tours with Shakespeare and his son Hamnet.

Stratford-upon-Avon: Of course, no Shakespeare-focused English vacation would be complete without a visit to the Bard's hometown. For all roads concerning Shakespeare lead to Stratford. It is where Shakespeare began and ended his life's journey. It is the town his parents and his wife lived their adult lives in, and the one in which his children (as far as we know) lived for their entire lives. Best of all, there is a lot to see and do in Stratford and its environs. To do it right, you will need between 2 and 3 days. If you are travelling from London, and you feel comfortable driving through roundabouts and on the left side of the road, you can rent a car for the journey. If you do are not comfortable driving, then you can take the train. Stratford is not the easiest place to get to, but it is well worth the trip.

The highlight of any trip to Stratford is a visit to the properties of The Shakespeare Birthplace Trust. Those properties include **Shakespeare's Birthplace** home on Henley Street, the site of the large home called **New Place** Shakespeare brought for his family during the height of his theatrical success in 1597, and the adjoining **Nash House** (housing an exhibit on Shakespeare and New Place), the home of Shakespeare's daughter, Susanna, and his son-in-law, Doctor John Hall (**Hall's Croft**), **Mary Arden's House** in nearby Wilmcote (the girlhood home of Shakespeare's mother), the adjacent **Palmer's Farm**, and the childhood home of Shakespeare's wife (**Anne Hathaway's Cottage**) in Shottery.

Until recently, Palmer's Farm was considered the birthplace of Shakespeare's mother.To everyone's surprise, a local historian's research revealed the much smaller Glebe House was the actual site. Glebe House was fortunately also owned by The Shakespeare Birthplace Trust, and it is now called Mary Arden's House. Palmer's Farm is run and maintained as a typical working farm of the Elizabethan Age.

As mentioned in the Recommended Reading section, an excellent official guide to the Shakespeare Birthplace Trust properties is available from the Shakespeare Birthplace Trust website at **Shakespeare.org.uk**. There is a very nice giftshop located at the Birthplace. Many of the gifts available there can be purchased online.

A further highlight of a trip to Stratford is a visit to **Holy Trinity**, the church where Shakespeare and most of his family were baptized and buried. It contains the monument featuring a bust of Shakespeare, quill and paper in hand, which was already installed by the time the First Folio of Shakespeare's plays was published in 1623. Holy Trinity sits on the banks of the Avon River and it has a characteristic English churchyard containing many weathered tombstones of Stratfordians from days gone by.

In the novel, the box-like base of the bust of Shakespeare in Holy Trinity Church is the place where Shakespeare's granddaughter Elizabeth decides to conceal the manuscript of his life story Shakespeare left for his heirs. Of course, there is no evidence Shakespeare ever wrote his life story. Keeping a diary was a very rare thing in Elizabethan and Jacobean times. There has, however, occasionally been speculation that some of Shakespeare's play manuscripts could be contained within the base of the monument. The statue (at least in its present form) does have Shakespeare holding a quill and a sheet of paper in his hands. The enigmatic inscription in the monument, that asks the passerby to stop, read, and contemplate the person (Shakespeare) placed within it, could certainly fuel such speculation.

As much as hope springs eternal, it is extremely doubtful any of Shakespeare's working papers are contained within the monument. The monument was already in place when the First Folio was published in 1623. In the introduction to the First Folio, Shakespeare's partners, John Heminges and Henry Condell, describe how they used his play manuscripts to construct the First Folio. At that point, the manuscripts were likely still the property of the King's Men, and they would remain so for many years. Once the First Folio (followed by the Second Folio in 1632) was published, there would be little reason to preserve the original manuscripts when their useful theatrical life was over.

As mentioned in the "Recommended Documentaries" section above, an excellent DVD that contains an armchair video tour of The Shakespeare Birthplace Trust Properties, Holy Trinity church, the King Edward VI school Shakespeare likely attended, and other sites of interest in and around Stratford is an ARTSMAGIC DVD, *Shakespeare's Stratford: An In-Depth Look at the City & Its Illustrious Native Son,* available from Artsmagic's distributor at **mvdshop.com**. When viewed in combination with the PBS distributed *In Search of Shakespeare* series hosted by Michael Wood (which, in addition to visiting certain Shakespeare Birthplace Trust properties, also contains visits to Hoghton Tower and Old Rufford Hall), it will provide you with all the background information required to greatly enhance your visits to England's historic Shakespearian sites.

Another premier, must-see Stratford attraction is the Royal Shakespeare Company's theatre complex located on the banks of the Avon River. The complex contains three theatres: the **Royal Shakespeare Theatre**, the **Swan Theatre** and **The Other Place**. In addition to a fairly constant run of Shakespeare's plays, the company offers a wide variety of interesting themed tours, including ones entitled: Audition Tour, Behind the Scenes, From Page to Stage, and Front of House. Ticketing, tour information, merchandise for sale, and other useful information is available on the Company website at **rsc.org.uk**.

If time allows, a visit to **Charlecote**, the impressive Tudor estate of Shakespeare's alleged nemesis and persecutor, Sir Thomas Lucy, is well worth the effort. Although the mansion is furnished in the Victorian manner, the home is filled with artwork from the Lucy family's long history of ownership. And the surrounding parkland is beautiful. A special attraction for someone in the mood for a real splurge is the three-room apartment (The Turret) on the second floor. It is available for stays of at least 3 nights, and it can be booked online. Learn more about the Lucy Family, Charlecote Park, and The Turret apartment at **nationaltrust.org.uk/charlecote-park**. Charlecote is only about four miles from Stratford, so you can use this as your base of operations if desired.

As one walks the present-day bustling streets of Stratford, one wonders what life was like in Shakespeare's day? Can we roll back the years and experience how it would feel to walk beside him? I believe snippets from his plays provide snap-shots. For instance, the "Winter Song," concluding Shakespeare's early play *Love's Labour's Los*t, paints quite a picture in words.

Icicles hang above the outside front wall of the Shakespeare family home on Henley Street. A shepherd named Dick hunches over, blowing upon the nails of his fingers to avoid frostbite. A blast of cold air rushes into the home as Tom the Woodman brings logs into the hall to feed the roaring fireplace. A kitchen maid returns from the barn with frozen milk in wooden pail. The winter winds howl down Stratford's snow-filled streets. A nasty cold virus spreads through town while birds brood within the snow. Over In Holy Trinity church, the Parson's sermon is constantly interrupted by hacking and coughing. Mother Marian's nose is raw and red.

As night falls, sister Joan stirs the stew simmering in the pot. Will Shakespeare sits down at the dinner table. He licks his lips, anticipating the sweet taste of the roasted crab apples simmering in the bowl before him. Just then, he hears the merry too-whit, too-who of the wide-eyed night owl that has of late stood watch over the Shakespeare homestead.

Other UK Sites of Interest: In the event you wish to retrace the journey Shakespeare may have taken to Lancashire to work with the Catholic Hoghton and Hesketh families, then you will want to visit the next two historic sites.

Hoghton Tower: By a stroke of good fortune, this historic stronghold of the Hoghton family still exists. The long roadway leading up to the fortress-like gate is very impressive. And the view of the surrounding countryside from the top of the high hill upon which the Tower is located is quite beautiful. As recounted in the novel, this has been a stronghold of the Hoghtons from the days of William the Conqueror. The Tower is open for general visitation from April until October 7th from 10 am to 4 pm, with tours starting every hour from 11 am to 4 pm.

An afternoon tea/tour package (or just an afternoon tea option) is available. In addition to the complex's historical significance, there is an extensive collection of Dolls' Houses. The estate also contains three walled gardens and beautiful grounds. There is a gift shop located in the stables. It is also possible to arrange an overnight stay in the "Irishman's Tower." More information and pictures of the Tower are available at the Tower's outstanding website: **hoghtontower.co.uk.**

Rufford Old Hall: If Shakespeare stayed with the Hoghtons, it is likely he subsequently went to work for the Hesketh at is what is now known as Old Rufford Hall, located in the town of Rufford, Lancashire. The William Shakeshafte mentioned in Alexander Hoghton's will appears to have been a musician or actor, and a tradition exists that Shakespeare did stay here and act in the Hesketh family's troupe of Catholic actors.

Rufford Old Hall was constructed by Sir Robert Hesketh around 1530. The Great Hall may be the only surviving part of the original building. It is likely the place where Shakespeare and his fellow actors would have performed. Rufford Old Hall also contains beautiful gardens of the Tudor and Edwardian eras. It has an informative website at **nationaltrust.org.uk/rufford-old-hall**.

Shakespeare in Washington, D.C.: **The Folger Shakespeare Library**, a stately white building housing perhaps the world's most extensive and valuable collection of historic books by and about Shakespeare, is located close to the U.S Capitol and Supreme Court.

Within the building is a large exhibition hall, a modern version of an Elizabethan Theatre, and a reading room. A number of Shakespeare's plays are performed every year in the Elizabethan Theatre. Docent led tours of the current exhibition and the theatre are given daily (11 am, 1 pm and 3 pm, Mon.-Sat.; 12 noon and 3 pm on Sun.). During the tour you will have an opportunity to view one of the many First Folios of Shakespeare's plays possessed by the Folger. What is unique about the First Folio I saw on display at the Folger is that, in addition to the actual open volume encased in glass, there was also a virtual First Folio that allowed you to turn the pages! More information, including how to register for a tour of the Folger's reading room, can be obtained at the Folger's website: **folger.edu**.

VI. THE PLAY'S THE THING

Shakespeare's plays were written for the stage and there is no better way to enjoy them than attending a live performance. Fortunately, there are an abundance of opportunities to do so. Most major metropolitan areas in North America have a Shakespeare Festival or Company that can be located with a simple internet search including Shakespeare's name and the closest city to where you live. Their web sites provide information on performance schedules and obtaining tickets. Some of them include the following:

Alaska, Fairbanks Shakespeare Theatre: fairbanksshakespeare.org
Ashland, Oregon, Oregon Shakespeare Festival: osfashland.org
Atlanta, The Shakespeare Tavern Playhouse: shakespearetavern.com
Boston, Shakespeare on the Commons: commshakes.com
Boulder, Colorado Shakespeare Festival: cupresents.org
Cedar City, Utah Shakespeare Festival: bard.org
Chicago Shakespeare Theater (on Navy Pier): chicagoshakes.com
Columbia, The South Carolina Shakespeare Company: shakespearesc.org
The Cleveland Shakespeare Festival: cleveshakes.com
Dallas: shakespearedallas.org
Detroit: shakespeareindetroit.com
Honolulu, Hawaii Shakespeare Festival: hawaiishakes.org
The Houston Shakespeare Festival, uh.edu.
Lenox, Massachusetts, Shakespeare & Company: shakespeare.org
Los Angeles, Shakespeare Center of Los Angeles: Shakespearecenter.org
Mesa, Arizona: Southwest Shakespeare Company: swshakespeare.org
Miami: shakespearemiami.com
Milwaukee, Free Shakespeare in the Park: optimisttheatre.org
Montgomery, Alabama Shakespeare Festival: asf.net
Montreal Shakespeare Theatre Company: themtsc.com
Nashville: nashvilleshakes.org
New Orleans Shakespeare Festival at Tulane: neworleansshakespeare.org
New York City, Shakespeare in Central Park: publictheater.org
North Carolina Shakespeare Festival: ncshakes.org
Orlando Shakespeare Theater: orlandoshakes.org

The Philadelphia Shakespeare Theatre: phillyshakespeare.org
Pittsburgh Shakespeare in the Parks: pittsburgshakespeare.com
San Diego, The Old Globe and Summer Shakespeare Festival: theoldglobe.org
San Francisco Shakespeare Festival: sfshakes.org
International Shakespeare Center Santa Fe: internationalshakespeare.center
Seattle Shakespeare Company: seattleshakespeare.org
Staunton, Virginia (Blackfriars Playhouse): americanshakespearecenter.com
Stratford, Ontario, Stratford Festival of Canada: stratfordfestival.ca
St. Louis, Shakespeare Festival St. Louis: sfstl.com
Toronto: summercanadianstage.com
Vancouver, Bard on the Beach Shakespeare Festival: bardonthebeach.org
Victoria, British Colombia, Greater Victoria Shakespeare Festival: vicshakespeare.com
Washington, DC, Folger Theatre: folger.edu; Shakespeare Theatre Company: Shakespeare theatre.org

As you can see from reading the various sections of this Afterword, the Universe of "All Things Shakespeare" is an ever-expanding one. At times it can be overwhelming. After spending years exploring it, researching and writing the novel you have read, I decided to use the knowledge gained to make the treks of those following in my footsteps easier and as enjoyable as my own. You readers will decide whether I achieved that goal. As I bid you each adieu, I hope your seas are calm and skies are blue!

A Note of Thanks: Finally, I wish to thank my Mother, Doris Gray, for the love, faith, advice, encouragement, and editorial expertise she has shared with me over the years. God Bless you Mom!

William ("Bill") Gray is an attorney and retired Naval Reserve Officer. His life-long interest in William Shakespeare led him to research and write the labor of love that is *Love's Labour's Won: The Secret Life of William Shakespeare*.

Old London Bridge

Holy Trinity Church, Stratford-upon-Avon

Made in the USA
Monee, IL
16 July 2020

36627861R00289